D1155416

Grimms' Tales around the Globe

SERIES IN FAIRY-TALE STUDIES

General Editor
Donald Haase, Wayne State University

Advisory Editors
Cristina Bacchilega, University of Hawai`i, Mānoa
Stephen Benson, University of East Anglia
Nancy L. Canepa, Dartmouth College
Anne E. Duggan, Wayne State University
Pauline Greenhill, University of Winnipeg
Christine A. Jones, University of Utah
Janet Langlois, Wayne State University
Ulrich Marzolph, University of Göttingen
Carolina Fernández Rodríguez, University of Oviedo
Maria Tatar, Harvard University
Jack Zipes, University of Minnesota

*A complete listing of the books in this series
can be found online at wsupress.wayne.edu*

Grimms' Tales around the Globe

THE DYNAMICS OF THEIR INTERNATIONAL RECEPTION

EDITED BY

Vanessa Joosen and Gillian Lathey

WAYNE STATE UNIVERSITY PRESS

DETROIT

© 2014 by Wayne State University Press, Detroit, Michigan 48201.
All rights reserved. No part of this book may be reproduced without
formal permission. Manufactured in the United States of America.
18 17 16 15 14   5 4 3 2 1

Library of Congress Control Number: 2014935683
ISBN 978-0-8143-3920-6 (pbk: alk. paper)—
ISBN 978-0-8143-3921-3 (ebook)

Published with the assistance of a fund established by Thelma Gray
James of Wayne State University for the publication of folklore and
English studies.

Designed by Keata Brewer
Typeset by E. T. Lowe Publishing Company
Composed in Adobe Garamond Pro, Raphael, and Scala Sans Pro

CONTENTS

Introduction 1

I. Cultural Resistance and Assimilation

1. No-Name Tales: Early Croatian Translations
of the Grimms' Tales 19
    MARIJANA HAMERŠAK

2. Polishing the Grimms' Tales for a Polish Audience:
Die Kinder- und Hausmärchen in Poland 39
    MONIKA WOZNIAK

3. The Grimms' Fairy Tales in Spain: Translation, Reception,
and Ideology 59
    ISABEL HERNÁNDEZ AND NIEVES MARTÍN-ROGERO

4. The Fairy Tales of the Brothers Grimm in Colombia:
A Bibliographical History 81
    ALEXANDRA MICHAELIS-VULTORIUS

5. "They are still eating well and living well":
The Grimms' Tales in Early Colonial Korea 99
    DAFNA ZUR

6. The Influence of the Grimms' Fairy Tales
on the Folk Literature Movement in China (1918–1943) 119
DECHAO LI

7. The Grimm Brothers' *Kahaniyan*: Hindi Resurrections
of the Tales in Modern India by Harikrishna Devsare 135
MALINI ROY

8. Before and after the "Grimm Boom": Reinterpretations
of the Grimms' Tales in Contemporary Japan 153
MAYAKO MURAI

II. Reframings, Paratexts, and Multimedia Translations

9. Translating in the "Tongue of Perrault": The Reception
of the *Kinder- und Hausmärchen* in France. 179
CYRILLE FRANÇOIS

10. Skeptics and Enthusiasts: Nineteenth-Century Prefaces
to the Grimms' Tales in English Translation. 199
RUTH B. BOTTIGHEIMER

11. German Stories/British Illustrations: Production Technologies,
Reception, and Visual Dialogue across Illustrations from
"The Golden Bird" in the Grimms' Editions, 1823–1909. 219
SARA HINES

12. Marvelous Worlds: The Grimms' Fairy Tales
in GDR Children's Films. 239
BETTINA KÜMMERLING-MEIBAUER

13. Retelling "Hansel and Gretel" in Comic Book and Manga
Narration: The Case of Philip Petit and Mizuno Junko 257
MARIANNA MISSIOU

14. Fairy-Tale Scripts and Intercultural Conceptual Blending
    in Modern Korean Film and Television Drama 275

    SUNG-AE LEE

Contributors 295
Index 299

Introduction

No German book has been translated into so many languages as the Grimms' tales, as the UNESCO translation index shows. And, although they appear below William Shakespeare, Agatha Christie, and Hans Christian Andersen, the Brothers Grimm are also listed in the top ten most frequently translated authors in the world. The international dissemination of their fairy tales started almost immediately after their publication in German. As early as 1816, four years after the first volume of the *Kinder- und Hausmärchen* (often abbreviated KHM) appeared, the first translation of a set of tales came out in Danish. Several additional translations followed during the 1820s and 1830s (Hennig and Lauer 565–67): after appearing first in Dutch (1820), Danish (a second set of tales appearing in 1821), English (1823), and French (1827 and 1836), the tales gradually spread through Europe and then the rest of the world.

The broad international reception of the *Kinder- und Hausmärchen* and the current status of a selection of their tales as global children's classics are the result of very diverse routes through which the stories have entered various languages and foreign cultures. It is certainly not the case, however, that the Grimm tales were immediately welcomed in all the countries where they were introduced; on the contrary, the inclusion of fantasy and cruel events often made them the topic of debate and they frequently required adaptation, especially when the Grimm tales were considered as literature for young readers.

The similarities and differences in the international reception of the *Kinder- und Hausmärchen* are the topic of this book. It builds on groundbreaking work in this area, for example, the work published in the journals and yearbooks of the Brüder Grimm-Gesellschaft (Brothers Grimm Society) in Kassel and Donald Haase's *The Reception of Grimms' Fairy Tales* (1993). Expanding the latter's focus on Western countries, this volume brings together a varied collection of essays from different parts of the globe, ranging from Japan to Colombia.

In the first part of this book, eight chapters shed light on the dissemination of the Grimm tales in a foreign culture, with its typical dynamics of assimilation and cultural resistance. Three chapters deal with the reception of the tales in Europe, specifically Croatia (Marijana Hameršak), Poland (Monika Wozniak), and Spain (Isabel Hernández and Nieves Martín-Rogero). That the European translations exerted their influence beyond their own continent becomes apparent in Alexandra Michaelis-Vultorius's contribution on the Grimm tales in Colombia. Another four chapters shed light on the tales' diverse manifestations in Asia, in particular in Korea (Dafna Zur), China (Dechao Li), India (Malini Roy), and Japan (Mayako Murai).

The six chapters in Part II shed light on how the Grimm tales were reframed when traveling abroad and affected by intermedial adaptation. Cyrille François examines how French translations of the Grimm tales were influenced by the fairy-tale language established there by Charles Perrault. Ruth Bottigheimer and Sara Hines are concerned with the nineteenth-century reception of the tales in Britain: whereas the former critically examines a selection of prefaces for their attitudes toward the Grimm tales as authentic renditions of an oral folk tradition, the latter considers British illustrations for "The Golden Bird" in the light of evolving printing techniques. Although still within Germany, Bettina Kümmerling-Meibauer shows that the German Democratic Republic provided a particular political climate in which the Grimm tales were revisited and recast—one that was quite distinct from the ideological context in which they first gained popularity. Her focus is on fairy-tale films produced during this era. The final two chapters once again help to shed light on the Asian reception of the Grimm tales: Marianna Missiou considers a French comic book and Japanese manga version of "Hansel and Gretel," and Sung-Ae Lee shows how Korean "Cinderella" adaptations for film and TV illustrate glocalized intercultural blending.

Glocalization is a fairly recent approach that studies the local adaptation of globalized products. When stories travel abroad, the foreign elements may cause friction with local elements, which can lead either to resistance or to innovation, or they may be smoothed out. Sung-Ae Lee uses glocalization as an explicit framework for her chapter, although other authors in this book come to similar conclusions about glocalization by using longer established concepts and methods from translation and reception studies. Taken together, these chapters show that the interaction between local and global that is central to glocalization studies is not unique to current globalization trends. Moreover, the Grimm tales with their interesting paradox between the universal and the local, as well as their long and world-spanning translation history, form a unique and exciting corpus to study these reception processes.

Although this book cannot possibly cover the entire world—Africa and the Middle East, for example, are not discussed—it unites historical and diachronic perspectives as reflections on the functioning of the tales in the contemporary society of a broad number of countries and languages. Considered side by side, the essays offer insights into the features of the Grimms' reception that are internationally constant as well as local particularities. In the rest of this introduction, we highlight five aspects of the common ground that individual chapters cover: the Grimms as a source of inspiration for folklorism, the tales as international classics of children's literature, common translation strategies, visual renderings of the tales, and political and ideological issues.

THE GRIMMS AS A SOURCE OF INSPIRATION FOR INTERNATIONAL FOLKLORISM

As soon as the Grimms' fairy tales moved beyond the German-speaking countries, their international dissemination had a profound impact on several receiving cultures in different corners of the world. Especially in the late nineteenth and early twentieth centuries, the pioneering work of Jacob and Wilhelm Grimm inspired folklorists worldwide to tread in their footsteps and save their own culture's folktales from oblivion. Several chapters in Part I illustrate this influence of the Brothers Grimm on international folklorists. Their impact is to some extent due to the persistent myths that pictured the Grimms as traveling fieldworkers and collectors of authentic tales among the German peasantry, as Dechao Li notes in early twentieth-century China and Malini Roy describes most recently in India with the works of Harikrishna Devsare. Cyrille François, too, shows that even in the 1960s, the editorial of the first complete French translation of the

Kinder- und Hausmärchen relied on assumptions that were proved wrong by scholars such as Heinz Rölleke. In addition, international folklorists relied on the Grimms' own writings on the tales as representative of the German folk spirit and wished to apply these ideals to their own countries of origin. Ruth Bottigheimer's contribution shows that reservations concerning the mythic origins and German roots of the Grimms' tales expressed by early British fairy-tale translators vanished toward the end of the nineteenth century under the influence of the compelling romantic ideal of transnational, ancient folktales. The romantic idealization of the Brothers Grimm as faithful spokespeople of the German folk proves to be persistent to date. Although we may deplore the lack of interest in the actual methods that the Grimms used to compile their fairy-tale collection, it is also partly thanks to this idealized picture that many folklorists once felt inspired to imitate the Grimms' example and that readers worldwide were and are still attracted to their tales.

Several chapters in Part I address the fact that the Brothers Grimm not only were interested in German folklore and literature but also maintained a broad international interest, which, during their lives, brought them into contact with a large number of scholars throughout Europe. Sometimes their influence was established through direct, personal contacts as well as by the launch of several appeals to send them folktales. In 1811, for example, Jacob Grimm published a request in a Dutch journal to send him folktales and epic stories, and in fact he maintained contact with several Dutch and Flemish scholars throughout his life. The Grimms were also members of various international societies and key figures in the Germanic Society of Frankfurt, which united linguists and literary scholars. From Marijana Hameršak's chapter, we learn that Jacob Grimm was an honorary member of the Croatian Historical Society founded in 1850; as Isabel Hernández and Nieves Martín-Rogero demonstrate, Fernán Caballero (1859) referred to the Grimms' interest in popular literature during the Spanish Golden Age in order to raise awareness in Spain of a collection of tales that in her opinion was international in its own right.

The Grimms' works and prefaces continued to inspire long after their initial publication. The prefaces often contained ambivalences that may have caused considerable debate and confusion but that also made their ideas flexible enough to appeal to foreign folklorists and translators occupying a wide range of positions. To the ambivalences for which the Grimms themselves are responsible, folklorists and translators in other countries added some of their own. The paradox that Hameršak points out in the Croatian reception of the tales is valid for several other countries: the Grimm tales were used abroad as models of national folklore, but by obliterating their national features and the Grimms' names, they often functioned as and blended with local folktales.

Several chapters in this volume draw attention to the fact that the Grimm tales were often published anonymously. The interpretation of the Grimms' folkloristic method and legacy by mediators abroad often involved interesting paradoxes and mind switching between the foreign and the local, between national and international, between oral and written transmission, and between high and low culture. For example, Zur indicates that in the colonized Korea of the 1910s the European tales by the Brothers Grimm, which were introduced through the Japanese colonizer, served the Korean people in strengthening their nationalist feelings and raising interest in their local folktales. Roy explains that although Harikrishna Devsare's recent Grimm translation relies heavily on the English translation history of the tales, he paradoxically also draws on their distinct German national character to deliver a panegyric on nationalistic feeling in the service of the modern Indian nation-state. And in Franco's Spain, Hernández and Martín-Rogero explain that the Grimms' tales were allowed to circulate as "harmless" stories for children but were imbued with added feelings of Spanish patriotism in spite of their German origin.

In several countries the Grimm tales were thus treated as written folklore when they appeared in translation. "Written folklore" is a term coined by Aleida Assmann and applied by Emer O' Sullivan to the translation of children's literature; it describes the transmission of literature in print with mechanisms and features that are usually associated with the more flexible transmission of oral tales. The usage of the Grimms' tales as written folklore abroad involved the obliteration of local German characteristics as well as the frequent omission of the Brothers Grimm's names. As is evident in the contributions by Hernández and Martín-Rogero, Hameršak, and Wozniak, this indeed was the case for the printed tradition of the Grimms in Spain, Croatia, and Poland, respectively. As a result, the Grimm tales were at times mistaken abroad for local tales and attributed to authors and collectors who were in fact their translators or adaptors. Although many folklorists relied heavily on romantic concepts of originality, authenticity, and local character in discussing the importance of the Grimms' legacy for their own culture, the international reception of the Grimm tales tells a recurrent story of borrowings, adaptations, and cultural hybrids.

Not all countries were eager to welcome the Grimm tales, however. In some countries, the tales by Hans Christian Andersen gained popularity before the Grimms', even though Andersen started publishing his *Eventyr* several decades later. Reasons for this delayed introduction vary. In the Netherlands there was a resentful attitude toward folktales, which were considered uninteresting nonsense (Joosen 40). Wozniak attributes the late acceptance of Grimm in Poland to political reasons. When Poland stood partly under Prussian rule in the nineteenth century, the Polish were unlikely to welcome a collection of tales that promoted itself as exemplifying the German national spirit.

AMBIVALENT INNOVATIONS AS CHILDREN'S LITERATURE

Despite the title *Kinder- und Hausmärchen*, the Grimms' purpose was a scholarly one, so the format of the 1812 edition of the tales was not designed to appeal to young readers. Soon after their appearance, however, the tales raised debate in Germany about their suitability as children's literature, a topic that the Grimms discussed with several of their friends (Rölleke). This concern for young readers led Wilhelm Grimm to omit certain erotic and confrontational tales and passages from the second edition of the *Kinder- und Hausmärchen*. A little later the success of the child-friendly English translation of 1823 by Edgar Taylor and David Jardine with illustrations by George Cruikshank inspired the Grimms to publish a small, illustrated collection of tales specifically aimed at young readers, the so-called *Kleine Ausgabe* (Rölleke 279–82). It is a noteworthy example of how a translation can influence the content and reception of an original source text.

The debate on the suitability of the tales for children was mimicked and continued in other countries, although outside of Germany such discussions were usually based on the later and already partly sanitized editions of the tales. In spite of recurrent adaptations in the translations, they served abroad as important sources of innovation for children's literature. From several chapters in this volume it becomes clear that literary and folkloristic magazines were a highly important medium to introduce selected Grimm tales abroad, yet it is mainly as tales in children's books and fairy-tale collections for children that they have captured the imagination of a broad audience. In Japan, the Grimms' tales played a central role in the golden age of children's literature in the early twentieth century, as Mayako Murai shows, when Japanese culture stood under a strong Western influence and was introduced to European Romanticism.

The Romantic ideals that the tales expressed often stood in competition with a strong Enlightenment tradition in countries abroad, which required didactic, realistic stories for children and was hesitant to accept fantasy as suitable for them. This tension frequently delayed a successful introduction of the Grimm tales in countries such as the Netherlands (Joosen 40) and Spain, as Hernández and Martín-Rogero demonstrate. In Spain, it required a daring publisher to make the tales available, and it is thanks to the editorial work of Saturnino Calleja that the Grimm tales became so successful there. Wozniak makes a similar case for the importance of the publishing house of Gebethner and Wolff in the innovation of children's literature in nineteenth-century Poland by introducing the Grimm tales, among others, to a broad public. The chapters by Li, Michaelis-Vultorius, and Murai demonstrate that in countries such as China, Colombia, and Japan, respectively, Grimm tales were imported for their pedagogical content, albeit in adapted form. Whereas the Grimm tales helped to make fantasy an acceptable form of children's literature in several countries, their cruelty was often disapproved of for a young audience. Just as translators have not shied away from localizing the tales and obscuring their German character, many have not hesitated to delete from the tales the scenes that might have frightened young children or provoked resistance in their parents.

It is evident that these varied appropriations of the Grimm tales in the supposed interests of a child audience served a number of purposes, from the imaginative to the ideological, and may have resulted in the paring down of any given tale to its essence. As Emer O'Sullivan has noted for many other classics of children's literature, the introduction of foreign stories for children often happens through a highly selective procedure, so that, for example, Carlo Collodi's rich account of "Pinocchio" is often reduced to a story about a wooden doll with a long nose (138–45). Indeed, the chapters in this volume confirm Donald Haase's statement from 1993 that "Hansel and Gretel—along with other fairy-tale characters—may live on, but they do not always play the parts given them by the Grimms" (10). In the international reception of the Grimms' fairy tales, innovation through translation and cultural context adaptation often go hand in hand.

Translation

As suggested above, the worldwide transmission of the Grimms' tales could not have taken place without the mediation of translators, whose work is sometimes anonymous and often taken for granted. Wilhelm and Jacob Grimm themselves were highly aware of the importance and difficulty of good translations. Although both commended Taylor and Jardine's English translation in response to Taylor's gift of a copy (letter to Taylor of 25 June 1823 qtd. in Hartwig 7–9), the general nature and purpose of translation had earlier been the subject of some dissension between the brothers. Jacob declared his reservations concerning the translation of ancient poetry in response to Wilhelm's German versions of the *Altdänische Heldenlieder, Balladen und Märchen* (Old Danish Heroic Songs, Ballads and Fairy Tales) of 1811. Jacob's conviction, as expressed in a letter to his former mentor Friedrich Carl von Savigny of 20 May 1811, was that any literary work is created in the form and language essential to it and that therefore its form and content (or rather its "Leib und Seele," body and soul; *Briefe der Brüder Grimm an Savigny* 102) should not be separated in the course of translation into another language. Since Jacob Grimm believed that no translation could approach the original in quality, he preferred a critical gloss, a crib or a deliberately "unfaithful" translation—in other words an adaptation or retelling (undated letter to Savigny; *Briefe der Brüder Grimm an Savigny* 116). Wilhelm argued that just as any text only comes into existence in the mind of a reader, a translation is simply the translator's individual response to the text in hand (letter to Savigny of 20 May 1811; *Briefe der Brüder Grimm an Savigny* 108). Both points of view were to have resonance in the complex translation history and transition of the Grimms' own best-known work, a transition that ranges from painstaking versions that remain close to the German text to free translations and even multimedia adaptations.

Crossing linguistic and cultural borders altered the status, context, medium, form, and genre of the Grimm tales, sometimes with changes so radical as to render them almost unrecognizable. A contemporary South Korean film of "Hansel and Gretel" featuring a grotesque orphanage director who tortures and starves abandoned children (Sung-Ae Lee) and the sensationalized Japanese retellings of the late 1990s (Mayako Murai) may be linked by the most tenuous of threads to the Grimms' tales, yet they are indicative of the challenge authors and adaptors relish in reworking stories that have long enjoyed universal currency. A spectrum of transformation now exists, from the mediator whose intention is to produce a faithful rendering that may nonetheless include degrees of domestication, censorship, and revision to the playful or subversive creator. Straightforward translation has gradually become the province of the scholarly edition, as adaptations and retellings dominate in meeting the undiminished demand for new versions of classic fairy tales.

The interlingual journey of the Grimms' tales has, moreover, been subject to stops along the way. It is striking to note just how often translators have not drawn on a German source text at all but rather on a translation into an intermediate language. Historically, relay translation (Dollerup) was an expedient means of conveying a text into a third language when a translation of the source text into a second, intermediary language was widely available or when the language of the source text was not particularly well known in the target culture. Thus the first edition of the Grimms' tales to appear in French was translated from the English of Edgar Taylor, as Cyrille François demonstrates here, probably because Taylor's one-volume format was readily accessible—and shorter—than the Grimms' two-volume work. For her part, Hameršak suggests that the first Croatian translation of the Grimms' "Robber Bridegroom" (1865) was possibly a relay translation via Czech.

Relay translation is also widespread in colonial contexts. Roy describes the dependence on English sources for translations of the Grimms' tales as standard practice for translations of texts of (non-English) world literature into the vernacular languages of India. Similarly, the Grimms' tales entered Korea via the language of the colonizer, in this case Japan, as Zur establishes. Naturally, economic considerations also come into play in the planning of new editions of fairy tales, so that a publisher will sometimes make use of an existing, successfully packaged translation rather than commission a new one. For example, as Michaelis-Vultorius has determined in the case of Colombia, a twenty-four-volume edition of fairy tales that had sold well in Italy, and that included tales by the Grimms, became the source for a comparable Spanish-language version published in Colombia. In this case, therefore, the Grimms became accessible to a Spanish-speaking audience through an Italian translation of German texts.

A second phenomenon that arises either from a cavalier approach to translation and editing or from the eclectic practice of retellers is that of the blending of tales from the French and German traditions. Given the overlap of material, it is not surprising that a common confusion of the Grimms' tales with those of Charles Perrault, particularly of "Cinderella" and "Sleeping Beauty," is replicated in written versions. Karen Seago has traced a gradual merging of Perrault and Grimm versions of "Sleeping Beauty" into hybrid English-language versions in the United Kingdom. In this volume Wozniak recounts similar instances of the combination of motifs from both sources by Polish authors, whereas François provides intriguing insights into how Perrault's heritage has influenced the choice, titles, and written style of Grimm tales translated into French. Evidence of a further dimension to intercultural integration can be found in Lee's account of the blending of the Grimms' tales with local analogues in Korea.

Once child readers became the target audience for the tales, translators began to adapt the Grimms' texts to prevailing expectations of child behavior and experience, practicing both cultural domestication and moral adjustment in the form of censorship. Read-aloud qualities, for example, are essential to the survival of the Grimms' tales as stories for children, and names of key characters have often been changed to those customary in the target language. Violence, references to sexuality, and religious material were toned down or deleted from translations from the nineteenth century onward (see Sutton for a detailed account of such practices in nineteenth-century English translations). One instance in which censorship occurs across a number of cultures is "The Frog King" with its frequently omitted scenario of a newly transformed prince spending a night with the princess: Zur cites a Korean version in which a wedding ceremony replaces any hint of suspect room sharing. In recent decades authors and retellers of adult versions have deliberately chosen to reverse this trend toward censorship, adapting the basic plot or theme of familiar tales formerly associated with childhood to create works that are both compelling and disturbing in their emphasis on violence and sexuality. Murai discusses this trend in detail for Japan.

THE VISUAL

Illustration, picture book versions, and—from the early twentieth century onward—film adaptations of the Grimms' tales have formed a tide of visual transformation that has spread across the world and sent powerful waves back to its German source. As mentioned above, Edgar Taylor's first translation into English of a limited selection of tales, illustrated by satirical caricaturist George Cruikshank, alerted the Grimm brothers to the potential popularity of a single volume with attractive images. Thus, thanks to a translation and its English illustrator, the *Kleine Ausgabe* came into being, an edition that was, according to Jennifer Schacker, to be responsible for the "bourgeois commodification" of the tales in their country of origin and across Europe. Cruikshank's scurrilous humor appealed both to the British reader and to the Grimms, but his was an idiosyncratic interpretation of the material. Indeed, all illustrators choose telling moments from a tale to enhance a reader's imaginative experience; they present their own vision of a particular incident that renews and invigorates the reading of the written word. Sara Hines reveals just how different these interpretations may be, both artistically and in terms of the development of printing techniques, with reference to Cruikshank's and other illustrated versions of a single tale, "The Golden Bird." High-quality illustration of the tales would not, of course, be possible without the advances in technology that Hines describes. Gradually, as technological progress gained pace and both the late nineteenth-century "gift book" and twentieth-century picture book became popular as keepsakes and stories to be read to children, the commissioning of an artist to illustrate collections or individual tales emerged as a leading factor in the publication of new editions.

Artists also become mediators, as their work is shaped by a complex system of influences. Wozniak points out that it was not only translators but also illustrators who domesticated the Grimm tales in order to obliterate their link with a detested Germany in postwar Poland. Later in the twentieth century, artists created revisions of Grimm tales to accompany retellings, whether for the purpose of entertaining young readers familiar with the Grimm pre-texts, or for ideological reasons. Feminist retellings, for example, required a very different artistic rendering of male and female characters, with Michael Martchenko's illustrations to Robert Munsch's *Paper Bag Princess* as a prime example. Not only does the text depart from the traditional, passive fairy-tale princess, but also the illustrations contribute to establishing a new kind of heroine who values character and independence over looks. As fairy-tale criticism developed in the 1970s, illustrators—like authors— often incorporated critical interpretations and layers in their illustrations.

The British illustrator Anthony Browne is a good example here—his work in particular seems to be indebted to psychoanalytic fairy-tale readings such as Bruno Bettelheim's (see Joosen). Although various German illustrators have worked intensely with the Grimm tales as international classics, countries that have welcomed the Grimms have also produced their own illustrated versions, which once again demonstrate the blending of the global with the local.

A turning point that was to have a new and radical effect on the international reception of the tales was the leap from static to moving pictures through the advent of cinema. Once film versions of particular tales and attendant publications appeared, cinematic images had the potential to supersede illustrations in children's imaginations. Debates on negative aspects of the appropriation of fairy tales by the Disney Corporation continue (Zipes), but the consequences of international film distribution on the reception of the Grimms' tales and their impact are not always predictable. As the detailed investigation into the reception of the Grimms' tales in Colombia by Michaelis-Vultorius suggests, it was the 1937 Disney adaptation of the Grimms' "Snow White" that inspired interest in the existence of tales previously little known in the country and that therefore had an unforeseen and beneficial effect. Later in the twentieth century, film versions of Grimm tales served a specific ideological purpose in the era of the German Democratic Republic or, in an entirely different context, have reflected in a macabre manner contemporary social concerns in South Korean films and TV series loosely based on Grimm motifs. And, in a rapidly developing visual narrative format that simulates the action and movement of the animated cartoon, recent manifestations of the ninth art in comic strip and manga versions have moved the Grimms' tales into entirely new genres. Today, Grimm tales and motifs appear in visual form in our lives on a daily basis, from advertisements to children's toys and clothing and even adult TV drama, in which one of the most recent examples, the American NBC police procedural series *Grimm*, features characters inspired by the tales.

POLITICAL AND IDEOLOGICAL ISSUES

The persistent belief that the Grimms rendered a faithful reflection of German folktales and of the German national identity appealed to states or cultures aspiring to establish or reinvigorate their own national consciousness.

As indicated, Zur cites parallels identified by a number of Korean scholars between the Grimm brothers' project of enhancing German national identity and the promotion of national culture by their Korean counterparts working under Japanese colonial subjugation in the 1920s. Moreover, authors have adapted the tales to address a range of social and ideological issues beyond those pertaining to the politics of nationality. Indeed, it is well known that the Grimms themselves labeled the *Kinder- und Hausmärchen* an "*Erziehungsbuch*," a book for education, and this notion is taken on in some surprising new contexts. As Roy shows, the award-winning children's writer Harikrishna Devsare was eager to stress the educational value of the collection when he recently published a translation in Hindi (*Grimm Bandhuon Ki Kahaniyan,* 2000). Not only does he attempt to relocate the political background of a united Germany to modern-day India, but he also performs a surprising revaluation of the collection's gender models. As Roy explains, his valuation of gender roles in tales by the Grimms runs counter to the former trend of critical opinion, for example in the work of Marcia Lieberman, Jack Zipes, and Ruth Bottigheimer, regarding the supposed prevalence of passive heroines.

Germany's own post-Grimm political history has also played its part in the tales' reception at home and abroad. In the aftermath of the Third Reich, the holocaust, and the Second World War, the tales were subject to accusations that they had promoted the violence and cruelty perpetrated by the Nazi regime; the allied forces occupying Germany even operated a temporary ban on their publication. Wozniak details the drastic strategy of removal of the *Kinder- und Hausmärchen* from Polish children's literature for over a decade. Only in 1956, after the end of the Stalinist era and when some of the anti-German resentment had faded, did it become possible to propose a new edition of the Grimms' tales in Poland. In the Communist German Democratic Republic, on the other hand, the tales were manipulated in film versions to represent Socialist ideals (Kümmerling-Meibauer).

Today the travels of the Grimms' tales into new forms and media continue apace. This volume cannot claim to be comprehensive in its coverage of their international reception; rather, it serves as an introduction to the range of cross-cultural reinterpretations to date. Little can the Grimm brothers, looking to the local German past to retrieve fast disappearing songs, tales, and legends (preface to the 1819 edition), have imagined the scale, the political, aesthetic, and sociocultural dimensions their collection was to achieve in the future in all corners of the globe. Yet by adapting and revising the tales for literary and didactic reasons, the Grimms themselves (particularly Wilhelm) began a process that became both a preoccupation and a challenge to their concept of the organic and sacrosanct origins or the folktale. On the one hand the 1819 preface unequivocally and at length condemns "*Bearbeitungen*"—the radical rewriting of folktale material to embellish and sentimentalize it—as superficial and short lived, while on the other there is a reluctant acceptance of new interpretations that re-create the tales as contemporary works of art: "denn wer hätte Lust, der Poesie Grenzen abzustecken?" (for who would want to set borders for poetry? Grimm 31).

That crossing of linguistic and cultural borders was, of course, unstoppable once the first translations appeared. Grimm scholars may have reservations about some of the appropriations of Grimm tales revealed in these pages, but the publication of scholarly editions and translations continues alongside a dynamics of cross-cultural reception that is as unpredictable as it is invigorating. New issues and contexts will undoubtedly emerge regarding the translation and adaptation of the *Kinder- und Hausmärchen* into different languages and media. Fairy tales as international classics are often preferred material when it comes to introducing new media. Over a century ago, that was the case for film, and now we can witness the same development for tablet computers and e-books. They too often implement fairy tales as well known and popular stories to demonstrate their technological possibilities and are bound to catch the attention of fairy-tale scholars soon. As was the case for Jacob and Wilhelm Grimm's bicentenary in 1985 and 1986, the 2012 anniversary gave rise to a new wave of publications, both literary and academic, and we also witnessed a new wave of fairy-tale films. At the beginning of the third century since the publication of the tales, we can only await with keen anticipation the next round of local and global transformations.

References

Assmann, Aleida. "Schriftliche Folklore. Zur Entstehung und Funktion eines Überlieferungstyps." *Schrift und Gedächtnis.* Eds. Aleida Assmann et al. Munich: Z. N., 1983. 175–93.

Dollerup, Cay. "'Relay' and 'Support' Translations." *Translation in Context. Selected Contributions from the EST Congress, Granada 1998.* Eds. A. Chesterman, N. San Salvador, and Y. Gambier. Amsterdam: John Benjamins, 2000. 17–26.

Grimm, Jacob, and Wilhelm Grimm. *Briefe der Brüder Grimm an Savigny. Aus dem Savignyschen Nachlass. Herausgegeben in Verbindung mit Ingeborg Schnack von Wilhelm Schoof.* Berlin: Erich Schmidt, 1953.

———. *Kinder- und Hausmärchen gesammelt durch die Brüder Grimm.* Illus. Otto Ubbelohde. Frankfurt: Insel, 1974.

Haase, Donald. *The Reception of Grimms' Fairy Tales: Response, Reactions, Revisions.* Detroit: Wayne State UP, 1993.

Hartwig, O. "Zur ersten englischen Übersetzung der *Kinder- und Hausmärchen* der Brüder Grimm. Mit ungedruckten Briefen von Edgar Taylor, J. u. W. Grimm, Walter Scott, und G. Benecke." *Centralblatt für Bibliothekswesen* 15.1–2 (1898): 1–16.

Hennig, Dieter, and Bernhard Lauer, eds. *200 Jahre Brüder Grimm: Dokumente ihres Lebens und Wirkens.* Kassel: Weber-Weidemeyer, 1986.

Joosen, Vanessa. *Wit als sneeuw, zwart als inkt: De sprookjes van Grimm in de Nederlandstalige literatuur.* Leuven: LannooCampus, 2012.

O'Sullivan, Emer. *Comparative Children's Literature.* Trans. Anthea Bell. London: Routledge, 2005.

Rölleke, Heinz. *Die Märchen der Brüder Grimm: Quellen und Studien. Gesammelte Aufsätze.* Trier: Wissenschaftlicher Verlag Trier, 2000.

Seago, Karen. "Nursery Politics: *Sleeping Beauty,* or the Acculturation of a Tale." *New Comparison* 20 (1995): 14–29.

Sutton, Martin. *The Sin Complex: A Critical Study of English Versions of the Grimms' 'Kinder- und Hausmärchen.'* Kassel: Schriften der Brüder-Grimm-Gesellschaft, 1996.

Zipes, Jack. "Breaking the Disney Spell." *Classic Fairy Tales.* Ed. Maria Tatar. New York: Norton, 1999. 332–52.

I

Cultural Resistance and Assimilation

1

No-Name Tales

Early Croatian Translations
of the Grimms' Tales

MARIJANA HAMERŠAK

According to bibliographical sources (See *Građa za hrvatskih retrospektivnu bibliografiju knjiga 1835–1940*), the oldest Croatian translations of a coherent selection from the Grimms' collection were published in the first decades of the twentieth century, almost a century after the *Kinder- und Hausmärchen* first appeared. At first glance, the situation is no better with Croatian translations of individual Grimm tales. As Milan Crnković (104) argues in his fundamental book on nineteenth-century Croatian children's literature, the first tale explicitly, although very discreetly (at the end of the tale), attributed to the Grimms appeared in Croatian in 1895, when a translation of "The Seven Ravens" (KHM 25) was published in a children's magazine. Moreover, a close look at Croatian children's magazines and books shows that this is not only the first but also the only tale explicitly ascribed to the Brothers Grimm in nineteenth-century Croatian children's literature.

The rather late translations of the Grimms' tales in Croatia may seem strange if you consider the country's social, political, and literary history. Croatia was part of the Habsburg Monarchy, and there were numerous cultural and social interferences between the Croatian and German cultural spheres (Goldstein 54–107). For example, Croatian secular primers were bilingual (Croatian and German) until the second half of the nineteenth century, and one of the first Croatian children's novels ever published was Anton Vranich's translation of Joachim Heinrich Campe's *Robinson der Jüngere* (Robinson the Younger, originally published in 1779/1780) in 1796. Writers such as Franz Friedrich Hoffmann and Christoph von Schmid were the most popular authors of nineteenth-century Croatian children's literature (see Crnković; Majhut). Hence it comes as no surprise that Crnković (104) found several Croatian translations or, to be more precise, appropriations of the Grimms' tales prior to the publication of the only nineteenth-century Croatian translation of signed Grimm tales in 1895. These Grimm tales were rewritten and published in Croatian in the 1880s, but without reference to their source text (104).

Broadening the scope of Crnković's corpus to include not only periodicals but also monographs from nineteenth-century Croatian children's literature adds dozens of tales and reveals that Croatian translations of the Grimms' tales had been published systematically, as well as anonymously, in the 1870s. Moreover, a variant of the Grimms' "Robber Bridegroom" (KHM 40) was published in 1865 in the oldest Croatian children's magazine, similarly appearing with no reference to its original author or source and mentioning only the following paratextual element: translated by M.V. ("Dvie pripoviedke"). Then again, significant differences in form and content between this variant and the Grimms' tale open up the possibility that another source text lies at the base—Marijan Šabić (96) suggests that it is probably a translation from Czech. The Croatian variant might well be a so-called chain or relay translation from German into Czech and from Czech into Croatian. However, the extensive international oral and print distribution of this tale (Goldberg 348–53; Lang 847–48) indicates that we cannot exclude the possibility that it was based on one or more source text independent of the Grimms' variant.

A very similar line of argumentation is viable for a significant number of other anonymous nineteenth-century Croatian children's tales, which could, at best, be labeled rewritings or retellings based on the Grimms' motifs and structures. Still, most of these motifs and structures already circulated in print and/or oral form before and especially after *Die Kinder- und Hausmärchen* was published. This further complicates an unambiguous determination of the source text(s) of these anonymous tales. Setting aside all the unambiguously attributable tales of Croatian children's literature as well as several dramatizations of the Grimms' tales published by Croatian authors (Crnković 104), we are still left with at least thirty-two translated or appropriated individual Grimm tales in Croatian children's literature before 1895. More than half of them are close or verbatim translations of Grimm (Hameršak,

"A Neverending Story?"), whereas the other half could be labeled appropriations.[1] Moreover, given that some of the Grimms' tales were translated several times in this period, and some translations were reprinted repeatedly, we are dealing with nearly one hundred Croatian translations of the Grimms' tales published before 1895[2]—all of them with no paratextual reference to the Brothers Grimm as the source text (see Appendix). Most of these tales were published in Croatian children's folktale collections, whereas several were appropriated for children's picture books, magazines, and anthologies.

In order to comprehend the significance of this abundance of Grimm tales it should be mentioned that during the nineteenth century, fairy tales, and folktales in general, were not a privileged genre in Croatian children's literature. Quite the contrary, they were introduced into this field as late as the 1860s. Until 1895 fairy tales were recognized as a relevant, but by no means a preferred, children's genre. However, fairy tales were privileged in Croatian picture books as soon as this genre was established in the 1880s. Therefore, when we adopt a genre-sensitive perspective, it can be readily observed that the Grimms' tales were marginal on the level of children's literature in general but dominant on the level of picture books. Setting aside the complexities of the material history of the Grimms' adoption and reception in Croatian children's literature,[3] this chapter will further on focus on the cultural, legal, and conceptual foundation of the anonymity of these translations or appropriations and their paradoxical role in the construction of Croatian national identity in the nineteenth century.

ONCE UPON A TIME: ANONYMITY

In our age of seemingly strict copyright practices, it may seem odd that nineteenth-century Croatian translations of the Grimms' tales have no reference to the Grimms as their original authors or editors. But, as is well known, literary discourse was not always, constantly, and universally endowed with the author function. In the Middle Ages, Michel Foucault explains, "The texts that we today call 'literary' (narratives, stories, epics, tragedies, comedies etc.) were accepted . . . without any question about the identity of their author" (109). Contrary to popular perception, which is also expressed in Foucault's work,[4] anonymity in literary discourse did not dissolve steadily and gradually, nor did this ever happen in the seventeenth or eighteenth century (Chartier 32).

The shift from anonymous to signed literary works depended on the cultural, economic, and political context of a given literary field, and it varied in this field according to genre, gender, class, and other characteristics. At the turn of the nineteenth century, for example, translations and satire were still mostly anonymous in the context of English literature (Erickson 267). Novels were more often anonymous than poetry books, and children's books more than books for adults (Feldman 282–87). In Zohar Shavit's words, "For quite a long time (long after adult writers had ceased the practice . . .), writers for children (especially men) would not sign their work. Most likely, they were interested in writing for children because of the chances for commercial success or because of ideological motivations" (38–39). Anonymity was particularly common in the field of children's literature translations. As Gillian Lathey demonstrated in her study of translators of children's literature as "invisible storytellers," in English-language children's literature "anonymity remained common well into the eighteenth century, with either no accreditation of the translation at all, or the use of initials or the formula 'translation by several hands'—a phrase that conjures up intriguing images of collective translation" (112).

LITERATURE AND LAW

When discussing anonymous Grimm tales in nineteenth-century Croatian children's literature, it is important to emphasize that, contrary to Foucault's suggestion (109), the common use of anonymity, as Gérard Genette argued, "did not die out even in the nineteenth-century as quickly as one might think" (45).[5] Nineteenth-century works by notable French writers such as Victor Hugo and Stendhal were also published anonymously. According to Robert Griffin, anonymity (conceived in the broadest sense as the absence of the proper name of the writer on the front page of the book) affected nearly every author at the time, including the Romantic poets (Griffin 882), who are most often unjustly credited with developing the oversimplified notion of the author as an autonomous genius (Bennett 55–71). Walter Scott's *Waverley,* all the books that Jane Austen published during her lifetime, and over half of Shelley's work, for example, were originally printed without reference to their proper names.

Over the course of time these and many other originally anonymous or pseudonymous works were attributed to their rightful authors. In her convincing deconstruction of the myth of anonymous female poets in the Romantic era, Paula Feldman showed that during Romanticism newspapers and periodicals customarily published contributions, including poetry, without the authors' proper names or under pseudonyms, whether they were male or female (282). However, as Lee Erickson (247) reported about Romantic poets in general, they eventually abandoned their anonymity when their poems were collected in books.

During the nineteenth century, anonymity was flourishing in English weekly and daily newspapers, whereas many monthly and quarterly journals employed signatures by the 1880s (Sagner Buurma 21). In Croatian journals and magazines many contributions were also anonymous during the nineteenth century. The form of anonymity varied, from a complete lack of identification to the use of pseudonyms or initials (Brešić 28). The most famous example of anonymity in Croatian literature is Juraj Šporer's (alias Jure Matić) *Almanah ilirski* (The Illyrian Almanac) published in 1823 with not a single signed contribution, with the exception of Baroque poems by I. Ivanišević, which were, in Šporer's words, substantially modified. The same was true in Croatian children's magazines; anonymity was also, if not a dominant, at least a common, practice and affected not just the Grimms. In her discussion of poems in the English Civil War, Ellen Gruber Garvey (160) suggests that anonymity in collective publications allows texts "to blend into a general field" of other contributions that may be perceived as similar by readers.

Similarly, entirely or predominantly anonymous contributions in nineteenth-century Croatian children's magazines and anthologies produced homogeneity and filiation on the level of the publication, not on the level of the author's name. In this medium the Grimms' tales blended in seamlessly with the other contributions in a magazine or the other tales or poems in a particular anthology, pushing away any thoughts about their authors or their original definition as German folktales and fairy tales. They were adopted in Croatian first of all to participate in, as Jack Zipes says, "discourse about mores, values, and manners so that children would become civilized according to the social code of that time" (3). They merged with the other anonymous and nonanonymous literary texts published in order to instruct and amuse Croatian child readers.

It must be admitted that the prevailing anonymity was sometimes the result of rather mundane reasons. As suggested in the introductory note to the oldest Croatian nonfunctional children's anthology, *Mali tobolac raznog cvětja* (A Little Knapsack Full of Flowers), published in 1850 by teacher, reformer, and writer Ivan Filipović: "The translated contributions are anonymous, not by a fault of my own. The fact that they were thus presented in the original publications is to be blamed" (7). Like most popular literature, Croatian children's literature was frequently based on free exchange, endless borrowings, and circulations. In this process, signatures were often lost, not only due to accidental omissions in rewriting but also because they were irrelevant to the producers and consumers of popular literature. In the case of collective works such as anthologies, almanacs, pamphlets, and popular magazines, it was the product and its genre, its layout, and possibly the editors' or publishers' rather than the authors' names that defined the readers' horizon of expectations.

Furthermore, the author's signature was irrelevant in the context of nineteenth-century Croatian literature because most Croatian translations from the period were in accordance with Klaus Roth's finding about translations of southeast European popular literature in general: "rewritings (or 'imitations') rather than translations; the foreign texts were acculturated to the tradition of the target society in such a way that in many cases the original language or culture were no longer recognizable by the Balkan reader. This 'domestication' was so common that it had its own names in the Balkan countries, such as *posrbe* (Milincevic 1984), *pobălgarjavane* (Mincev 1912) or Hellenization, and was considered necessary by the educated elites and the translators, at least until the beginning of the 20th century" (Roth 250).

Pohrvaćenje (Croatization), the Croatian word for this kind of domestication (Venuti 31), was a standard procedure in both adults' and children's nineteenth-century Croatian literature. According to Crnković, the majority of nineteenth-century Croatian children's literature was "more or less an adaptation and 'Croatisation' of texts read in children's journals from all over the Monarchy, primarily in Czech or German" (104). Almost all the appropriations of the Grimm tales (i.e., half of all individual Grimm tales) in Croatian children's literature until 1895 followed this line of adoption. And in this process, it was much more difficult to keep a signature than to lose it.

The anonymity of nearly one hundred published Croatian translations and appropriations of Grimm tales turns out to be a norm, rather than a deviation, if we take into consideration the legislative framework of authorial rights in which it was developed. In this respect, Griffin's conclusion about a lack of any cause and effect relation between naming the author and affirmation of copyright in England is of particular importance. Publishing and copyright regulations in England were primarily imposed on printers, publishers, and distributors, which goes to show that naming and copyright protection operated on two different levels of discourse and required authors to make separate (and unrelated) decisions (Griffin 889). After all, as David Šporer (73) reminds us, the institution of copyright laws emerged at the beginning of the eighteenth century and was primarily a result of the aspiration of London publishers to protect their interests, not the authors'.

The status of translations in nineteenth-century copyright legislation in Croatia also shows that the regulations were designed to protect producers, distributors, and books viewed as material entities distributed for profit, rather than to protect the author's name or the aesthetic identity of the author. Thus, the regulations focused on the violation of rights for those products that could financially jeopardize the distribution of original editions. Publications in a different language were not in direct competition with the original and were therefore out of the scope of these legislative acts. In the legislative framework ("Zakonski" § 1 and "Austrian" § 7.3) relevant for the Croatian translations or appropriations of the Grimms' tales as anonymous, the consent of authors or their successors was a prerequisite for translation only in exceptional cases (when authors or their successors have explicitly reserved the right to arrange for its translation)—and only within one to three years of the original publication. When, as was the case with the Grimms' collection, the authors did not explicitly claim the right to arrange for the translation, anyone was free to translate and publish the work in Croatian. Thus the Grimms' collection or individual tales from it could be circulated in Croatian regardless of "a lawsuit that was brought after Wilhelm [Grimm]'s death, when pirated versions threatened to erode the income to Wilhelm's heirs deriving from sales of *Die Kinder- und Hausmärchen*" (Bottigheimer, *Grimms' Bad* 7). In other words, in contrast to the situation in the German-speaking part of the Monarchy, where *Die Kinder- und Hausmärchen* was protected by copyright until the beginning of the twentieth century (Bottigheimer, "Publishing History" 87), in Croatia the tales were freely appropriated and translated completely legally.

Moreover, according to the same legislation that was in effect during the period when nearly one hundred Croatian translations or appropriations of the Grimms' tales were published as anonymous tales, the name of the author was required only for the extracts selected from the works of various writers and put together into a collection for a specific literary purpose or to be used in church, in school, or for teaching purposes in general ("Zakonski" § 9.1.; "Austrian" § 5.c). In all other instances, the legislative framework mentions no requirement to include information about the original source (such as the author's name). It was up to authors to decide whether their work would be signed or not because, according to the law, "No author may be forced to sign his work against his will" ("Zakonski" § 1). Signing or not signing was at the authors' discretion or at the discretion of the translator or editor in the case of a translation. Therefore, some of them did include the names of the source text authors, whereas others did not.

NATION AND FOLK NARRATION

Whether or not an author's name was revealed depended on gender, genre, publication, and social class, as well as the author's status. It is precisely because of their status that some names were commonly referred to in Croatian publications, despite legislative voluntarism and a tendency toward anonymity in translations and collective works. For example, in contrast to the publishing history of the Grimms, the names of extremely popular writers such as Hoffmann and von Schmid and cultural and intellectual coryphaei such as Johann Gottfried Herder, Pavel Jozef Šafárik, Alexander Pushkin, Božena Němcová, and Hans Christian Andersen were regularly featured in the nineteenth-century Croatian translations of their texts (see Brešić). The ideas and works of these authors were well known in Croatia (directly or indirectly) or, as is the case with Herder, Pushkin, Šafárik, and Němcová, they were recognized as well known at least by the intellectual elite. Therefore, featuring their names enabled their (further) acceptance in nineteenth-century Croatian culture and promoted the translation and reception of their works.

On the other hand, Jacob and Wilhelm Grimm's work was presented as anonymous (except for the abovementioned "exception," i.e., the translation of "The Seven Ravens" published in 1895), even though the brothers were far from unknown to nineteenth-century readers in Croatia. As the Croatian folklorist Maja Bošković-Stulli (*Priče* 93) reminds us, the Grimms' usage of the term "*Sagen*" had been adopted in the Croatian context as early as the 1830s. The death of Jacob Grimm was promptly announced and commented on in a Croatian newspaper (Rački). This comes as no surprise, taking into consideration that his work was regularly referred to in *Danica ilirska* (Ilyrian Hesperus), the most important Croatian literary and cultural magazine of the first half of the nineteenth century. Moreover, Jacob Grimm was an honorary member of the Croatian Historical Society (see *Arkiv*), which was founded in 1850. Finally, during the second half of the century his name was commonplace among educated Croatian readers (Basariček 70) and his theories were praised and widely supported by Croatian intellectuals (e.g., Valjavec).

Keeping in mind the widespread reception of the Grimms' work and the parameters of the production of folktales in Croatian children's literature in general, we come to the paradoxical conclusion that the Grimms' names were omitted from the Croatian translations of their tales precisely because of their presentation of *Volkspoesie* (folk poetry) as the embodiment of the national spirit, an idea derived from the work of Gottfried Herder (Wilson). Jacob Grimm's notion of folktales as broken ancient myths and as the embodiment of the German national spirit (Holbek 221) was generally accepted in Croatia in the second half of the nineteenth century (Bošković-Stulli, "Usmena" 279–86). Moreover, this Herderian notion was a cornerstone of nineteenth-century Croatian national mobilization on (folk) literary grounds. It also provided a framework in which acknowledging the Grimms' authorship/editorship of a particular text meant acknowledging its German heritage (and divulging it to the Croatian readers), and this was unacceptable as long as Herder's notions of the nation as a distinct organic entity different from every other nation held sway.[6] German fairy tales and folktales, conceived according to the Herderian view of folk literature as the best expression of the national soul (Wilson 28), could have national integrative effect only for German readers, not for the readers of the emerging Croatian nation. As long as mythological theories of folktales and the ideas of Slavic unity and nation building were embedded in Croatian literary production for children, referring to the Grimms or to German folklore in general was counterproductive.

More precisely, because the Grimm tales were accepted as a broader type of tale, sometimes even as examples of Slavic folktales, as will be argued later, the attribution to the Grimms and to Germany would make further publication difficult—hence the difference in the presentation of Andersen's and the Grimms' tales in nineteenth-century Croatia. Whereas the first were conceived of as authorial tales, the second were considered German folktales and in the framework of Herderian notions of folklore useless or irrelevant to Croatian readers. Attribution to a single author, for example Andersen, who was not connected in popular discourse to folk literature, was not contentious. In contrast, the publication of German folk literature was problematic because it meant the promotion of a competitive culture in the sphere of nineteenth-century Croatian processes of national integration. Whereas until the first half of the nineteenth century the German language was imposed from Vienna in administrative and public services, after the 1860s it was promoted primarily from below through intercultural connections and bourgeois practices and values. Although in the 1880s, 72 percent of the urban population in northern Croatia declared Croatian to be their native language, German still functioned as the everyday language of private communication in urban areas (Hameršak, *Pričalice* 94–95). Therefore German national symbols, including folktales, were in fact a threat for the project of national integration on a Slavic basis, and as such they were either evaded in Croatian print for children or, as shown in the case of the Grimm tales, presented as if they had no connection to the German language and culture.

At the end of the nineteenth century, the literary and political climate changed: the notions of nation and folk literature developed and employed by the Grimms and their intellectual successors began to lose their general appeal, and the ideas of Slavic unity were abandoned in the Croatian political arena as well as in academic and popular discourse (see Stančić 107–30). In short, during the 1880s and 1890s a Croatian, not Slavic or south Slavic, identity came into the foreground of cultural and political life.[7] It was then that non-Slavic European tales began to be explicitly labeled as such.

Setting aside the abovementioned example of the first and only, as well as very timidly signed and therefore questionable, explicitly Grimm tales published in Croatian nineteenth-century children's literature, the first explicitly non-Slavic European folktale, as far as we know today, was published in 1899 in the Croatian children's journal *Bršljan* (Ivy). The full title and subtitle of this first explicitly non-Slavic Croatian children's tale was "The Marvelous Jar: An Irish Tale" (Čudnovata).[8] In the meantime, many of the Grimms' tales were presented as Croatian, Serbian, and/or Slavic: the first Croatian collection of vernacular folktales for children (Stojanović) and several subsequent popular collections appearing in several editions during the 1880s and 1890s (see Appendix and Literature) included translations of a substantial number of individual Grimm tales with no reference to their authors/editors (and their declared German folk literature origin). Some of these were even verbatim translations, such as "Snow White and Rose Red," published in 1879 in the oldest Croatian folktale collection for children (Hameršak, "A Neverending Story?").

As was the case with the publication of anonymous Grimm tales in Croatian children's magazines, the Grimm tales were included to teach children the mores, values, and manners of the time. Their attribution to the Grimms was probably lost in the process of relay translations or denied in accordance with the legal framework and the predominance of an organic conception of nation and folk literature. Their presentation as anonymous was, furthermore, prompted by the fact that the Croatian collections contained a substantial number of illustrations with motifs from the Grimms' tales—all purchased abroad, probably in Germany. For example, Franjo Bartuš, the editor of numerous late nineteenth-century illustrated Croatian collections of folktales for children (see Appendix and Literature), erased any reference to the brothers in order to secure at least the illusion of the national "purity" of his collection. The result was astonishing. Although overflowing with Grimm tales, Bartuš's collections emphasized the names of notable Croatian and Serbian folktale collectors in the paratext (subtitle), leaving out the names of the Grimms.

With their inclusion in these collections, which were also referred to as collections of Croatian, Serbian, or simply Slavic tales in their titles and prefaces, the anonymous individual Grimm tales were labeled once again folktales but this time with a Slavic, Croatian, and/or Serbian determinant. These are extreme, radical examples of domestication—presenting the culture of others as one's own. Consequently, in these collections, German names for characters, towns, rivers, and so forth were regularly replaced by Croatian ones. For example, Hans became Vaso (Bartuš, *Četrnaest* 25–29), and Bremen was turned into Frkljevci (Bartuš, *Dvadeset* 35–38). Translations were sometimes domesticated with additional reference to Croatian cultural contexts. For example, in the tale "Snow White and Rose Red" (Stojanović 98) the phrase "huge pieces of rock" was explained in parenthesis: "as in Lika" (one of the Croatian regions). The Grimms' tales in these collections thus blended with the corpus of presumably vernacular folk literature and became regarded as genuine examples of Croatian, Serbian, or generally Slavic folktales. In this they paradoxically helped to oil the wheels of national integration.

Legislative framework, translational practices (relay translation), the status and implied functions of children's literature, and above all processes of national integration based on the language, folklore, and folk literature fostered the first Croatian appropriation of Grimm tales without references to their names. Presented simply as tales or even as Croatian or in general Slavic folktales, almost 100 nineteenth-century Croatian publications of Grimm tales were adopted as part of a larger civilizing discourse and functioned as instances of cultural domestication and national integration. At the end of the nineteenth century and the collapse of the ideal of Slavic unity in the Croatian political realm, tales defined as non-Slavic folktales were for the first time introduced in Croatian children's literature with explicit reference to their original background. Shortly after, the first Croatian translation actually attributed to the Grimms appeared, and at the beginning of the twentieth century the first Croatian selections of the *Kinder- und Hausmärchen* were published in book form. Then as well as for most of the twentieth and twenty-first centuries, the Grimms' tales were only rarely presented as German folktales in Croatian popular discourse. Even today, in a Croatian context the Brothers Grimm are most often conceived of as authors of fairy tales rather than as collectors and editors of folktales. Translation is always a process of cultural negotiation, and the Croatian translation history of the *Kinder- und Hausmärchen* continues to influence their perception to this day.

Appendix

Most of the Croatian children's literature translations or appropriations of the individual Grimms' tales published until 1895 with no reference to their authorship or editorship were also included in the so-called *Kleine Ausgabe* of the Grimms' collection, that is, they were part of the standard repertoire for children (cautionary tales, animal tales, moral tales) and/or were highly imaginative (fairy tales). The following bibliography of pre-1895 Croatian children's literature translations or appropriations of the individual Grimms' tales emphasizes the specificities of the publishing format of these tales.

Croatian Children's Magazines

Bršljan (Ivy): "Little Red Cap" (1875, 5, KHM 26, ATU 333—according to *Školski prijatelj*),[9] "Hansel and Gretel" (1892, 2: 55–58, KHM 15, ATU 327A), and

"Table-Be-Set," "Gold Donkey," and "Cudgel-out-of-the-Sack" (1894, 10: 307–9, KHM 36, ATU 563).

Smilje (Immortele): "The Bremen Town Musicians" (1876, 11: 162–63, KHM 27, ATU 130), "Hansel and Gretel" (1878, 1: 5–9; 1889, 3: 39–44), "Little Red Cap" (1878, 2: 23–25), "Cinderella" (1879, 11: 174–75, KHM 21, ATU 510A), "The Six Swans" (1880, 6: 82–84, KHM 49, ATU 451), "Little Snow White" (1890, 7: 101–7; 8: 118–23, KHM 53, ATU 709), "The Goose Girl" (1890, 4: 53–62, KHM 89, ATU 533).

Children's Anthologies

"The Bremen Town Musicians" (Tomšić 119–23).
"The Wolf and the Seven Young Kids" (Tomšić 99–102, KHM 5, ATU 123).

Children's Collections of Slavic, Croatian, and/or Serbian Tales and Folktales

"The Bremen Town Musicians" (Bartuš *Dvadeset* 35–38 and Bartuš *Zanimive*).
"The Carnation" (Bartuš *Četrnaest* 9–14, KHM 76, ATU 652).
"Cinderella" (Bartuš *Četrnaest* 39–46).
"The Elves" (Bartuš *Dvadeset* 28–30 and Bartuš *Zanimive*, KHM 39, ATU 503, etc.).
"Frau Holle" (Bartuš *Trinaest* 18–22 and Bartuš *Zanimive*, KHM 24, ATU 480).
"The Frog King, or Iron Heinrich" (Bartuš *Dvadeset* 22–25 and Bartuš *Zanimive*, KHM 1, ATU 440).
"Godfather Death" (Bartuš *Trinaest* 34–36 and Bartuš *Zanimive*, KHM 44, ATU 332).
"The Golden Bird" (Bartuš *Dvanaest* 27–31 and Bartuš *Zanimive*, KHM 57, ATU 550).
"The Goose Girl" (Bartuš *Trinaest* 30–33 and Bartuš *Zanimive*).
"Hans in Luck" (Bartuš *Četrnaest* 25–29, KHM 83, ATU 1415).
"Hansel and Gretel" (Bartuš *Trinaest* 24–27 and Bartuš *Zanimive*).
"The Hare and the Hedgehog" (Bartuš *Četrnaest* 53–56, KHM 187, ATU 275C).
"Jorinde and Joringel" (Bartuš *Dvanaest* 22–24 and Bartuš *Zanimive*, KHM 69, ATU 405).
"Little Brier Rose" (Bartuš *Dvadeset* 7–13 and Bartuš *Zanimive*, KHM 50, ATU 410).
"Little Brother and Little Sister" (Bartuš *Trinaest* 18–22 and Bartuš *Zanimive*, KHM 11, ATU 450).
"Little Red Cap" (Bartuš *Dvanaest* 40–44 and Bartuš *Zanimive*).
"Little Snow White" (Bartuš *Dvanaest* 10–18 and Bartuš *Zanimive*).
"The Old Grandfather and His Grandson" (Bartuš *Dvadeset* 49–50 and Bartuš *Zanimive*, KHM 78, ATU 980).
"Old Sultan" (Bartuš *Četrnaest* 29–30, KHM 48, ATU 101).

"The Poor Man and the Rich Man" (*Trinaest* 42–46 and Bartuš *Zanimive*; Stojanović 85–90, KHM 87, ATU 750A).

"The Poor Miller's Boy and the Cat" (Bartuš *Dvanaest* 24–27 and Bartuš *Zanimive*).

"Rumpelstiltskin" (Bartuš *Dvanaest* 19–22 and Bartuš *Zanimive*, KHM 55, ATU 500).

"The Seven Ravens" (Bartuš *Dvadeset* 50–52 and Bartuš *Zanimive*; Stojanović 124–27, KHM 25, ATU 451).

"Snow White and Rose Red" (Bartuš *Dvanaest* 34–40 and Bartuš *Zanimive*; Stojanović 92–100, KHM 161, ATU 426).

"The Star Talers" (Bartuš *Dvadeset* 13–14 and Bartuš *Zanimive*; Stojanović 77–78, KHM 153, ATU 779H*).

"The Three Brothers" (Bartuš *Dvadeset* 45–46 and Bartuš *Zanimive*, KHM 124, ATU 654).

"The Three Children of Fortune" (Bartuš *Četrnaest* 6–9, KHM 70, ATU 1650).

"The Three Feathers" (Bartuš *Dvanaest* 9–10 and Bartuš *Zanimive*, KHM 63, ATU 402).

"The Twelve Brothers" (Bartuš *Četrnaest* 21–25, KHM 9, ATU 451).

"The Two Brothers" (Bartuš *Trinaest* 1–11 and Bartuš *Zanimive*, KHM 60, ATU 303).

"The White Bride and the Black Bride" (Bartuš *Trinaest* 37–40 and Bartuš *Zanimive*; Stojanović 150–55, KHM 135, ATU 403).

"The White Snake" (Bartuš *Četrnaest* 34–38, KHM 17, ATU 673, 554).

Picture Books

"Cinderella" (1879, approx. 1882), "Little Brier Rose" (1879), "Little Red Cap" (1879), "Snow White and Rose Red" (approx. 1882). Except for "Cinderella" (approx. 1882), these picture books are lost today and known only by the secondary sources (*Danica* 161–62; *Najveći*). Their definition as appropriations or translations of the Grimms' tales on their titles in this chapter is founded on their comparison with the same name contributions in Croatian children's magazines as well as on the insight of oral and print international distribution of a particular tale. Early editions of Franjo Bartuš's collections of tales and folktales are also mostly lost today. In this chapter they are listed according to the information from publishers' catalogs from the nineteenth century (*Najveći*) and the relevant bibliographies (*Građa*) and biobibliographies (Pleše).

NOTES

1. In contrast to adaptations, "appropriated text or texts are not always as clearly signaled or acknowledged as in the adaptive process" (Sanders 26). As stated, all

the Croatian tales discussed in this chapter were published without reference to the Grimms' source text.

2. The year 1895 and the publication of the first authorized translation of one of the Grimms' tales is a provisional turning point for the publication and attribution of the Grimms' tales in Croatia for several reasons. It is provisional, first, because anonymous translations of the Grimms' tales were published later, long into our age, and, second, because the Grimms' authorship of the tale "The Seven Ravens" published in 1895 was indicated very discreetly, at the end of the tale, not next to the title. Although the publication of this first signed Grimms' tale was obviously accidental and had no structural founding, the focus of this chapter has been directed at the abundant corpus of tales published before 1895 in order to provide the basis for its historically grounded analysis.

3. This has been dealt with elsewhere (Hameršak, "Przekłady baśni").

4. According to Foucault (109), a radical reversal of the medieval status of the author function happened in the seventeenth or eighteenth century.

5. Foucault's (109) thesis that in the seventeenth or eighteenth century a radical reversal of the medieval status of the author function occurred has been rebutted on the level of periodization (Sagner Buurma), mechanisms (Chartier; Erickson), and the validity of the dichotomy literary/scientific (Chartier 58–59).

6. As William Wilson summarizes, Herder applied Giambattista Vico's concept of cultural patterns to the historical stages of individual nations and argued "that since each nation was organically different from every other nation, each nation ought to be master of its own destiny. 'Every nation,' he said, 'contains the center of its happiness within itself'" (23).

7. During the 1880s and 1890s the extremely popular Party of State Right played "an important role in fomenting the disorders, channeling popular anger at the increasing gap between the wealth of the middle class and the poverty in both towns and villages into resistance to Hungarian domination, and singling out representatives of the Hungarian government as targets. Their receptivity to propaganda based on national arguments clearly showed that a politically Croatian nation" had been integrated and emancipated (Goldstein 92–93).

8. The first Croatian children's literature translation of an individual Grimm tale with explicit reference to their authorship/editorship (Grimm and Grimm, "Sedam"), did not explicitly (in its paratext) emphasize the Grimms' conception of it as a German folktale. But, having in mind the status and connotations of the Grimms in Croatia at the time, this tale could be implicitly recognized as such by some Croatian readers; probably not many of them, however, because it was, after all, published in a children's book.

9. ATU is short for the fairy-tale index compiled by Aarne, Thompson, and Uther.

References

Arkiv za povjestnicu jugoslavensku. Vols. 1–3 (1851, 1852, 1854). http://dnc.nsk.hr/
Journals/LibraryTitle.aspx?id=8d336349–9ee8–498d-8387–57ca296e820a. 10 Jan.
2012.

"Austrian Copyright Act (1846). Imperial Patent of 19 October 1846." *Primary
Sources on Copyright (1450–1900).* Eds. L. Bently and M. Kretschmer. Trans. Luis
Sundkvist. www.copyrighthistory.org/cgi-bin/kleioc/0010/exec/showTransla-
tion/%22d_1846b%22/start/%22yes%22. 10 Jan. 2012.

Bartuš, Franjo, ed. *Četrnaest najljepših priča i narodnih pripovijedaka: po Karadžiću,
Stojanoviću i po drugim izvorima.* Zagreb: Lav. Hartman (Kugli i Deutsch), s. a.,
1892, 1893, 1895.

———, ed. *Dvanaest najljepših priča i narodnih pripovijedaka: po Karadžiću, Stojanoviću i po drugim izvorima.* Zagreb: Lav. Hartman (Kugli i Deutsch), s. a.,
1887.

———, ed. *Trinaest najljepših priča i narodnih pripovijedaka: po Karadžiću, Stojanoviću i po drugim izvorima.* Zagreb: Lav. Hartman (Kugli i Deutsch), s. a.,
1887.

———, ed. *Zanimive i zabavne narodne priče: pedesetdevet najljepših i najkrasnijih
narodnih pripovijedaka—po Karadžiću, Stojanoviću i po drugim izvorima.* Zagreb:
Lav. Hartman (Kugli i Deutsch), s. a., 1887.

Basariček, Stjepan. "Moje putovanje i hamburžka učiteljska skupština." *Napredak:
časopis za učitelje, odgojitelje i sve prijatelje mladeži* 14.5 (1873): 66–70.

Bennett, Andrew. *Author.* London: Routledge, 2005.

Bošković-Stulli, Maja. *Priče i pričanja: stoljeća usmene hrvatske proze.* Zagreb: Matica
hrvatska, 2006.

———. "Usmena književnost." *Povijest hrvatske književnosti u sedam knjiga. I—
Usmena i pučka književnost.* Zagreb: Liber and Mladost, 1978. 7–353, 641–51.

Bottigheimer, Ruth. *Grimms' Bad Girls and Bold Boys.* New Haven: Yale UP, 1987.

———. "The Publishing History of Grimm's Tales: Reception at the Cash Register."
The Reception of Grimms' Fairy Tales. Responses, Reactions, Revisions. Ed. Donald
Haase. Detroit: Wayne State UP, 1993. 78–101.

Brešić, Vinko, ed. *Bibliografija hrvatskih književnih časopisa 19. stoljeća.* 4 vols. Zagreb: Filozofski fakultet, 2006.

Chartier, Roger. *The Order of Books: Readers, Authors, and Libraries in Europe between
the Fourteenth and Eighteenth Centuries.* Trans. Lydia G. Cochrane. Stanford:
Stanford UP, 1994.

Crnković, Milan. *Hrvatska dječja književnost do kraja XIX stoljeća.* Zagreb: Školska
knjiga, 1978.

"Čudnovata staklenka: irska priča." *Bršljan: list mladeži* 14.9 (1899): 258–66.

Danica ilirska: 1835–1836–1837. Zagreb: Liber.

Danica: koledar i ljetopis Društva svetojeronimskoga za prestupnu godinu 1880. Zagreb: Društvo sv. Jeronima. 161–62.

"Dvie pripoviedke." *Bosiljak: list za mladež* 1.7 (1865): 188–89.

Erickson, Lee. "Unboastful Bard: Originally Anonymous English Romantic Poetry Book Publication, 1770–1835." *New Literary History* 33.2 (2002): 247–78.

Feldman, Paula R. "Women Poets and Anonymity in the Romantic Era." *New Literary History* 33.2 (2002): 279–89.

Filipović, Ivan, ed. *Mali tobolac za dobru i pomnjivu mladež naroda srbsko-ilirskoga.* Vol. I. Zagreb: Franjo Župan, 1850.

Foucault, Michel. "What Is an Author?" *The Foucault Reader.* Ed. and Trans. Paul Rabinow. New York: Pantheon, 1984. 101–20.

Gavrin, Mira. "Pjesništvo narodnog preporoda u odnosu na njemačko i austrijsko pjesništvo." *Hrvatska književnost prema evropskim književnostima: od narodnog preporoda k našim danima.* Eds. Aleksandar Flaker and Krunoslav Pranjić. Zagreb: Liber, Izdanja instituta za znanost o književnosti Filozofskog fakulteta u Zagrebu, 1970. 51–119.

Genette, Gérard. *Paratexts: Thresholds of Interpretation.* Trans. Jane E. Lewin. Cambridge: Cambridge UP, 1997.

Goldberg, Christine. 2003. "Der Räuberbräutigam." *Enzyklopädie des Märchens.* Vol. 11.1. Ed. Rolf Wilhelm Brednich. Berlin: Walter de Gruyter, 348–53.

Goldstein, Ivo. *Croatia: A History.* Trans. Nikolina Jovanović. London: Hurst, 2004.

Građa za hrvatsku retrospektivnu bibliografiju knjiga 1835–1940 [Materials for the Croatian Retrospective Bibliography: 1835–1940]. 25 vols. 1982–1999. Zagreb: Nacionalna i sveučilišna biblioteka.

Griffin, Robert J. "Anonymity and Authorship." *New Literary History* 30.4 (1999): 877–95.

Grimm, Jacob, and Wilhelm Grimm. *Kinder- und Hausmärchen.* 4 vols. 1857. Ed. Hans-Jörg Uther. Munich: Diedrichs, 1996.

———. "Sedam gavrana." *Smilje: list za mladež obojega spola* 23.10 (1895): 136–38.

Gruber Garvey, Ellen. "Anonymity, Authorship and Recirculation: A Civil War Episode." *Book History* 9 (2006): 159–78.

Hameršak, Marijana. "A Neverending Story? Permutations of Snow White and Red Rose Narrative and Its Research across Space and Time." *Narodna umjetnost: Croatian Journal of Ethnology and Folklore Research* 48.1 (2011): 147–60.

———. *Pričalice: o povijesti djetinjstva i bajke.* Zagreb: Algoritam, 2011.

———. "Przekłady baśni pomiędzy mobilizacją narodową komodyfikacją: Niemieckojęzyczna literatura dla dzieci w dziewiętnaestowiecznym społeczeństwie chorwackim." *Przekładaniec: Półrocznik Katedry UNESCO do Badań nad Przekładem i Komunikacją Międzykulturową UJ* 22/23.2.1 (2009–2010): 130–45.

Holbek, Bengt. *Interpretation of Fairy Tales: Danish Folklore in a European Perspective.* Helsinki: Suomalainen Tiedeakatemia, 1987.

Lang, Milan. *Samobor: narodni život i običaji.* Samobor: Grad Samobor, Gradska knjižnica Samobor, Izdavačka kuća Meridijani, 2009.

Lathey, Gillian. *The Role of Translator in Children's Books: Invisible Storytellers.* London: Routledge, 2010.

Liddle, Dallas. "Salesmen, Sportsmen, Mentors: Anonymity and Mid-Victorian Theories of Journalism." *Victorian Studies* 41.1 (1997): 31–68.

Majhut, Berislav. *Pustolov, siroče i dječja družba: hrvatski dječji roman do 1945.* Zagreb: FF Press, 2005.

Najveći i najpodpuniji sistematički popis hrvatskih knjiga i muzikalija koje se dobivaju u Akademijskoj knjižari Lav. Hartmana (Kugli i Deutsch). Zagreb: Hartman (Kugli i Deutsch), 1884.

Pepeljuga: Pričalice. Vol. 5. Zagreb: Albrecht and Fiedler, s. a.

Pleše, Mladen. "Bartuš, Franjo." *Hrvatski biografski leksikon.* Vol. 1. Ed. Nikica Kolumbić. Zagreb: Jugoslavenski leksikografski zavod, 1983. 497–98.

Rački, Franjo. "Žaloba na grobu Jakova Grimma." *Pozor* 220 (1863): 878.

Roth, Klaus. "Crossing Boundaries: The Translation and Cultural Adaptation of Folk Narratives." *Fabula* 39.3–4 (1998): 243–55.

Šabić, Marijan. *Iz zlatnog Praga: češka književnost i kultura u hrvatskoj književnoj periodici 1835.–1903.* Zagreb: Sveučilište u Zagrebu—Filozofski fakultet—Hrvatski institut za povijest—Podružnica za povijest Slavonije, Srijema i Baranje, 2009.

Sagner Buurma, Rachel. "Anonymity, Corporate Authority, and the Archive: The Production of Authorship in Late Victorian England." *Victorian Studies* 50.1 (2007): 15–42.

Sanders, Julie. *Adaptation and Appropriation.* London: Routledge, 2006.

Schacker, Jennifer. *National Dreams: The Remaking of Fairy Tales in Nineteenth-Century England.* Philadelphia: U of Pennsylvania P, 2003.

Shavit, Zohar. *Poetics of Children's Literature.* Athens: U of Georgia P, 1986.

Školski prijatelj: časopis za promicanje pučkog školstva 9.23 (1875): 287–88.

Šporer, David. *Status autora: od pojave tiska do nastanka autorskih prava.* Zagreb: AGM, 2010.

Stančić, Nikša. *Hrvatska nacija i nacionalizam u 19. i 20. stoljeću.* Zagreb: Barbat, 2002.

Stojanović, Mijat, ed. *Narodne pripoviedke: sabrao i priredio za mladež.* Zagreb: Hrvatski pedagogijsko-književni sbor, 1879.

Tomšić, Ljudevit. *Djetinji vrtić: zabavne pripovjesti dobroj djeci. Svezak II.* Zagreb: Mučnjak and Senftleben, 1877.

Valjavec, Matija Kračmanov. "O rodjenicah i sudjenicah." *Književnik* 2 (1865): 52–61.

Venuti, Lawrence. *The Scandals of Translation: Towards an Ethics of Difference.* London: Routledge, 1998.

Vranich, Anton. *Mlaissi Robinzon: iliti jedna kruto povolyna, y hasznovita pripovezt za detczu. Prvi del.* Zagreb: Novoszelska slovotizka, 1796.

Wilson, William. "Herder, Folklore and Romantic Nationalism." *Folklore Groups and Folklore Genres.* Ed. Eliott Oring. Logan: Utah State UP, 1989. 21–37.

"Zakonski članak o autorskom pravu." *Sbornik zakonah i naredabah valjanih za kraljevinu Hrvatsku i Slavoniju* 30 (1884): 221–31. http://alex.onb.ac.at/cgi-content/anno-plus?apm=0&aid=lks&datum=18840304&zoom=2&seite=00000221&x-=11&y=6. 10 Jan. 2012.

Zipes, Jack. *Fairy Tales and the Art of Subversion: The Classical Genre for Children and the Process of Civilization.* New York: Routledge, 1991.

2

Polishing the Grimms' Tales for a Polish Audience

Die Kinder- und Hausmärchen in Poland

MONIKA WOZNIAK

While today the name Grimm is almost synonymous with the classic fairy tale, the Grimms' canon in Poland is by no means identical to the original German canon or the Grimms' canon in other countries.[1] Of the more than two hundred German tales, only a small portion became really popular in Poland. Furthermore, they reached the Polish audience mainly in the form of retellings and adaptations. This fact, by itself, is not unusual, since fairy tales are generally subject to retellings and transformations, but for a long time Polish readers did not have access to the alternative of (reasonably) faithful translations of the Grimms' work. The first, by Zofia Kowerska, appeared in 1896, but since it was intended as an academic publication, it did not reach a broader audience and was never reprinted; the second complete edition of the Grimms' tales in Poland was published as late as 1982. These faithful translations have not played a decisive role in the Grimms' assimilation into Polish culture. Furthermore, many Polish retellings of the most popular tales had been literally appropriated by the adaptors and became known as "Anczyc's *Sleeping Beauty*," "Porazińska's *Cinderella*," "Krüger's *Snow White*," and so forth.

Until very recently, the development and outlook of children's literature in Poland was in fact heavily conditioned by extratextual factors of various kinds, and they all contributed to the Polish reception modes of the Grimms' work. In what follows I will present a diachronic survey of the Grimms' reception in Poland, split into two parts, the first covering the period until 1918, and the second stretching from the 1920s to the present. The reason for choosing this precise delimitation mark is very simple: although both periods are by no means internally homogenous and can be further divided into different phases, Poland's nonexistence as an independent state was a factor of decisive importance for Polish literature up to 1918.

The Grimms' Reception in Poland before 1918

In the eighteenth century, the French literary fairy tales that had first amused adults of the upper classes were appropriated by a young audience and began to penetrate other European countries successfully, first of all England and Germany.[2] At that time, the Polish–Lithuanian Commonwealth, which had fallen into decline and was threatened by powerful neighbors, concerned itself with an attempt at radical internal reforms, especially in the field of education. Polish reformers were intent on creating an efficient learning system, with the primary aim of raising a new generation of enlightened citizens conscious of a patriotic obligation toward their motherland. They had little patience for texts ill suited to such purposes. The Commission of National Education, created in 1773 in order to enact a radical reform of the Polish education system, generally did not approve of works of fiction and explicitly forbade reading texts at school that were not included in the imposed curriculum (Kaniowska-Lewańska 29–49). Most publications for young readers reflected this general educational trend. The publishers favored books with a clear moral message and didactic purpose that conformed to the official education policy. Therefore, although some French writings for young readers, for example, François Fénelon's *Les Aventures de Télémaque, fils d'Ulysse* (The Adventures of Telemachus, Son of Ulysses), had been rapidly translated and not only became popular but also inspired a conspicuous number of imitations, others, among them fairy tales, remained virtually absent in the panorama of Polish literature.[3]

In 1795 a major political disaster struck: after the third partition undertaken by the three neighboring countries of Prussia, Austria, and Russia, the Polish state effectively ceased to exist and would not regain its independence until 1918. It was a long period of desperate struggle to preserve a national identity within the increasingly repressive policies of the partitioning powers. In the face of the failure of several military rebellions and uprisings as well as the fiasco of diplomatic attempts to restore self-government, cultivating the cultural and literary heritage became of crucial importance to safeguard the Polish language, traditions, and sense of nationhood. Children's literature that could function as a tool of patriotic education assumed, therefore, even more weight in the nineteenth than it had in the eighteenth century. Given the restrictions that the occupying powers imposed on the use of the Polish language in schools and public life, contact with Polish books—preferably by a Polish author—became a fundamental element in cultivating national and linguistic identity. Through the entire period of the partition this moral obligation remained a prime concern of Polish educators, writers, publishers, and parents and consequently became a decisive factor in the development of policies regarding children's literature in Poland.

This preference for national topics and authors does not mean that foreign works did not penetrate Polish literature for children. Children's literature in Poland had always depended heavily on imported works and although national writers were privileged, the demand for texts grew more rapidly than the domestic literary potential. Nonetheless, the selection and the accommodation of foreign texts for Polish readers were very much influenced by the priorities generated by the historical context, and these priorities could not but clash with the message conveyed by the *Kinder- und Hausmärchen.* The implied ideological message of the *Märchen,* believed by the Brothers Grimm to be an expression of a specific German sensibility (Zipes 276), was hardly endearing to Polish readers, especially those who lived under Prussian and Austrian rule and were subjected to Germanization policies. It is quite telling, indeed, that while the Grimms' first Polish translations and adaptations only appeared in the 1890s, Andersen's tales, which were written later, had already been translated in the 1850s and became increasingly popular in subsequent decades.[4] Another deterrent to the Grimms' reception in Poland was undoubtedly the religious character of many tales and the incompatibility of their Protestant values with the Polish Catholic orientation, which in the 1800s became identified with a fundamental element of national identity. Once the Grimms' tales began to be translated into Polish, the religious tales were usually omitted or their Protestant values altered to accord with the Catholic sensibility (Krysztofiak 155–56).

If we look at the cultural climate of the nineteenth century, it is important to note that Romanticism arrived in Poland at the beginning of the 1820s, heralded by Adam Mickiewicz's *Ballady i romance* (1822, Ballads and

Romances). A typical romantic interest in folktales as well as the idea that the folk tradition is the source of spiritual truth featured prominently in his poetry, as declared in the opening ballad "The Romantic." In the following years romantic trends spread rapidly through Polish literature, but although they shared many traits with German and English Romanticism, and in fact were strongly influenced by them, there were also some significant differences. In the first place, the Polish literary tradition had always been predominantly oriented toward poetry, prose being both secondary and regarded as an inferior kind of literature. This supremacy was confirmed in the period of Romanticism, characterized by an explosion of poetic masterpieces by such writers as Adam Mickiewicz and Juliusz Słowacki. As a consequence, among numerous new literary genres introduced or evolving in that period in Poland, there were very few narrative ones, and the fairy tale was certainly not one of them. Furthermore, although fantastic and fairy-tale motifs are present in Mickiewicz's early works and in Słowacki's dramas (most notably in his tragedy *Balladyna,* strongly influenced by Shakespeare's *A Midsummer Night's Dream*), they were never valued very highly by literary critics.[5]

Another factor that may have worked against the interest in fairy tales in Poland is the strong tradition of fables in verse derived from Aesop's epigrammatic fables and, later, those of La Fontaine. Already very popular during the Polish Enlightenment, they found their insuperable embodiment in Ignacy Krasicki's *Bajki i przypowieści* (1779, Fables and Parables), initially targeted at adult readers but soon to become the fundamental model of Polish children's literature. The popularity of the poetic fables endured in Polish Romanticism, with excellent new contributions by Aleksander Fredro, Adam Mickiewicz, and many others. Finally, and most importantly, Polish writing for children was not part of the literary vanguard of its time but was, rather, still anchored in the literary currents of the preceding age of Enlightenment. Therefore it naturally favored already established genres, especially Krasicki's model of the allegorical fable. The first important Polish author for children, Stanisław Jachowicz (1796–1857), created a considerable corpus of such texts, some of them still popular today. Other less talented writers followed his example. It was not until the 1850s that the first narrative fairy tales for children began to appear.

The almost complete lack of direct translations from the *Kinder- und Hausmärchen* in Polish until the last decade of the nineteenth century does not mean that the Grimms' works were totally unknown in Poland or that their theories did not influence Polish writers. They did, at least indirectly. However, the scarcity of archival studies on this topic makes it very difficult to establish, especially as far as Romanticism is concerned, which literary phenomena were inspired by the Grimms' ideas and texts and which were merely products of general Romantic trends and interests.[6] It is, therefore, highly probable—if not well documented—that the impulse to collect traditional tales in order to preserve national cultural heritage was kindled in Poland by the Grimms' model. The first compilation, *Klechdy, starożytne podania i powieści ludu polskiego i Rusi* (Tales, Ancient Legends, and Narratives of Polish and Russian Folk)[7] by Kazimierz Wojciech Wójcicki, appeared in 1837. Although the Grimms' name is never mentioned in the ample preface to the volume, Wojcicki's general theories and approach to the tales bear a strong resemblance to their theories. The fact that one of the reviewers of *Klechdy* called Wójcicki "a Polish Grimm" (Simonides 32) without any further explanation suggests that in spite of a lack of translations, the fame of the *Kinder- und Hausmärchen* had already been well established in Poland at that time.

Wójcicki's volume, for all its shortcomings,[8] had the merit of stimulating a general interest in folktales. Other, similar publications soon followed by Lucjan Siemieński, Karol Baliński, Roman Zmorski, Ryszard Berwiński, and Józef Lompa. Curiously enough, the tales collected by Lompa in the region of Silesia, strongly influenced by German culture, share surprisingly few motifs with the Grimms' fairy tales, even if the practice of editing the style and uniting different variants into one clearly recalls their modus operandi. Nevertheless, none of these authors stated explicitly that they pursued the model proposed by the Grimms in their work. In 1853 *Bajarz polski* (The Polish Tale Teller) by Antoni Józef Gliński appeared, a compilation of tales in four volumes. Different from the earlier compilations, it was conceived not so much as a scholarly work but rather as a pleasant read for all.[9] The formula proved successful and the book became extremely popular among Polish readers. Universally acclaimed by critics and readers alike, it had eleven editions in Poland and seven translations into other languages. Gliński's work was undoubtedly of crucial importance in the development of Polish children's literature. Since he addressed his book specifically to children and popularized for the first time the model of the classic fairy tale, it soon became the most popular collection of Polish folk stories.[10]

Paradoxically, it was precisely the popularity of *Bajarz polski* that delayed by many decades the direct assimilation of the Grimms' fairy tales in Poland

and later interfered with the variants of the most popular tales. In fact, several of Gliński's tales bear a distinct resemblance to the Grimms' tales: such texts as "O zwierciadełku gadającym i o uśpionej królewnie" (About a Talking Mirror and a Sleeping Princess), "O staruszku i staruszce i o złotej rybce" (About an Old Man, An Old Woman, and a Goldfish), and "O macosze i pasierbicy" (About a Stepmother and a Stepdaughter) are in fact variants of, respectively, "Snow White," "The Fisherman and His Wife," and "One-Eye, Two-Eyes, and Three-Eyes."

However, not only are they much longer than the German tales (about 15–17 pages each), but the style of narration is also very different and there are several divergent points in the development of the stories. For example, in "About a Talking Mirror and a Sleeping Princess" the protagonist meets twelve outlaws in the woods, instead of seven dwarfs; the evil queen is not a witch herself, but to get rid of the young princess she hires a "professional" witch; and the princess is prevented from eating the poisoned apple by her faithful dog. When she finally succumbs to the curse, it is because of a be-witched pin in her hair, and when the prince finds her, he does not manage to wake her with a kiss, so he takes her to his castle, where he hides her in a locked bedroom. In the end, it is the prince's mother who successfully wakes up the princess and agrees to her marriage with the prince.[11]

Similarly, the fisherman's story follows Alexander Pushkin's variant of the tale; in fact, the Russian version has been the point of reference for all the Polish adaptations up to the present day and it seems unlikely that the faith-ful translation included in the recent complete Grimms' collection published by Media Rodzina (2009) could supplant the version already appropriated by the Polish literary tradition.

In the second half of the nineteenth century the demand for children's texts began to grow, and accordingly some publishers broadened their range of books in order to meet the needs of a larger audience. The first to do so was Gebethner and Wolff, an important publishing house founded in 1857, later to be joined by many other smaller publishers, especially Michał Arct, founded in 1887. The publishing policy they all followed, in a more or less coherent way, was to reconcile the patriotic and pedagogical goals that chil-dren's texts were expected to fulfill with more practical, commercial consid-erations.[12] Fairy tales were a natural choice for publishers, given their appeal to young readers, but the prejudice against magical and fantastic elements in texts for children was slow to dissipate,[13] and therefore even in the 1870s and 1880s the assimilation of foreign tales was still very partial and limited to single, universally known titles heavily rewritten by Polish adaptors.

Typical of these early publications is *Trzy Baśnie* (Three Fairy Tales, 1878)[14] by Władysław Ludwik Anczyc, a peculiar blend of motifs taken from the Grimms, Charles Perrault, and Wójcicki, with the addition of the adaptor's own inventions. For example, the beginning of Anczyc's "Cinderella" loosely resembles the Grimms' "Aschenputtel" in the scene with the dying mother who asks her daughter to be always kind and good, in the motif of the protagonist praying every day at the mother's grave, and in the presence of the dove. The dialogues between Cinderella and her sisters before the ball are taken, however, from Perrault, as are the arrival of the fairy godmother and the transformation of the pumpkin. Finally, the tale also reelaborates the elements taken from Wójcicki's collection: the prince is arrogant, and when he visits the castle where Cinderella lives, he behaves rudely toward her; later, when he asks her where she comes from during the ball, she answers with a riddle. After the ball he searches in vain for the owner of the lost slipper but finally understands the riddle and guesses Cinderella's true identity. Therefore, he arrives at her castle already knowing who he is looking for, and trying on the slipper has a purely symbolic function.

The practice of adapting, rather than translating, foreign texts, had always been a distinctive trait of Polish literature in general; in fact, a great part of its early corpus consists of adaptations, imitations, and paraphrases. Jan Kochanowski (1530–1584), who effectively and almost single-handedly created the Polish literary language, borrowed in his work abundantly from Latin poets, especially Horatio. *Dworzanin polski* (1566, Polish Nobleman), a masterpiece by Łukasz Górnicki (1527–1603), is in fact a free adaptation of Baldassare Castiglione's well-known Italian treatise *The Book of the Courtier*. Piotr Kochanowski's (1566–1620) translation of Tasso's *Gerusalemme liberata* (1618), which had a huge impact on the evolution of epic poetry in Poland, transformed the original text to such an extent that it is known as Tasso–Kochanowski's work.

It is therefore not surprising that adaptation became a key procedure in Poland also as far as children's literature was concerned, in particular regarding fairy tales, which in any case are subject to retellings and transformations more than any other literary genre. Since the first to be published were the most famous classic tales such as "Cinderella," "Little Red Riding Hood," and "Sleeping Beauty," it is often extremely difficult to discern if a given

Polish author was inspired by Perrault or by the Grimms. In fact, tales frequently combine motifs from both variants, as seen in the example of the Anczyc adaptation, or retellers have transformed the narrative so radically as to render it almost a different story. For example, in some variants of "Cinderella" the protagonist, instead of going to the ball, goes to church for Sunday mass and the prince has to perform heroic deeds before winning her. Many retellings underwent such radical changes that they began to circulate as their adaptor's own creations. Such was the case, for example, with Anczyc's version of "Sleeping Beauty" titled "Princess of Hawthorn," which was soon included in collections of "Polish" fairy tales and even today is listed under his name as a "traditional Polish tale."

The first unmistakably Grimm tales to appear on the Polish book market were "Hansel and Gretel," published as *Jaś i Małgosia: baśń braci Grimm dla polskiej młodzieży* (1880, Hansel and Gretel: Grimms' Fairy Tale for Young Polish Readers) and *Śnieżna różyczka: baśń dla polskiej młodzieży* (Snow White: a Fairy Tale for Young Polish Readers), published in 1878 and reissued in 1880 (Boczar 129). Both were translated, or rather retold, by Wanda Reichsteinowa.

It was not until the 1890s, however, that the first compilations of selected Grimms' fairy tales actually appeared in Poland: in 1895 Gebethner and Wolff published *Baśnie dla dzieci i młodzieży* (Fairy Tales for Children and Young Readers) translated by Cecylia Niewiadomska. It was followed in 1899 by another small volume issued in Cracow by Jan Deubler, *Baśnie i powiastki dla dzieci* (Fairy Tales and Stories for Children) by Maria Kreczowska. Niewiadomska's translation had three more editions in the next twenty years (1901, 1909, 1916) and can probably be considered the most successful volume of the Grimms' fairy tales published in Poland up to the end of the First World War. However, the information "według oryginału niemieckiego opracowała" (based on the German original) on the front page is misleading. Niewiadomska's version cannot be considered a translation, even in a very liberal sense of the word: what she created are in fact free variations on themes from tales by the Grimms. For example, in the well-known fairy tale "King Thrushbeard," the original tale's incipit states simply: "A King had a daughter who was beautiful beyond all measure, but so proud and haughty withal that no suitor was good enough for her" (Grimm, *Complete* 52). In Niewiadomska's version, renamed "Dumna Księżniczka" (A Proud Princess), the text begins, however, as follows: "Lovely, the loveliest in the world was princess Mockspirit. She was so lovely that anyone who ever saw her beautiful black eyes, her forehead whiter than snow, her coral lips, would never forget her. Each time she let her black, silky hair down, it covered her like a mantle; when she looked at someone with pity, even the most unhappy would smile and forget their hardships; but when she glared proudly and angrily, the most courageous knights trembled and they did not dare to raise their eyes" (Grimm and Grimm, *Baśnie* 200, my translation).[15] Considering that what Niewiadomska did was a rule rather than an exception as far as the concept of "translating" the Grimms' fairy tales into Polish was concerned, there is no doubt that the bibliographical information about the Grimm editions in Poland cannot be taken for granted, nor may they be used as an objective indicator of the popularity of the tales and their assimilation into the literary canon.

The name Grimm became increasingly popular in the Polish children's book market between 1900 and 1920; apart from the reprints of Niewiadomska's book, at least six other compilations of tales were published (Buras 225). In addition, more or less Grimm-like tales multiplied in books published under the names of Polish authors, such as Juliusz Starkel, Teresa Prażmowska, Mieczysław Rościszewski, and, especially, Artur Oppman, who created multiple versions of the most popular plots. Only a small number of the Grimm tales made it into these first collections. Niewiadomska's book contained only sixteen tales, whereas other selections did not usually exceed twenty titles. The selection of tales varied, but some reappeared frequently, whereas others would emerge only sporadically or would be entirely left out, especially those that were specifically religious. Many of these tales are not very popular in other countries, either, but it is striking that among the tales that never entered the Polish children's canon there is also the famous "Rumpelstiltskin."

An important aspect of the Grimms' reception in Poland in the late nineteenth century was the impact of their work on Polish folklorists. Polish ethnographers studied the Grimms' methods and theories, as explained in numerous prefaces to their works, with great interest and drew inspiration for their own research from Jacob Grimm's *German Mythology* (1835) in particular. Among the most enthusiastic Polish supporters of the Grimms were Oskar Kolberg, Ryszard Berwiński, and above all Jan Karłowicz. Oskar Kolberg (1814–1900), author of the monumental compilation of Polish folktales in thirty-three volumes, followed closely the methodological approach proposed by the Grimms and used in his work their division of tales into six categories.

The ethnographer Jan Karłowicz (1836–1903) studied in Germany and had the opportunity to read the Grimms' work in great detail. Deeply impressed by their theories on mythology, he used them in order to develop a comparative analysis of Polish folklore and followed the Grimms' method in his own quest for new folktales (Simonides 36). Most importantly, Karłowicz was well aware of the high status of the *Kinder- und Hausmärchen* within the field of European folklore studies and was convinced that it was imperative to translate the entire collection into Polish.

To find a publisher interested in a serious and unabridged translation of the Grimms' work was not an easy task, however. Initially, Karłowicz tried to negotiate with Gebethner and Wolff, but they turned down his proposal, opting instead for Niewiadomska's more commercially profitable book. Not deterred by this first defeat, Karłowicz eventually managed to publish the integral edition of the *Kinder- und Hausmärchen* in 1896, translated by ethnographer Zofia Kowerska. Kowerska's translation was valued highly by folklorists, who emphasized its philological faithfulness and good style (Kapełuś 400), but the academic context of the publication and its unattractive graphic form limited its appeal. It did not attract a larger audience and was never reprinted.[16] Therefore, up to the end of the First World War, knowledge of the Grimms' fairy tales in Poland remained not only very incomplete but also inaccurate, as they were based on lighthearted retellings by authors who often did not even speak German and limited themselves to approximate reproductions of the original stories.

The Grimms' Reception in Poland up to the Present

At the end of the First World War in 1918, Poland finally regained its independence after more than a century of foreign rule. This had a profound impact on all aspects of social and cultural life. With regard to children's literature, the new political situation eliminated or at least attenuated the imperative to use texts for young readers as a principal tool of patriotic education and as a vehicle for national awareness. However, a number of dramatic political changes did have an effect on Polish children's literature. The short interlude between the two world wars was probably the only period of "normality" in the sense that children's literature was not shaped under political or ideological pressure. The book market began to operate on a commercial basis and it experienced an enormous growth due to the rise of literacy among children. It is hardly surprising that the number of compilations of fairy tales, one of the most sought after publications for small children, also increased exponentially: a bibliographical compendium of children's books published in Poland between 1918–1919 lists over 150 editions under the name "Brothers Grimm" (Krassowska and Grefkowicz 153–62).

The Second World War interrupted this flourishing activity. For six years (1939–1945) the publishing market froze almost completely. After the war, however, the situation of children's literature once again changed radically. The long period of Communist rule in Central and Eastern Europe, from 1945 to 1989, was characterized by a rigid state control over the children's book market, although ideological censorship passed through different stages: the relative liberality in the years 1945–1948 was followed by a fanatical stage of Stalinism from 1949–1955, whereas over the following decades the state's supervision of publication gradually became less oppressive. Nonetheless, the elimination of all private publishing houses after 1949 meant that the state maintained an exclusive authority over the book market and the power to shape it according to the political trends of the moment. Children's literature was monopolized almost completely by the publishing house Nasza Księgarnia.

The political transition of 1989 and the subsequent end of Communist rule in Poland also brought a radical change to the children's book market, which in the 1990s underwent a period of violent transformation. While the gargantuan state publishing houses struggled to survive in the free market milieu, dozens of small private publishers were established. Initially interested almost exclusively in financial success, many of them specialized in the field of children's literature, as that was considered one of the most profitable sectors of the publishing industry. To cut down costs, the publishers used old and antiquated translations, no longer covered by copyright, or commissioned new adaptations from whoever would do it at the lowest price. As a result, for almost a decade the editorial standards of children's literature in Poland worsened dramatically.

At the beginning of the twenty-first century, however, the situation gradually began to improve. Once the book market had been saturated, the public became more exigent and more attentive to the quality of the text.

Accordingly, the publishing houses had to modify their press strategies and to search for new ways of attracting buyers. Today the Polish children's book market has reached a certain equilibrium, and although cheap, low-quality publications are still quite common, in recent years there has also been an impressive number of valuable publishing initiatives, among them some new, ambitious translations of children's classics.

What position did the Grimm tales hold in this dynamic literary climate? The massive increase in the presence of the Grimms' fairy tales on the Polish book market in the 1920s and 1930s did not come with an improvement of respect toward the original texts. Although the profile of the publications became more diverse—ranging from cheap editions of single tales (the so-called *biblioteka groszowa* or one-penny library) to the lavish hard-cover volumes enriched with colorful illustrations by famous artists—the texts themselves were still just free adaptations, more or less readable depending on the literary talent of a given adaptor. The most popular and extensive Grimm compilation from this period, by Marceli Tarnowski (1924), has been, and indeed still is, thought of as a faithful translation of the German text, but in fact it can be considered at best a free translation, and some tales (such as "Cinderella" and "Sleeping Beauty") are dramatically different from the Grimms' versions.

The boom of individual variants of the most famous tales published as original creations of Polish authors that began in the nineteenth century continued in the interwar period and even remained a constant in post-war children's literature, with retellings by such authors as Antoni Gawiński, Janina Porazińska, Magdalena Samozwaniec, Ewa Szelburg-Zarembina, Witold Zechenter and later Jan Brzechwa, Czesław Janczarski, Kazimiera Jeżewska, and Maria Krüger, to name just the best known. Some became very popular and had numerous reprints, thus competing successfully with the versions included in the compilations of the Grimms' fairy tales.

In the immediate postwar period, fairy tales and fantastic elements in children's literature in general had yet again fallen into disgrace with those educators and pedagogues who thought them not compatible with the goals of Communist education. The Grimms' tales in particular became the object of violent attacks. Given the appropriation of the Grimms' fairy tales by Nazis, who used and interpreted them in accordance with National Socialist ideology, they were often considered the expression of all the negative characteristics associated with the German national character that the Poles had come to hate during the Second World War. Many critics maintained that "in

Germany the young Fritz read Grimms' fairy tales and then the adult Fritz went out to kill, annihilate, and steal" (Szczepańska 11, my translation),[17] and they protested that "for far too long we allowed Polish children to have their ethical and social ideas shaped by such books" (Osterloff 8, my translation).[18]

It is hardly surprising, therefore, that for almost a decade after the war the *Kinder- und Hausmärchen* were banned completely from children's literature in Poland. Most popular tales were published in variants signed by Polish authors, often stylized in a way to make them resemble Polish folktales and with illustrations that suggested a distinctly Polish setting. This tendency, always present in Polish adaptations, was even intensified in the Communist period. Some stories were further modified in order to meet educational standards imposed by the new regime. For example, in Ewa Szelburg-Zarembina's "Cinderella" (1947), the protagonist refuses to marry the prince, because he has "no useful profession" and chooses instead to wed a poor shoemaker. In Jan Brzechwa's "Hansel and Gretel" (1967) the witch turns out to be a janitor in a candy factory who just wants to teach the children a lesson for having eaten candies that had fallen from a lorry and belong to the plant.

Only in 1956, after the end of the Stalinist era and when some of the anti-German resentment had worn off, did it become possible to propose a new edition of the Grimms' tales in Poland. The compilation, prepared by a well-known Polish scholar of children's literature, Stefania Wortman, included, however, only twenty-two tales. Although in theory the translation used in the book was the prewar version of Marceli Tarnowski, the information given on the front page is misleading. In fact the book was based on a purged GDR 1954 edition of the Grimms, and the texts had been modified accordingly.[19]

Nonetheless, this new edition, attractively illustrated by Małgorzata Truchanowska, soon grew to be one of the most popular fairy-tale compilations in postwar Poland and has been reissued ever since, reaching eleven reprints by 1989. As the only accessible Grimm version on the monopolized children's book market, the volume effectively shaped the Polish Grimm canon in postwar Poland, although a two-volume complete edition of the Grimms' tales appeared in 1982 (in the version of Marceli Tarnowski and Emilia Bielicka, who translated the tales not included in earlier editions). This book, however—which was published by Ludowa Spółdzielnia Wydawnicza rather than Nasza Księgarnia and was not very attractive from a visual point of view—was not particularly successful and did not result in significant changes to the reception of the Grimms' work in Poland.

The "wild capitalism" found in Poland in the 1990s was characterized by a massive increase in the publication of fairy-tale books, combined with a sharp fall in editorial quality. Given the conservative tastes of Polish consumers, whose preferences, as far as books for small children are concerned, still lean decidedly toward traditional Polish fables and classical fairy tales (Zając 33), it is not surprising that the market was inundated with cheap and sloppy pseudo-Grimm and pseudo-Andersen compilations. In addition to obsolete adaptations, the market also underwent an eruption of coprints, low-quality illustrated books bought from foreign publishers (in particular Italian ones such as De Agostini), which were translated summarily into Polish and released in great numbers. The rapid development of audiovisual technologies and private TV channels in the second half of the 1990s also considerably changed the reception and the perception of fairy tales. For example, between 1999 and 2002 Polish television transmitted twenty-six episodes of the successful German animated series *Simsala Grimm,* which was accompanied by books based on the individual episodes.

The 1990s were also the time of Disney's effective arrival on the Polish book and audiovisual market. In the Communist period the presence of Disney products in Poland was very limited and therefore their influence on children's culture and literature had been delayed for several decades. Before the war, *Snow White and the Seven Dwarfs* was shown in the cinema in Polish dubbing and was novelized by Irena Tuwim. The most tangible impact of the film on fairy-tale reception was the canonization of the title: from that moment Snow White became "Królewna Śnieżka" (in earlier adaptations and translations the most frequent translation was "Śnieżyczka" or "Śnieżna różyczka" but also "Białoskórka" or "Białośnieżka").

In the Communist period, Disney's full-length animated films were occasionally shown in the theaters only in the 1960s,[20] although in the 1970s and 1980s short cartoons appeared on rare occasions (usually at Christmas) on television. What is important, however, is that until 1989 there were no Disney books, toys, or gadgets available in Poland; therefore, the impact of Disney imagery on Polish writers and illustrators for children, and in consequence on the young audience, was minimal. That all changed, of course, in the 1990s. The liberalization of the book market resulted, among other things, in a rapid growth of Disney products in Poland. A massive importation of Disney coprints and the quick growth of the DVD market had a huge impact on the reception of fairy tales in Poland and as a consequence

Poland has caught up, at an accelerated rate, with the same tendencies that in Western Europe had begun decades earlier.

After the chaotic decade of the 1990s, the beginning of the new century brought a revival in the interest in quality books for children, as far as both their literary and visual quality were concerned. It did not result, however, in new translations of classic texts but rather in a series of retellings of the most famous tales, some of which were written by well-known writers for children, such as Grzegorz Kasdepke and Jarosław Mikołajewski, and enhanced by innovative illustrations. Quite recently, however, an ambitious publishing house specializing in children's literature, Media Rodzina, decided to launch a faithful translation of the Grimms' tales. In 2009 a compilation of fifty of the most popular stories appeared, followed by a two-volume edition of all the tales in the next year. The translator, Eliza Pieciul-Karmińska, followed principles that maintained rigorous fidelity to the original texts. The return to the original, "true" version of the tales, highlighted by the decision to enrich the book with the traditional, very "German" illustrations by Otto Ubbelohde, a policy carefully explained in the prefaces and afterwords to the books, was an important element in the promotional campaign organized by the publisher. This new translation was warmly received by the critics and met with modest success with its audience, but only the passage of time will allow us to determine whether it will acquire the status of a new canonical version of the Grimms' tales in Poland.

CONCLUSION

The particular dynamics of the assimilation of the *Kinder- und Hausmärchen* into Polish literature clearly produced a situation that, for all the similarities with the dynamics present in other countries, diverges in a number of ways from other national canons of children literature. Some of the general attitudes to fairy tales, such as the tendency to edit and expurgate the elements deemed not suitable for children, are naturally also present in Polish culture, even though the objections toward the Grimms' work had been exacerbated by the historical circumstances of Polish–German relations, as becomes particularly clear in the postwar period.

A combination of religious, political, social, and literary factors made the *Kinder- und Hausmärchen* subject to radical modifications as a rule rather than as an exception and shaped the Polish canon of the Grimms' fairy tales.

Consequently, some tales were excluded, whereas others were assimilated in a form completely different from the original text. In short, the Polish "Cinderella" and "Hansel and Gretel" differ from their German counterparts, not only because they have been abridged and rendered less explicit but above all because they were turned into "Kopciuszek" or "Jaś i Małgosia" and were thus transferred and became deeply rooted in the Polish cultural context and narrated in line with the Polish stylistic and literary tradition.

Logically, one may presume that similar discoveries and surprises will emerge from research into other national contexts, especially as far as so-called minority cultures are concerned. Only after having drawn a detailed and exhaustive map of the reception of the *Kinder- und Hausmärchen* in many different countries will it be possible to distinguish clearly between the phenomena that are unique to a given culture and those that tend to manifest themselves throughout all contexts and historical circumstances. In any case, to go beyond the abstract concept of an international Grimms canon in favor of a comparative approach that is inclusive of these lesser known cultural realities—such as the Polish one—promises to open new perspectives in general studies on the Grimms' fairy tales and even to change some of the long-established dogmas and assumptions in Grimm scholarship.

Notes

1. To establish precisely which Grimm texts may be included in the corpus of canonical fairy tales in Poland is extremely difficult, if not altogether impossible, since there are simply not enough data to rely on. So far, no detailed research on reader response to the most popular tales has been carried out: in 2002, in a great plebiscite launched in the media as the "readers' canon of children's literature in Poland," the Grimms' tales took eighth place in the ranking of twenty-five; first place went to Andersen, and Perrault did not enter into the ranking at all (Leszczyński 261). This generic recognition of the Grimms' importance by a large audience does not reveal much either about the popularity of given tales or about the real knowledge of the texts. Therefore, the considerations and the conclusions presented in this chapter are based mainly on the study of the publishing history of fairy tales in Poland; on bibliometric indicators, such as number of publications, reprints, adaptations, and so on; and on reviews, comments, prefaces, and other paratextual sources. The "Grimms' canon" in Poland is intended as the corpus of the tales that have effectively penetrated into the mainstream of Polish children's literature.

2. The boom of fairy tales as a genre in England and in Germany in the 1700s has been relatively widely studied and analyzed by scholars such as Manfred Grätz, Jack Zipes, Ruth Bottigheimer.

3. Although in 1775 Adam Czartoryski, cofounder of the Commission of National Education, included Perrault's tales in the list of recommended readings for schools (Sinko 36), throughout the entire eighteenth century only a handful of French fairy tales had been translated into Polish (Sinko 42–44) and not one of them by Perrault or Madame d'Aulnoy.

4. The first collection of selected tales by Andersen, adapted into Polish by Fryderyk Henryk Lewestam, was published in 1858, but individual tales began to appear in different journals starting in 1852. For a detailed bibliography of Andersen's reception in Poland, see Brzozowska (86–109).

5. In fact *Balladyna*, today considered one of Słowacki's chief works, was violently attacked and criticized, particularly for its fantastic elements.

6. Some information about Grimms' early reception in Poland may be found in the volume *Bracia Grimm i folklor narodów słowiańskich* (1989), especially in the two introductory essays by Helena Kapełuś and Dorota Simonides, but this early period of the Grimms' reception in Poland has never been thoroughly investigated and is still waiting for an in-depth analysis based on serious archival research.

7. The term "*klechda*," used by Wójcicki, was his invention based on a false interpretation of an ancient Polish word. It is quite telling, however, that he did not want to use the word "*bajka*" (tale), which in the Polish language had acquired a strong negative connotation, as a synonym of "lie" or "invention."

8. It has been pointed out by many scholars that some of Wójcicki's tales do not derive from authentic folk narratives but were in fact "borrowed" from foreign literary sources such as Vuk Karadžić's works (Wojciechowski 44).

9. "When collecting our *Bajarz* we thought about a wide public of readers, and it is well known that a strictly scientific approach often discourages them from reading the book," explained Gliński in the preface (xi).

10. It has often been observed that "Polish fairy tales are characterized by a certain rationalism, while the wonderful and marvelous elements remain in the background" (Haase 877). Gliński, however, was not really interested in reproducing true folktales but rather borrowed freely from the existing literary versions, especially in Russian.

11. Some elements of the tale recalls motifs present in folktales of other nations, for example, the Sicilian tale "Maria, die böse Stiefmutter und die sieben Räuber" (Maria, the Wicked Stepmother, and the Seven Robbers) included in Laura Gonzenbach's volume of Sicilian tales, collected from the people (1870).

12. Since the failure of the January Uprising in 1863, the anti-Polish measures introduced by the Russian and Prussian occupiers made the struggle for a national identity of even more crucial importance than before.

13. Even in the 1880s Polish educators were still convinced that "fantasy . . . is something we should rather restrain than encourage in children" (qtd. in Kuliczkowska 71).

14. The tales included are "Puss in Boots," "Sleeping Beauty," and "Cinderella."

15. "Śliczna, najpiękniejsza na świecie była królewna Drwidusza, tak piękna, że kto raz ujrzał jej przecudne czarne oczy, czoło bielsze nad śniegi, koralowe usta, ten już do końca życia zapomnieć jej nie mógł. Gdy rozpuściła czarne, jedwabiste włosy, osłaniały ją one niby płaszczem; gdy spojrzała z litością, nieszczęśliwi się uśmiechali i zapominali o swoich cierpieniach, a gdy błysnęła dumnym i gniewnym spojrzeniem, drżeli najodważniejsi rycerze i oczu podnieść nie śmieli."

16. It is important to bear in mind this situation when comparing the Grimms' reception in Poland with the situation in other countries. In Italy, for example, the first compilation of fifty Grimm tales was published in 1897 by Hoepli in a faithful (though inelegant) translation by Fanny Vanzi Mussini. In contrast to Kowerska's forgotten version, however, it was an instant success and became a canonical Italian version of the *Kinder- und Hausmärchen*. Regularly reprinted ever since, it remains in circulation even today.

17. "W Niemczech mały Frycek zaczytywał się w bajkach Grimmów, a duży Fryc szedł mordować, grabić, unicestwiać i bogacić się w sposób nieprawy."

18. "Zbyt długo pozwalaliśmy polskiemu dziecku, by na takich wzorach kształtowało swoje poglądy społeczne i etyczne."

19. This becomes clear when comparing the 1956 book with Tarnawski's prewar editions. Some fairy tales were subject only to minor editing, whereas others had in fact been completely rewritten. A typical example of these modifications is the ending of "Snow White": in the postwar edition the queen is not forced to dance in iron shoes until she drops dead, but rather she is so vexed that she becomes very ugly and flees the country.

20. Only in 1961 did such films as *Bambi* (1942), *Cinderella* (1950), *Alice in Wonderland* (1953), and *Peter Pan* (1953) arrive in Poland. *The Sword in the Stone* (1963), shown in 1969, was the last Disney film to be released in Poland until 1989.

References

Anczyc, Władysław Ludwik. *Trzy baśnie,* Warsaw: Gebethner i Wolff, 1878.

Boczar, Elżbieta. *Bibliografia literatury dla dzieci i młodzieży.* Vol. 19. Warsaw: Wydawnictwo Uniwersytetu Warszawskiego, 2010.

Brzozowska, Zdzisława. *Andersen w Polsce.* Wroclaw: Ossolineum, 1970.

Buras, Jacek. *Bibliographie deutscher Literatur in polnischer Übersetzung: vom 16. Jahrhundert bis 1994.* Wiesbaden: Harrasowitz, 1996.

Gliński, Antoni Józef. *Bajarz polski: baśnie, gawędy, powieści ludowe.* 2nd rev. ed. Vols. 1–2. Wilno: Drukarnia Gubernialna, 1862.

Grimm, Jacob, and Wilhelm Grimm. *Baśnie dla dzieci i młodzieży.* Trans. Cecylia Niewiadomska. Warsaw: Gebethner i Wolff, 1895. http://jbc.bj.uj.edu.pl/dlibra/ dlibra/docmetadata?id=664. 6 Sept. 2013

———. *The Complete Grimm's Fairy Tales.* Digireads.com. 2009. 6 Sept. 2013

———. *Grimms Märchensammlung. Für E-book reader optimiert.* N.p.: Sonne + Wind Verlag, 2011.

Haase, Donald, ed. *The Greenwood Encyclopedia of Folktales and Fairy Tales.* Vols. 1–3. Westport: Greenwood Press, 2008.

Kaniowska-Lewańska, Izabela. *Literatura dla dzieci i młodzieży do roku 1864.* Warsaw: WsiP, 1980.

Kapełuś, Helena. "Posłowie." *Baśnie domowe i dziecięce zebrane przez braci Grimm.* Vols. 1–2. Trans. Emilia Bielicka and Marceli Tarnowski. Warsaw: LSW, 1982. 379–405.

Krassowska, Bogumiła, and Alina Grefkowicz. *Bibliografia literatury dla dzieci i młodzieży 1918–1939.* Warsaw: Biblioteka Publiczna m.st. Warszawy, 1995.

Krysztofiak, Maria. *Przekład literacki a translatologia.* Poznań: Wydawnictwo Naukowe Uniwersytetu im. Adama Mickiewicza, 1999.

Kuliczkowska, Krystyna. *Literatura dla dzieci i młodzieży w latach 1864–1918.* Warsaw: Wydawnictwa Szkolne i Pedagogiczne, 1981.

Leszczyński, Grzegorz. "Kanon książek—pojęcie i sprzeczności." *Książka dziecięca 1990–2005. Konteksty kultury popularnej i literatury wysokiej.* Eds. Grzegorz Leszczyński, Danuta Świrszczyńska-Jelonek, and Michał Zając. Warsaw: SBP, 2006. 255–68.

Osterloff, Waldemar. "Kryminalistyka i bajki Grimmów." *Odrodzenie* 19 (1946): 8.

Simonides, Dorota. "Jakub i Wilhelm Grimmowie a folklor polski." *Bracia Grimm i folklor narodów słowiańskich.* Eds. Jerzy Śliziński and Maria Czurak. Wroclaw: Ossolineum, 1989. 25–50.

Szczepańska, Hanna. "Niemieckie bajeczki." *Odrodzenie* 21 (1946): 11.

Wojciechowski, Ryszard. "Kazimierz Władysław Wójcicki i jego Klechdy." *Klechdy, starożytne podania i powieści ludu polskiego i Rusi.* Kazimierz Władysław Wójcicki. Warsaw: Państwowy Instytut Wydawniczy, 1974. 12–67.

Zając, Michał. *Raport o książce dla dzieci i młodzieży.* Warsaw: Biblioteka Analiz, 2006.

Sinko, Zofia. *Powiastka w oświeceniu stanisławowskim.* Wroclaw: Ossolineum, 1982.

Zipes, Jack. "The Grimms and the German Obsession with Fairy Tales." *Fairy Tales and Society: Illusion, Allusion and Paradigm.* Ed. Ruth Bottigheimer. Philadelphia: U of Pennsylvania P, 1986. 271–78.

3

The Grimms' Fairy Tales in Spain

Translation, Reception, and Ideology

ISABEL HERNÁNDEZ AND NIEVES MARTÍN-ROGERO

The way in which the Brothers Grimm compiled German fairy tales was an important landmark, not only for popularizing folklore but also for the development of children's literature.[1] Due to the importance of the Enlightenment tradition, the beginning of Romanticism was held back in Spain until the 1830s and lasted not more than just over a decade. Whereas in Germany, Romantic ideals had fostered collections of local folk heritage, in Spain the philological interest in folktales came late and the tales compiled by the Grimms also made a late appearance.[2] When popular folktales were collected, for example by Fernán Caballero (1796–1877) and Father Coloma (1851–1915) in the second half of the nineteenth century, they became reading material for children only after stylistic adaptation. Their oral character was not retained.

At the end of the nineteenth century, Spanish children's literature was conditioned by didacticism, Catholic religiosity, and fin-de-siècle Realist literature. This is the time when the works by the Brothers Grimm were disseminated by Saturnino Calleja (1853–1915), a publisher who was instrumental in the extension of recreational reading beyond the canon imposed by schools. Throughout the twentieth century, translations of the Brothers Grimm's stories into Spanish continued to be published; how these translations were carried out and published is of great importance in understanding the historical evolution of their reception in Spain. In relation to other studies, such as those of the folklorist A. Rodríguez Almodóvar, which accentuate the similarities of the German model with the Spanish oral tradition, this chapter emphasizes the imprint left by the Brothers Grimm in light of cultural and ideological studies. This historical, ideological–cultural, and comparative approach allows us to draw conclusions regarding the reception of a founding genre in the area of children's books and its adaptation to a country that, in spite of its variety of languages, maintains an identity of its own.

THE WEIGHT OF DIDACTICISM IN FOLKTALES

Literature intended for readers in their formative years has always been conditioned by adult views in order to establish certain codes of social and moral behavior within the system of values prescribed by that particular culture, a system that usually coincides with the oligarchies and groups in power. After the Brothers Grimm published their *Kinder- und Hausmärchen* in 1812, they felt obliged to make certain modifications in form and content with respect to children: "The tales [Wilhelm] Grimm chose to set before young people are especially good examples of what he considered socially desirable and safe for their eyes" (Bottigheimer, *Fairy Tales* 20).[3] These adaptations appear in the editions that followed, especially in the second edition of 1819 and in the so-called *Kleine Ausgabe* (Small Edition) of 1825.

If we look at the Spanish context in that same period, there was no movement to recover folklore or original legends, partly, as mentioned, because of the delayed arrival of Romanticism in Spain. The political circumstances did not help, as the reign of Ferdinand VII, after the Peninsular War (1808–1814), was a period of intellectual stagnation in which the borders were closed to foreign ideas. Furthermore, at the time when the Brothers Grimm published their collection of stories, there existed in Germany a nationalist feeling that demanded cohesion with regard to German traditions. In Spain no equivalent need emerged, perhaps because the unity of the state had been attained many centuries earlier. Furthermore, the late arrival of Romanticism in Spain presents contradictions, with one liberal ideological current and another advocating a return to the Catholic–monarchic tradition.

The task of recuperating folkloric material, carried out in later years, reached a compromise with the bourgeoisie of the period, which had ties to the traditional Catholic spirit. According to the Hispanist A. Rodríguez Almodóvar, this is why there was no interest in following the philological method of the Grimm brothers. Undertaking a project similar to the

Grimms' would have revealed a common, international folkloric heritage, something that conflicted with the desires of the bourgeoisie and other hegemonic groups of the period, who saw nothing positive in anything from abroad: "The transnational character of the authentic rural culture could come to light," they feared (Rodríguez Almodóvar 175), and that would mean its revitalization as opposed to institutional culture. For this reason, the Spanish authors who turned to popular narratives attempted to accommodate them to the ideology of the moment, emphasizing Christian and family values of the most traditional kind.[4]

The work undertaken by the writer Fernán Caballero (the pseudonym of Cecilia Böhl de Faber) shows the greatest concordance with that of the Brothers Grimm. Indeed, the Grimms are cited in the preface to her book *Cuentos y poesías populares andaluces* (1859, Popular Andalusian Tales and Poems) as a model to follow in compiling folktales: "Among the collections of popular and children's stories and legends that we have always read with delight there is a German one, in three volumes, compiled by the erudite Grimm brothers, in which they did not limit themselves to collecting those of their own country but did the same thing with the tales and legends of other countries" (Caballero xi, our translation).[5]

Caballero also points out the Grimms' interest in Spain, focusing especially on the literature of the Spanish Golden Age, in which parts of popular stories appear.[6] She attempts to justify her work by alluding to the fact that, in spite of the rich Spanish popular tradition, no one had yet undertaken the task to form a collection. No doubt her German origins led Fernán Caballero to commit herself to this enterprise. Nevertheless, the folk character of the tales she compiled was influenced by her desire to create a national Spanish anthology of popular literature similar to those of other European countries. As a result, she "literaturized" the material she gathered. In 1877, Fernán Caballero published *Cuentos, oraciones, adivinanzas y refranes populares e infantiles* (Popular Children's Stories, Prayers, Riddles, and Proverbs), now aimed at children, and its division into "stories of enchantment" and "religious stories" is an indication of the moral intent of this anthology.

The literary treatment of oral sources also characterizes Antonio de Trueba's collection (1865), which centers on the tradition of the Basque Country and other Spanish regions such as Andalusia and Catalonia; similar projects were carried out between 1870 and 1880. Testifying to the lack of consideration toward popular culture, Trueba writes: "Those tales, which roll as pebbles across the fields, are of no use, unless seasoned with a tasty sauce" (393).[7]

Several years later, other authors, such as Father Coloma, undertook the compilation of folklore reshaped for children, with a didactic and moralistic focus, which does not preclude the appearance in their stories of amusing local customs, manners, and scenes. One evident example is the story *Periquillo sin miedo,* which was included in the undated collection *Cuentos para niños* (Tales for Children). In this Spanish version of "The Story of the Youth Who Went Forth to Learn What Fear Was" the main character, now turned into an altar boy, has to deal with a wild bull, which he tries to fight with a cassock. The moral nature of the tale becomes evident toward the end of the story, as the main character feels fear for the first time when being shown his own flaws.

THE CALLEJA VERSIONS

At the end of the nineteenth century, one can speak of a new period in Spain, marked by the restoration of the constitutional monarchy. During that period, the predominance of a conservative bourgeoisie favored the consideration of childhood as a stage with needs of its own, a stage of education. The foundation of the publishing house Calleja in 1876 was a decisive factor in the popularization of books intended specifically for children, and, with time, it gradually published works that were more recreational as opposed to those with a marked instructional and scholastic tone (García-Padrino, *Libros* 18–20). The success achieved by the famous "tales of Calleja" in the Spanish-speaking countries,[8] in part thanks to the massive circulation permitted by its low cost, is significant if it is compared with other works of a pedagogical nature. It must be pointed out that the percentage of translations soon eclipsed the Spanish creations, because in the stories from abroad children could find humor, fantasy, and entertainment, elements that stood in contrast to nineteenth-century Spanish productions, which offered models of conduct in everyday surroundings. Thanks to Calleja, the tales of the Brothers Grimm and of other authors, such as Charles Perrault and Hans Christian Andersen, were disseminated, and representative works such as *The Thousand and One Nights, Gulliver's Travels,* and *Robinson Crusoe* reached young Spanish readers.

There were also anthologies with Grimm tales available in Spain prior and parallel to their diffusion by Calleja, most notably *Cuentos escogidos de los hermanos Grimm* (1863, Selected Stories of the Brothers Grimm), translated by José S. Viedma and *Cuentos escogidos de los hermanos Grimm* (1896, Selected Stories of the Brothers Grimm), translated by José Muñoz Escámez. Yet, at the beginning of the twentieth century, Calleja would provide the greatest dissemination of the tales in the form of cheap adaptations. The stories, published as offprint booklets, were at times quite altered and the author was not even mentioned, so that they could be confused with other national creations; not only the text but also the titles of the most famous tales were changed and domesticated for the Spanish reader. Examples include *La princesa Camelia* (c. 1900, Princess Camelia), an imitation of "Cinderella"; *La rueca, el telar y el bastidor* (c. 1900, The Distaff, the Loom, and the Spinning Frame), a version of "The Three Spinners"; and *La envidia de una reina* (c. 1900, The Jealousy of a Queen), an adaptation of "Snow White." In the context of the conservative Catholic society that Spain was at the time, translators frequently made the moral lessons of the tale explicit. For example, at the end of *La envidia de una reina*, it is added that the protagonist went to heaven because of her goodness. Calleja was not interested in preserving a faithful version of the Grimms' tales. Instead, many of their adaptations were published anonymously and became confused with other popular Spanish tales.

The same publisher produced the selection *Cuentos escogidos* (1920, Selected Tales, by the Grimms) as part of the collection Biblioteca Perla (Pearl Library), one of the most carefully and exquisitely presented by the publisher (García-Padrino, *Libros* 37). If we stop to consider the changes made by Calleja, we perceive a residue of the religious and conservative ideology of the period and, at the same time, a clear desire to innovate children's publications, giving them a more literary character. The transformations of the Grimms' tales are sometimes clear to see and instrumental for the new generations to socialize in a world where virtue, work, and effort are paramount and where masculine and feminine roles are well delimited.

Although Calleja belonged to a process of modernization in Spain, it should not be forgotten that, especially in its early period until 1915, orthodox Catholic values predominated in its publications (Ruiz-Berrio 196). In addition, there is an evident desire to suppress or soften the most violent details or episodes. Spanish domestication of the stories is another characteristic that is noticeable in the translation of certain titles and expressions. Calleja included local references in order to facilitate identification and reading pleasure for a broad audience. Some of the illustrated stories were accompanied by jokes, pastimes, and, sometimes, pictures alluding to the history of Spain and to Spanish stereotypes. Without a doubt the maxim of "instruction by delight" also meant that doses of patriotism were added to the tales, in accordance with the regenerationist spirit of the period.

Among the tales most widely circulated in Spain is "Hansel and Gretel," translated by Calleja as *Juanito y Margarita* (c. 1910). The modification of the opening situation, the abandonment of the children in the forest, alters the sense of the whole story. In the Spanish adaptation, brother and sister are lost when they go out to pick strawberries, whereby the not very edifying cause for the parents' guilt is eliminated, and the stepmother's role is played out by the mother, who does not die at the end.[9] This denouement attempts to attract the reader of the period by way of direct appeal and anachronism: "With the money that Juanito and Margarita had, everyone's troubles were over, and with time, Margarita had a good dowry to take with her when she married, and Juanito, who worked hard, was able to study for a profession. . . . Many younger architects were his followers. When in your city you see one of those buildings, usually very large, that look like a confectioner's bouquet, you can say, . . . 'That building is in the style of Juanito, the one who, together with his sister Margarita, got lost in the woods and reached the candy house of the ogress.'" (n.p., our translation).[10]

Another tale adapted by Calleja, "Snow White," had two versions. In one of them, translated as *Blanca Nieves* (c. 1910), the text adheres to the original, although the editor's alterations are evident, adding drama to the story while they emphasize its literary quality. The abundant adjectives and the use of metaphors are proof of that: "As the dwarfs have the head of a man and the body of a child, their grown-up tears came running down to the ground, without drying out on their way. So they sprinkled all over the room" (n.p., our translation).[11] In the other, the title *La envidia de una reina* (c. 1908, The Jealousy of a Queen) is representative of the mitigation of violence in the tales, beyond the transformations made by the Grimms in their day. In this narrative, unlike in the previous version, passages that might be too frightening for children were expurgated. For example, the fact that the stepmother eats the liver and lungs of a deer (believing that they are Snow White's) is omitted from the Spanish version. Likewise, the Grimms' violent ending is modified, so that the stepmother is no longer condemned to die dancing in red-hot shoes. Instead, her punishment is to eat and live in a cage like an animal. Apart from this, there is also the substitution of certain elements, such as the replacement of the coffin by a carriage made of gold and precious stones. Of particular notice is the extension with which the story ends: "Little White Snow lived happily for many years, and when she died, she went straight to heaven, which she had earned so well with her good deeds" (n.p., our translation).[12]

As for the Spanish domestication that the tales underwent, several examples can be cited. In *Juanito y Margarita,* the house that the children find is not made of gingerbread and sugar but of the typically Spanish *turrón,* a kind of nougat usually eaten at Christmas. An expression that would even provoke a smile in a Spanish speaker is "*picaronaza,*" used to refer to the stepmother in *La envidia de una reina:* "In those days the 'picaronaza' of a queen still believed that Snow White was as dead as her mother" (n.p., our translation).[13] This adjective contains two augmentative suffixes with respect to *pícaro* (rogue, knave),[14] and the fact that they are used in relation to the stepmother is indeed atypical, since in Spanish "*pícaro*" tends to be used in a more ironic and humorous context.

Evolution of the Adaptations in the Twentieth Century

When examining the adaptations from a chronological point of view, the names of the publishing houses must be underlined, since, as García-Padrino ("El libro infantil" 299) points out, they greatly influence how children's literature was accepted in the Spanish social realm, as has been proven in relation to Calleja. Among the fairy-tale collections that appeared on the Spanish market at the beginning of the century, the one issued by Ramón Sopena publishers in 1918 is most noteworthy. "Hansel and Gretel" is this time translated as *Juanito y Anita,* a title that shows a higher degree of Spanish domestication than Calleja's version, since the name Margarita (Spanish for Gretel) was not very frequently used at that time. The translation is more faithful in content than Calleja's, but one can also observe alterations made by the "translator/narrator."[15] At no time does the translator render the original literally. Rather, the story of "Hansel and Gretel" is retold, with the addition of expressions typical of oral narration, exaggerating the use of adjectives and including phrases of didactic–moral content that gradually lead the young reader along the path that the editor has determined. The wisdom, courage, and intelligence of the children are continually emphasized. They are the real protagonists, and so the tale finishes in quite an abrupt way, with the two children embracing each other while the witch (who is an ogress in the Spanish version) burns in the oven.

Similar, although with less formal freedom, is the translation of this same tale included in the anthology *Cuentos de Grimm* (Grimms' Tales) told for children by Amy Steedman and published by Araluce between 1910 and 1920. In this case at least, the reader knows from the beginning that the book is not a direct translation from the German original, but a selection "retold" by someone whose name is indicated. Though it is not indicated, the source text is probably *Stories from Grimm. Told to the Children* by Amy Steedman, published in London in 1906 by E. C. and T. C. Jack. The editor does not translate the names of the children but leaves them as "Hansel y Gretel"— replacing only the "a" with an umlaut, which is unknown to the Spanish reader. What is more, the narrator displaces the story in space: "At a great distance from our country, near a dark forest" (*Cuentos de Grimm*, 1910–1920 109, our translation),[16] so that the foreign names are justified and the story is read as something unthinkable in Spain.

The text bears great similarities to the earlier versions of Calleja and Sopena when it comes to the valuation and exaltation of certain childhood virtues; the children are capable of acting and thinking like adults, which even leaves its mark on their vocabulary: " 'Oh, Hansel!' exclaimed Gretel, 'We are going to die of starvation' " (166, our translation)[17]—a word a child would never use. Nevertheless, this edition maintains the original ending of the tale, that is, the children's return home and the reunion with their father, although the narrator cannot resist putting in a personal final comment: "And even though the diamonds and rubies were very lovely, Hansel and Gretel did not consider them as beautiful as the pretty little pebbles that shone like little silver coins when they were bathed in the silver moonlight" (124, our translation).[18] At least on this occasion a certain poetic intention can be perceived in contrast to mere moral teaching.

It is noteworthy that in the 1930s a translation appeared that respects the Grimms' original. This is the collection titled *Cuentos* (Stories) published by Juventud in 1935, just a year before the beginning of the Spanish Civil War. Compared with previous editions, in this anthology the passages considered most violent, such as the stepmother's cannibalism and her death in red-hot shoes, have not been expurgated. The context of the Republican period favored an interest in a more progressive education, and the publications intended for children began to be more highly valued: they were not considered to be merely a vehicle for moral and didactic transmission.

The flourishing of children's literature also attracted attention with respect to the autochthonous creation of both folktales and children's books. This expansion had already begun at the end of the 1920s, and in its wake various prizes for and exhibitions of children's books appeared. The growing interest on the part of authors motivated by literary intentions revitalized the productions intended for children and connected them with the avant-garde movements in general literature. But this respectful attitude underwent a brusque change after the end of the Civil War, and one of the explanations for this was the inevitable exile of writers who had advocated a modernization of Spanish children's literature.

With the establishment of the Franco regime, education also became a concern for the new government but for reasons that were completely different from those of the Republican period. Now it was a matter of shaping the new generation with the objective of perpetuating the regime and avoiding any hint of criticism. The ideals of national Catholicism led to the imposition of a system of values based on pillars such as love of the fatherland and religious traditions. Thus, there arose an urge to legislate and control all publications intended for children, from school texts to the most recreational reading, and as a result prescriptive catalogs were distributed. The censorship of the period found fertile ground in children's books, since young readers were deemed more susceptible to the views of the world that were offered to them.[19] The Grimms' tales continued to be published because they were not considered harmful for children. An examination of the *Catálogo crítico de libros para niños* (1945, Critical Catalog of Children's Books), prepared by the so-called Santa Teresa de Jesús reading room, identifies which stories were considered to be of "recognized merit and morality" and which required caution. Some tales by Charles Perrault were considered inappropriate, especially "Donkey Skin," because of its "immoral" theme.

The selection of *Cuentos de Grimm* (Grimms' Tales), published in 1941 in Calleja's Biblioteca Perla,[20] is one of the books recommended in the catalog. And it is certainly surprising to read the comment that "the translation is very good" in spite of its multiple transformations. From the beginning, *Juanito y Margarita* attempts to capture the young reader with a tone that denotes a certain sentimentality and affectation:

In a little cottage that was situated close to a great leafy forest there lived a woodsman with his wife and two young children. When our tale begins, the evening of a beautiful spring day was drawing to a close. In the uncertain light of dusk, the woodsman, sitting at the door of his house, was resting from the day's labors, lost in profound meditation, without conceding a glance at the lovely panorama before him. Nearby Juanito and Margarita, the two children that the woodsman had from his first marriage, were playing and running about with that delightful unawareness of children. With bare feet and legs, and dressed in poor, very humble clothing, they were, nevertheless, so happy and enchanting that anyone who saw them felt attracted to them by irresistible affection. (91–92, our translation)[21]

The description fits well with the idea of Spain in that period as a country of incomparable beauty, and at the same time it serves as a mirror for many children of the postwar era, who were obliged to survive with very limited means. All the actions performed by the protagonists could be considered feats, so that the tone of the translation coincides with a traditionalist patriotic spirit: "To make matters worse, work was noticeably scarce that year. The family had already been *defending itself heroically* for several months, but as of a short time ago their economic situation had become unsustainable" (93–94, translation and italics ours).[22] Not only does the description of the children differentiate between them in their masculine and feminine roles, but the role of the mother is also perfectly defined from the very beginning of the narrative, since the woodsman considers it necessary, after the death of his wife, to have "the presence of a woman to take care of the children and attend to domestic tasks" (93, our translation).[23]

It is not the purpose of this study to enter into a discussion of gender stereotypes in fairy tales, which is denounced from feminist positions; this is a topic that has been treated by various critics, such as Ruth Bottigheimer, Cristina Bacchilega, and Elizabeth Wanning Harries, to name a few.[24] Nevertheless, Francoist ideology clearly affects Spanish variants of the Grimms to reaffirm conservative notions of gender.

Another element that is borrowed from Calleja and that had appeared in Sopena's adaptation is the exaltation of charity. Some critics have seen in the promotion of this theological virtue a sign of the Catholic faith (Alcubierre-Moya 40). In contrast, one finds the commission of cardinal sins a characteristic attribute of the wicked characters. The witch of the cottage in the woods, who is described as an "ogress," provides a vivid example: "Her face had widened, and her mouth stretched in a smile of fierce satisfaction. At the same time the gaze of voracious gluttony that with wide open eyes she directed at Margarita was so eloquent" (113, our translation).[25] The influence of the Catholic religion is evident not only in this passage but also in the development of Spanish children's literature in general and has ties with Francoist ideology. Several titles of popular tales in Calleja's version from the beginning of the century suffice as examples, such as *El castillo de la caridad* (The Castle of Charity) and *El palacio de las virtudes* (The Palace of Virtues). In the latter, Prudence, Justice, Fortitude, and Temperance become characters in the manner of the morality plays of the Spanish Golden Age.

In the same decade, Hernando, another key publisher in the history of Spanish children's books, brought out the collection *Cuentos infantiles* (1947, Children's Stories). The prologue clearly indicates what was considered valuable at the time: "The Brothers Grimm were always united by an intimate affection. Their collaboration and the similarity of their feelings have allowed them in posterity to be considered a true model of brotherhood. They were, as is said, two hearts beating as one, and this enlightening and exemplary fact, together with their fruitful and persevering work, is the best example for young people today" (7, our translation).[26] Furthermore, in the prologue it says that these stories are "very much to the children's liking" (7).[27] The transformations they underwent recall the adaptations of other times. The ending of *Blancanieves,* for example, is similar to Araluce's version (1910–1920), making the dwarfs' goodness more explicit: "Snow White and her husband were very happy, and they never forgot the unselfish protection of the seven dwarfs. In their palace they reserved two rooms for them, and whenever they wanted to, the dwarfs would go there to spend a few days of rest, attended and entertained with the splendor that befitted the goodness of their hearts" (56, our translation).[28]

A complete edition of the Grimm stories was published for the first time by Labor in 1955. The translation was the work of Francisco Payarols, with a prologue by Eduardo Valentí, which situated the figures and the work of the Grimms in the place that they deserved as authors of a philological work aimed not only at children but also at all those interested in popular stories. It was, furthermore, the first time that a work of translation and editing in Spain was undertaken with respect to the original texts in all the tales without considering them exclusively addressed to a young readership. Only expressions such as those that appear at the end of some stories like "Hansel and Gretel" were replaced by Spanish ones with the same meaning, for example "y colorín colorado, este cuento se ha acabado" (185), which means "and bright color, color red, this story here ends." Such expressions, which come from the Spanish oral tradition, became very famous after a while, which is a sign of the complete edition's success.

In the 1960s, numerous pocketbook collections for children began to appear. Among them was the series published by Bruguera. In the 1958 edition, the editor included, in addition to the original text, a version in pictures, like a comic book, to make it easier for the youngest children to read. Bruguera's selection contains eighteen of the Grimms' tales, some of them already well known to the Spanish public, such as "Juanito y Margarita" and "Blancanieves." Apart from dividing the story into chapters in order to adapt it to the structure of the collection, the editor made only a few alterations in the narrative, so that the language is brought closer to that of the young reader, who would probably read the complete version of the text. That is to say, that the sometimes unrefined language of the German original is softened here by a more varied use of adjectives as well as by more detailed descriptions of characters, actions, and situations. Thus, although the cruel end of Snow White's stepmother is respected, a few phrases are added to mitigate the effect of her sentence and to emphasize the future happiness that awaits both the protagonist and those who helped her in her misfortune: "And the wicked stepmother had to dance in them [the red-hot shoes] until she fell to the ground, dead, while Snow White and her young husband lived many years of happiness in the company of the seven dwarfs, who had loved and protected the unfortunate little princess" (56, our translation).[29]

In 1962, Noguer also published a collection. The changes that can be found correspond, in a way, to those seen in previous works, but they tend to respect the endings of the original; this occurs too with the endings of "Juanito y Margarita" and "Blancanieves." One modification affects the famous "mirror, mirror on the wall," which becomes "espejo de luna, espejo de estrella" (mirror of moon, mirror of star) in order for the final word to rhyme with the adjective "bella" (beautiful); thus the original image of a mirror hanging on a wall is altered. In this way, the reader can think of a little hand mirror, so the Grimms' emphasis on the mirror being on the wall is literally lost in translation. With the translator's poetic additions, the plain and often unrefined language employed by the Grimms is modified and in this text acquires tones that are typical of an oral narrative fused with a written one—a combination that results in a text that is easier to read. In this edition, the elements of the exaltation of childhood values have disappeared, and the language has lost the added exaltation of the fatherland that was so necessary in the difficult postwar period. This is clearly related to the unquestionable fact of the opening up of the Franco regime in the 1960s, which was also more generally reflected in the cultural and educational systems.

The field of translations for children did not develop in the same way as that of books for adults, and that explains why in 1975 the publisher Everest, with its Lecturas Everest 2000 (Everest Readings 2000), brought out a collection to be read at schools, a book titled *Cuentos de los hermanos Grimm* (Tales by the Brothers Grimm), selected by Antonio Roche Navarro. What is curious about this is that the publisher makes use of the translation that Juventud had issued back in 1935. The text, as noted earlier, was faithful to the original, but it was already forty years old. This phenomenon of old Grimm translations being recycled was repeated on numerous occasions throughout the century. Until well into the 1970s the name of the translator was seldom mentioned because the occupation of translator was generally considered to be one of little merit—a situation that is by no means unique to Spanish children's literature, as Gillian Lathey has noted in *The Role of Translators in Children's Literature: Invisible Storytellers*. For this reason, the translators also approached the texts rather casually, making lexical and structural changes wherever they considered them necessary.

A noteworthy case is found in a 1976 edition published by Lumen. It seems strange that a change should be made in the final passages of the stories it contained, although the selected texts try to come closer to a literary language, leaving aside the typical characteristics of the oral narrative. The translation of "Blancanieves," conducted by Feliú Formosa, one of the most productive translators of the 1970s and 1980s, differs from the original in the same way it did in earlier periods:[30] "And when she [the stepmother] arrived at the palace and recognized Snow White, who was smiling happily and was more beautiful than ever beside the prince, her fury was so terrible that she died of rage" (68).[31]

In 1976, Alianza also published a new selection in the collection El libro de bolsillo (The Pocketbook), translated by Pedro Gálvez. The books in this collection are not intended for a young readership, and they respect the original text from the beginning to the end. It can be seen, then, that Spanish publishers considered the Grimms' stories works that need not be adapted for children and felt adults could also be included in their potential readership. Gálvez's translation even maintains the endings of the German originals, without replacing them with the overworked Spanish functional equivalent "y colorín colorado." Thus he introduces the reader to expressions that are not common in Spain. For example, Gálvez includes the phrase at the end of "Hansel and Gretel" that states: "My story is finished; there is a mouse running around over there; whoever catches it can make himself a large, very large fur cape" (27), a literal translation of the Grimms' ending.[32] Such faithful translations with foreign elements are found in many other pocket editions, such as the one published a year later by Magisterio Español.

Once democracy had been reestablished after Franco's death in 1975, the 1980s represented a new landmark in children's literature, so that there was a publishing boom that affected the different languages of Spain. As regards the presence of the Brothers Grimm, Anaya brought out a complete edition of their tales in three volumes in its famous Laurín collection. The translation was by María Antonia Seijo, who followed the German original very closely in a desire for precision that, at times, makes some expressions or syntactic constructions seem strange to the Spanish reader.

This was also the decade in which Carmen Bravo-Villasante translated many nineteenth-century German authors, including the Brothers Grimm. Her work in making German literature known in Spain, as well as her studies on the history of Spanish literature for children, is praiseworthy, although it must be said that sometimes in translating she solves the problems presented by nineteenth-century German in a somewhat unorthodox manner. She has the habit of doing away with anything that seemed difficult by rewriting the text rather than translating it. She is also responsible for the interesting anthologies published in the attractive Olañeta editions, such as *El rey de la montaña de oro y otros cuentos de los hermanos Grimm* (1985, The King of the Gold Mountain and Other Fairy Tales by the Brothers Grimm), in which we find some of the stories less well known in Spain. In her very interesting anthology based only on folktales' feminine characters titled *Hadas, princesas, brujas, curiosas, caprichosas, compasivas, madrastras, protectoras, guerreras, valientes . . . y otras heroínas de Calleja* (1994, Fairies, Princesses, Witches, Curious, Capricious, Compassionate Women, Stepmothers, Protective, Warlike, Valiant Women . . . and Other Calleja Heroines), Bravo-Villasante recaptures characters from famous tales, including some versions of the Grimms' tales. The importance of this anthology lies in emphasizing the centrality of female characters. Bravo-Villasante shows that they play a decisively active part—unlike the traditional passive and submissive role—in folktales.

CONCLUSION

To sum up, it can be stated that the history of the Brother Grimms' translations into Spanish in Spain reflect the country's changing sociopolitical conditions. In times of prevailing conservative ideology, preserving the country's idiosyncrasy and/or traditional values while at the same time appealing to the reader prevailed over literary fidelity. From today's perspective, for example, it seems strange to contemplate the former ingenuous, moralizing adaptations, because present-day recipients hold other ideas of what children's literature is or should be.

In times when progressive ideological winds predominated, accurate translating, as a sign of respect for the aesthetic value of literature per se—regardless of its moralizing power—became increasingly valued. This especially applies to contemporary Spain, where faithful translations are considered part and parcel of the country's opening up to the world. In this context, the rendering of the Grimms' tales into Spanish in Spain has ripened into more and more accurate renditions of the original text. María Antonia Seijo's version is undoubtedly the most reliable one. However, the need is felt for a revision and updating of all previous translations in light of the new criteria of translatology. Why? Because many of the changes made in markedly conservative times still predominate in the collective imagination. In the Spanish world of print, the Grimms' ending of "Snow White," for example, is quite unknown to the nonspecialized audience.[33]

The flood of versions disseminated via various channels offers products of all kinds, for different ages. The versions that preserve the stamp of the original are not usually addressed to the young reader. Thanks to the circulation of carefully prepared editions that give special attention to the illustrations, the tales of old have come back to life, variously dressed in the clothes of artistic postmodernism. Their message of far-reaching effect is apparently not obsolete, and the translations that are faithful to the originals share the field with the most provocative and humorous new versions. Sometimes the stories are adapted to today's prevailing system of values, but their main elements remain unaltered. All in all, they have stood the test of time and, their versatility being proven, it is no wonder the Brothers Grimm's tales have become part of humankind's cultural heritage.

Notes

1. This chapter will deal with those stories translated into Castilian or Spanish. Nevertheless, it should be considered that since 1975, once the dictatorship was over, children's literature also started to blossom in the regional languages that had been more or less silenced up to that time, namely Catalan, Galician, and Basque. Folktales, both as translations of classical works, such as the collection by the Brothers Grimm, or as a part of their own oral tradition, meant a great boost for the development of those vernacular languages (see Roig-Rechou, Soto-López, and Neira-Rodríguez's *Reescrituras do conto popular*).

2. The exile of the liberal intellectuals after the absolutist Fernando VII acceded to the throne brought about a late and short-lived Spanish Romanticism. It can be said that it prevailed from 1833, with the return of the exiled intellectuals, and lasted until approximately 1845, when the esthetics of Realism and *costumbrismo* began to gain ground.

3. Not only did the Brothers Grimm remove inappropriate elements, but they also chose tales they considered suitable for children's ears.

4. In the final decades of the nineteenth century, authors belonging to the canon of Spanish literature and associated with the aesthetic of the new currents of Realism and Naturalism—Emilia Pardo Bazán (1851–1921), Juan Valera (1824–1905), Vicente Blasco Ibáñez (1867–1928), and Leopoldo Alas Clarín (1852–1901)—were aware of the relevance of compiling collections of traditional tales, just as the Brothers Grimm had done. Nevertheless, none of them carried out a similar task but instead simply borrowed from them certain elements and characters that fitted most easily into their narratives.

5. "Entre las colecciones de cuentos y leyendas populares e infantiles que siempre hemos leído con encanto existe una alemana, en tres tomos, formada por los eruditos hermanos Grimm, en la que no se han contentado con recoger las de su patria sino que han hecho otro tanto con los cuentos y leyendas de otros países."

6. The Brothers Grimm offer examples from Cervantes's *Coloquio* and Calderón's comedy *Peor que estaba* (Worse than Before).

7. "Los cuentos que andan rodando por el campo son guijarros que de nada sirven si no se les adereza con una buena salsilla."

8. Evidence of the enormous success of the collection is the existence of a saying in Spain that directly refers to it: "Tienes más cuento que Calleja" (You have more

tales than Calleja). This saying means that someone is making excuses or giving explanations that sound like lies or the products of fantasy. Calleja also came up with the best-known ending for fairy tales in Spanish: "y fueron felices y comieron perdices, y a mí no me dieron porque no quisieron," which literally means "and they were happy and ate partridges, and they did not give me any, because they did not want to" (Fernández de Córdoba 93).

9. However, it should be pointed out that this is in keeping with the 1812 edition of the story, in which it was the mother—not the stepmother—who abandoned the children in the forest.

10. "Con el dinero que Juanito y Margarita llevaban, salieron todos de apuros y, andando el tiempo, Margarita, al casarse, pudo llevar una buena dote, y Juanito, que era estudioso, seguir una carrera. . . . Muchos arquitectos más jóvenes siguieron su escuela. Cuando en vuestra ciudad veáis uno de estos edificios, por lo general muy grandes, que parecen un ramillete de confitería, ya podéis decir. . . . 'Esta casa es del estilo de Juanito, del que con su hermana Margarita se perdió en el bosque y llegó a la casita de turrón de la ogresa.'"

11. "Como los enanos tienen cabeza de hombre y cuerpo de niño, sus lágrimas de persona mayor llegaron completas al suelo, sin secarse en el camino. Así es que con ellas regaron la habitación."

12. "Blanquita vivió muchos años feliz, y fue siempre muy buena, y cuando murió se fue derechita al cielo, que tan bien tenía ganado con sus buenas acciones."

13. "Por entonces la picaronaza de la reina seguía creyendo a Blanca Nieves tan muerta como su madre."

14. The term has literary connotations, as it was the origin of a characteristic genre of Spanish Golden Age literature: the picaresque novel.

15. When critics identify manipulations in translations, these are often described and analyzed in terms of the differing norms governing the source and the target languages, cultures, and literatures. Emer O' Sullivan has shown that the translator usually has a very important presence in the translated text, as far as he becomes the creator of a new text for readers of the target text. This process can be observed in all translated narrated literature, but due to the asymmetrical communication in and around children's literature, the implied translator is particularly present (O'Sullivan 197–207).

16. "A mucha distancia de nuestro país, cerca de un tenebroso bosque."

17. "—Oh, Hansel!—exclamó Gretel,—nos vamos a morir de inanición."

18. "Y aún cuando los diamantes y rubíes eran muy hermosos, Hansel y Gretel no los consideraban tan bellos como las piedrecitas que brillaban como moneditas de plata al ser bañadas por la plateada luz de la luna."

19. In those years, ideology was seen very clearly in the prologues and other preliminary passages that accompanied texts; we find an obvious example in a school

edition of *Don Quijote*, in which together with a portrait of Cervantes appear one of Franco and another of José Antonio Primo de Rivera, the leader of National Syndicalism. The desire to disseminate among pupils the works that best demonstrated the values of the fatherland, represented perfectly by the heroes of the medieval epic, such as El Cid Campeador and the literature of the Golden Age, was no barrier to the popularization of other foreign champions, to a great extent characters from adventure novels far removed from the reality of the moment, such as *Tarzan of the Apes* and the pirates of Salgari (Martín-Rogero 175).

20. When its founder Saturnino Calleja died in 1915, the publishing house was taken over by his two sons at different times, but the greatest period of the publishing house was in the first quarter of the century. In 1941, the edition that Calleja had published in his Biblioteca Perla in 1935 was reissued. The new reprint did not cause him any difficulties given that the content fully matched the spirit of the new dictatorial regime established in Spain by General Franco.

21. "En una casita, que estaba situada al lado de un extenso y frondoso bosque, vivía un leñador, con su esposa y dos hijos de corta edad. Cuando comienza nuestra narración, declinaba la tarde de un hermoso día de primavera. A la indecisa luz del crepúsculo, el leñador, sentado a la puerta de su vivienda, descansaba de las faenas del día, sumido en profunda meditación, sin conceder una mirada al bello panorama que se ofrecía a sus ojos. Cerca de él jugueteaban y corrían con esa deliciosa inconsciencia de los niños, Juanito y Margarita, los dos hijos que el leñador había tenido en su primer matrimonio. Descalzos de pie y de pierna, y cubiertos con pobres y humildísimos vestidos, eran, sin embargo, tan lindos, tan alegres y encantadores que quienquiera que les contemplase sentíase atraído hacia ellos por irresistible simpatía."

22. "Para colmo de males, el trabajo escaseó notablemente aquel año. Ya hacía unos meses que venía *defendiéndose heroicamente*, pero de poco tiempo a esta parte, la situación económica de aquella familia llegó a hacerse insostenible."

23. "La presencia de una mujer que cuidase de los niños y atendiese a los quehaceres domésticos."

24. Elizabeth Wanning Harries has offered a broad overview of the numerous critical studies that have dealt with feminist perspectives on fairy tales in recent decades. Also worthy of note are Bottigheimer's *Grimms' Bad Girls and Bold Boys: The Moral and Social Vision of the Tales* (1987) and Bacchilega's *Postmodern Fairy Tales: Gender and Narrative Strategies* (1997). In Spain, the controversy was revived in 2010 because of certain recommendations made by the ex-minister of equality Bibiana Aído regarding the use of fairy tales in schools.

25. "Su cara se había dilatado, y su boca se ensanchó en una sonrisa de feroz satisfacción. Al mismo tiempo eran tan elocuentes las miradas de gula voraz que con los ojos enormemente abiertos dirigía sobre Margarita."

26. "Los hermanos Grimm estuvieron siempre unidos por un cariño entrañable. Su colaboración y afinidad de sentimientos los ha hecho pasar a la posteridad como verdadero modelo de hermanos. Fueron lo que se dice dos corazones y un latido, y esto tan aleccionador y ejemplar, unido a su trabajo fecundo y perseverante, es lo mejor que podemos destacar para los muchachos de hoy."

27. "Muy del gusto de los niños."

28. "Blancanieves y su esposo fueron dichosísimos y no olvidaron nunca la desinteresada protección de los siete enanitos. En su palacio destinaron dos habitaciones para ellos, y éstos, siempre que querían, iban a pasar unos días de descanso a ellas, siendo atendidos y agasajados con la esplendidez que correspondía a la bondad de sus corazones."

29. "Y la malvada madrastra hubo de bailar con ellas hasta que cayó al suelo, muerta, mientras Blancanieves y su joven esposo vivieron largos años de venturas, rodeados de los siete enanitos que habían amado y protegido a la desgraciada princesita."

30. It is hence plausible that the translator could not have based his work on the original text but was working from a text that had been translated previously.

31. "Y cuando llegó al palacio y reconoció a Blancanieves, que sonreía feliz y más hermosa que nunca junto al príncipe, fue tan terrible su furia que murió de rabia." Formosa seemed to pay little attention to the source he was translating from.

32. "Mi cuento se ha acabado; por allí corre un ratón; quien lo coja podrá hacerse una capa grande, muy grande, de pieles."

33. In 2012, the publishing house Nórdica released an edition of "Snow White" illustrated by Iván Barrenetxea and translated by Isabel Hernández. This version is faithful to the original text as included in the *Kinder- und Hausmärchen* edition from 1857. In an interview with the newspaper *Diario de Álava*, the illustrator declared that "more than one reader has been shocked when reading this version of the story" (Barrenetxea).

References

Primary Sources

Grimm, Jacob, and Wilhelm Grimm. *Blanca Nieves*. Madrid: Calleja, c. 1910.

———. *Cuentos*. Barcelona: Juventud, 1935. Cuentos de Calleja en colores, IV serie [a collection].

———. *Cuentos*. Barcelona: Bruguera, 1958.

———. *Cuentos*. Madrid: Alianza, 1976.

———. *Cuentos completos*. Barcelona: Labor, 1955.

———. *Cuentos de Grimm*. Barcelona: Araluce, 1910–1920.

———. *Cuentos de Grimm*. Madrid: Calleja, Biblioteca Perla, 1941.

———. *Cuentos de Grimm*. Barcelona: Lumen, 1976.

———. *Cuentos de los hermanos Grimm*. Barcelona: Sopena, 1918.

———. *Cuentos de los hermanos Grimm*. Barcelona: Noguer, 1962.

———. *Cuentos de los hermanos Grimm*. Madrid: Everest, 1975.

———. *Cuentos de los hermanos Grimm*. Madrid: Magisterio Español, 1977.

———. *Cuentos de niños y del hogar*. Madrid: Anaya, 1985–1986.

———. *Cuentos escogidos*. Madrid: Calleja, 1920. Biblioteca Perla [a collection].

———. *Cuentos escogidos de los hermanos Grimm*. Madrid: Gaspar Editores, 1863.

———. *Cuentos escogidos de los hermanos Grimm*. Madrid: s.n., 1896.

———. *Cuentos infantiles*. Madrid: Hernando, 1947.

———. *El castillo de la caridad*. Madrid: Calleja, c. 1908. Serie juguetes instructivos, ser. 5 [a collection].

———. *El palacio de las virtudes*. Madrid: Calleja, c. 1908. Serie juguetes instructivos, ser. 3 [a collection].

———. *El rey de la montaña de oro y otros cuentos*. Palma de Mallorca: José J. de Olañeta, 1985.

———. *Hadas, princesas, brujas, curiosas, caprichosas, compasivas, madrastras, protectoras, guerreras, valientes . . . y otras heroínas de Calleja*. Palma de Mallorca: José J. de Olañeta, 1994.

———. *Juanito y Margarita*. Madrid: Calleja, Cuentos de Calleja en colores, c. 1910. IV serie [a collection].

———. *La envidia de una reina*. Madrid: Calleja, c. 1908. Serie Juguetes instructivos, ser. 10 [a collection].

Secondary Sources

Alcubierre-Moya, Beatriz. "El cuento de hadas como código de conducta y sus adaptaciones en el contexto hispanoamericano." *Boletín del Instituto de Investigaciones Bibliográficas* 1–2 (2005): 23–50.

Bottigheimer, Ruth B. *Grimms' Bad Girls and Bold Boys: The Moral and Social Vision of the Tales*. New Haven: Yale UP, 1987.

———. *Fairy Tales. A New History*. Albany: State U of New York P, 2009.

Bacchilega, Cristina. *Postmodern Fairy Tales: Gender and Narrative Strategies*. Philadelphia: U of Pennsylvania P, 1997.

Barrenetxea, Iban. "Quiero crear libros que puedan crecer al mismo tiempo que el lector." www.noticiasdealava.com/2012/05/21/ocio-y-cultura/cultura/quiero-crear-libros-que-puedan-crecer-al-mismo-tiempo-que-el-lector. 9 June 2012.

Caballero, Fernán. *Cuentos y poesías populares andaluces*. Seville: Imprenta de la Revista Mercantil, 1859.

Fernández de Córdoba, Enrique. *Saturnino Calleja y su editorial*. Madrid: Ediciones de La Torre, 2006.

"Gabinete de lectura 'Santa Teresa de Jesús.'" *Catálogo de libros para niños*. Madrid: Editora Nacional, 1945.

García-Padrino, Jaime. *Libros y literatura para niños en la España contemporánea*. Madrid: Fundación Germán Sánchez Ruipérez, and Pirámide, 1992.

———. "El libro infantil en el siglo XX." *Historia ilustrada del libro español*. Modern ed. Vols. 19–20. Ed. Hipólito Escolar. Madrid: Fundación Germán Sánchez Ruipérez, 1996: 229–343.

Harries, Elizabeth Wanning. *Twice upon a Time: Women Writers and the History of the Fairy Tale*. Princeton: Princeton UP, 2001.

Lathey, Gillian. *The Role of Translators in Children's Literature: Invisible Storytellers*. New York: Routledge, 2010.

Martín-Rogero, Nieves. "El exilio interior de la posguerra en la narrativa y la recuperación de la memoria." *Pequeña memoria recobrada. Libros infantiles del exilio del 39*. Ed. A. Pelegrín, M. V. Sotomayor, and A. Urdiales. Madrid: Ministerio de Educación, Política Social y Deporte, 2008. 169–84.

O'Sullivan, Emer. "Narratology Meets Translation Studies, or, the Voice of the Translator in Children's Literature." *Discourse* 48.1–2 (2003): 197–207.

Rodríguez-Almodóvar, Antonio. *El texto infinito. Ensayos sobre el cuento popular*. Madrid: Fundación Germán Sánchez Ruipérez, 2004.

Roig-Rechou, B., I. Soto-López, and M. Neira-Rodríguez, eds. *Reescrituras do conto popular (2000–2009)*. Vigo: Xerais, 2010.

Ruiz-Berrio, Julio, ed. *La editorial Calleja, un agente de modernización en la Restauración*. Madrid: UNED, 2002.

Trueba, Antonio de. *Cuentos campesinos*. Barcelona: Librería de Llordach Hijos, 1865.

4

The Fairy Tales of the Brothers Grimm in Colombia

A Bibliographical History

ALEXANDRA MICHAELIS-VULTORIUS

The *Kinder- und Hausmärchen,* or *Children's and Household Tales,* are probably the best-known collection of folktales worldwide. Two centuries after the first printed edition appeared (1812), selected tales continue to enjoy broad popularity; yet their enduring success and lasting appeal do not suggest a homogeneous reception. The reception of a story—that is, how it is understood and reacted to—can differ significantly both at an individual and at a collective level. A unique combination of historical, sociopolitical, and cultural factors produces, in a given reader, a very particular response to a single tale. That response is also influenced by the way an edition is constructed. Editors, collectors, and translators play a role as coauthors of the texts they are transmitting; devices such as prefaces, introductions, and other discursive paratexts as well as story selection, arrangement, and contextualization are used, whether intentionally or unintentionally, to shape a reader's understanding and response.

Several surveys and studies have examined the reception of the German fairy-tale collection in a localized manner; among the most recent is *Os contos de Grimm em Portugal: a recepção dos* Kinder- und Hausmärchen *entre 1837 e 1910* (The Grimm Stories in Portugal: A Reception of the *Kinder- und Hausmärchen* between 1837 and 1910) by Maria Teresa Cortez, published in 2001.[1] Broad-based studies of this kind, however, are limited for Latin America. This chapter seeks to illuminate the afterlife of the Grimms' tales in Colombia by exploring the dynamic process of reception based on a historical bibliographical analysis. To document the introduction, avenues of transmission, and reception of the *Kinder- und Hausmärchen* in Colombia, I turned to the national and public libraries, where I examined the existing inventory of Grimm tales and other printed materials related to the siblings and their work published until the year 2000. Taking into account textual and paratextual elements, I looked at individual editions, tales published in Colombian magazines and anthologies, articles in newspapers and reference books, critical pieces by Colombian scholars, and locally authored retellings.

Fully aware of the challenges of collecting information on a national scale, my point of departure was to create a database inventory of the Grimm publications that are held in Colombian libraries.[2] Since the tales of the Brothers Grimm and their related translations and reactions do not exist in isolation but in a context involving the works of other authors and collectors, I also considered the so-called classical European fairy tales and other writings cataloged as children's and youth literature. The collected bibliographic data were arranged chronologically by dates of publication. If we assume that these works were circulating around the time of their publication, this classification helped to discern authors, genres, and styles that were favored over others during a specific period, thus providing initial indications of reception. Drawing on the economic principles of supply and demand, a surplus of publications by a particular author at a given time is indicative of positive reception; conversely, a limited supply suggests a lack of interest among readers. Because the time frame covers a period of more than 150 years, this study was divided into two sections: the first section focuses on the earliest publications up to 1955; the second section covers publications from 1955 until 2000. The 1950s marked a turning point in the reception of the Grimm tales in Colombia; I chose to end the first interval halfway in the decade to denote two distinct phases of reception.

To provide a historical context of the reception of the Grimms' tales, it is important to address first the response that other European authors of literature for children have met with in Colombia. The identified bibliographical data published until 1955 suggest that works for children that convey Catholic teachings and strict moral codes were better received during the first half of the twentieth century than classical fairy tales. A combination of aspects including number of volumes per author; scope, quality, and provenance of the editions; available translations; and reprints in Colombian publications gave insights into this notion. Fairy-tale editions are outnumbered by works from authors such as the German Catholic priest Christoph von Schmid (1768–1854), the Italian novelist and short story writer Edmondo de Amicis (1846–1908), and the French author Sophie Comtesse de Ségur (1799–1874), best known for her realistic novels for children.

Characteristic of these writers is their highly ethical intention and promotion of values consistent with the Catholic faith. In Colombia, Catholicism has been the established religion since the early sixteenth century, and the Roman Catholic Church has permeated all levels of politics and society throughout the history of the country. Its central role in the field of education is a plausible explanation for the disparity in the high number of children's works imbued with religious doctrine and stern morality versus more secular ones.

Most of the relevant materials published through 1955 were imported from Europe and came in a variety of languages. Particularly noticeable is the number of French editions, from both French authors and non-French authors translated into French. The oldest located copy by Christoph von Schmid, for example, is *La Chartreuse* (The Carthusian), a French translation of *Das Kartäuserkloster* from 1836. The surplus of texts in French can be explained by a perception of Paris as the center of European culture that prevailed in Colombia, and elsewhere in Latin America, in the late nineteenth and early twentieth centuries. Within this mind frame, works coming from France were regarded as valuable literary pieces to be read at home. Yet, the accessibility of such works was limited to an educated elite versed in that foreign language.

The official language in Colombia is Spanish, hence translations into Spanish clearly have a much broader reach. If we can assume that the publishing dates of the located volumes reflect their circulation at roughly that time, then Spanish translations of the stories and novels by Schmid, Amicis, and Ségur have been available in the country since the late nineteenth century.[3] In addition to the ease of access that a Spanish translation affords, texts from these authors were reprinted in early Colombian literary anthologies and reading books, which further suggests their positive reception.[4]

In light of the availability of works by authors such as Schmid, Amicis, and Ségur, the fairy-tale genre appears to have been less popular during the first half of the twentieth century. Nonetheless, the existing fairy-tale inventory can give us clues about the introduction and dissemination of fairy tales in Colombia, which points to France. About one third of all the located fairy-tales volumes published until 1955 are French editions, and of the identified editions in French, about 13 percent are tales by Andersen, about 17 percent are tales by the Grimms, and about 55 percent are tales by French fairy-tale authors.[5]

If we now turn to editions by French fairy-tale authors held in Colombian libraries, we see that they are quite old and abundant in number; this suggests that the French tales not only have been readily available but also have had a prolonged exposure among Colombians. The oldest volumes located are two copies of *Le Magasin des enfants* (1757; The Young Misses' Magazine) by Jeannne-Marie Leprince de Beaumont (1711–1780); one is a 1768 French edition and the other a Spanish translation from 1829. I found nearly 20 percent more editions of French tales than the Grimms' tales from this early period, that is, published in or before 1955. Most of the existing volumes are of substantial quality and scope. About 23 percent were acquired through donations from family libraries, which increases the likelihood that they were being read in Colombian homes at the time of their publication; their reach, though, is limited due to the language barrier (more than half of the editions are in the original French). Of the French fairy-tale authors, the best represented is Charles Perrault (1628–1703), whose works account for nearly 64 percent of the identified inventory.

Within this early period, however, the most prominent of the classical fairy-tale writers is not Perrault but the Danish Hans Christian Andersen (1805–1875). Titles by Andersen outnumber both the French tales and those by the Grimms. A significant portion of his materials is in Spanish (about 67 percent), and 21 percent of the located items came from private donations. Andersen's works are available in a variety of formats that range from comprehensive high-quality editions to inexpensive single-story booklets. His "Historia de una madre" (1848; Story of a Mother), which appeared in a leaflet from 1893 that was distributed for free in post offices, is evidence of how widely accessible his tales were.

Moreover, the reprinting of numerous Andersen stories in Colombian literary anthologies and journals from the late nineteenth and early twentieth centuries indicates a favorable reception.[6] The popularity of Andersen may be attributed to two main factors. On the one hand, there seemed to be a preference for the literary tale over the folktale, which made the literariness of Andersen's works much more appealing to Colombian readers than retellings of stories from the common folk (like the Grimm tales). On the other hand, the degree of sorrow and sentiment displayed in Andersen's oeuvre was appealing to the overwhelmingly Catholic population. His narratives emphasize the liberating character of pain and suffering, and like the works of Amicis and Schmid, Andersen's writings evoke empathy and compassion—emotions that resonate strongly among the devout public.

In contrast to the literary tales by Andersen and the French fairy tales, the Grimms' tales—commonly thought to rely more heavily on oral traditions—appear to have been less popular in Colombia during the first half of the twentieth century. I found fewer Grimms editions than Perrault's or Andersen's published up to 1955, and over 60 percent of the located items are in foreign languages so that they could only be read by a minority of the Colombian people. In all but one case the origin of the editions (i.e., how they became part of a library's collection) is unknown. The scope and overall quality of the Grimm publications is generally more modest than the identified editions of Andersen, Perrault, and Mme de Beaumont.

The oldest located Spanish translation for example, *Cuentos y leyendas de los hermanos Grimm* (Stories and Legends of the Brothers Grimm) from 1893, contains a selection of merely seven tales.[7] This booklet for popular consumption is part of the series *Biblioteca ilustrada: cuentos populares* (Illustrated Library: Popular Stories)—a collection of stories from various countries and authors that appeared biweekly in two separate volumes. The seven Grimm tales made up the eleventh and final chapter of Volume I. The narratives in *Cuentos y leyendas de los hermanos Grimm* present noticeable editorial liberties in their translation, which is evident in titles that bear little or no resemblance to the original, such as "Los dos pollos" (The Two Fowls, an adaptation of "Clever Gretel"). I did not find any tales by the Brothers Grimm in Colombian publications from this early period, even though pieces by other German writers contemporary to the Grimms were being published at the time; for instance, the mermaid tale by Friedrich de la Motte Fouqué *Undine* (1811) that appeared in several Colombian literary anthologies.[8]

Most of the located editions with Grimm tales published until 1955 are translations imported from Europe, and nearly 40 percent came from Spain. In Colombia, the fairy tales of the Brothers Grimm from the Casa Editorial Calleja (founded in 1876) are among the oldest editions to be found. Saturnino Calleja (1853–1915) and his publishing empire made a major contribution to the rise of children's literature in Spain and was highly influential in Colombia. A variety of Calleja's publications, ranging from deluxe editions of considerable scope to inexpensive single-tale booklets, were circulating early on in the country. The popularity of these publications was captured in the 1976 article titled "Calleja" by the Colombian film critic Hernando Salcedo Silva (1916–1987), in which the author remembers the tiny booklets as one of the most gratifying dimensions of his childhood in the 1920s.

The Grimm texts in the Calleja editions were freely translated and modified to cater to the Spanish market: the characters were given Spanish names, spoke in the most "*castizo*" (Castilian) style, or appeared in Spanish geographical settings. The stories were also censored to avoid any sexual overtones; for example, "La rana encantada" (The Enchanted Frog, an adaptation of "The Frog King, or Iron Heinrich") omits the scene where the newly transformed prince and the princess fall asleep together.

Several tales from Calleja's *Cuentos escogidos* (Selected stories)—a deluxe edition with fifty-five Grimm stories estimated to be from 1896—were reprinted in the Colombian children's magazine *Chanchito* (1933–1934; Piglet), albeit without acknowledging the authors. *Chanchito* is one of the few children's magazines from this early period and perhaps the best and most complete yet published in the country. Most stories are verbatim transcripts of Calleja's adaptations; however, in some cases, the narratives in *Chanchito* present additional modifications to the already altered Spanish versions, going one step further in censoring the tales. *Chanchito* avoids not only sexual connotations but also allusions to nudity and certain parts of the human body. In "El caballo prodigioso" (The Prodigious Horse, an adaptation of "The Goose Girl"), for example, the princess puts her mother's handkerchief in her pocket instead of her bosom, as it appears in Calleja's and in the original tale; and when it comes to the punishment, which calls for throwing the impostor naked inside a barrel full of nails and having two horses drag her through every street until she dies, the word "naked" is omitted. The removal of such references offered Colombian children a very "chaste" version, much in line with expectations of the hegemonic Catholic Church.

Calleja's *Cuentos escogidos* includes a brief preface that portrays the Brothers Grimm roaming the countryside and stopping at every hamlet to collect stories from the simple folk. The preface also claims that the edition at hand offers its readers the complete and unaltered fairy-tale collection of the German siblings. Prefaces like this one, with their inaccuracies about the brothers' fieldwork, informants, and method of collection; the authenticity of the tales; and the completeness of the published volumes are not uncommon and have contributed in Colombia to a misconception about the Grimms and their work. The long disproven image of the wandering brothers, along with the old peasant woman of prodigious memory as main contributor of the tales, has been perpetuated through newspaper articles and editorials, scholarly publications, and even the most recent reference books.[9]

An area that causes a lot of confusion is the French origin of some of the Grimms' tales. This becomes apparent in the newspaper article "Jacobo y Guillermo Grimm, padres adoptivos de Blanca Nieves y Caperucita" (1985; Jacob and William Grimm, Adoptive Parents of Snow White and Little Red Riding Hood) by the respected Colombian journalist Daniel Samper Pizano. Samper uses the word "adoptive" in his title to denote the foreign origin of these tales. He writes that many of the stories that the Grimms collected from the lips of peasants are not of German but French origin, adding that Perrault had already compiled them a century and a half before. Although Samper makes correct allusion to the French provenance of "Cinderella," "Little Red Riding Hood," and "Sleeping Beauty," he indiscriminately casts into the same group the equally popular tale of "Snow White," which certainly did not come from Perrault. Possible explanations for this misperception are the prolonged exposure that French tales seem to have enjoyed in Colombia during the first half of the century and the influence of Disney with its first three filmic adaptations of fairy tales.[10]

The presence of the Disney Corporation was felt in Colombia early on, almost a decade before the release of its first animated feature based on a classical fairy tale. The title story of "Colombia y el mundo en 1928" (Colombia and the World in 1928), a segment in the periodical *Revista credencial historia* (Magazine Credential History) that appeared on 19 September 1928, for instance, was already informing Colombians about the release of *Steamboat Willie* (starring Mickey Mouse) one month before it came out in the United States. The ascendance of Disney was ensured through the aggressive promotion of its movies. Several weeks before the release of *Snow White and the Seven Dwarfs* (1937) in Colombia in late 1939, the national press launched an advertising campaign that created unprecedented anticipation among the public. The film became an instant hit. The extensive press coverage that focused on Walt Disney and his creation remained mostly oblivious to the written source on which the movie was based—a tale by the Brothers Grimm. Despite the marginal reference to the Grimms, the massive publicity of *Snow White and the Seven Dwarfs* indirectly made people aware of the German fairy-tale collection. Subsequent Disney productions, especially *Cinderella* (1950) and *Sleeping Beauty* (1959), both adaptations of tales by Perrault, were equally successful in the country.

Even though *Snow White and the Seven Dwarfs* was the only film based on the Grimms', there appears to be a strong correlation between Disney's adaptations of classical fairy tales and the rising popularity of Grimm tales in printed form. An outpouring of Grimm editions published after 1950 flooded the Colombian libraries. Compared to the Grimms', the post-1950 inventory of tales by Andersen and Perrault grows at a considerably slower rate.

The increased importance of the Grimm tales after 1950 may also be attributed to the pertinence of their messages to modern society. By the mid-twentieth century Colombia was experiencing significant socioeconomic changes caused by industrial growth and political turmoil. Traditionally, agriculture and manufacturing were the two leading areas in the country's economy; however, after 1950 the share of the gross domestic product generated by the agricultural sector started to decline, whereas that of manufacturing gradually increased. This resulted in a migration toward the main urban areas, where most manufacturing centers were located. The demographic displacement was further fueled by "La violencia" (The violence)—a prolonged period of rural violence that started in the mid-1940s as a consequence of a feud between the two traditional political parties (Conservatives and Liberals). More and more people were drawn into the cities either looking for jobs or attempting to escape the violence or both—Colombia was on its path toward a modern society.

As the Grimms' collection also emerged from a modern bourgeois society in the wake of an industrial revolution, the cultural and ideological messages embedded in the stories became relevant. Through their editing, the Grimms modified the tales they had collected to make the narratives more proper and prudent and to promote social and cultural values that were appealing to a growing bourgeois audience. The values that once suited Germany's nineteenth-century bourgeoisie still speak to the needs, wishes, and hopes of Colombia's present society; and corporations like Disney have recognized the tales' relevance in order to profit greatly from filmic adaptations and spin-off products.

In Colombian libraries, Grimm tales published and edited in the Americas start to emerge in the inventory around 1950; these editions are predominantly in Spanish and no longer exclusively European. In fact, my database shows a general decline in the number of European editions from the 1940s onward, due to the negative effect on trade between Europe and America caused by the Spanish Civil War (1936–1939) and the Second World War. Particularly noticeable for post-1950 publications edited in the Americas is the influence of Disney. The selection and arrangement of stories (usually including and foregrounding all three tales adapted by Disney) and the general tendency to minimize or avoid violent episodes are indicative of this influence.

While editions with Grimm tales published before 1955 have "generic" titles, more recent books are frequently headed with *Snow White*. Take for example the Mexican publication *Blanca Nieve y otros cuentos* (Snow White and Other Tales)—the oldest Latin American edition that I could locate, issued in 1959. This book title stands in contrast with that of older publications such as Calleja's *Cuentos escogidos* (1896?), *Cuentos de Grimm: ilustrados por Arthur Rackham* (1935; Grimm Stories: Illustrated by Arthur Rackham), *Libro de cuentos ilustrado* (1950?; Illustrated Storybook), and *Cuentos y leyendas de los hermanos Grimm* (1893), which did not even include the tale of Snow White. A close inspection of the Mexican *Blanca Nieve y otros cuentos* and several other editions published in Latin America reveals that these are not local (domestic) adaptations of the Grimms' tales; instead they have clear ties to Europe, particularly to Spain. With the outbreak of the Civil War many Spanish authors and publishers fled the country and relocated predominantly to Mexico City and Buenos Aires, which eventually became the main publishing centers. It is therefore not surprising that manipulations to the original narratives that inscribe the values, interests, and linguistic expressions specific to Spanish culture resurface again in these Latin American editions.

Tales of the Grimm brothers published in Colombia appeared only later. In the 1970s Editorial Norma—a leading publisher in the country—made available a series of high-quality kinetic collections. *Blanca Nieves y los siete enanitos* (Snow White and the Seven Dwarfs) was one of the oldest titles that I found; this edition does not mention the Grimms and was published anonymously in Bogotá in 1975. In 1976, Norma issued another pop-up book called *El festival de Blanca Nieves* (The Festival of Snow White); this time, though, the publisher specified Walt Disney as corporate author. Omitting the name Grimm from the 1975 edition, while designating Disney as corporate author in a subsequent edition published just one year later, is telling of the colossal influence of the Disney Corporation. What is more, it undermines the work of the German Brothers and ultimately contributes to the misperception regarding authorship that already prevails in Colombia.

The confusion about which tales are actually Grimm tales is evident in *Los mejores cuentos infantiles del mundo* (The Best Children's Stories of the World)—an anthology of stories from Andersen, Perrault, and the Grimms published in Bogotá and estimated to be from 1970. Eight out of the fourteen tales in this edition are indeed Grimm tales, but only three are attributed to the brothers; for the remaining five no author was specified.[11] "Blanca Nieves" (Snow White) is one of the tales identified as being from the German brothers, along with "Hansel y Gretel" and "El lobo y los 7 cabritos" (The Wolf and the Seven Kids)—both of which are common stories in earlier editions of the Grimms (and therefore easy to associate with the siblings).

Los mejores cuentos infantiles del mundo differs from others in both its distribution channel and the wording of the spoken exchanges. Unlike many of the other editions published in Colombia, the dialogues in these stories do not make use of the second person plural (*vosotros*)—a speech form common in Spain but rarely used in Latin America; this suggests that the stories may be Colombian adaptations. Unfortunately the origin is difficult to prove given the limited information in the edition itself, which lacks a publisher, editor, and date of publication. On the back cover the remark "Exclusive distributors: Almacenes LEY" gives us a hint about the way this product was made available to consumers; and in so doing, it also illuminates the link between the reception of the fairy tales and their role as commodities. Almacenes LEY, the first self-service store in Colombia, was an affordable supermarket chain of produce and household items founded by Luis Eduardo Yepes in 1922. Perhaps following Disney's lead, Yepes took the initiative to "commodify" the classical fairy tales and sell them at a cheap price in his nationwide retail store; however unconventional a channel of distribution, it was a viable way to make the tales widely accessible in the 1970s.

The 1970s marked an important decade for children's literature in Colombia, which until then had shown only few and sporadic instances of development. An unparalleled stimulus came from the Premio Enka de Literatura Infantil—a writing contest for children's and young adult literature. This influential contest, which later extended its call to neighboring countries, not only encouraged the production of quality works for children but also helped to disband the existing prejudice in Colombia that literature for children is an "inferior genre."

In addition to helping professionalize writing for children, the Enka contest was an incentive for local publishers to reprint classical works. The proliferation of Colombia-published editions, however, offered mostly tale versions that show close ties to Europe. In 1979, the renowned Colombian publishing house Editorial Bedout issued *Cuentos infantiles* (Children's Stories) with over fifty Grimm tales; the tales were transcribed from an earlier Mexican volume titled *Cuentos de Grimm* (Stories by Grimm), which, in turn, appears to be based on a Spanish edition.[12]

In 1986 Educar Cultural Recreativa came out with the twenty-four-volume *Biblioteca fantástica* (Fantastic Library), one of the most complete collections of classical literature for children ever published in Colombia. The comprehensive collection, rooted in an Italian production bearing the same name (*Biblioteca fantástica,* issued by Gruppo Edittoriale Fabbri in Milan in 1979),[13] contains numerous Grimm tales. The tales were translated into Spanish from the Italian, and the Italian texts depart considerably from the originals. One of the most noticeable changes is the enhancement of the narratives to create a more dramatic effect, as "Los músicos de Bremen" (The Bremen Town Musicians) demonstrates. This version gives a detailed description of the donkey's unwavering loyalty to his master, his hardworking life, his hopes, dreams, and youthful illusions—all modifications that elicit in the reader pity and compassion for the aging animal (and brings to mind the stories by Andersen, Amicis, and Schmid that were popular in Colombia earlier in the twentieth century).

To continue now with editions published in Colombia, in the 1980s and 1990s Edilux Ediciones issued a number of fairy-tale collections in a variety of formats and qualities. Among them is *Hermanos Grimm: Cuentos* (1990; Brothers Grimm: Stories), a selection of fifteen stories that was advertised as being endorsed by teachers.[14] Like many of the other examined editions of the Grimms' tales, these are, once again, not local creations but essentially European productions. Nevertheless, traditional Colombian publishers like Norma and Bedout must have recognized the demand (and economic potential) of classical children's literature in general, and the Grimm tales in particular, to offer such an array of editions.

The rising demand was also being met by editions from smaller and lesser known publishers. For example, Latinopal issued twelve affordable booklets, mostly Grimm tales, marketed as the "best selection of stories for the Colombian child." Among the titles is *Blanca-Nieves y los siete enanitos* (Snow

White and the Seven Dwarfs). This anonymous adaptation of "Snow White" presents certain details and subtleties in the language that suggest it may be a local revision of the famous Grimm tale. The witch, here a separate character that acts as adviser and instigator of the stepmother, is named Patecabra.[15] The term "*patecabra*" in colloquial language refers to the hoof (*pata*) of a goat (*cabra*), but in the Colombian popular tradition it is associated with witchcraft (the goat's hoof is an ingredient to produce concoctions used for spells).

Another variation concerns the story ending. This version bypasses the final punishment and adds instead a religious dimension that would appeal to the pious Colombian readership. A final moralizing paragraph states that virtuous behavior will always triumph and will be rewarded not only by society but also by God, the supreme judge of our earthly conduct. Despite the lack of information about this edition, the fact that this story merges into its narrative traditional elements of Colombian culture and language suggests that this could be a local revision and as such illustrates, to some extent, the incorporation of the tales into Colombian society.

Colombian scholars of children's literature disagree to what extent the *Kinder- und Hausmärchen* has been assimilated in the country. Some scholars, including Rafael Díaz Borbón, maintain that the classical tales have become firmly rooted and fully integrated into Colombian culture and society. Others, such as the writer and critic Rocío Vélez de Piedrahita, see their repercussions as only marginal. Assessing with accuracy the degree of integration of the tales into Colombia and the effect they may have exerted on the culture is a complex undertaking. The few editions that were circulating during the first half of the twentieth century, mostly accessible to the elite, may lead us to believe that the stories could not have had a real influential power on the domestic culture. Furthermore, the unfamiliarity with the stories that prevails in Colombia, where the general public seems to be aware only of the few adaptations made by Disney, may corroborate this view. However, as the twentieth century progressed, and especially in the final two decades, the strong presence of the Grimms' tales in Colombia's print culture becomes more and more tangible. Some of the previous examples are indicative of their influence, such as *Hermanos Grimm: Cuentos*. The selection by teachers suggests that the tales have entered the educational institutions and, in that sense, have achieved, to a certain degree, canonical status in Colombian culture.

The mark left by the Grimms is also evident in contemporary productions from Colombian authors. Examples include the Enka award-winning novella *Los amigos del hombre* (1979; The Friends of Man) by Celso Román, whose cast of protagonists—a horse, a dog, a cat, and a rooster—echoes the tale "The Bremen Town Musicians." Román's story tells about a weak old horse and a limping dog that set out to find help for their destitute dying master, who lives in a self-made shanty of tin plates next to the train tracks. The two animals come across a magical star that reunites them with their long-lost friends, the cat and the rooster. The star heals the abused animals and reveals that the cure for the ailing old man is found in the heart of the humans. With their regained health and strength the four friends set forth on their journey in search of the human heart.

Another example is Triunfo Arciniegas's publication *Caperucita Roja y otras historias perversas* (1997, Little Red Riding Hood and other Perverse Stories)—a volume that includes several tales by the Grimms rewritten from the perspective of different characters. Among them is "Little Red Riding Hood" focalized through the wolf, supposedly a well-intentioned admirer of beauty and misunderstood creature. Acting in the name of love, he gets caught in the scheme of the mischievous teenager Red Riding Hood and is judged and condemned by the world without a fair trial. Another recast version of a Grimm tale is "El sapito que comía princesas," (The Little Frog That Ate Princesses, an adaptation of "The Frog King"), in which Arciniegas shifts the focus from the princess to the frog. Tired of waiting for a princess to lose her golden ball and relieve him of his spell with a magical kiss, the frog goes out in search of a princess and soon sees one walking in the forest. Determined to approach her, it leaps with such force that it accidently gobbles her up, and realizing that princesses are very tasty the frog becomes a dangerous yet elusive princess-eater. Arciniegas's appropriation of the Grimms' stories is telling of their resonance among the Colombian audience; it is because the author can assume that his readers are familiar with these stories that he is able to play with the narratives.

In general, recastings of the tales by authors such as Arciniegas and Román, critical pieces by Colombian scholars, and secondhand adaptations edited in Colombia without apparent foreign intervention are not readily found in the national and main public libraries, at least not for the period covered in this study, which extends only until 2000. But however limited these few retellings, interpretations, and responses, they attest to the positive and still growing reception of the Grimms' tales in the country. The tales by the Brothers Grimm have come a long way in Colombia since the early twentieth century, and their resonance is very much perceptible in the twenty-first century, although this is beyond the scope of this study.

Stage arrangements such as "Los tres pelos del diablo" (The Devil's Three Hairs) by the storyteller Jaime Riascos Villegas continue to carry the legacy of the Grimm brothers. Riascos conflates colloquial expressions and elements of indigenous oral tradition with the most *castizo* style to give a global dimension to the story. The "globalization" of the Grimms' tales is especially evident in recent years when they were picked up by the Colombian mass media. Since 2009 the national television channel Caracol Television has offered the animated series *Los cuentos de los hermanos Grimm* (The Tales of the Brothers Grimm) as part of the morning programming for children. Produced by the Japanese company Nippon Animation (1987–1989), dubbed into Spanish in Mexico, and aired in Colombia, this cartoon series shows the impact of the new media and the global reception of the Grimms' tales—a reception that transcends national boundaries. Broadcasting the tales on national television will further ensure their dissemination in versions that are not necessarily transmitted directly from the German originals but that have a truly international or transnational dimension.

Most Colombians have come to know the Grimms' tales only secondhand, in translations, adaptations, movies, and cartoons that can be widely divergent from the original stories. But, it is precisely the tales' malleability that accounts for their longevity and staying power. The flexibility of the tales to adapt to any medium and to any land, language, and culture and to assume new meanings and identities has conferred on the stories the ability to bridge generations. The increased importance that the Grimm stories attained in Colombia in the past decades demonstrates that the folktales collected in Germany two centuries ago continue to enthrall audiences throughout the world, while inviting us to engage with characters, events, and conflicts that still matter to us today.

NOTES

1. Other examples include Kwon-Ha Ryu's dissertation on the Grimms' reception in Korea (1993), Marek Halub's "Die Märchen der Brüder Grimm in Polen"

(1986; Grimms' Fairy Tales in Poland), and Lucia Borghese's "Zur Geschichte der Rezeption und der frühsten Übersetzung Grimmischer Märchen in der Toskana" (1984; On the History of the Reception and the Earliest Translations of Grimms' Fairy Tales in Tuscany).

2. I surveyed the catalogs of Colombia's National Library and numerous public and university libraries across the country. However, most of the pertinent materials for this study were located in the main libraries in Bogotá; specifically at the Biblioteca Luis Angel Arango and the Biblioteca Nacional de Colombia.

3. I found Spanish editions by Christoph von Schmid as old as 1876 (e.g., *Itha*: *Condesa de Toggenbourg* published by Calleja) as well as one of the first published Spanish translations of Edmondo de Amicis's best-known novel *Cuore* (Heart) from 1887.

4. Stories by Amicis, for example, appeared in the literary anthology *Colección de grandes escritores nacionales y extranjeros* (Collection of Grand National and International Writers, edited and published by Jorge Roa in Bogotá in 1909), the reading book *Libro de lecturas escogidas en prosa y verso, para niños y niñas* (Book of Selected Readings in Prose and Verse for Girls and Boys, edited by Rodolfo D. Bernal and published by Tipografía de Lleras y Compañía in Bogotá in 1891), and the children's magazine *Chanchito* (Piglet, edited by Victor E. Caro in Bogotá in 1933), among others.

5. The percentages that I am citing here (and elsewhere) are based on the existence of editions counted in the documented library holdings; the actual data are substantial and thus difficult to include. Detailed information on these works can be found in Tables 1–3, Appendices 1–3, and the Bibliography in my dissertation titled "The Tales of the Grimm Brothers in Colombia: Introduction, Dissemination, and Reception."

6. For example, "La sirena" (1837; The Little Mermaid) and "Ib y Cristina" (1855; Ib and Little Christina) appeared in the 1899 edition of the literary anthology *Colección de grandes escritores nacionales y extranjeros*. "La niña de los fósforos" (1845; The Little Match Girl) appeared in the periodical *El Liberal Ilustrado* (1914; The Illustrated/Illustrious Liberal). "El Gnomo y la Hortera" (1852; The Goblin and the Huscktser) was published in *Revista Pan* (1935; Magazine Bread); and a selection of tales titled "Ramo de cuentos" (Bouquet of Stories) was printed in *Revista de las Indias* (1947; Magazines of the Indies).

7. The tales included in *Cuentos y leyendas de los hermanos Grimm* are the following: "Seis soldados de fortuna" (Six Soldiers of Fortune, an adaptation of "How Six Came through the World"; "La corneja" (The Crow, an adaptation of "The Raven"); "Juan Fiel" (Faithful John); "Pulgarín" (Little Thumb); "El almendro" (The Almond Tree, an adaptation of "The Juniper Tree"); "El perro viejo y el gorrión" (The Old Dog and the Sparrow); and "Los dos pollos" (The Two Fowls, an adaptation of "Clever Gretel").

8. The tale "Ondina" appeared in the literary anthologies *Colección de grandes escritores nacionales y extranjeros* (1894) and *Narraciones populares de la selva negra* (1893; Popular Narrations of the Black Forest) among others.

9. For example, in *Literatura infantil sus forjadores y cultivadores* (1991; Children's Literature, Its Pioneers and Cultivators) by Silvio Modesto Echeverría Rodríguez, which includes a brief paragraph on the Grimms and their work; and the entry "Jakob [*sic*] y Wilheim [*sic*] Grimm" in the reference book *2.000 años de literatura universal* (1994; 2000 Years of World Literature) edited by Fanny Zamora Nieto.

10. Movie ads appearing in Colombia's newspapers at the time contributed to this misperception in that they fully disregarded the written sources on which the films were based (*Snow White and the Seven Dwarfs* was based on a Grimm tale, while *Cinderella* and *Sleeping Beauty* were based on tales by Perrault).

11. This edition includes the following Grimm tales: "Los músicos de Brema" (The Bremen Town Musicians); "El ahijado de la muerte" (The Godson of Death); "El pájaro Grifo" (The Griffin Bird); "El sastrecillo listo" (The Clever Little Tailor); and "El agua de la vida" (The Water of Life), all of which were published anonymously. Only "Blanca Nieves," "Hansel y Gretel," and "El lobo y los 7 cabritos" were attributed to the Grimms.

12. *Cuentos de Grimm*—the basis for the Colombian-published *Cuentos infantiles*—was issued by Editorial Porrúa in 1969. *Cuentos de Grimm* contains seventy-two tales selected and introduced by the Mexican author and educator María Edmée Alvarez (1896–1992). No specific information about the translator is provided on the edition; nonetheless, and judging by the dialogue (featuring the second person plural *vosotros*), the tales appear to be transcripts of a previous Spanish translation or at least the work of a translator from Spain.

13. The Grimm tales in the Italian *Biblioteca fantastica* were, in turn, taken from a previous series by Fabbri called *Fiabe sonore* (Audible Fairy Tales) that was first published in 1966. The popular *Fiabe sonore,* which has been republished repeatedly, consisted of single-story illustrated books accompanied by a nonmusical record (45 rpm).

14. The selection of tales in this edition was reprinted from the earlier mentioned Mexican edition *Cuentos de Grimm* (1969) issued by Editorial Porrúa—the same edition that served as the basis for *Cuentos infantiles* (1979) published by Editorial Bedout (see note 11).

15. As the friend and confidant of the stepmother, the witch Patecabra provides advice on how to get rid of Snow White, prepares the poisonous apple, and entices the stepmother to seek revenge.

References

Amicis, Edmondo de. *Corazón: Diario de un niño.* Trans. H. Giner de los Rios. Madrid: Librería de D. Fernando Fe, 1887.

Andersen, Hans Christian. "El gnomo y la hortera." *Revista Pan* 5 (1935): 71.

———. "Historia de una madre: Cuento de Andersen." *Folletines de "El Correo Nacional."* Bogotá: n.p., 1893.

———. "Ib y Cristina." *Colección de grandes escritores nacionales y extranjeros.* Vol. 19. Bogota: Jorge Roa, 1899.

———. "Ramo de cuentos." *Revista de las Indias* 30.96 (1947): 446–49.

———. "La Sirena." *Colección de grandes escritores nacionales y extranjeros.* Vol. 19. Bogotá: Jorge Roa, 1899.

Arciniegas, Triunfo. *Caperucita Roja y otras historias perversas.* 2nd ed. Bogotá: Panamericana Editorial, 1997.

Biblioteca fantástica. Milan: Edittoriale Fabbri, 1979.

Biblioteca fantástica. Illus. Barilli et al. Trans. Jesús Villamizar and Consuelo Gaitán G. Bogota: Educar Cultural Recreativa, 1986.

Blanca-Nieves y los siete enanitos. Bogotá: Latinopal, 1980.

Blanca Nieves y los siete enanitos. Un libro mágico. Bogotá: Norma, 1975.

Borghese, Lucia. "Zur Geschichte der Rezeption und der frühsten Übersetzung Grimmischer Märchen in der Toskana." *Brüder Grimm Gedenken* 4 (1984): 135–47.

"El caballo prodigioso. Part 1." *Chanchito: Revista ilustrada para niños* 1.9 (1933): 15–16.

"El caballo prodigioso. Part 2." *Chanchito: Revista ilustrada para niños* 1.10 (1933): 10–15.

"Colombia y el mundo en 1928." *Revista Credencial Historia* 2006. 8 May 2009. www.lablaa.org/blaavirtual/revistas/credencial/julio2006/mundo1928.htm.

Cortez, Maria Teresa. *Os contos de Grimm em Portugal: a recepção dos* Kinder- und Hausmärchen *entre 1837 e 1910.* Coimbra: MinervaCoimbra, 2001.

Díaz Borbón, Rafael. *La literatura infantil: Crítica de una nueva lectura.* Bogotá: Tres Culturas Editores, 1986.

Disney, Walt. *El festival de Blanca Nieves.* Bogotá: Norma, 1976.

Echeverría Rodríguez, Silvio Modesto. *Literatura infantil sus forjadores y cultivadores.* Medellín: Editorial Lealon, 1991.

Fiabe Sonore. Milan: Edittoriale Fabbri, 1966.

Fouqué, Friedrich de la Motte. *Cuentos escogidos.* Madrid: Saturnino Calleja, 1896.

Grimm, Jacob, and Wilhelm Grimm. *Blanca Nieve y otros cuentos.* Mexico City: Ed. Renacimiento, 1959.

———. *Cuentos de Grimm.* Trans. Maria Luz Morales. Illus. Arthur Rackham. Barcelona: Editorial Juventud, 1935.

———. *Cuentos de Grimm.* Ed. María E. Alvarez. Mexico City: Editorial Porrúa, 1969.

———. *Cuentos infantiles.* Medellín: Editorial Bedout, 1979.

———. *Cuentos y leyendas de los hermanos Grimm.* Barcelona: J. Roura, 1893.

———. *Hermanos Grimm: Cuentos.* Medellín: Edilux, 1990.

———. "La rana encantada." Grimm and Grimm, *Cuentos escogidos:* 264–67.

———. *Libro de cuentos ilustrado: 10 láminas en color con los más bonitos cuentos de los hermanos Grimm.* Trans. Brigitte de Stöter. Madrid: A.A.A., 1950.

———. "Los dos pollos." Grimm and Grimm, *Cuentos y leyendas:* 85–97.

———. "Ondina." *Colección de grandes escritores nacionales y extranjeros.* Vol. 5. Bogotá: Jorge Roa, 1894.

———. "Ondina." *Narraciones populares de la selva negra.* Bogotá: Librería Nueva, 1893.

Halub, Marek. "Die Märchen der Brüder Grimm in Polen." *Brüder Grimm Gedenken* 6 (1986): 215–40.

Leprince de Beaumont, Jeanne-Marie. *Almacén y biblioteca completa de los niños ó diálogos de una sabia directora con sus discípulas de la primera distinción.* Trans. Matias Guitet. Madrid: Don Julian Viana Razola, 1829.

———. *Magasin des enfants ou dialogues d'une sage gouvernante avec se élèves de la première distinction.* Lyon: Jacquenod Père et Rusand, 1768.

Los mejores cuentos infantiles del mundo. Bogotá: n.p., 1970.

Michaelis-Vultorius, Alexandra. "The Tales of the Grimm Brothers in Colombia: Introduction, Dissemination, and Reception." Diss. Ann Arbor: ProQuest, 2011.

Román, Celso. *Los amigos del hombre.* N.p.: Panamericana, 1996.

Ryu, Kwon-Ha. "Die 'waltende Spur' im Lande der Morgenfrische: Eine Untersuchung zur Rezeption und Wirkung von Grimms Märchen in Korea." Diss. University of Wuppertal, 1993.

Salcedo Silva, Hernando. "Calleja." *Consigna* 1.48 (1976): 17.

Samper Pizano, Daniel. "Jacobo y Guillermo Grimm, padres adoptivos de Blanca Nieves y Caperucita." *El Tiempo* 27 Oct. 1985: 8–9.

Schmid, Christoph von. *Itha: Condesa de Toggenbourg.* Trans. Méndez Bringa. Madrid: Saturnino Calleja, 1876?.

———. *La Chartreuse.* Trans. L. Friedel. Tours: A. D. Mame, 1836.

Vélez de Piedrahita, Rocío. *Guía de la literatura infantil.* Medellín: Secretaría de Educación y Cultura, 1983.

Zamora Nieto, Fanny, and Alvaro Cáceres Ramirez, eds. *2.000 años de literatura universal: Consultor biográfico y literario A–Z.* Bogotá: Zamora Editores, 1994.

5

"They are still eating well and living well"

The Grimms' Tales in Early Colonial Korea

DAFNA ZUR

DAFNA ZUR

INTRODUCTION: "COLLECTION CONTEST"

In 1922, an announcement appeared at the back of the August issue of the Korean literary magazine *Kaebyŏk* (The Dawn of Civilization). It was written by Pang Chŏnghwan,[1] a man famous for his activism for children's rights as well as for his best-selling collection *Sarang ŭi sŏnmul* (Gift of Love), a book of ten translated folktales including three German tales, two of them by the Brothers Grimm, published a month earlier.[2] The announcement, "Hyŏnsang mojip" (Collection Contest), was subtitled "Chosŏn korae tonghwa mojip" (Collection of Old Stories of Chosŏn) and read as follows:

All nations are built on the foundation of their nation's character and life which, in turn, produces a nation's folk tradition, folk songs, children's stories and children's songs. The Americans and British have their own folktales and children's songs; The Germans and French have theirs.... *Consider the great contributions that the tales of the Brothers Grimm made to the strength and courageous character of the German people*... and you will re-experience the sublime nature of folktales and myths. Ah, brethren! What do we have to show for the next generation? Because no one has paid heed, our folktales, our unique children's stories and songs, have been buried before our very eyes; in our cities and in the countryside, the new generations know and recite nothing other than

[Japanese tales]. . . . We must gather our strength and uncover those tales that have been buried in every corner of the land for the sake of the revival of children's literature, which is the source of our people's spiritual character. It is for this purpose . . . that I propose and announce this collection contest. (Pang, "Hyŏnsang mojip" 112, emphasis added)

The call for a tale collection quoted above was voiced a decade after the official annexation of Korea to Japan in 1910 and followed on the heels of the exuberant anticolonial resistance movement in 1919 that resulted in a relative relaxation of colonial cultural policies. As he intimates in his "collection contest," Pang perceived fairy tales as critical to the preservation of Korea's colonized voice. The glaring absence of Korean fairy tales—or rather, of commercial publications of such tales, since Korea certainly had a storytelling tradition—was viewed as symbolic of Korea's loss of sovereignty. The project of translating foreign tales into Korean and of collecting Korea's own tales, which began with enthusiasm in Korea in the 1920s, can thus be viewed as a reflection of Korea's struggle to sustain its national identity in the face of colonial subjugation.

Yet this impassioned attention to fairy tales was not motivated by anticolonial sentiment alone. It was informed by Japan's own developing interest in fairy tales and in the perceived role of these tales in the development of an authentic "folk" voice. Japan's interest in the Grimms' tales and the tales' contribution to the production of the national subject is reflected in translations published from 1887; and it was these early translations that served as the source texts for the Korean translators. Therefore, an examination of Korean translations of the Grimms' tales cannot ignore the fact that the originals that fueled them were conduits of Japanese ideas of national identity and storytelling. At the same time, these tales functioned as a means for Korean writers to reinvent their nation's storytelling traditions by infusing them with linguistic expressions that marked them as decidedly modern, and that paved the way for the development of Korea's own genre of the modern folktale.

The two translators of the Grimms' tales in Korea in the 1920s were Ch'oe Namsŏn (1890–1957) and Pang Chŏnghwan (1899–1931). Ch'oe was a leading figure of the Enlightenment in Korea, a man who boasted of abundant tomes that expounded forceful arguments regarding the modern (and largely European) knowledge that Korea needed to embrace. He published his translations in the literary magazine that he edited, *Tongmyŏng* (Eastern Light). Pang, by contrast, was a leading children's rights activist who sought to create a new kind of children's culture and literature that would offer children comfort and entertainment but that would also draw public attention to children's issues. Pang published his translations in the children's magazine that he edited, *Ŏrini* (Child). The two men's different positions within the literary establishment, and their sensitivity to their audiences, resulted in the production of dissimilar translations, as I will demonstrate below. Yet in spite of the divergent outcomes, they shared a perceived inherent potential in the Grimms' tales that made them conducive for the development of national identity and children's culture. Recent scholarship on the Grimms' tales (Bauman and Briggs; Zipes, *Fairy Tales*; Haase, "Decolonizing Fairy-Tale Studies") argues convincingly that the tales were projects of constructed tradition and invented modernity. In Korea, too, translators developed a fairy-tale language that both created a timeless connection with the mythical past and bolstered modern tropes of storytelling.

THE JAPANESE CONNECTION

An analytic engagement with the emergence of fairy tales in the second decade of twentieth-century Korea must be framed by a discussion of the political and social context of their appearance and also by a consideration of the Japanese translations that inspired them. Korea had a rich tradition of storytelling, of course, well before it was colonized by Japan in 1910. But the introduction of the Grimms' tales to a child and adult readership in Korea was done during a time when the folktale was consciously revived as a simultaneously modern narrative genre—modern in its ability to capture colloquial voices and modes of expression particular to the Korean language—and an authentic and indigenous narrative form that captured a true and timeless folk character.

Two Japanese literary figures played a particularly significant role in setting the stage for Korea's development of its repertoire of folktale translations. The first of these was Iwaya Sazanami (1870–1933), who exercised a direct influence on the above-mentioned author of the "collection contest," Pang Chŏnghwan. Iwaya spent two years in Germany and other cities in Europe, where he gathered stories for his folktale collections (Ōtake 53). He was credited with publishing the first volume of Japanese folktales in 1894, founding the children's magazine *Shōnen Sekai* (Children's World) in 1895, and writing Japan's first children's story—published in 1891 and inspired, in part, by folktales such as the Grimms' tales (Carter 61; Henry 219; Piel 215). A second influential figure in Korean translations of folktales was Yanagita Kunio (1875–1962). Yanagita played an important role in the repositioning of folktales as an important genre in Japan: he founded Japanese folklore studies and *minzokugaku* (native ethnology) and published a collection of short tales and local songs in his book *Tōno monogatari* (Tales of Tōno) in 1910 (Ortabasi, "Narrative Realism" 127).

Tanigawa Ken'icihi explained that Yanagita's work contributed to a reconceptualization of Japanese culture: in his scholarship, he sought to expose the "deep structures of the culture of the common people as transmitted from antiquity" (qtd. in Morton 100).[3] Yanagita was hugely influential in his time, and his work would have been familiar to Korean intellectuals in Japan in the first few decades of the twentieth century.[4] These Japanese scholars had an immeasurable influence on the abovementioned Korean translators, who approached the folktale genre as a medium of preservation of an authentic folk voice as well as an appropriate and desirable genre for young readers.

Not only did Japan's preoccupation with folktales predate that of Korea; Japan's own process of adaptation of the Grimms' tales also exerted a direct influence on the outcome of the Korean translations. The first Japanese Grimm translation, which was published in 1887, was aimed at adults and is said to have been a faithful translation that lacked editorial interference and didactic interpretation (Tsuzukihashi 19). However, Tsuzukihashi claims that the two translations of "The Wolf and Seven Young Kids" that came out in 1889 indicated a departure from the literal translational approach and reflected the burgeoning nationalism of the Meiji era that was concerned with reform and enlightenment. For example, a version of "The Wolf and Seven Young Kids" published in September of 1889 in the children's magazine *Shōgokumin* (Young Citizen) was translated as a cautionary tale; it was altered to reflect the concern with morality and the promotion of a sense of national identity among young Japanese readers (Tsuzukihashi 19).[5] Yoshito Takahashi also notes that the translators in this period removed gruesome scenes, inserted Japanese elements, and emphasized the moral lessons of each tale (333).

The source text used by Ch'oe Namsŏn—and probably also by Pang Chŏnghwan—was a Japanese translation of the Grimms' tales from 1916. *Gurimu otogibanashi* (Grimm Tales)[6] was one of several translations popular at this time in Japan. In its introduction, the translator and compiler Nakajima Kotō explained that the forty-one tales were difficult to edit and compile because of moralistic and nationalist considerations (Tsuzukihashi 21). It is therefore important to underscore that the Japanese versions that Pang and Ch'oe were working with had been interpreted and adapted by their Japanese translators to suit the needs of a Japanese society that was undergoing its own creation of a modern national identity and developing an authentic folk voice.

THE GRIMMS' TALES IN KOREAN TRANSLATION

A month before Pang Chŏnghwan announced the Collection Contest, he published *Sarang ŭi sŏnmul,* a book of ten translated fairy tales.[7] Pang did not reveal the source of his translations; instead, he identified the tales by country of origin. Of the ten, three are "German tales," and of these two are Grimm tales: "Cham chanŭn wangnyŏ" (Brier Rose), and "Ch'ŏndang kanŭn kil" (The Master Thief). This was the second time a Grimm tale was published in Korean; the first was translated by a prominent educator named O Ch'ŏnksŏk, who published his translation of "How Six Made Their Way in the World" (Changsa ŭi iyagi) in the magazine *Haksaenggye* (Students' World) in 1920 (Ch'oe Sŏkhŭi 240). Pang's *Sarang ŭi sŏnmul* marked a turning point in the consumption of fairy tales because it enjoyed unprecedented sales. It also stimulated discussions among translators and literary figures about the role of translation in literature and reflected the keen interest in collecting foreign and local tales.[8] The publication of *Sarang ŭi sŏnmul* was followed by the simultaneous publications of the Grimms' tales in two important literary magazines. In 1923, the abovementioned children's rights activist Pang Chŏnghwan included several Grimm tale translations in *Ŏrini,* a magazine published for children. In the same year, the prolific intellectual Ch'oe Namsŏn published his own translations of the Grimms' tales in the literary magazine *Tongmyŏng* among his other essays on literature, history, and culture.

Pang and Ch'oe translated the Grimms from a Japanese translation and probably used the same Japanese source text. In any case, Pang (translating specifically for young readers) and Ch'oe (translating for adults) produced two distinctly different translations, and the question arises as to what guided their approach. A response can be partially found in essays they themselves wrote with respect to the task of the translator as they saw it. Another response, supported by theories of narratology in translation as proposed by Emer O'Sullivan, can be found in considering the way that their imagined audiences shaped their translation craft. Both of these possibilities will be explored, as will this underlying question: What was it about the Grimms' tales in particular that made them conducive to the modernizing project of literature for adults and children?

CH'OE NAMSŎN'S TRANSLATIONS IN *TONGMYŎNG*

The literary magazine *Tongmyŏng* was published on a weekly basis from September 1922 to June 1923 (Kim and An 333). As the editorial on the front page explains, the mission of *Tongmyŏng* was to examine the nation's internal and external state of affairs and to be a "national magazine" by placing emphasis on the arts and by featuring original and translated fiction, poetry, and plays. Literary translations were included in each volume, which ran about twenty pages in length. Translations included the works of Anton Chekhov, Jack London, and Sir Arthur Conan Doyle. From 14 January 1923 onward, each volume also contained a Grimm tale in translation. Altogether, fifteen tales were published in *Tongmyŏng*. While the translator of the tales is not mentioned, it has been convincingly suggested that all were translated by the editor of the magazine himself, Ch'oe Namsŏn (Ch'oe; Kim and An). The source Ch'oe used for his translations was *Gurimu otogibanashi* (Grimm Tales) published in 1916 (Kim and An 345).[9]

Although his dense prose indicates that the target group of this magazine was a literate adult audience and not a child readership, the large number of essays about child rearing and home economics alongside essays about Korean history and culture suggests that this magazine targeted the entire family. A call for young people's submissions in *Tongmyŏng* on 1 October 1922 for the sake of promoting their creative writing skills also suggests that the magazine envisioned itself playing a part in the development of young readers and writers. Altogether, the magazine's analytic essays and translations of European literature position it solidly within the overarching trajectory of the oeuvre of Ch'oe Namsŏn, who was a tireless advocate for Korea's acquisition of modern knowledge. In this sense, then, *Tongmyŏng* was another channel through which Ch'oe promoted the knowledge and culture that he believed indispensable to Koreans of all ages.

A comparison of his translations with his Japanese source text reveals his intentions more clearly. In his translations, Ch'oe tampered with certain details to make the texts readable and palatable to Korean readers. In certain stories, the characters' German (or their Japanese equivalents) names are replaced by Korean ones; for example, Cinderella is called Kyŏnghŭi, and she rides a horse-drawn carriage through Chongno, the main intersection in the city of Seoul. Red Cap goes to visit her grandmother who lives not alone— for this would offend Korean sensibilities—but with Red Cap's uncle.[10] The Bremen musicians call each other by familiar Korean titles (*Yŏboge! Ku Sŏbang!*). The seven kids, in their escape from the wolf, hide behind furniture one would typically find in a Korean home; for example, the youngest kid hides successfully behind the folding screen (*pyŏngp'ung*) and not the clock as in the original German and the Japanese intermediary translation.[11]

Ch'oe not only adjusted his translations with respect to proper nouns but also adapted the overriding narrative, editing and expanding it. For example, Ch'oe omitted from his "Frog Prince" the entire ending with loyal Heinrich and the snapping bands around his heart. Yet in the opening, he adds that the well underneath the old tree was narrow in circumference but deep beyond imagination and that "from ancient times it is said that its water pours in from the sea." The narrator goes on to explain that "from time to time the water from the well shoots up into the air" and "even on a hot summer day, the well seems like another world." The translator thus offers an explanation of the fascination that the princess has with this well and also gives the readers extra details to marvel at.

Ch'oe's language does more than embellish the translation. Certain expressions such as "long, long ago" (*yennal yetch'ŏk*) or "they are still eating well and living well" contributed to the coining of certain generic expressions that added to a new arsenal of Korean fairy-tale literary language. One might argue that they mimic, to a certain extent, the formulaic expressions in Japanese; the result, however, is that these terms were coined in Korean. The use of speech levels and dialogue markers was also borrowed to a certain extent from the Japanese and, as in the Japanese case, mimicked real speech, thus bringing the text to life. Indeed, there was considerable debate in Korea at the end of the nineteenth and early twentieth centuries over the need to unify forms of speech and writing, or *ŏnmun ilch'i* (King 35).[12] However, some scholars (e.g., Hŏ 463) have pointed out that fairy tales have a certain propensity toward orality, as reflected in Ch'oe's lively dialogue ("Open the door, oh Princess!"/*mun yŏl'ŏ chushyu, mangnae kongjunim!*), so that the spoken quality of the text is less a product of the Japanese translation and more a property of the fairy-tale genre.

Although Ch'oe remained generally faithful to his Japanese source text, he added to and subtracted from it to create a bridge between the foreign and familiar. Some scholars have condemned Ch'oe's translation style—marked by long, descriptive, and detailed free prose—as a "fictionalization" of the original narrative (Kim and An 347). Yet Ch'oe was not unaware of the deliberate decisions he made as a translator, which he addressed in "Weguk ŭlossŏ kwihwahan chosŏn kodam" (Old Korean Stories Domesticated from Overseas) published in *Tongmyŏng*. In this essay, Ch'oe insists that all Korean stories, even those considered indigenous, have their roots in foreign tales. He demonstrates the way in which these stories evolved when they came to Korea and explains his translational approach, saying that original stories must be adapted—and made readily accessible—for the benefit of the reader: "Stories are only entertaining when the objects described in them are clear. It is only when they are suitable for their national culture that they are powerful and can enjoy longevity. Each country has its own natural landscape, so that when stories travel from one part of the world to another, they must be adapted [*pyŏnt'ong*]. . . . As long as the basic narrative is not shattered, there is a need to adapt stories so that their readers can recognize and understand them at first sight" (6).

Ch'oe justifies his tampering with the narrative to better suit the readers' national character by arguing that a story will inevitably fail to convey meaning if readers are unfamiliar with its basic elements. Ch'oe sees storytelling as a deeply nationalistic endeavor, and therefore it is not only the privilege but also the duty of a translator to imbue the text with Korean elements. As Kim and An explain, his view was that translation without transformation—without a basic shifting of narrative to suit "national" tastes—is not possible (337). Ch'oe was convinced of the transformational power of literature and fairy tales and believed in them as educational vehicles that would propel Korea toward modernity.

PANG CHŎNGHWAN'S TRANSLATIONS IN *ŎRINI*

The same year that Ch'oe Namsŏn began publishing his Grimm translations, Pang Chŏnghwan published five of his own translations in the children's magazine *Ŏrini* (Child). These included "The Golden Goose" (Hwanggŭm kŏu),[13] "The Seven Ravens" (Ilgop mari skamakwi),[14] "The Wolf and the Seven Young Kids" (Yŏmso wa nŭktae),[15] "Rumpelstiltskin" (Chakŭni ŭi ilhom),[16] and "The Frog King" (Kaeguri wangja).[17] Pang, too, took generous liberties with his source text, adding, omitting, and embellishing the narrative, and nowhere does he identify his stories as Grimm tales. In fact, Pang's translations take such liberties that it is hard to discern what source text he was using exactly, although one supposes that he is likely to have used the same 1916 text that served Ch'oe Namson and that he might have used Ch'oe's translation as a source as well.

Pang's personal biography and *Ŏrini* attest to the long-lasting influence of German culture and education on his work. Take, for example, an essay in one of the first volumes of *Ŏrini* titled "Those Pitiful Yet Frighteningly Well-Disciplined German Children—Schools That Make Children Nap Once a Day."[18] Here Pang describes his impressions following a classroom visit. "There are few people like the Germans," he begins: "Healthy, robust, knowledgeable, yet also refined and full of love" (*Ŏrini* 1 [1923]: 4). He notes their remarkable discipline, orderliness, and enthusiasm and the freedom with which they can move from one activity to the next. They play, dance, sing, draw, sculpt, and listen to stories. "Ah!" he sighs at the end of his essay, "How can the future of these children, who grow up sturdy and free, be anything but happy?"

Inspired as he may have been by the Japanese fascination with German culture and its emphasis on strength and national identity, Pang's main preoccupation in this period was the creation of a new kind of children's literature. He sought to depart from the typically dry, didactic, and moralizing reading materials of the time and advocated the creation of a new space for children. This new space was both physical—he established youth group organizations—and cultural—he initiated a new holiday called "Children's Day" and published *Ŏrini*. This magazine in particular intended to entertain children, call attention to their economic and social plight, and offer alternative role models for children, picturing them as resourceful yet pitiful, precocious yet endearing. He made a conscious break with the discourse of the Korean Enlightenment by promoting literature that had aesthetic parameters, not just intellectual and/or didactic ones.

Pang's approach to translation is reflected in the page layout and in his narrative voice. In comparison with Ch'oe's dense prose and closely packed sentences, Pang's page has wide margins and greater spacing between the sentences. The sentences themselves are shorter, and Pang employs far more indigenous Korean expressions and onomatopoeia in his writing, as opposed to vocabulary of Chinese origin: the princess sobs (*hulchŏk hulchŏk*); the wolf snores (*k'ulŭlŭng k'ulŭlŭng*); the kids squirm in his belly (*mungk'ul munk'ul* and *pulluk pulluk*). Another method used by Pang is that of rhythmic repetition: "deep" (*kip'ŭn*) is *kiptŭi kiphŭn*, and pathetic (*kuch'ahan*) is *kuch'ahadŭi kuch'ahan*. He often included a common punctuation marker, a long dash (—), which indicated that the first syllable was meant to be drawn out for emphasis. Small or *chokŭman* is *chok—koman*, yellow or *noran* is *nu—rŏn*, and white or *hayan* is *ha—yŏn*. These are but a few examples from Pang's translations in which he uses a generous number of musical expressions that bring the narrative to life. Pang also keeps the rhymes in his translation of the wolf's dying elegy in "The Wolf and the Seven Kids," something that Ch'oe ignored. Pang's translations are clearly meant not only to be read in silence but also to be heard.

Besides employing such musical narrative techniques to charm his young readers, Pang does something else that exposes his awareness of his young audience: he omits and edits the less than palatable content in accordance with what he deemed appropriate for his young readers. For example, in "The Frog Prince" in its original and Japanese translations (as well as in Ch'oe's), the princess hurls the frog against the wall with a violence that is immediately glossed over when the frog is transformed into a beautiful prince who explains that he was put under a spell from which only she could release him. The princess and frog are joined according to her father's wishes; they wake up in the morning together and leave to claim his kingdom. In Pang's translation, the transformed prince first explains that the evil spell necessitated a princess's brutal behavior to free him; this excuses her violence. Instead of the ambiguous reference to the couple sleeping together, Pang immediately marries off the two in a large wedding ceremony. Pang's sanitized editing is evidence of his intention to (properly) educate and amuse his young readers.

If Pang's first mission was to promote a new culture of childhood, his second, Yŏm Hŭigyŏng ("Minjokchuŭi ŭi naemyŏnhwa," "Neisyŏn") argues, was to promote nationalist, anticolonial sentiment. In her analysis of Pang Chŏnghwan's translations in *Sarang ŭi sŏnmul*, Yŏm concludes that what drove Pang's translations was his desire to convey to children a sense of national identity. She argues that some of the subtle ways in which he communicated messages of empowerment were in his table of contents; for example, a tale that is attributed to Sicily rather than Italy offers a slight tip of the hat to this struggling nation (Yŏm, "Neisyŏn" 164–65).

Such anticolonial sentiments are also reflected in the abovementioned Collection Contest, in which Pang underscores the connection between the survival of Korean culture and its stories. However, an examination of Pang's Grimm tale translations in *Ŏrini* yields little evidence to support the argument that they were explicitly nationalistic. To be fair, there were few public venues in which one could resist the colonial government, despite the relaxation of cultural policies that followed the March First Movement of 1919. One might argue that Pang's choice of works was the message: "The Seven Ravens," "The Golden Goose," "The Frog Prince," "Rumpelstiltskin," and "The Wolf and Seven Young Kids" are all celebrations, to a certain extent, of an unlikely hero or heroine that overcomes a formidable challenge against great odds.

Perhaps the nationalist argument is not as convincing, then, as this: in his translations, Pang tried to create a pleasurable space for young readers and to draw sympathy to their plight through depictions of children struggling against adult oppression. And by creating a musical storytelling voice in his translations, Pang was encouraging the establishment of a genre that would eventually revive Korea's own tales in a modern voice, thus maintaining its cultural legitimacy against a backdrop of colonial and cultural assimilation policies.

LITERARY LANGUAGE AND MODERNITY, ADAPTATIONS, AND NARRATOLOGY

The translations and essays written by Pang and Ch'oe attest to the critical relationship they perceived between storytelling and national identity. They viewed the act of storytelling as one of both social significance—it reinforced the national identity of the reader by celebrating sounds and images native to Korea—and literary significance—it enriched Korean narrative through the establishment of storytelling language and through the domestication of unfamiliar storylines. It is interesting to note that the domestication of foreign texts through translation, which both Pang and Ch'oe subscribed to in their work, was a practice that was already underway in Japan. Wakabayashi explains that translators domesticated unfamiliar imports in an attempt to accommodate readers' perceived understanding rather than as a form of resistance to foreign culture ("Foreign Bones, Japanese Flesh" 227). She adds, "It was translations that offered models to writers of original works, rather than the reverse. . . . Translations opened up new vistas in terms of content, language and presentation in a process that continued long after the appearance of the first original works fitting the definition of modern children's literature" (243–54). Both Pang and Ch'oe, who spent significant time in Japan working with literary scholars involved in translation and adaptation, would have no doubt been inspired by these trends.

When reading Pang's and Ch'oe's translations, however, it is clear that there is more at play than their sensitivity to the formative role that language plays in enforcing Korean national identity or in establishing modern literary tropes. Their translations reveal that they negotiated their interpretations with a keen awareness of the perceived needs of their audiences. Ch'oe's subscription to social Darwinist principles and belief in the superiority of modern (European) knowledge made the translation of the Grimms' tales a natural choice. And Pang's translations were dictated very clearly by the child image in his mind and his culturally determined ideas about what was appropriate for children. Emer O'Sullivan offers a convincing model of the way that translators reprocess the original; she effectively applies the work of Giuliana Schiavi, who argues that the translator "intercepts the communication [of the original] and transmits it—reprocessed—to the new reader who will receive the message" (qtd. in O'Sullivan 102). O'Sullivan points to the "audibility of the translator"—the places in the text in which the translator's voice can be located in the act of communication.

These moments—for example, the sanitation of the content and transformation of certain details to make them more palatable to Korean audiences—are apparent when reading the German and Japanese source texts alongside the Korean translations. O'Sullivan's theorization can be further nuanced by drawing attention to the fact that in this case, the process of translation is mediated also by a power differential: the ideas that are being "reprocessed" about the individual and nation in the Grimm tales were filtered through the language of the colonial oppressor. This complicates her linear diagrams and demands a more complex visualization of the transference of language and knowledge in translation within a context of unequal power relations.

This question remains: Why the Grimms? Some Korean scholars have already pointed to the nationalistic aspect of the texts (Yŏm "Neisyŏn") and have drawn on the similarities between the project of preserving national identity undertaken by the Brothers Grimm and their Korean counterparts working under colonial subjugation in the 1920s (Ch'oe). One might also argue that for Pang and Ch'oe, translation was a tool of resistance (Kim and An; Cho 212): the Korean translators used the colonial language (Japanese) as a foundation only to build upon it in order to form and strengthen the Korean language.

However, Bauman and Briggs, Zipes (*Fairy Tales*), and Haase ("Decoloniz-ing Fairy-Tale Studies") offer a more theoretically complex view of the Broth-ers Grimm's tales by suggesting alternative readings. They turn their attention to the manipulative power of the language of these tales and highlight their role in the construction of tradition and modernity. Zipes argues that despite its apparent subversive potential as an allegory of overthrowing authority, oral storytelling was appropriated and converted into literary discourse with the deliberate purpose of socializing its adult and child readers. The Grimm tales guided their readers "to use one's powers rightly to be accepted in society or re-create society in keeping with the norms of the status quo" (*Fairy tales* 70). They were less subversively manipulative than they were a commodity of the middle class; the tales were not only the "products of the struggles of the common people to make themselves heard in oral folktales [but also] literary products of the German bourgeois quest for identity and power" (62–68).

It is perhaps this quality—the tale as a literary commodity—that ap-pealed to Ch'oe Namsŏn as an advocate of modernity and a forerunner in the development of modern literature in Korea.[19] At the same time, Bau-man and Briggs explain that the Grimms engineered a language of fairy tales that tried to reveal that a "shared national voice had been there all along" (220). Haase, too, argues that "in becoming convincing ventriloquists for the folk, the Grimms not only created the enduring idea that folktales give direct expression to national identity, but they also created a fairy-tale lan-guage whose apparent artlessness, purity, and simplicity seemed completely transparent and facilitated the translation of their tales as universal stories" ("Decolonizing" 28). This aspect of linguistic engineering and the coinage of fairy-tale tropes as universal language corresponds with Pang's and Ch'oe's translational approaches and with their desire to create an illusion of the existence of continuity in the midst of colonial rupture.

Bauman and Briggs demonstrate that in the process of rendering their texts more scientific, the Grimms in fact severed "the indexical links that connected tradition to localities" so that texts could come to define a national and universal space. This universal quality, incidentally, is what granted them an intrinsic propensity toward translation-ness.[20] And it was the supposed intrinsic character of their folktales that made the stories into such potential fodder for the translation and rediscovery of Korea's own folktales. As Bauman and Briggs explain, folktales, epics, legends, and other folk texts are crucial to the construction of the status of a nation as a modern entity in order to "embody continuities with the traditional base that (in theory) preceded it." They argue successfully that "producing and consuming traditional texts became a crucial part of the process of imagining the nation and making it seem to be real, a natural phenomenon with deep historical roots" (224). Herein lies the source of attraction offered to the Korean translators by the Grimms' tales.

Ten years after Korea's humiliating absorption into the Japanese empire, the Grimm tales offered their translators a site from which to reclaim tradition—with the illusion of transparency offered by the fairy-tale language developed by the Grimms[21]—and, at the same time, forge a modern language that imitated contemporary speech and modern voices. Under their skillful hands, the Korean "transcultural"[22] folktale genre was reborn—and continues to enjoy multiple rebirths to the present day.

Notes

1. Pang (1899–1931) secured his place in the history of children's literature through his writing, editing, and publication of the children's magazine *Ŏrini* (1923–1931) and his establishment of Children's Day in Korea in 1923.

2. Three tales in the collection are "German tales," and of these two are Grimms' tales: "Cham chanŭn wangnyŏ" (Brier Rose) and "Ch'ŏndang kanŭn kil" (The Master Thief). The book sold about 200,000 copies, a remarkable number for the period (Yŏm, "Minjokchuŭi ŭi naemyŏnhwa" 149–50).

3. One of the central concepts of his work was that of the *jōmin*, which is a descriptive category of the everyday life of the common people living in the villages (Morton 138).

4. The connection between Yanagita and Iwaya is addressed by Ericson (xii); Ortabasi explains that Yanagita made a few references to Iwaya's writings in his own work on folklore and had a number of disciples working in Korea (personal communication, 17 May 2011).

5. Ericson notes that "the Japanese embrace of folktales as both emblematic of cultural identity and fundamental for the construction, through children, of national citizens reflects many similarities with the Brothers Grimm and nineteenth-century German nationalism. Meiji educators championed the morals and ethics embedded in retold folktales, while writers and publishers celebrated the popularity and effectiveness of the tales, stripped of the extraneous through countless retellings, conveying what they argued was the 'essence' of literature" (ix–x).

6. I am indebted to Shirin Eshghi for her invaluable help in finding these materials.

7. The original 1922 publication is no longer to be found; the earliest version available is its eleventh printing published in 1928 (Yŏm, "Minjokchuŭi ŭi naemyŏnhwa" 150).

8. Despite the local interest in fairy tales marked by Pang's Collection Contest, the very first publication of collected Korean folktales was published not by Koreans but by their Japanese colonizers: the *Chōsen dōwa shū* came out in 1924 and was intended less for the consumption of the locals and more for the benefit of the colonizers.

9. Kim and An's analysis of the translations is incomplete because of their (admitted) lack of access to the Japanese translation.

10. This detail is missing from the Japanese translation, which stays quite faithful to the original text.

11. Some of these details have been pointed out also by Kim and An.

12. The movement toward the unification of speech and writing took place in Japan too; Melek Ortabasi explains that the movement *genbun itchi* in Japan privileged a vernacular style that would "produce a modern idiom that more closely approximated everyday speech" (Ortabasi, "Brave Dogs" 187; Tomasi).

13. *Ŏrini* (1.4): 10–12.

14. *Ŏrini* (1.8): 2–6.

15. *Ŏrini* (1.9): 3–7.

16. *Ŏrini* (2.1): 13–15 and *Ŏrini* (2.2): 15–17.

17. *Ŏrini* (2.7): 2–7.

18. "Pulsanghamyŏnsŏdo musŏpkae k'ŏganŭn tok'il ŭi ŏrini: maeil hanbŏnsik natcham ŭl chaeunŭn hakkyo" in *Ŏrini* 4 (1923): 4.

19. Bauman and Briggs argue that the Grimms contributed not only to the creation of the fairy tale as a middle-class commodity but to the shaping of the image of the modern child. They contributed to this discussion by noting that the Grimm tales "played at least a small role in *shaping* a romantic image of the child as embodying the same sort of naiveté associated with both the past and contemporary peasants. Traditional texts thus bear value for constructing the idealized affective

parameters of a bourgeois childhood as well as imparting instructions on how to become a responsible national subject" (222; italics in original).

20. "The Grimms actively encouraged translation of the KHM . . . they conceived of the KHM as providing a model that specialists in other countries should emulate in collecting and publishing folktales and other genres. . . . Just as the KHM could embody a national prototype that they had largely created, the *Märchen* were readily comparable to narratives that were cut on the same mold" (Bauman and Briggs 223).

21. Bauman and Briggs note that the Grimms crafted an "illusion of intertextual fidelity" that "made the texts into powerful devices" (214).

22. Haase acknowledges the discussion regarding translation of the folktale as an act of trespassing and omission; he adds that not only is the question of translation one of omission and trespassing, but it also "produces something new—a transcultural text that communicates more than the sum of its cultural parts" ("Decolonizing" 30).

REFERENCES

An, Kyŏngsik. *Sop'a pang chŏnghwan ŭi adong kyoyuk undong kwa sasang* [The Children's Activism and Educational Philosophy of Pang Chŏnghwan]. Seoul: Hakchisa, 1999.

Bauman, Richard, and Charles L. Briggs. *Voices of Modernity: Language Ideologies and the Politics of Inequality.* Cambridge: Cambridge UP, 2003.

Carter, Nona L. "A Study of Japanese Children's Magazines 1888–1949." Diss. University of Pennsylvania, 2009.

Cho, Jaeryong. "Traduction en face de la modernité et du nationalisme: La post-colonialité en traduction et la transformation de l'écriture à l'époque de l'ouverture au monde." *Hanguk p'ŭrangsŭhak nonjip* 73 (2011): 205–20.

Ch'oe, Sŏkhŭi. "Tokil tonghwa ŭi hanguk suyong: Kŭrim (Grimm) tonghwa rŭl Chungsimŭro" [The Reception of German Tales in Korea Focusing on the Grimms' Tales]. *Hese yŏngu* 3 (2000): 240–63.

Chu, Chongyŏn. "Hanguk tonghwa wa tokil Marchen ŭi pigyo yŏngu: Kŭrim tonghwa ŭi iip kwajŏng e kwanhayŏ" [A Comparison of Korean Tales and German Märchen: On the Importation of the Grimms' Tales]. *Hangukhak nonch'ong* 3 (1980): 193–220.

Ericson, Joan. Introduction. *A Rainbow in the Desert: An Anthology of Early Twentieth Century Japanese Children's Literature.* By Yukie Ohta. Armonk: M.E. Sharpe, 2000.

Gonzenbach, Laura. *Beautiful Angiola: The Great Treasury of Sicilian Folk and Fairy Tales.* Trans. and ed. Jack Zipes. Illus. Joellyn Rock. New York: Routledge, 2004.

Grimm, Jacob, and Wilhelm Grimm. *The Complete Fairy Tales of the Brothers Grimm.* 3rd expanded ed. Trans. Jack Zipes. New York: Bantam, 2003.

———. *Gurimu otogibanashi.* Trans. Kotō Nakajima. Tokyo: fuzanbō, 1916.

Haase, Donald. "Decolonizing Fairy-Tale Studies." *Marvels & Tales* 24.1 (2010): 17–38.

———. "Framing the Brothers Grimm: Paratexts and Intercultural Transmission in Postwar English-Language Editions of the *Kinder- und Hausmärchen.*" *Fabula* 44.1–2 (2003): 55–69.

Henry, David. "Japanese Children's Literature as Allegory of Empire in Iwaya Sazanami's Momotarō (The Peach Boy)." *Children's Literature Association Quarterly* 34.3 (2009): 218–28.

Hǒ, Chaeyǒng. "Kǔndae kyemonggi ǒnmunilch'i ǔi ponjil kwa kukhanmunch'e ǔi yuhyǒng" [The Unification of Written and Spoken Language and the Mixed Style of Writing in the Modern Enlightenment Period]. *Ǒnmunhak* 114.12 (2011): 441–67.

Kawada, Minoru. *The Origin of Ethnography in Japan: Yanagita Kunio and His Times.* London: Kegan Paul International, 1993.

Kim, Hwasǒn, and An Miyǒng. "1920 nyǒndae sǒgu chǒllae tonghwa ǔi pǒnyǒk kwa chuch'e ǔi yokmang: *Tongmyǒng* e sogaedoen kǔrim tonghwa chungsim ǔro" [The Grimm Tales in Tongmyǒng: The Desire and Form of Translations of Western Fairy Tales in the 1920s]. *Imun yǒn'gu* 53.4 (2007): 331–55.

King, Ross. "Nationalism and Language Reform in Korea: The Questione della lingua in Precolonial Korea." *Nationalism and the Construction of Korean Identity.* Ed. Timothy Tangherlini and Hyung-il Pai. Berkeley: U of California P, 1998. 33–72.

Kwǒn, Hyǒngnae. *Chosǒn Tonghwajip: Uri nara ch'oech'o chǒllae tonghwajip (1924 nyǒn) ǔi pǒnyǒk, yǒn'gu* [Chosǒn Fairy Tales: Translation and Research on Korea's First Fairy Tale Collection]. Seoul: Chimmundang, 2003.

Melek, Ortabasi. "Narrative Realism and the Modern Storyteller: Rereading Yanagita Kunio's Tōno Monogatari." *Monumenta Nipponica* 64.1 (2009). 127–66.

Mitsuru, Hashimoto. "Chiho: Yanagita Kunio's 'Japan.'" *Mirror of Modernity: Invented Traditions of Modern Japan.* Ed. Stephen Vlastos. Berkeley: U of California P, 1998. 133–43.

Morton, Leith. *Modern Japanese Culture: The Insider View.* South Melbourne: Oxford UP, 2003.

Ortabasi, Melek. "Brave Dogs and Little Lords: Thoughts on Translation, Gender, and the Debate on Childhood in Mid-Meiji." *Translation Modern Japan.* Ed. Indra Levy. London: Routledge, 2011. 186–212.

———. "Narrative Realism and the Modern Storyteller: Rereading Yanagita Kunio's Tōno Monogatari." *Monumenta Nipponica* 64.1 (2009): 127–66.

O'Sullivan, Emer. "Narratology Meets Translation Studies, or the Voice of the Translator in Children's Literature." *Translation of Children's Literature*. Ed. Gillian Lathey. Buffalo: Multilingual Matters, 2006. 98–110.

Ōtake, Kiyomi. *Kundae Han-Il Adong Munhwa Wa Munhak Kwangyesa, 1895–1945* [Exchange of Modern Korea–Japan Children's Culture and Literature, 1895–1945]. Seoul: Ch'ongun, 2005.

Pak, Hyesuk. "Sŏyang tonghwa ŭi yuip kwa 1920 nyŏndae hanguk tonghwa ŭi sŏngnip" [The Inflow of Western Fairy Tales and the Establishment of Korean Fairy Tales in the 1920s]. *Ŏmun yŏngu* 125.3 (2005): 173–92.

Pang, Chonghwan. "Hyŏnsang mojip." *Kaebyŏk* 8 (1922): 112.

———. *Sarang ŭi sŏnmul* [Gift of Love]. Seoul: Kaebyŏk, 1922.

Piel, L. Halliday. "Loyal Dogs and Meiji Boys: The Controversy over Japan's First Children's Story, Koganemaru (1891)." *Children's Literature* 38 (2010): 207–22.

Takahashi, Yoshito. "Japan und die deutsche Kultur: Die Rezeption der Grimmschen Märchen und der deutschen Bildungsidee seit der Meiji-Zeit." *Wie Kann Man Vom "Deutschen" Leben? Zur Praxisrelevanz Der Interkulturellen Germanistik*. Ed. Ernest W. B. Hess-Lüttich and Richard Watts. Frankfurt: Oxford, 2009. 331–42.

Tomasi, Massimiliano. "Quest for a New Written Language: Western Rhetoric and the Genbun Itchi Movement." *Monumenta Nipponica* 54.3 (1999): 333–60.

Tsuzukihashi, Tatsuo. "Nihon ni okeru gurimu siyōkai no reikishi" [The History of the Introduction of the Grimms in Japan]. *Nihon jidō bungaku* 31.10 (1985): 18–25.

Underwood, Horace Grant. *An Introduction to the Korean Spoken Language*. 2nd ed. New York: MacMillan, 1914.

Wakabayashi, Judy. "An Etymological Exploration of 'Translation' in Japan." *Decentering Translation Studies: India and Beyond*. By Wakabayashi and Rita Kothari. Amsterdam: John Benjamins, 2009. 175–94. Benjamins Translation Library 86.

———. "Foreign Bones, Japanese Flesh: Translations and the Emergence of Modern Children's Literature in Japan." *Japanese Language and Literature—Journal of the Association of Teachers of Japanese* 42.1 (2008): 227–56.

Yŏm, Hŭigyŏng. "Minjokchuŭi ŭi naemyŏnhwa wa 'chŏllae tonghwa' ŭi model ch'ahki: Pang Chŏnghwan ŭi *Sarang ŭi sŏnmul* e taehayŏ (2)" [Internalization of Nationalism of the Fairy Tale Model: Pang Chŏnghwang's *Gift of Love* (2)]. *Hangukhak yŏngu* 16 (2007): 147–71.

———. " 'Neisyŏn' ŭl sangsanghan pŏnyŏk tonghwa: Pang Chŏnghwan ŭi *Sarang ŭi sŏnmul* e taehayŏ (1)" [Fairy Tales as a Means of Imagining the Nation: Pang Chŏnghwang's *Gift of Love* (1)]. *Tonghwa wa pŏnyŏk* 13 (2007): 157–88.

———. "Pang Chŏnghwan ŭi ch'ogi pŏnyŏk sosŏl kwa tonghwa yŏngu: saero ch'ajŭn p'ilmyŏng kwa chakp'um ŭl chungsim ŭro" [A Study on Pang Chŏnghwan's

Early Translated Novels and Fairy Tales with a Focus on His Newly Discovered Pennames and Works]. *Tonghwa wa pŏnyŏk* 15 (2008): 145–68.

Zipes, Jack. *The Brothers Grimm: From Enchanted Forests to the Modern World.* New York: Routledge, 1988.

———. *Fairy Tales and the Art of Subversion: The Classical Genre for Children and the Process of Civilization.* 2nd ed. New York: Routledge, 2006.

6

The Influence of the Grimms' Fairy Tales on the Folk Literature Movement in China (1918–1943)

DECHAO LI

THE FOLK LITERATURE MOVEMENT IN CHINA

In 1918, a group of Chinese progressive scholars, including Zhou Zuoren and Gu Jiegang, initiated the Chinese Folk Literature Movement (hereafter "the Movement"), which called for the collection and compilation of folk songs by "going to the people." They first called for the collection of Chinese folk songs that were later published periodically in the *Beijing daxue rikan* (Beijing University Daily; Hung 1). These published folk songs soon attracted the attention and contributions of quite a number of other intellectuals, which led to the formation of the Folk Song Research Society (Geyao yanjiu hui) at Peking University in 1920. This society, together with a series of journals, monographs, and essays its members had published, ushered in "a great movement of folk literature in China"[1] (Zhong, "*Dao*" 3) that exerted a great influence on the intellectuals, writers, and students of that time.

The Movement, after reaching its peak in the 1920s, did not subside until 1937, when the Sino–Japanese War (1937–1945) broke out. It gradually lost its momentum at the beginning of the 1940s, when the contributions dwindled and many of its journals became moribund. The Movement finally came to an end when its flagship quarterly *Minsu* (Customs), published by Zhongshan University, wound up in 1943. Though it only lasted twenty-five years (1918–1943), the Movement had far-reaching effects on the literary sphere at the time and has also been instrumental in the formation of contemporary Chinese literature.

In addition to collecting and compiling various Chinese folk literary works, the Movement encouraged the creation of a kind of literature that could easily be understood by the general public. To put it simply, the main achievements of the Movement are fourfold. First, it successfully encouraged a number of Chinese intellectuals and writers to use the rich folk resources they discovered as inspiration or material for new works that were different from Chinese literature before 1918 in style, theme, and language. Second, the Movement partially fulfilled its aim of educating the masses through its promotion of fine Chinese traditions as revealed in collected folk literature and also reinforced the sense of national identity of the May Fourth scholars, including Zhou Zuoren and Liu Bannong. Third, it promoted the use of the "lively spoken language of the people" to create a new literature that was inherently different from the traditional highbrow literature written in classical Chinese. Finally, it gave "due recognition to traditional folklore stories or plays" (Zhong, "Wusi" 1) that were usually scorned by the Chinese literati.

Overseas scholars such as Hung Chang-tai pointed out that the Movement was largely an offshoot of a more sweeping national reform called the New Culture Campaign (*Xīn wénhuà yùndòng*) in 1912 that called for China to embrace Western standards and values to replace Confucian culture and for the creation of a new Chinese culture mainly based on science and democracy (see, e.g., Hung and Wang). No literary movement can escape the influence of the domestic social, political, and poetical contexts within which it happens. In this regard, Zhong and Hung were quite right in pointing out that it was mainly the intellectuals' discontent with traditional Chinese culture and upper-class literature that kick-started the Movement. But other than these internal causes, are there any external impetuses from other countries or thinkers that helped trigger the Movement? Hung Chang-tai clearly outlines two different sources of foreign influence (18): foreigners who lived in China at the turn of the twentieth century (including Baron Guido Amedeo Vitale and Isaac Taylor Headland) and Western folklore scholarship translated into Chinese, for example Andrew Lang's *Custom and Myth* (1884) and *Myth, Ritual and Religion* (1887); Charlotte S. Burne's *The Handbook of Folklore* (1914); and Arthur R. Wright's *English Folklore*.

But as the Movement became more widespread and influential and its collection targets gradually expanded from folk songs to other genres of folk literature such as legends, children's literature, and proverbs, there must have been other external influences. Of special importance is the translation of the Grimms' fairy tales. The Chinese translations of the *Kinder- und Hausmärchen* not only helped to precipitate the development of the Movement but also furnished the theoretical framework, the inspiration, and the direction for further development of the Movement at later stages as well as providing valuable samples of tales for imitation by the first-generation Chinese children's literature authors who were inspired by and took an active part in the Movement.

THE GRIMMS' FAIRY TALES AND THEIR INFLUENCE ON THE MOVEMENT

Scholars have already attempted to map out the influence of the translation of the Grimms' fairy tales on the Movement, although they sometimes express conflicting views. Hung indicated that the influence of the Grimms' fairy tales on the Movement was an indirect one. Rather than helping to initiate the Movement, he argued, this influence was mainly at work when the Movement was on the upswing during the middle of the 1920s, helping to widen its scope. When the Movement first started in 1918, its major purpose was to collect folk songs while excluding other types of folk literature, as reflected in the title of the leading journal of the Movement: *Geyao* (Folk Song). But in 1924, Zhou Zuoren suggested that fairy tales should also be collected, an idea that other members supported unanimously (Hung 108–9). Zuoren was an early translator of some of the Grimms' tales and had also made comparisons between the value of the Grimms' tales and other fairy tales (such as those written by Hans Christian Andersen). Moreover, he had quoted the name of the Grimm brothers in some of his articles, so it seemed to Hung quite reasonable to assume that the work of the brothers had influenced Zuoren's proposition.

Wu ("Tonghua Chuanbo de Wenhua Zhengzhi"), Fu and Xi, and Fu and Yang, on the other hand, argued that the influence of the Grimm collection came into play earlier and actually helped to start the Movement. Inspired by the Brothers Grimm's goals of using fairy tales as a means to establish a common German heritage and to educate children and the general populace with "childlike powers and nature" (Peppard 41), Chinese intellectuals also started the Movement with the same aspiration of using folk literature—a genre that is easily accessible to most of the lower-class masses—to appeal to the Chinese people to rise to the national crisis resulting from China's humiliating defeats in the wars with Japan and other Western powers at the beginning of the twentieth century. Even the background and aims of the Movement to "go to the people" to collect folk literature share much common ground with the practice of the Brothers Grimm (as it was then understood) of collecting folktales and fairy tales when the culture and the language of their nation were at a historical crossroads.

Both of these arguments seem quite plausible, at least based on the evidence the researchers have provided. But to answer the question of exactly how the Chinese translation of the Grimms' tales influenced the Movement, we need to conduct a more comprehensive study of the history of the translation and reception of the Grimms' tales in China and consider how the translations fare at every stage of the Movement, which supporters of the Movement were influenced by the Grimms' tales (rather than focusing on Zhou Zuoren alone), and whether and in what ways the translations have directly affected Chinese children's authors.

A Brief History of the Translation of the Grimms' Fairy Tales in China at the Beginning of the Twentieth Century

The earliest Chinese translation of the Grimms' fairy tales was Zhou Guisheng's *Xinan xieyi* (Interesting Stories Translated by Xinan), which was published in Shanghai in 1903. However, only six Grimm tales, including "Der Froschkönig oder der eiserne Heinrich," "Die drei Männlein im Walde," "Der Wolf und die sieben jungen Geißlein," "Der Wolf und der Mensch," "Der Bärenhäuter," and "Der wunderliche Spielmann," were translated in Guisheng's book (Wu 156). Conforming to the literary convention of that time, all the translations were written in classical or literary Chinese, which was used in formal correspondence or literary works in China until the early twentieth century. The language also differs drastically from vernacular Chinese, the modern spoken form that was used later to render the Grimm collection. Other classical Chinese translations of the *Kinder- und Hausmärchen* in book form produced at that time include Sun Yuxiu's *Tonghua* (Fairy Tales, 1909) and *Hongmaoer* (Little Red Cap, 1917) and Shen Dehung's *Tonghua* (Fairy Tales, 1918). Yuxiu's and Dehung's translations included more than ninety stories from the fairy tales of the Brothers Grimm. From 1909 to 1916, around two dozen classical Chinese translations of the Grimm tales also appeared in magazines that were mostly published in Shanghai and Beijing (Fu and Yang, "Gelin tonghua" 96–97).

Comparatively speaking, vernacular Chinese translations of the Grimm tales were all the rage after 1920, with the publication of several collections that contain quite a number of stories from the Grimm collection and two complete Chinese translations of the tales. Among these translations, Wei Yixin's translations (1934) were also the first Chinese version based on German source texts (the other translations were based on English source texts). In addition, around two hundred translations of different stories from the Brothers Grimm's fairy tales were published in various newspapers and magazines. Given the fact that a large number of Chinese translations of the Grimm tales were published before and after 1918, it seems possible that these translations, as separately argued by Hung and Wu ("Tonghua Chuanbo de Wenhua Zhengzhi"), exerted influence both before and during the Movement. My research shows that the Chinese translation of the Grimm tales influenced the Movement at least in the following three aspects: the proponents' conceptions and perceptions of folk literature, the polemic about the function of children's literature during the Movement, and the creations of the first-generation children's literature writers of China.

An important document to trace this influence specifically is a position paper of the Movement written by Hu Yuzhi (1896–1986), who made an early attempt to theorize the concept and the important characteristics of folk literature as well as differences from its supposed counterpart—book literature—by drawing on ideas from the Brothers Grimm. In his highly influential essay "Lun minjian wenxue" (On Folk Literature) from early 1921, he wrote:

> The meaning of folk literature, which is more or less the same as "folklore" in English and "Volkskunde" in German, refers to the literature that is popular among ethnic communities. . . . Folk literature has two features. First, its authors are the whole community, not individuals. Generally, literary works are created by individual writers, as each work should have its author. But this is not the case with folk literature: its creator is not an individual A or B, but an entire community. . . . Second, folk literature is an oral literature and not a book literature. Book literature has fixed texts, which are difficult to change once finished.

Folk literature is different. This is because the popularity of stories and folk songs relies completely on oral narration. Thus folk literature is in a fluid, but not fixed state. (Hu 3–4)

In this article, Hu Yuzhi famously summarized two important characteristics of folk literature—communal creation and oral production—which were to become the creeds of the Movement from that point onward. The feature of the "communal creation" of folk literature readily reminds us of the famous folk theory as proposed by the Brothers Grimm. In fact, Hu himself did not conceal that this idea was borrowed from the Grimms as he continued to argue what should be, in his opinion, the scientific methods to write and collect folklore: "Folk literature is a part of the study of folklore, or in fact the most important part. It was from the early nineteenth century that Westerners began to use scientific methods to study folklore. The pioneers of folklore study are the Brothers Grimm, who coauthored the *Kinder- und Hausmärchen*, 1812–1815, and *Deutsche Mythologie*, 1835. In these books, folk stories were faithfully recorded without any embellishments in order to retain their true face. This [writing] method [used in folk literature] was initiated by them" (Hu 5–6).

Again, Hu reiterates his assumption that the Brothers Grimm adopted the principle of "trying their utmost to maintain the plain and unornamented style of spoken literature" when collecting folklore or stories. Although it subsequently proved to be erroneous, this interpretation of the Grimms' methods of collecting and writing folk literature was widely heralded as "pointing out the correct way for the Movement" in China and was strictly adhered to by many of the later participants.

The importance of Hu Yuzhi's theorizing about folk literature, which only appeared in 1921—three years after the launch of the Movement—cannot be exaggerated. The activities of the Movement before the publication of Hu's paper were rather disorganized, and the qualities of the contributions varied greatly. The purpose of the research activity was just collecting for its own sake, with few people realizing what could be defined as folk literature (see Zhong, *Minjian Wenxue Lunji*). Part of the reason for this was the dearth of quality theorizing about the study of folklore or folk literature, which was then a fairly novel research area for Chinese intellectuals. Only with the publication of Hu Yuzhi's paper, which draws heavily on the Brothers Grimm's ideas—as understood at the time—did the Movement develop into a more self-conscious activity with a clearer understanding about the nature and principles of folk literature, including the genre of folk song, which was the focus of attention during the early 1920s. The influence of Hu's paper is also evidenced by the fact that the number of contributions to folk literature collections and the publication of collections of folklore, legends, and folk songs soared when compared with the first three years of the Movement.

The view of the Brothers Grimm that folk literature should be written down in a plain and straightforward style and a contemporary understanding of their method of faithfully recording folk literature without any distortion (although the Grimms, especially Wilhelm, did in fact amend the tales they collected) were so influential that Zhou Zuoren in 1927 also echoed their views when comparing the merits of the fairy tales of the Brothers Grimm and Hans Christian Andersen:

> When we first read foreign literature, most of us must have encountered fairy tales written by the Brothers Grimm and Hans Christian Andersen. At first I thought these stories naive, ridiculous and not interesting at all. But I dare not depreciate the value of the work for fear that I have too little knowledge to understand its merits. Later after I read some books related to folklore, I began to appreciate the value of the Grimms' fairy tales: the Brothers Grimm were scholars. They collected and recorded folklore without adding or deducting any content and made folklore suitable for scholarly research. (Zuoren, "Andersen" 149)

What impressed Zuoren was the alleged representation of the stories as they were told in real life and the sources of inspiration of the stories, namely, the general public, two features that were greatly emphasized during the whole course of the Movement.

As one of the earliest translators of the Grimm tales, Zuoren also frequently used them to illustrate some basic theoretical concepts in the study of either folklore literature or children's literature. The following is an example in which he quoted the Brothers Grimm's tales in 1922 to explain the difference between what he called "communal" and "literary" children's literature, emphasizing that only the former was the target of the Movement:

> Although communal children's literature is also literature, it actually differs from the so-called literary children's literature: the former is

communal, narrative, and natural; while the latter is personal, creative, and individual. Whereas the former is "the childhood of fiction," the latter is the embodiment of fiction, a combination with emotion and narration. People who record communal children's literature are folklorists, among whom the Brothers Grimm are famous examples; people who create literary children's literature are men of letters, among them [Oscar] Wilde. (Zuoren, "Wangerde Tonghua" 48)

The above review of articles by different activists of the Movement shows that although the Grimms' tales had been translated long before 1918, they did not exert much influence until the early 1920s. It was the launch of the Movement that triggered Chinese intellectuals' gradual attention to the Grimm tales, and not the other way round as claimed by Wu ("Tonghua Chuanbo de Wenhua Zhengzhi") and Fu and Yang.

The Movement's appreciation for the Brothers Grimm also led its participants to recognize the value of children's literature more than before, thus directly leading to the inclusion of children's literature as one of the targets for collection at the later stage of the Movement, after 1924, when Zhou Zuoren formally suggested that fairy tales be included in the Movement of folklore study.[2] The Chinese translation of the Grimms' tales instigated a polemic about whether children's literature is always moralizing or educational or whether value-free children's books can exist. If there are indeed two types of children's literature, the debate goes on as to which one should be read by children and modeled by China's indigenous writers.

While inspired by some of the ideas expressed by the Brothers Grimm about the study of folk literature, Zhou Zuoren actually held an ambivalent attitude to some of their stories, considering them to have too many moral overtones. When exchanging views with Zhao Jingshen, a Chinese expert on children's literature of that time, Zuoren argued that fairy tales should be free from teaching or indoctrination, especially of a moralistic or political nature. In his opinion, if fairy tales were to perform any function in children's education, "it should be literary rather than moral" (qtd. in Hung 123). His words seemed to be a direct attack on the popular acceptance of the Grimms' tales as a pedagogical tool in China at that time, where moral and educational intentions were usually highlighted. This pedagogical instrumentalization was not imposed by the Chinese translators but originates with the Grimms themselves. Indeed, the Brothers Grimm actually made it very clear in the preface to their *Kinder- und Hausmärchen* that they regarded it as an *Erziehungsbuch* (an educational book).

To some of the supporters of the Movement, such as Zhao Jingshen, the educational nature of the tales gave an extra incentive to introduce the Grimm tales rather than other foreign fairy tales to China, as their pedagogical purpose coincided with the aim of reforming the existing traditional Chinese culture by educating the Chinese masses through popular literature. In fact, Chinese scholars and translators liked the moral and educational intentions of the tales so much that they called them "educational fairy tales" (Hung 124) when they were translated on a large scale in China during the early 1920s. One scholar lauded the moralistic potential of the tales as follows: "In the tales there is a story entitled 'The wolf and the seven kids,' which a lot of German educators used to evoke the affection between mothers and their children. It is the most superior way of teaching to give children moralistic lessons by drawing on the stories in the Grimm collection" (Zhang, "Lun Tonghua" 6).

We do not know where the author learned of the use of the tale in Germany, but this pedagogical interpretation of the stories was gaining ground. The selection criteria of "containing no ridiculous, frightening, or offensive pieces" adopted by the Brothers Grimm already indicated that their tales "were suitable as references for pedagogical research. And their rigorous way of selecting tales is also worth learning by us" (Zhao 186). Even the language and the length of each story had a pedagogical function for Chinese children: "The sentences of the stories in the tales are short and concise. Each story is also of moderate length. All these fit into the mentality of children. . . . If somebody wants to use something as supplementary materials for teaching and as reading materials for children, he or she had better do some research on the Grimm tales" (Zhao 187). Zhao even called the Brothers Grimm "educational children's literature writers" (177).

However, it is largely this educational tendency as exhibited in the popular tales that prompted Zhou Zuoren to argue vigorously against children's literature that was tinged with moralistic or political teaching and that, in his opinion, lacked any value for Chinese children. To him, the true merit of fairy tales lay in "the meaning of meaninglessness" ("Ertong de Shu" 57). He went even further to claim that fairy tales should be devoid of "traditional moral norms" ("Tonghua yu Lunchang" 719) or "any political views" or "patriotic feelings" ("Guanyu" 713). When one of the most popular children's magazines *Xiao pengyou* (Little Child) published a special issue to promote products made in China and to advocate the boycotting of Japanese goods in 1923, Zhou raised an outcry against the practice and argued that "temporary political views should not be instilled into children's minds" ("Guanyu" 712). According to him, fairy tales, including children's literature, should be totally "value-free," excluding any explicit or implicit moral or political issues.

Zuoren's views stirred heated debates among Chinese intellectuals (including prominent scholars of that time such as Zhao Jingshen, Zhang Zisheng, Tai Shuangqiu, and Yan Jicheng), who were also attracted to the study of fairy tales and children's education partly because of the influence from the Movement. Some of these discussions appeared in the form of letters in magazines and newspapers. Most notable are the nine letters exchanged between Zhao Jingshen and Zhou Zuoren that were published in *Chenbao fukan* (the literary supplement to the *Chenbao* newspaper) in 1922 and the vehement exchanges between Zhao Jingshen and Zhang Zisheng in *Funü zazhi* (The Women's Magazine) in the same year (Wu, *Tonghua Beihou* 246). Their discussions aroused the general interest of the Chinese public and attracted more noted intellectuals to join the debate, which resulted in the very first serious discussion on children's literature (especially fairy tales) in China. Topics included the definition, function, and educational significance of fairy tales, methods for the translation and collection of Western fairy tales, and the merits and demerits of works by some of the well-known Western fairy tale writers, including the Grimm brothers, Hans Christian Andersen, and Oscar Wilde.[3]

Although some scholars seem to agree with Zuoren's proposal of value-free fairy tales and children's literature, most of them argued for upholding its moral and educational intentions. A full discussion of each writer's views is certainly beyond the scope of the present chapter, but it suffices to know that the Grimm tales sparked the above debate, which greatly deepened the general public's understanding about fairy tales—this new literary genre in China—as well as laying down a solid theoretical foundation for the study of contemporary fairy tales in China.

The Influence of the Grimms' Fairy Tales on the First-Generation Fairy-Tale Writers of China

To further explore how the tales have influenced the Movement, we shall briefly indicate how a story by Zhang Tianyi (1906–1985), a prominent author of modern literature (as opposed to traditional literature) whose fairy tales were among the earliest vernacular Chinese tales considered to be important landmarks of children's literature, shows clear traces of the Grimm tales in its subject matter and narrative structure.

Dalin he Xiaolin, one of the most famous fairy tales written by Zhang Tianyi in the early 1930s, tells a story about the adventures of ten-year-old twin brothers Dalin and Xiaolin after their parents die. One day they flee from a monster and lose contact with each other. Dalin is adopted by a millionaire and becomes a parasite only fond of eating and doing nothing. At the end he drifts to the Island of the Rich Man, where numerous treasures can be found but no food. Dalin dies of hunger on the island in the end because he does not know any practical survival skills. By contrast, Xiaolin works extremely hard and overcomes numerous hardships. He has a good heart and is always ready to help others. As a result, he earns his colleagues' respect and is able to make a good living.

Dalin he Xiaolin was lauded as one of the important landmarks of Chinese fairy tales. Ever since its publication, it has won high accolades from Chinese critics for its rich imagination, gripping plot, straightforward language and style, novel subject matter, and profound moral lessons. It is no overstatement when one scholar claimed that the story of *Dalin he Xiaolin* was "a brand new work that has opened a new chapter in the history of children's literature in China" (Jiang 357). But despite its revolutionary nature, we can actually find familiar traces from the Grimm tales in the story. First there is a similar narrative structure to that of the Grimms' "The Three Sons of Fortune." Both stories begin with children staying beside the deathbeds of their parents, listening to their final words.

The instructions are more or less the same too: Dalin and Xiaolin's parents ask them to bring something useful from home and to go to other places to look for jobs, whereas in "The Three Sons of Fortune," the father gives his three sons items to convey to places where they will be greatly valued and thus earn them a lot of money. In "The Three Sons of Fortune," the third son leaves his cat in a royal palace on a remote island—which reminds us of the rich man's island in *Dalin he Xiaolin,* as both of them are grand and full of treasures. Given these similarities, we may conclude that Zhang's story *Dalin he Xiaolin* has at least drawn some inspiration from the Chinese translation of "The Three Sons of Fortune," which was already available to the Chinese general public in the 1910s.

A second structural similarity to that found in many of the Grimms' tales is the use of numbers in *Dalin he Xiaolin*. The Grimms' tales frequently make use of symbolic numbers, especially the patterns of "three," "seven," and "twelve" (Zhang and Yang 291), for the title, the total number of characters, the frequency of events, or the number of times an event takes place. This tendency has also been imitated in *Dalin he Xiaolin,* in which the use of symbolic numbers abounds.[4] The ample use of figures in *Dalin he Xiaolin,* such as the chanting of *yi, er, san* (one, two, three) to indicate the character's preparation or run-up to an important event, mimics the language of children.

Third is the linear progression of the story. In Grimm tales, stories are usually organized according to the "linear–temporal narrative structure" (Zhang and Yang 292). Other temporal narrative structures, for example flashback or inserted narration, and other narrative frameworks, such as spatial narrative structure, were seldom used in the Grimm tales. These techniques keep the story lines and major plots arranged on a simple temporal dimension, which makes the story easily understandable, especially to children.

All these narrative features were also faithfully reproduced in *Dalin he Xiaolin,* as the story has a fixed temporal structure: first is the story of Xiaolin and what he encounters, which is followed by Dalin's adventures. Both their stories are organized strictly chronologically and the endings of the stories are natural consequences of the temporal narrative developments. Indeed, Zhang's use of the linear temporal narrative structure in the story was so successful and influential that it has almost become the default narrative scheme used by other contemporary Chinese writers of fairy tales, particularly longer ones. Although the linear narrative structure was also used in traditional Chinese folktales, typically through an omniscient third-person narrator, the narrator frequently juxtaposes one story with another and "constantly shifts his focus in storytelling" (Ding 1). In fact, very few Chinese folktales had observed the linear–temporal narrative structure so stringently as Tianyi did in *Dalin he Xiaolin.*

CONCLUSION

As one of the "most widely disseminated and translated works of German literature" (Blamires 163), Jacob and Wilhelm Grimm's *Kinder- und Hausmärchen* exerts enormous influence in many countries of the world. The impact of the

Grimm collection is not limited to the creation, together with the fairy tales of Hans Christian Andersen, of "the core of a new literary genre: the international fairytale" (Dollerup ix) but also helps to effect many changes in language, history, and national politics both at home and abroad. Whereas in Germany the Grimm tales also "proved to be a powerful element in the development of national consciousness" (Blamires 164), the Chinese translation of the tales fueled a nationwide Folk Literature Movement in the early 1920s.

The charting of the reception and impact of the tales in China as illustrated above amply demonstrates the seminal role played by the *Kinder- und Hausmärchen* in inspiring the proponents of the Movement to reexamine their rich folklore traditions and in influencing Zhang Tianyi to create a masterpiece of a modern Chinese fairy tale—*Dalin he Xiaolin.* It may be true that the activists of the Movement might, intentionally or unintentionally, have misinterpreted the Grimms' methodology and their stated intentions (as revealed, for example, in research by Heinz Rölleke)[5] to advance and promote their literary and political agenda, but their work testifies to the eternal charm and power of the *Kinder- und Hausmärchen* to influence the course of developing children's literatures.

NOTES

This research was supported in part by the Erasmus Mundus Action 2 program MULTI of the European Union, grant agreement number 2009-5259-5.

1. All translations from Chinese are my own.

2. This does not mean that before 1924, no fairy tales whatsoever were published in the magazines. In fact, in the early 1920s, Chinese and Western fairy tales were also frequently seen in some literary magazines of that time (see Hung 109). But the serious study of this genre did not begin until 1924, when Zhou Zuoren made an appeal to expand the subject of research in the Movement to children's literature.

3. Some of the notable contributors are Feng Fei, Yan Jicheng, Zheng Zhenduo, Guo Moruo, Hu Yuzhi, Zhang Wentian, Wang Fuquan, Xia Mianzun, Rao Shangda, Dai Weiqing, Zhou Bangdao, Chen Xuejia, Zhang Songling, and Zhong Fu (see Wu, *Tonghua Beihou* 249–53).

4. Different numbers are mentioned more than 1,700 times out of a total of 48,000 characters, accounting for 3.5 percent of the total words in the story.

5. I would like to thank the editors Dr. Gillian Lathey and Dr. Vanessa Joosen for drawing my attention to this point.

References

Bettelheim, Bruno. *The Uses of Enchantment: The Meaning and Importance of Fairy Tales.* New York: Vintage, 1977.

Blamires, David. "The Early Reception of the Grimms' *Kinder- und Hausmärchen* in England." *The Translation of Children's Literature: A Reader.* Ed. Gillian Lathey. Clevedon: Multilingual Matters, 2006. 163–74.

Ding, Naitong. *Zhongguo Minjian Gushi Leixing Suoyin.* Beijing: Zhongguo Minjian Wenyi Chubanshe, 1986.

Dollerup, Cay. *Tales and Translation: The Grimm Tales from Pan-Germanic Narratives to Shared International Fairy Tales.* Amsterdam: John Benjamins, 1999.

Fu, Pinjin, and Xi Yang. "Gelin Tonghua zai Zhongguo de Jingdianhua Yanjiu." *Masterpiece Review* 24 (2011): 150–52.

Fu, Pinjin, and Yang Wuneng. "Gelin tonghua zai Zhongguo de Yijie yu Jieshou." *Comparative Literature in China* 2 (2008): 94–101.

Haase, Donald. *Fairy Tales and Feminism: New Approaches.* Detroit: Wayne State UP, 2004. Fairy-Tale Studies.

Hu, Yuzhi. "Lun Minjian Wenxue." *Ershi Shiji Zhongguo Minsuxue Jingdian—Minsu Lilun Juan.* 1921. Ed. Li Yuan. Beijing: Shehui kexue wenxian chubanshe, 2002. 3–9.

Hung, Chang-tai. *Going to the People. Chinese Intellectuals and Folk Literature, 1918–1937.* Cambridge: Council on East Asian Studies, Harvard University, 1985.

Jiang, Feng. "Zhang Tianyi he Ta de Dalin he Xiaolin." *Zhang Tianyi Yanjiu Ziliao.* Ed. Shen Chenkuan. Beijing: Zhonguo Shehui Kexue Chubanshe, 1982. 357–60.

Peppard, Murray. *Paths through the Forest, a Biography of the Brothers Grimm.* New York: Holt, Rinehart and Winston, 1971.

Wang, Lijun. " 'New *Youth*' and the Provenance of Modern Children's Literature in China." *Collection of Research on Modern Chinese Literature* 5 (2010): 167–76.

Wu, Hongyu. *Tonghua Beihou de Lishi—Xifang Tonghua yu Zhongguo Shehui (1900–1937).* Taipei: Taiwan Student Book Company, 2010.

———. "Tonghua Chuanbo de Wenhua Zhengzhi—Lun Gelin Tonghua de Deguo Shengchan yu Zhongguo Zaisheng." *Journal of Sino-Western Cultural Studies* 1 (2007): 153–55.

Zhang, Qin, and Yang Min. "Gelin Tonghua zai Zhongguo." *The World Literature Criticism* 1 (2007): 290–93.

Zhang, Zisheng. "Lun Tonghua." *Tonghua Pinglun.* 1921. Ed. Jinshen Zhao. Shanghai: Xinwenhua chubanshe, 1928. 1–8.

Zhao, Jingshen. "Tonghuajia Gelin Dixiong Zhuanlue." *Tonghua Lunji.* Ed. Zhao Jingshen. Shanghai: Xinwenhua chubanshe, 1928. 177–88.

Zhong, Jinwen. "*Dao Minjian Qu* Zhongyiben Xu." Trans. Dong Xiaoping. *Dao Minjian Qu: 1918–1937 Nian de Zhongguo Zhishifenzi yu Minjian Wenxue Yundong*. Ed. Hong Chang-tai. Shanghai: Shanghai wenyi chubanshe, 1993. 1–16.

———. "Wusi Shiqi Minsu Wenhuaxue de Xingqi." *Journal of Social Science of Jiamusi University* 4 (1999): 1–9.

———. *Zhong Jingwen Minjian Wenxue Lunji*. Shanghai: Shanghai wenyi chubanshe, 1982.

Zuoren, Zhou. "Andersen de 'Shi zhi Jiu.'" *Tan Long Ji*. 1927. Ed. Zuoren Zhou. Shijiazhuang: Hebei jiaoyu chubanshe, 2002. 148–53.

———. "Ertong de Shu." *Ertong Wenxue Xiaolun*. 1923. Ed. Zuoren Zhou. Shijiazhuang: Hebei jiaoyu chubanshe, 2002. 55–58.

———. "Guanyu Ertong de Shu." *Zhou Zuoren Wenleibian·Shangxiashen*. 1923. Ed. Shuhe Zhong. Changsha: Hunan wenyi chubanshe, 1998. 712–15.

———. "Tonghua yu Lunchang." *Zhou Zuoren Wenleibian·Shangxiashen*. 1924. Ed. Shuhe Zhong. Changsha: Hunan wenyi chubanshe, 1998. 719–20.

———. "Wangerde Tonghua." *Ziji de Yuandi*. 1922. Ed. Zuoren Zhou. Beijing: Renmin wenxue chubanshe, 1998. 47–50.

7

The Grimm Brothers' Kahaniyan

Hindi Resurrections of the Tales
in Modern India by Harikrishna Devsare

MALINI ROY

> I hope that this timeless achievement of world literature will
> be welcomed by the world of Indian children's literature, and
> by Indian child readers, as a unique gift on the occasion of the
> golden anniversary of India's Independence.
>
> Devsare I.10

Fairy tales and folklore, whenever discussed in relation to India, usually conjure up visions of ancient folktale collections such as *The Panchatantra,* whose
tales have long circulated in medieval and modern Europe owing to early
routes of traffic, trade, and military conquest (Bottigheimer 1). In modern
times, however, the fairy tales of the Brothers Grimm have also found a *Heimat* in India. The excerpt above is from a selection of tales from the *Kinder-
und Hausmärchen,* translated into Hindi as *Grimm Bandhuon Ki Kahaniyan*
(2000, The Grimm Brothers' Tales) by children's author Harikrishna Devsare
and concludes one of his four essays that accompany the tales.[1] Devsare is an
award-winning children's author and holds a doctorate in Hindi children's
literature. He has also translated Hans Christian Andersen's tales, and his
oeuvre for children includes science fiction and television drama.[2] *Grimm
Bandhuon* is published by the Sahitya Akademi (the Indian National Academy of Letters); thus, the text bears connotations of a certain measure of
literary quality in the Indian book market. Devsare's translation has won

a dedicated readership: there have been successive reprints (in 2004, 2007, 2008, and 2009) as well as plagiaries and piracies in a market with loose enforcement of copyright laws in publications attributed to authors such as Shravani Mukharji and Chitra Varerkar.

This chapter aims at a critical appreciation of Devsare's translation, which addresses reading communities unfamiliar with the Grimms' tales as direct reading material or in broad cultural circulation through other media. Devsare, advertising the métier of his publication, observes that *Grimm Bandhuon* is the first comprehensive translation in Hindi, signifying a "supremely important endeavour" to bring out "these achievements of world children's literature in Indian languages" and aimed particularly at children. Devsare admits that the Grimms' tales have been known in India but as "expensive sets in English" (*Grimm Bandhuon* I.7–8). As with many translations of the Grimms' German collection in Asian languages, these tales were probably introduced to the Indian subcontinent through English translations, particularly through the mechanisms of the former British Empire (Dollerup 278–79; see also Lathey 162–70). However, Devsare overstates his claim for *Grimm Bandhuon* as a first in "Indian languages": translations of the tales in Bengali, for instance, have long been available.[3] Nonetheless, there is some justice in Devsare's claim that his Hindi translation, in contrast to "expensive sets in English," vastly widens access to the Grimms' tales for "Indian children" (*Grimm Bandhuon* I.7). This is a phenomenon that can only be fully understood with reference to the surrounding nexus of linguistic, historical, and sociocultural determinants.

Way back in the 1830s, colonial politician and orator Thomas Babington Macaulay famously argued for his program "to form a class" who might become "interpreters between us [the colonial rulers]" and the "millions whom we govern; a class of persons, Indian in blood and colour, but English in taste, in opinions, in morals, and in intellect" ("Macaulay's Minute on Indian Education"). The post-Independence educational system in India has largely continued to perpetuate the formation of this "class of persons" with English minds, as demonstrated by postcolonial scholar Gauri Viswanathan in his 1989 *Masks of Conquest* (3–12). The readers of the Grimms' tales in English are likely to be children from "English-medium" schools (that is, schools where pupils learn English as a first language), and the tales themselves are often known colloquially as "English Fairy Tales," despite the historical origins of the collection within the cultural currents of German Romanticism.[4]

Today, a stark class divide still persists (with some modification) between the English-educated classes and the masses attuned to "Indian languages" such as Hindi: publishers and booksellers observe that English books tend to cost at least twice the price of Indian vernacular-language books, while glitzy pan-Indian lifestyle bookstore chains (such as Crossword) often stock a majority of English titles and a nominal number of vernacular books. The latter are sold in less upmarket outlets such as roadside stalls and bought by readers commonly based in semiurban areas or the rural interiors.[5]

The magnitude of Devsare's task can be gauged by appreciating that his translation addresses this less privileged milieu, which remains underrepresented on the global stage in proportion to its size and local significance, in contrast to the (pan-Indian) English-educated classes. Folklore scholar Sadhana Naithani has observed incisively that the legacies of the British Empire from "the late nineteenth and early twentieth centuries" remain instrumental to modern geopolitics in the positions of nations ranging from the United States to India; today, the "postcolonial world" is largely "the world after the Empire" (*Story-Time* ix). In folktale and fairy-tale scholarship dominated by the Euro-American academy (historically linked to the continued leverage of the West), English-language texts in postcolonial sites are more accessible than texts in other languages such as Hindi, which are liable to be overlooked, although Hindi is today (potentially) one of the five most commonly spoken languages in the world.

Of a modern Indian population of over a billion, native speakers of Hindi alone (not counting the many who speak it in addition to their mother tongues) constitute at least double the number of (native or nonnative) English speakers in India. Even though regular readership for pleasure in Hindi is probably practiced by only a part of the total, this part still comprises a readership at least comparable in size to English-language readers in India.[6] In reflecting in a nuanced way on the demographics of Devsare's readership, this chapter is conceptually indebted to recent trends in postcolonial scholarship that have foregrounded important sociocultural differences within postcolonial sites (Jain 21; Spivak 1–13, 136).

Devsare's *Grimm Bandhuon,* produced at the turn of this century, exhibits some anachronistic continuities with reading formations of the Grimms' tales in India from the colonial era. But in introducing a new range of reading material from world literature into the local book market, his translation also deviates from these formations as he appropriates the source texts in the process of translation, working to socialize child readers growing up under the aegis of the modern Indian nation-state. Jack Zipes, in his extended studies of the impact of the Grimms' tales especially in Germany and the United States, has noted that the Grimms' tales have been co-opted into the sociopolitical values of modern nation-states to enforce respective hegemonic norms. My aim is to extend the scope of such critical under-standings of the Grimms' tales, weighted toward Western contexts, into that of modern India (Zipes, *Fairy Tales* 59–60; *Brothers Grimm* 21–22). Some of Devsare's readings of the tales are startling in view of current critical tenets in the field of global folktale and fairy-tale studies, even as he brings unfamiliar interpretations to bear on the texts and in the process opens up possible aspects to the tales not covered in the current critical literature. For instance, Devsare gestures toward the potential deployment of the tales to promote the cause of gender equality. Furthermore, even as he professedly welcomes these fairy tales, he rings a note of caution at the relevance and usefulness of the genre within his vision of a contemporary India, moored in a landscape of secular modernity. Devsare's idiosyncratic views are expressed chiefly in his vocal and voluminous prefatory material—which this arti-cle therefore foregrounds—rather than the tales themselves, which follow the plot and content of the Grimms closely.

A key factor to consider about Devsare's translation is the timing of his publication with respect to genre. Although "English fairy tales," as noted above, have had a presence in India since colonial times, recent trends in the book market have led to "retellings" of Indian-origin folktales receiving a fresh lease on life through innovative publishing ventures and new media. In the global market, Indian publishers have released collections of Indian folk-tales augmented by quality illustrations based on folk art traditions. These include Tara, with its exquisitely handcrafted books and Tulika, which of-fers bilingual books with text in English and a vernacular Indian language. Karadi Tales has brought out a growing repertoire of audiobooks based on folktale collections, including *The Panchatantra* and the *Jatakas* and episodes from the epics *Ramayana* and *Mahabharata*. Correspondingly, the local mar-ket appears to be less receptive to European fairy tales.[7] Devsare's translation inhabits a space in the Indian book market that is in the process of becoming marginal, although the Grimms' tales remain vibrant, if limited presences in creative arts communities, such as the performance repertoire of the World Storytelling Institute based at Chennai in Southern India.[8]

That English-language translations, rather than the German originals, have largely contributed to the global dissemination of the Grimms' tales was mentioned above, and Devsare's translation fits into this model, as he admits freely, although he does not mention his exact source text (*Grimm Bandhuon* I.9). Indeed, the dependence on English sources has been standard for translations of texts of (non-English) world literature into vernacular languages in India since colonial times (Ahmad 243–85).[9] However Devsare, unlike many other translators, is also keenly self-aware of this historical linguistic aspect of his translation (probably expressing his scholarly proclivities) and foregrounds this aspect in his essays by discussing the first English translation of the Grimms' tales by Edgar Taylor, with illustrations by George Cruikshank, "a well-known artist of the era." He grounds the ensuing popularity of the tales in England by invoking an early scholarly study in English, *A Critical History of Children's Literature* from 1969 (Devsare, *Grimm Bandhuon* I.13, 18). Devsare further observes that the Taylor–Cruikshank translation was followed by a number of other translations in England, mentioning especially those illustrated by Victorian artists Walter Crane and Arthur Rackham (see Zipes, *Brothers Grimm* 156–59). He goes on to imply that these English translations were the sources for "translations into other languages over the world" and that "this is an ongoing process"—a claim with some empirical basis, even as it serves to subtly justify Devsare's own dependence on English-language sources (Devsare, *Grimm Bandhuon* I.19; see Dollerup 278–79).

Naturally, the "English fairy tales" by the Grimms, in Devsare's translation, carry implications beyond the accident of a linguistic choice conditioned historically through a colonial past; these implications include the politics of translation borne out for an audience unfamiliar with the cultural vocabulary of the European source texts. Devsare usually renders elements of local color from his sources faithfully. These elements, culturally specific to nineteenth-century, Christian, northwestern (rather than specifically German) Europe are left as normative and unexplained (unannotated) to the contemporary north Indian readership, which is unlikely to be familiar with the religious and social significance of these elements, composed as it is of a largely Hindu population with some Muslim and other minorities.

Among the Christian elements, the paraphernalia of institutional religion in the Grimms such as churches may not present problems of comprehension to the target audience.[10] In "The Two Travelers," when a good tailor and an evil cobbler must pass through a deep forest to reach a city, Devsare retains the simile of the forest being as silent "as a church" and the context makes the simile self-explanatory (*Grimm Bandhuon*, II.167). However, when Devsare repeats popular iconographic or folkloric elements, key meanings of the tales get lost in translation. "The Two Travelers," for instance, features a talking stork that brings a baby to the queen in order to help the tailor out of his predicament. Here, the stork seems to perform the feat out of mere coincidence, instead of having lived up to its reputation in European folklore as a bringer of babies (II.166–76). In "The Three Journeymen," the protagonists meet a stranger on the street. One of the journeymen, noticing that the stranger's feet have hooves, concludes that he is the devil. This surmise, however, would not be self-evident to a reader unversed in the relevant visual references. Moreover, Devsare does not clarify the stranger's identity after the journeyman's observation but merely refers to him as a "bad person" henceforth; the clumsy epithet misses out the theological resonance of the stranger's true identity (I.67–70).

Other folkloric beings, too, get diffused into an unhelpful vagueness, failing to communicate the vivid quality of the Grimms' tales. In "The Elves: First Tale," which relates the story of the shoemaker and his wife who are helped out of poverty by elves, the everyday earthiness of these uncanny little folk is regrettably sublimated in the Hindi equivalent *devdoot*, which signifies angels or cherubs (Devsare, *Grimm Bandhuon* I.190–91). An accurate translation may prove difficult here because the fine categories of European little folk—pixies, elves, sprites, and so on—are absent in the pantheon of supernatural beings in Indian folklore.[11] This is not to suggest that Devsare ought to have weighed his translations down with explanatory marginalia— after all, any text presented to an audience unfamiliar with the source may get lost in translation, and adventurous readers are often willing to take on this risk.

However, the problematic neocolonial implications of Devsare's presentation of a Western text for an Indian audience can be illuminated by a contrast with collections of Indian folktales for a Western audience. *Folktales from India* (Pantheon, 1994) by the well-known poet and scholar A. K. Ramanujan was published in New York in the same decade. Ramanujan supported his collection with an exhaustive introduction to the volume and explanatory notes to each tale, and Western readers appreciated his presentation of material from a distant culture in a manner that avoided possibilities of "confusion"

("Customer Reviews"). Without perhaps intending to, Ramanujan's deliberate urge to prevent "confusion" has exoticized and simplified his source culture as a cultural "other" to his primarily English-speaking American readership and lends itself to the critical discussion inaugurated by postcolonial scholar Tejaswini Niranjana in her seminal study *Siting Translation* (1992).

Niranjana has demonstrated that the translation of Indian-origin texts perpetuated cultural imperialism in the process of constructing and appropriating the other. With regard to Ramanujan's translation of a medieval Kannada poem from Southern India, Niranjana (drawing on poststructuralist theory) criticizes his tendency to "smooth over the heterogeneous text" for his readers, offering an alternative translation of her own that preserves the "disruptive" force of the original (Niranjana 163–86). Devsare's corresponding lack of desire, therefore, to "smooth over" the culturally specific elements within his source texts can be placed within the neocolonial legacies of inherited unequal positions between the West and the Rest. His translation does not treat the knowledge needs of the target audience with the same solicitude as Ramanujan; Ramanujan's annotations were welcomed by Western readers. Devsare's Hindi translation thus preserves and perpetuates the epistemological violence wreaked by colonial legacies of cultural imperialism, originally exercised in English.

The neocolonial provenances in Devsare's English-language sources make for but one aspect of *Grimm Bandhuon*. An equally important, if contradictory, aspect to his work is his appropriation of the tales to deliver a panegyric on nationalistic feeling in the service of the modern Indian nation-state. This he accomplishes through his appreciation of these tales as artifacts of distinctly German (rather than English) culture and heritage. Certainly, his enterprise is bolstered by the support of his publisher, the state-accredited Sahitya Akademi. Despite his admission that he used English sources, Devsare stakes out his sensitivity to the German aspect of the tales by claiming fidelity to the Grimms' original work, professing that his objective has been to "keep the soul of the Grimm brothers intact." He credits this claim by citing his own research at the Max Mueller Bhavan in New Delhi (the cultural wing of the German Embassy in India) and his consultation of experts on German literature (Devsare, *Grimm Bandhuon* 1.9).

In order to situate the importance of the Grimms' tales to German national identity, Devsare frames their lives and work as a seamless and ahistorical myth, evading disruptions and contradictions in his narrative. The very

title of his translation hints at this process. He characterizes the Brothers as *bandhuon*, which is, technically, a mistranslation of their sibling relationship, more properly meaning "kin" in Hindi, but his poetic term enlivens a sense of their strong mutual attachment. Furthermore, with a creative writer's practiced élan, Devasare offers a superlative eulogy of the Grimms' work as a nation-building project as he sketches the arduous process of their collection and recording of the tales. His second essay, titled "Preservers of Immortal Folklore: The Brothers Grimm," discusses the Grimms' scholarly interest in folk culture. Here he recapitulates the Grimms' claim, as put forth by Wilhelm in the preface to the 1819 edition, that they gathered their stories from peasants in the countryside (*Grimm Bandhuon* 1.11–17).

Devasare invests the collection with the textual authority of a document that was a true record of the results of an ethnographic exercise by two neutral observers of simple, unpolished, and homely tales. In situating the Grimms' archival work, Devasare's account remains underwritten by the nostalgic myth of a unified, seamless culture of the *Volk* as expressed in oral sources, which evinced faded but pure, authentic, and uncontaminated remnants of a supposedly shared German past that went back to ancient Germanic roots (Bottigheimer 5). In gesturing toward the Grimms' attempts to recover this heritage, Devasare remarks that the Grimms' work was not produced in iso-lation but formed part of a general privileging of folk culture within the his-torical and cultural tendencies of German Romanticism. He also mentions the Grimms' differences with Clemens Brentano in their attempts to remain more faithful to their source material (*Grimm Bandhuon* 1.15).

Devasare thus promotes a critically regressive view of the Grimms' work that has been seriously interrogated in twentieth-century scholarship, espe-cially since the 1970s (Zipes, *Brothers Grimm* 10–11).[12] His privileging of the Grimms' collection, posited upon a nostalgic and essentialist construct of the *Volk* made up of peasants, has itself been recognized now by folklore scholars as problematic; as folklorist Frank Korom has clarified, "folklore" does not exist "as an empirical bit of reality" apart from its "academic crea-tion." There is "nothing in the realm of human experience that is intrinsi-cally folkloric" (9).

Although Devasare considers the textual alterations made by the Grimms in their editorial methods, particularly by Wilhelm, he tends to stake out their fidelity to their sources. Devasare underplays the extent of the Grimms' alterations and envisages them in a merely cosmetic role, portraying the tenor

of their work as an anthology rather than an act of creative engagement with their source material reflecting their own ideological leanings. He mentions the successive editions of the *Kinder- und Hausmärchen* but explains them in terms of their progressively child-friendly orientation—or at least what adults thought was so—through the gradual removal of content and language deemed inappropriate. Deosare also gestures with nuance at variants of tales with similar plots in the Grimms' collection as texts created through their recording of different storytelling performances (*Grimm Bandhuon* 1.13; see Korom 1–15). But he does not tease out the possible implications of this phenomenon to consider that each folktale presented in the collection might be a palimpsest of different tellers, nor does he consider the literary sources (books, journals, letters, and such) that the Grimms' occasionally drew their stories from (Zipes, *Brothers Grimm* 50–51).

Unsurprisingly, Deosare's discussion of the Grimms' collection remains bounded within national borders in line with the Grimms' attempts to unify the three hundred different warring German states into a single nation, as a response to the French occupation following the Napoleonic Wars (*Grimm Bandhuon* 1.9; Zipes, *Brothers Grimm* 78). Deosare presents German culture as unitary, praising the Grimms' efforts to preserve an imagined and shared Germanic mythic past through a cultural sense of authentic Germanness, as he subscribes to the political fiction of the nation as an "imagined community," to invoke Benedict Anderson's watershed theorization of such social constructions (6–9). Thus, Deosare's account resurrects a latter-day nationalism as he reads the Grimms' collection as an authentic national record, downplaying the brothers' transnational sources and correspondences and transformations from French, Italian, and other European (and possibly non-European) cultures.

Tellingly, when Deosare brings in a hint of French influence, it is only to mark the Grimms' affinity with French counterparts in terms of style rather than content: he notes that the "tellers of the tales . . . must have been influenced by the popularity of French fairy tales and their flair for entertainment" (*Grimm Bandhuon* 1.21) although scholarly commentary on the Grimms elsewhere has emphasized the French Huguenot ancestry and culture of one of the Grimms' chief sources for their tales, the Hassenpflug family (Zipes, *Brothers Grimm* 10–11, 114). Deosare's admiration and consequent appropriation of the Grimms' nationalism thus unriddles his comfortable accommodation of this key text of German Romanticism as

"a unique gift on the occasion of the golden anniversary of India's Indepen-dence" (*Grimm Bandhuon* I.10). In this context it is striking that Devsare's account marks the traffic of these tales from Germany into world literature, and thus to Indian children's literature, but remains silent on the voluminous and recurrent discussions on ancient Indian culture in German works of the late eighteenth and early nineteenth centuries.[13]

In appropriating the Grimms' tales for the Indian state in *Grimm Band-huon*, Devsare's essays express the pedagogical hope that the Grimms' tales, in the avatar of children's literature, will "acquaint" young readers "with the truths of life," informing them about "society, people and traditions" (*Grimm Bandhuon* I.7, 13), although he does not envisage the tales primarily for classroom use, accenting their qualities of imaginative largesse instead. Accordingly, he indicates certain paradigms for the socialization of children, in the vein that the Grimms themselves hinted at when they referred to their own early edition as an *Erziehungsbuch*, or childrearing/educational manual (Bottigheimer 4; Zipes, *Fairy Tales* 59–79). This hint has been enthusiasti-cally taken up in critical commentary on the Grimms, not least on the score of the (allegedly) sexist messages of the tales. Devsare considers the gender politics of the tales at some length and, in tune with state ideologies favoring women's empowerment, veers off from recent critical trends in his outright claim that the Grimms wished to "erase gender disparity" (*Grimm Band-huon* II.8). His observations are occasionally more remarkable for verve than persuasiveness; nevertheless, they are worth consideration for their alternate interpretive perspectives.

Key to Devsare's readings is these tales' potential to underline the "impor-tance of the girl child in society," instrumentally endorsing progressive lines for a highly topical concern in India from the late twentieth century onward. The issue has been the focus of rising public awareness and state attention in a largely patriarchal society in which female feticide remains a rampant and horrifying reality ("Female foeticide"). Devsare's observation seems justified, to some extent, in the case of the female characters he identifies as picaresque or wanderer heroes similar to young men.

Comparing the story variants "The Twelve Brothers" and "The Seven Ravens" with similar plotlines (and ascribing their disjunctures to different storytelling performances recorded by the Grimms), Devsare notes that the presence of a newborn sister is the source of the brothers' banishment and subsequent miseries in both tales. Yet, when the sisters grow up and learn of

their brothers' situations, they set out in search of them, proving their equal strengths (*Grimm Bandhuon* II.9). Elsewhere, Devsare points to the many wanderer heroes in the Grimms, male or female, who are presented as models to be emulated, recapitulating what many scholars of the Romantic period have observed about the cultural privileging of the wanderer hero as a bourgeois entrepreneur, capable of endless self-transformation (*Grimm Bandhuon* I.19; Zipes, *Magic Spell* 74–79; Henderson 60–62). Devsare's reading controverts the critical tendency of a canonical study on the subject of the Grimms' gender politics such as Ruth Bottigheimer's *Grimms' Bold Girls and Bad Boys,* which reads "male transgressors" as occupying a privileged position compared to their female counterparts. According to Bottigheimer, the former escape the consequences of trespassing social mores, much like folkloric trickster figures, while the latter are invariably punished for similar acts of rebellion (82).

In another instance, Devsare, observing the story variants "The Twelve Brothers," "The Seven Ravens," and "The Seven Swans," readily concedes that they show wandering girls suffering "in silence" as they attempt to relieve their brothers through expiatory vows of muteness. He notes that such silence is ultimately rewarded at the end of the tales, as the female protagonists rescue their brothers at the last minute before being burnt at the stake for witchcraft and win back their royal husbands' love as well (*Grimm Bandhuon* I.23). Devsare highlights these protagonists' silence in the aspect of suffering rather than reward, positing that these tales push for women's equality by eliciting readers' sympathetic identification through the strategic representation of violence against women. By contrast, Bottigheimer notes that these three tales progressively "weaken the figure of the sister" in the Grimms' "numerically ordered sequence," pointing to female silence as a desired value for women in the brothers' patriarchal schema (36–39). Devsare observes a similar indictment of violence against women by the Grimms in the cases of Cinderella and Snow White, noting that they bear their stepmothers' and stepsisters' merciless sarcasm "in silence" (*Grimm Bandhuon* I.23). For Bottigheimer, instead, the Grimms' Cinderella exemplifies the "textual silence and powerlessness" of the "titular protagonist," while the vulnerability of both heroines is accentuated by the "narrative, textual, and lexical silence" of their birth mothers, whose deaths lead to the plot complications whereby their daughters are abused by their stepmothers (35–36).

While Devsare reads (potentially) emancipated gender politics into the Grimms' tales, his enthusiasm for the genre is tempered by a sense of their ambivalent possibilities, as he presents the translation to his readership with critical distance toward the collection. Referring to international public discourse on the UNESCO International Year of the Child in 1979, Devsare quotes the views of Ecuadorian writer Jorge Enrique Adoum with approval.[14] Here, Devsare recalls Adoum's anxious hypothesis: fairy tales might delude young women into familiar and restrictive models of female domesticity. Consequently, young women might start living in fantasy worlds and lose their belief and capacities for transformative self-empowerment in the real world: "For most women the dream of Cinderella turns into the cruel reality of Snow White." The latter earns shelter by her consent to "make the beds, cook food, wash clothes, sew and knit for the dwarves and keep everything clean" (*Grimm Bandhuon* I.23). Devsare goes on to second Adoum's view that children in underprivileged contexts might be especially vulnerable to the beguiling dreams of fairy-tale plots—a claim that perhaps reflects social realities in large parts of Latin America, mirroring conditions of poverty and deprivation present in modern India.

Devsare frames Adoum's invective within a general critique of fairy tales, pointing out that the genre inhabits a contested site, potentially harmful in its delusive power and out of step with the zeitgeist of "modern culture" and the values of "civilized societies." Eschewing a commercially minded spirit (for his publication of a fairy-tale collection), and recalling perhaps his own experience in writing science fiction, Devsare articulates doubt about the genre's relevance and usefulness in his perception of a contemporary world of primarily secular values. Indeed, some of his arguments run counter to the current vogue for folktales in Indian children's publishing. Quoting his own article from 1962, Devsare rejects outmoded "epics and folktales" for "the kind of literature that acquaints children" with "the changing age" of "rockets, the moon, citizenship and ethics."

In a more tendentious vein, Devsare questions the relevance of tales with "kings and queens" as protagonists, pointing out that monarchy is a remnant of courtly and feudal culture, outworn in a world of democratic, capitalist modernity (*Grimm Bandhuon* I.24–25). Possibly, Devsare has in mind here the Indian state's derecognition of princely kingdoms and their maharajas (from colonial times) as political forces in 1971, together with their formal incorporation into national parliamentary democracy (Ramusack 66–89). In view of Devsare's sympathies with the bourgeois values of the modern Indian nation-state, his skepticism toward fairy tales and his engagement with twentieth-century ideological concerns about the form and function of fairy tales (such as the UNESCO-related debate about the delusive rather than transformative potential of the genre) can be appreciated in terms of a similarly socially constructivist agenda.

CONCLUSION

Devsare does not stand alone in his skepticism toward the Grimms' tales; his incertitude about the genre voices a collective cultural concern in modern India. Some current publishers feel a sense of overkill with the enthusiasm for folktales and fairy tales, especially those of Indian origin, in the global/Western (and the local) market and share Devsare's support for stories of contemporary modernity. Manasi Subramaniam, editor at folktale publisher Karadi Tales, regrets that "innovation" is not highly valued in Indian children's publishing today, observing that the rise of "homegrown folklore" appears to have consigned "contemporary, original children's writing in India" to obscurity (Subramaniam).[15] These writers' and publishers' discontented voices register, it appears, a resistance to what they perceive to be a conservative Eurocentric elision of narratives of secular modernity from the Indian subcontinent by means of a simultaneous dwelling on tales from a seemingly frozen and static past.

The paradigm appears to work today in the publishing industry as a modified form of the cultural phenomenon of "Orientalism," famously identified and critiqued by Edward Said, and subsequent postcolonial theory, whereby the East has been stereotyped as the timeless repository of the traditional and the West perceived as the abode of modernity and innovation. Devsare's troubled preface, favoring stories about twentieth-century astronomical wonders of journeys to the moon over the archaic adventures of kings and queens, ends up subverting his enthusiasm for the Grimms tales' offer of "endless entertainment, romance, [and] curiosity" (*Grimm Bandhuon* I.7, 25).

Despite Devsare's professed fidelity to his sources and his reluctance to tinker with the tales themselves—which he treats as a hallowed original source—his Hindi translation is framed with resistance to his source texts. His tempered celebration of the Grimms totters on the brink of cancelling the raison d'être for his translation and requires their internationally validated status as a "timeless achievement of world literature"—an avowal of Matthew Arnold's classic, culturally elitist slogan in favor of "the best which has been thought and said in the world." In overriding his own hesitancy in presenting his translation to millions of readers on the Indian subcontinent, Devsare's *Grimm Bandhuon* hovers within a peculiar marriage of loyalty and compromise between the cultures of the local and the global.

NOTES

All translations from the Hindi are my own.

1. Volume 1 contains three essays, titled "Foreword: This Timeless Achievement" (7–10), "Preservers of Immortal Folklore: The Brothers Grimm" (11–14), and "Tales by the Brothers Grimm" (15–26), and Volume 2 has one essay titled "Foreword."

2. Harikrishna Devsare, *Hans Andersen Ki Kahaniyan*; "Non-governmental Awards"; "H K Devsare Wins First 'Vatsalya Award' for Children's Literature."

3. Discussing Hindi translations of the Grimms, Devsare lists some previous translations in ephemeral media such as magazines, but he presents these translations as desultory productions, rarely attributed to the Grimms (*Grimm Bandhuon* I.7–8). For an example of a Bengali translation of the Grimms' tales, see Gangopadhyay, *Grimm Bhaider Rupkatha* (1963, The Fairy Tales of the Brothers Grimm). It may well be that Devsare is unaware of such translations in Indian languages other than Hindi. The lack of information is plausible in a country as linguistically and culturally diverse as India—the state recognizes at least twenty-two major languages ("Abstract of Speakers' Strength of Languages").

4. This view is largely based on anecdotal evidence. Writer Rumjhum Biswas, who has published a retelling of "Rumpelstiltskin" titled *Batul and the Rumpel* in an online literary magazine, observes that according to some people she has "interacted" with, many European "fairy tales were adapted for children's text books" in India, presumably during colonial times and beyond. Based on this observation, Biswas has her protagonist, Batul, invoke this pedagogical material as "English fairy tales" in the retelling.

5. Meera de Condappa, e-mail message to the author, 18 Aug. 2011; Coonoor Kripalani-Thadani, personal interview, 27 Aug. 2011.

6. According to the Indian government's census reports in 2001, over 400 million people claimed Hindi as their mother tongue, while the number of Hindi speakers (native and nonnative) constituted at least 550 million. In comparison, the number of native or nonnative speakers of English was only 125 million, though this number may have increased with global traffic in a growing economy.

7. Manasi Subramaniam, editor at Karadi Tales, offers an authoritative, historicized perspective on the current rise of Indian folktales with the decline of European

fairy tales in this market. Subramaniam recalls that historically until the 1980s, the children's publishing sector was underwritten by "educational content" in a market in an industry almost entirely constituted by "textbook publishers." In the 1990s, radical alterations in state policy led to the opening up of the previously nationalized market, and the entry of multinational companies gave a boost to trade publishing but made little impact on the "textbook hangover." Even today, the notion of "fun for its own sake" has not proved popular in this market; the "major demand" is for books related to school syllabi or as bearers of "knowledge." According to Subramaniam, this deep-rooted fondness for didacticism may be understood as a vestige of Indian "fable culture," which continues to find expression in the revived popularity and abundance of retellings of stories from *The Panchatantra* and the *Jatakas* in the "children's section" of contemporary bookstores. Subramaniam also feels that these folktales seem to "appeal more to the desire of parents for 'moral stories,'" as opposed to the less overtly didactic fairy tales of the Grimms and Andersen, which appear to have "dwindled in the market."

8. Eric Miller, e-mail messages to the author, 2 May, 4 May, 5 May 2011.

9. Very often, such translations emerge from a hack culture in which linguistic fidelity to the source text is rarely a concern for the publisher or bookseller. Anil Varma, well-known New Delhi-based distributor of Devsare's works and other Hindi books, sums up the activity of such translators as just "doing the job" (Anil Varma, e-mail message to the author, 27 Apr. 2011).

10. See Bottigheimer (143–55). She offers an illuminating discussion of scholarly traditions of Christian exegesis of the tales. Indian Christians, although a significant presence, form a religious minority of just over 2 percent of the entire population ("Census Data 2001").

11. See note 9.

12. Zipes draws attention especially to Heinz Rölleke's edited *Die älteste Märchensammlung der Brüder Grimm* (1975), which shows the successive changes that the texts of the Grimms' handwritten manuscripts went through (once they were recovered in the early twentieth century). See also John Ellis's *One Fairy Story Too Many* (1983) and Maria Tatar's *The Hard Facts of the Grimms' Fairy Tales* (2003).

13. The Schlegel brothers' work was key to these indological drifts: Friedrich Schlegel's interest in myths and his study of the Sanskrit language led him to argue, in the tract "On the Language and Wisdom of the Indians," for linguistic and philological affinities between the then newly conceived German nation and ancient India. As premier linguists, the Grimms would have been aware of these currents (Figuiera 517–26).

14. Devsare's Hindi transliteration of the name of the Ecuadorian writer leaves some room for doubt, but the context makes it likely that he is referring to the well-known Latin American poet.

15. Manasi Subramaniam, e-mail message to the author, 17 Aug. 2011; Sayoni Basu, e-mail message to the author, 11 Aug. 2011.

References

"Abstract of Speakers' Strength of Languages and Mother Tongues—2001." *Government of India, Ministry of Home Affairs*, 2010–11. http://censusindia.gov.in/Census_Data_2001/Census_Data_Online/Language/Statement1.htm. 21 Sept. 2011.

Ahmad, Aijaz. *In Theory: Classes, Nations, Literatures.* London: Verso, 1992.

"Ancient Christians in India." *Religion and Ethics Newsweekly, PBS.* 24 Apr. 2009. www.pbs.org/wnet/religionandethics/episodes/april-24–2009/ancient-christians-in-india/2754. 10 Sept. 2011.

Anderson, Benedict. *Imagined Communities: Reflections on the Origin and Spread of Nationalism.* London: Verso, 1983.

Arnold, Matthew. Preface. *Culture and Anarchy.* 1882. *University of Toronto English Library,* 1998. www.library.utoronto.ca/utel/nonfiction_u/arnoldm_ca/ca_ch-1.html. 17 June 2012.

Basu, Sayoni. "Roundtable: Of Naga and Bidadari—Asian Stories for Global Kids." Panel discussion, Asian Children's Media Summit. Asian Festival of Children's Content, Singapore, 28 May 2011.

Biswas, Rumjhum. "Batul and the Rumpel." *Enchanted Conversation,* 24 Mar. 2011. www.fairytalemagazine.com/2011/03/batul-and-rumpel-by-rumjhum-biswas.html. 2 May, 2011.

Bottigheimer, Ruth. *Grimms' Bad Girls and Bold Boys: The Moral and Social Vision of the Tales.* New Haven: Yale UP, 1987.

"Census Data 2001>>India at a Glance>>Religious Composition." *Government of India,* Ministry of Home Affairs, 2010–2011. http://censusindia.gov.in/Census_Data_2001/India_at_glance/religion.aspx. 14 Sept. 2011.

"Customer Reviews." *Folktales from India.* Pantheon Fairy Tale and Folklore Library. 15 Feb. 1999. www.amazon.com/Folktales-India-Pantheon-Folklore-Library/dp/0679748326/ref=sr_1_1?ie=UTF8&qid=1339970434&sr=8–1&keywords=folktales+from+india. 28 Sept. 2011.

Devsare, Harikrishna. *Grimm Bandhuon Ki Kahaniyan* [Tales by the Brothers Grimm]. 2 vols. New Delhi: Sahitya Akademi, 2000.

———. *Hans Andersen ki kahaniyan* [Tales by Hans Andersen]. 2 vols. New Delhi: Sahitya Akademi, 2008.

Dollerup, Cay. *Tales and Translation: The Grimm Tales from Pan-Germanic Narratives to Shared International Fairytales.* Amsterdam: John Benjamins, 1999.

Ellis, John M. *One Fairy Story Too Many.* Chicago: U of Chicago P, 1983.

"Female foeticide in India." *UNICEF India Media Centre*. www.unicef.org/india/media_3285.htm. 15 Sept. 2011.

Figuiera, Dorothy. "Myth in Romantic Prose Fiction." *Romantic Prose Fiction*. Eds. Gerald Ernest Gillespie, Manfred Engel, and Bernard Dieterle. Amsterdam: John Benjamins, 2008. 517–26.

Frere, Mary. *Old Deccan Days; or, Hindoo Fairy Legends Current in Southern India*. With Anna Liberata de Souza. 1868. Rev. ed. Ed. Kirin Narayan. Santa Barbara: ABC-Clio, 2002.

Gangopadhyay, Mohanlal. *Grimm Bhaider Rupkatha*. Calcutta: Abhyuday Prakas Mandir, 1963.

"H K Devsare Wins First 'Vatsalya Award' for Children's Literature." *Oneindianews*, 8 Feb. 2007. http://news.oneindia.in/2007/02/08/h-k-devsare-wins-first-vatsa-lya-award-for-childrens-literature-1170938517.html. 8 June 2011.

Henderson, Andrea K. *Romantic Identities: Varieties of Subjectivity 1774–1830*. Cambridge: Cambridge UP, 1996.

"Indiaspeak: English Is Our 2nd Language." *The Times of India* 14 Mar. 2010. http://articles.timesofindia.indiatimes.com/2010–03–14/india/28117934_1_second-language-speakers-urdu. 13 Sept. 2011.

Jain, Kajri. *Gods in the Bazaar: The Economies of Indian Calendar Art*. Durham: Duke UP, 2007.

"Karadi Tales." www.karaditales.com. 6 Jul. 2011.

Karim-Ahlawat, Mariam. *Saanp aur Medhak/The Snake and the Frogs*. Illus. Nancy Raj. Chennai: Tulika, 2010. Panchatantra Series.

Korom, Frank J. *South Asian Folklore: A Handbook*. Westport: Greenwood, 2006.

Lathey, Gillian. *The Role of Translators in Children's Literature: Invisible Storytellers*. New York: Routledge, 2010.

Macaulay, Thomas Babington. "Macaulay's Minute on Indian Education." 2 Feb. 1835. Department of English, U of California Santa Barbara. www.english.ucsb.edu/faculty/rraley/research/english/macaulay.html. 5 Sept. 2011.

Meigs, Cornelia Lynde, ed. *A Critical History of Children's Literature*. 4 vols. London: Macmillan, 1969.

Mukharji, Shravani. *Grimm Brothers: Kaljayi Kahaniyan*. New Delhi: Rashtrabhasha Sansthan, 2008. Grimm Brothers: Timeless Tales.

Naithani, Sadhana. *In Quest of Indian Folktales: Pandit Ram Gharib Chaube and William Crooke*. Bloomington: Indiana UP, 2006.

———. *The Story-Time of the British Empire: Colonial and Postcolonial Folkloristics*. Jackson: UP of Mississippi, 2010.

Niranjana, Tejaswini. *Siting Translation: History, Post-Structuralism, and the Colonial Context*. Berkeley: U of California P, 1992.

"Non-governmental Awards." *Culturopedia,* 2009–2012. www.culturopedia.com/awards/awards_nongovernmental.html. 9 June 2011.

Pathak, R. C., comp and ed. *Bhargava's Standard Illustrated Dictionary of the Hindi Language (Hindi–English).* Rev. ed. Varanasi: Bhargava, 1991.

"Population." *World Bank, World Development Indicators.* http://data.worldbank.org/indicator/SP.POP.TOTL. 29 Oct. 2011.

Raghunath, Jeeva. *The Talkative Tortoise/Baatuni Kachhua.* Illus. Shailja Jain. Chennai: Tulika, 2010. Panchatantra Series.

Ramanujan, A. K. *Folktales from India.* New York: Pantheon, 1994.

Ramusack, Barbara N. "The Indian Princes as Fantasy: Palace Hotels, Palace Museums, and Palace on Wheels." *Consuming Modernity: Public Culture in a South Asian World.* Ed. Carol A. Breckenridge. Minneapolis: U of Minnesota P, 1995. 66–89.

"Sahitya Akademi." National Academy of Letters. http://sahitya-akademi.gov.in/sahitya-akademi. 27 June 2011.

Said, Edward W. *Orientalism.* London: Routledge and Kegan Paul, 1978.

Spivak, Gayatri Chakravorty. *Other Asias.* Malden: Blackwell, 2008.

Subramaniam, Manasi. "Asian Content for the World's Children." *Karadi Tales Blog.* June 2011. http://karadionline.blogspot.de/2011/06/asian-content-for-worlds-children.html. 10 July 2011.

"Tara Books Blog." Tara Books. www.tarabooks.com/blog. 6 July 2011.

Tatar, Maria. *The Hard Facts of the Grimms' Fairy Tales.* Rev. ed. Princeton: Princeton UP, 2003.

"Top 30 languages of the world." *Vistawide World Languages and Cultures.* 2004–2011. www.vistawide.com/languages/top_30_languages.htm. 5 May 2011.

Varerkar, Chitra. *Grimm Brothers Ki Rochak Kathayen* [The Entertaining Tales of the Grimm Brothers]. New Delhi: Parashuram Hindi Sansthan, 2010.

Viswanathan, Gauri. *Masks of Conquest: Literary Study and British Rule in India.* New York: Columbia UP, 1989.

World Storytelling Institute. http://storytellinginstitute.org. 1 May 2011.

Zipes, Jack. *Breaking the Magic Spell: Radical Theories of Folk and Fairy Tales.* London: Heinemann, 1979.

———. *The Brothers Grimm: From Enchanted Forests to the Modern World.* New York: Routledge, 1988.

———, trans. and introd. *The Complete Fairy Tales of the Brothers Grimm.* 2 vols. Toronto: Bantam, 1987–1988.

———. *Fairy Tales and the Art of Subversion: The Classical Genre for Children and the Process of Civilization.* 2nd ed. New York: Routledge, 2006.

8

Before and after the "Grimm Boom"

Reinterpretations of the Grimms' Tales
in Contemporary Japan

MAYAKO MURAI

INTRODUCTION

The fairy tales of the Brothers Grimm experienced a great vogue among adult readers in Japan at the end of the twentieth century, a phenomenon often referred to as the "Grimm boom." A collection of sensationalized retellings of the Grimms' tales by Misao Kiryū titled *Hontō wa osoroshii Gurimu dōwa* (Grimms' Tales Really Are Horrific)[1] was published in 1998, and, together with its sequel in 1999, sold more than 2.5 million copies. This huge commercial success led to the publication of numerous books with similar titles emphasizing the cruel and sexual aspects not only of the Grimms' tales but also of folktales and fairy tales from around the world.

Owing to its misleading title, Kiryū's collection has spread the faulty impression that these rewritings are the "real" versions of the Grimm tales that "really are horrific."[2] Although it only lasted for about two years, the vogue for fairy tales radically changed the perception of Grimm in Japan, where the tales had been circulating widely but mostly in heavily sanitized versions intended for a young audience. The Grimm boom itself for the most part was a commercially driven phenomenon, but it certainly helped liberate the Grimms' tales from classrooms and nurseries as well as from the general belief in the monolithic nature of the "traditional" tales, inspiring a wide adult audience, especially women, to discover hitherto unexplored implications of the tales.

Although the Grimm boom was clearly triggered by the translation of the new kind of research in fairy-tale studies since the late 1970s by such scholars as Bruno Bettelheim, Heinz Rölleke, Maria Tatar, and Jack Zipes, it is also related to the way in which the Grimms' tales had been received in Japan since the late nineteenth century. This chapter first gives an overview of the reception and translation of the Grimms' tales in Japan, also paying attention to the illustrations accompanying the translations as exemplary of cultural transformation, and then explores the ways in which this historical background gave rise to the Grimm boom and later artistic and literary works.

The Reception of the Grimms' Tales since the Late Nineteenth Century

One explanation for the recent widespread interest in unexpurgated or sensationalized versions of the Grimms' tales among adult readers in Japan is that it is a reaction against a more general repression imposed on Japanese society, a repression that is reflected in the ways in which the Grimms' tales have been received and transformed in the course of Japan's modernization since the late nineteenth century. The Grimms' tales were first introduced to Japan as teaching materials in primary schools practicing the educational method advocated at the beginning of the nineteenth century by Johann Friedrich Herbart, a German philosopher and founder of pedagogy as an academic discipline. Herbart's theory emphasizes moral and intellectual development through literary appreciation, for which the Grimms' tales are given as a practical example. On the one hand, Herbart's systematic educational method was welcomed by Japanese educators at a time when Japan was eager to catch up with the modernity of the West. On the other hand, Herbart's theory was not out of accord with the rising nationalism apprehensive of losing national identity in the process of modernization; his key concepts were mapped onto Confucian ideas and made suitable for nationalistic moral education (Nagura 12).

The first tale by the Brothers Grimm to appear in Japanese was "The Nail," which was translated in 1873 from an English textbook, *Sargent's Standard Reader,* published in America in 1868. From then on, the Grimms' tales were published in various translations and adaptations in teaching materials and magazines intended for children's moral education. The most frequently translated tale during the early stage of the reception of the Grimms' tales was "The Wolf and the Seven Young Kids," which was the first example introduced to Japanese educators in the course of explaining Herbart's method (Nakagawa 96). Most of the translations before the First World War followed the policy laid out by the Imperial Rescript on Education of 1890, which regarded the development of loyalty and filial devotion as the principal aim of education. The fact that the Grimms' tales first became popular as teaching materials for children's moral education was a formational factor in the reception of the Grimms' tales in Japan.

The first actual collection of Grimm tales in Japanese, however, was aimed mainly at adult readers intent on absorbing Western culture, which flooded the country after 1868, when the Meiji Restoration marked the end of a period of national seclusion lasting more than 200 years. In 1887, Ryōhō Suga published *Seiyō koji: Shinsen sōwa* (Western Folklore: A Collection of Supernatural Tales), which contained eleven stories from the Grimms' collection, including "Cinderella" and "Faithful John." Although no source is shown—not even the names of the Brothers Grimm are mentioned—Yoshiko Noguchi (2005) infers from the stylistic and editorial characteristics that Suga used Mrs. H. B. Paull's English version (1868), from which Paull removed some of the violent and sexual expressions that she considered to be inappropriate for Victorian readers. As the expression "Supernatural Tales" in the subtitle suggests, Suga's translation underlines the magical and exotic aspects of the tales, a tendency also evident in the title of each story: "Cinderella," for example, is rendered as "The Strange Fate of Cinderella."

This emphasis on the exotic in old stories seems to derive from the oral tradition of *otogi*. *Otogi* originally means telling stories at bedtime but came to be associated with stories told by feudal lords' attendants to entertain their masters in sixteenth-century Japan. Suga, a Buddhist monk who studied philosophy at Oxford University and later became a politician, wrote in a sophisticated literary style, not only introducing new expressions to describe Western social and cultural customs but also adding the moral messages suitable for the dominant feudalistic and Confucian ideas of his time. In "The Strange Fate of Cinderella," for example, the king, only a marginal figure in the Grimms' tale, is portrayed as a person of great moral integrity worthy of the loyalty of his subjects. The virtue of diligence is even more emphasized than in the original, and devotion to one's parents becomes the most important lesson of the story. In translating the Grimms' tales, Suga thus both exoticized—as is evident in his emphasis on the "supernatural" and "strange" aspects of Western culture in the titles—and domesticated them for a Japanese adult readership, a process of cultural transformation that is also characteristic of the Grimm boom.

Although the first collection to appear in Japanese was intended primarily for adults, children continued to be the main readership of the Grimms' tales inside as well as outside the classroom. In the 1890s, Sazanami Iwaya, often considered the pioneer of children's literature in Japan, began to translate the Grimms' tales from German for children's magazines; it is Iwaya who first used the term *otogibanashi* (*banashi* meaning "a tale") to refer to literary fairy tales such as those of the Grimms and Andersen and who played a leading role in establishing a new genre of literary fairy tales especially for children. Iwaya promoted the use of fairy tales not so much for moral education as for the entertainment of children, whose enthusiastic reception brought about the vogue for literary fairy tales for children in the 1890s. His translations, which were the most widely read versions at the time and which had a significant impact on subsequent translations of the Grimms' tales, are more adaptations than translations. In his "Koyukihime" (1896, Snow White), for example, not only is the whole setting, including characters, places, and customs, transported to Japan, as the illustration makes clear (Figure 1), but some major structural elements of the story are also altered: the prince, for example, makes no appearance at all throughout the story, and the wicked stepmother receives no punishment other than mild ridicule for her vanity. At the abrupt ending of the story, after breaking the magic mirror in a rage, she asks herself who the most beautiful woman in the world is and answers that it is she herself. Iwaya's adaptations of the Grimms' tales are generally imbued with this kind of playful irony.

One of the common characteristics of these early Japanese translations is that they are generally not as punitive as the Grimms' tales. As Maria Tatar points out in *The Hard Facts of the Grimms' Fairy Tales* (2003), the Grimms did not consider the cruel punishment inflicted on evildoers inappropriate for children; they even tended to intensify violence in the stories they collected from their informants (Tatar 20–21). In the early Japanese translations, however, the emphasis is placed more on the reward that would follow good conduct. Violence, even when inflicted on evildoers in the original, tends to be removed or at least alleviated in the Japanese version. In the

少女

第八説 （二五）

第貮巻 （七四九）

小雪姫

小波

むかし〳〵まづある處に、其名を小雪姫といふ、それは〳〵美しいお姫様がありましたとさ。

その阿母様は繼母で、月の前と云ふ方でしたが、此の方の中々奇麗な方で、又御自分も、大層容貌自慢で居らっしゃいました。

處がそのお邸に、不思議な鏡が一面でございました。それはどんなに不思議かと云ふと、誰でもその鏡に顔をうつしながら、何か物を尋ねれば、直ぐに返事をするといふ、まとに奇体な鏡でしたから、その名も辻占鏡とつけてありました。

それで月の前は、毎「朝鏡にひかひまして、自分の美しい顔を見ながらも、

（月）世の中に誰が一番美しき

と尋ねますと、鏡は直ぐに、

（鏡）月の前には如くものもなし

と答へますから、月の前は大岩悦で、さては世界一番の美人だなど、姿こそ、獨りで好い氣に成て居りました。

するど、或朝の事で、例の様に月の前は、

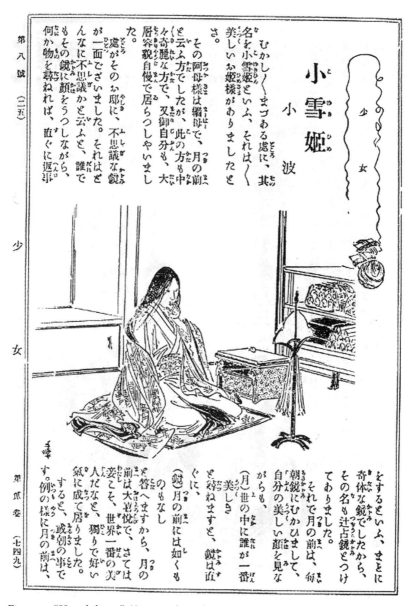

Figure 1. "Koyukihime" (Snow White) by Jacob and Wilhelm Grimm and translated by Sazanami Iwaya. Illustrator unknown. *Shōnen sekai*, 1896. Courtesy of Hakubunkan Shinsha Publishers.

translations of "Snow White," for example, the wicked queen's attempt to kill her stepdaughter three times and the cruel punishment inflicted on her at the end are often omitted, as they are in Iwaya's version; instead of the mother–daughter antagonism, the otherworldliness of such motifs as the magic mirror and seven dwarfs is foregrounded. Any element that might suggest sexuality also tends to be erased, so that heroes and heroines sometimes do not reach marriageable age even at the end of the story, as is the case in Iwaya's "Snow White."

This considerable license that early translators took with the Grimms' tales became a tendency common to the majority of later Japanese translations of children's literature. Editors and translators apparently believed that, because the tales were translated mainly for children, educational considerations should be given priority over faithfulness to the original text and that, because the Grimms' tales were supposed to represent the folk mentality of the German people, they could adapt the tales to suit what they regarded as its Japanese equivalent. The changes made to the tales range from culture-specific details, such as names, places, social customs, clothes, food, animals, and plants to major structural, stylistic, and ethical elements of the stories.

The rigorous method of the Herbart school combined with feudalistic ideology, to which Iwaya tried to offer an alternative by publishing non-educational literature for children, gradually began to be taken over by a more liberal theory of education that would allow more freedom and independence on the part of children in the early twentieth century. As ideas imported from the West such as democracy and liberal humanism began to take root, the importance of education and self-cultivation at a higher level than basic literacy increased among the middle class in the 1910s and the 1920s. Under the growing influence of Western culture, many innovative initiatives were taken in diverse areas such as education, art, literature, architecture, and city planning. This wave of Westernization also brought about a drastic change in the concept of childhood itself, and the role of education was now not to discipline "childish" thoughts and behavior but to cultivate pure, "childlike" sentiments and creativity uncontaminated by adult society. In light of this new understanding of childhood and education, the Grimms' tales, now reinterpreted within the framework of European Romanticism, were regarded as a privileged source of poetic imagination especially suitable for children and soon came to be incorporated into a newly defined genre of children's literature. With this redefinition of children's literature, the fairy tale was renamed *dōwa* (children's stories), severing the genre from *otogi,* the storytelling tradition for adults' entertainment (Kawahara 61). The translations of the Grimms' tales published during this period tend to be even freer than those in the previous era; translators re-created the Grimms' tales to fit them into their idealized notion of children.

A major redefinition of children's literature is represented by *Akai tori* (Red Bird), a children's magazine established by Miekichi Suzuki in 1918. *Akai tori* featured classic fairy tales such as those of Hans Christian Andersen and the Brothers Grimm as well as newly created stories for children by major Japanese literary figures of the time such as Ryūnosuke Akutagawa and Jun'ichirō Tanizaki. *Akai tori* was part of an educational movement that placed emphasis on children's subjectivity and creativity and reacted against what they considered the vulgarization of literature by the rising commercialism in the publishing industry, especially in the field of popular magazines for children. Yoshio Shimizu's illustrations for *Akai tori* (Figure 2) reflect their romantic notion of children—a child so pure and one with nature that she can communicate with birds on a tree—as well as their Westernizing artistic aspirations.

The Grimms' tales lay at the core of this liberal educational movement and thus played a central role in the Golden Age of children's literature in early twentieth-century Japan. Although the *Akai tori* approach to fairy tales puts more emphasis on aesthetic and creative values than on moral and regulatory functions, it is as emphatically educational and censorious as the previous approach; its editorial policy is to remove elements unsuitable for the romantic notion of *dōshin* (children's minds), which is conceived to be fundamentally different from the impure minds of adults. *Akai tori*'s idealization of children as a symbol of innocence valued by the Romantics, however, hardly corresponded to the real lives of children themselves and was later criticized as too abstract and elitist. Nevertheless, many of the picture books, magazines, and story collections for children published since the 1920s have followed this approach to some extent, and the expurgation of passages that adults regarded as too immoral or ugly for children in the Grimms' tales continued throughout the twentieth century.

At the same time, however, a folkloristic approach to the translation of the Grimms' tales also began to develop in the 1920s.[3] Kiichi Kaneda, a scholar and translator of German literature, published the first complete

Figure 2. Cover of *Akai tori* 12, no. 3 (1924). Illustration by Yoshio Shimizu. Reproduced on CD-ROM by Ōzorasha in 2008. Courtesy of Ōzorasha.

translation of *Die Kinder- und Hausmärchen* in two volumes in 1924 and 1927 as a part of *Sekai dōwa taikei* (An Anthology of World Children's Literature). Kaneda translated 248 tales altogether, including not only all 211 tales in the seventh edition (1857) but also 22 tales that the Grimms excluded after the first edition, nine posthumous tales, and six fragments. Kaneda's intention was to translate the Grimms' tales in such a way that both children and adults could enjoy them; he rejected the *Akai tori* view of children's literature shared by many educators and writers of the time, stating in the introduction that "it is a truly lamentable phenomenon that adults are gradually damaging children's pure minds with the almost demonic goodwill arising from their conscious and unconscious sense of privilege" (7). His translation, therefore, makes no attempt to remove or alter the violent or sexual elements previously regarded as unsuitable for children.

Kaneda's unabridged and faithful translation of the Grimms' collection was influenced by the rise of scholarship on children's literature that began to incorporate a folkloristic perspective and can be seen as an early attempt to bridge the gap between the educational and folkloristic approaches to the Grimm tales. His approach was followed by translators such as Genkurō Yazaki, who translated the Grimms' seventh edition for children in 1954. Yazaki, in line with the view that violence in fairy tales is harmless to children because it is put in an obviously unrealistic context, does not tone down the cruel elements; his "Snow White," for example, makes no changes to the often modified scene of punishment in which the wicked queen is forced to dance in red-hot iron shoes. His simple and rhythmic style is apparently intended to be read aloud by or for children, but its poetic elegance balanced with folkloric naiveté can be appreciated also by adults.

Translations of the older editions of the Grimms' collection began to appear in the latter half of the twentieth century. The Ölenberg manuscript was translated first in 1949 and then again in 1989. A translation of the second edition of the *Kinder- und Hausmärchen* appeared in 1985, a complete translation of the first edition in 1997, and more than five different complete translations of the seventh edition have been published since Kaneda's groundbreaking work. Although not intended to emphasize the immoral elements, this vogue for translating the older editions certainly laid the foundations for the Grimm boom in the late 1990s, in which the writers, however free or distorted their versions, invariably claim that their rewritings and reinterpretations are based on the Grimms' "original" or "unexpurgated" versions.

The ways in which the Grimms' tales have been received and transformed during the period of rapid Westernization reflect the conflictual process of Japan's attempt to reinvent itself as a modernized and democratic nation. It can be said that the Grimm boom in the late 1990s originated in adult readers' desire to rediscover what had been repressed by the process of alteration and expurgation executed by previous generations of adults in their roles as educators and parents. As mentioned above, the process of uncovering the older, more "original" versions of the Grimms' tales became an attempt to reach beyond the Grimms' text for the "truths" that were supposed to have existed before the moral repression enforced by modern Japanese society, and this seems to have been especially the case with women writers and readers who have been subjected to more severe social and sexual repression in a male-dominated society.

ANTICIPATING THE GRIMM BOOM

A series of substantial critical works on the *Kinder- und Hausmärchen* by Japanese scholars began to appear after 1985, the year in which Jacob Grimm's bicentenary anniversary was celebrated. This was also the year in which several "new," "true," or "complete" translations of the Grimms' collection, intended mainly for an adult readership, began to be published. The translation of Heinz Rölleke's seminal essay "The 'Utterly Hessian' Fairy Tales by 'Old Marie': The End of a Myth" appeared in 1985 in a collection of scholarly essays titled *Gendai ni ikiru Gurimu* (The Grimms Still Living Today), which also included philological, linguistic, historical, folkloristic, literary, and psychological (Jungian) analyses of the Grimms' tales by five Japanese scholars. Although this collection played a significant role in making the public aware of new approaches to the Grimms' tales, it failed to incorporate perceptive insights provided by feminist criticism. For example, although Yoshiko Noguchi had first introduced Rölleke's essay in a Japanese journal as early as 1977, her article was not even mentioned by Toshio Ozawa, who translated Rölleke's essay for the above-mentioned collection. Nor did Noguchi's critical works on the Grimms' tales from a feminist perspective receive wide attention until much later; a collection of the essays she wrote after the late 1970s, *Gurimu no meruhyen: Sono yume to genjitsu* (Grimms' Märchen: Dream and Reality), was finally published in 1994, on the eve of the Grimm boom. It can be said that the vogue for Grimm scholarship among Japanese folklorists and literary critics that laid the foundation for the Grimm boom was not as female-centered as the Grimm boom itself.

At the same time, innovative rewritings of the Grimms' tales for an adult readership that precede the Grimm boom also began to appear. A work often regarded as the Japanese equivalent of Angela Carter's seminal feminist fairy-tale revisions in *The Bloody Chamber and Other Stories* (1979) was published in 1984 by Yumiko Kurahashi. Despite its title, Kurahashi's recasting of folktales and fairy tales from around the world in *Otona no tame no zankoku dōwa* (Cruel Fairy Tales for Adults) is not primarily an attempt to sensationalize the cruel and sexual aspects of traditional tales as would be the case of the works related to the Grimm boom that are generally classified as popular or commercial fiction rather than as literary fiction. Kurahashi's playful irony and black humor are directed at the absurdities of people adhering to gender stereotypes, both men and women alike.

In her "Snow White," for example, the prince marries the wicked queen, who is more sexually attractive and intelligent than her pretty but dull stepdaughter. Nevertheless, we are told that Snow White lived "fairly" happily ever after with the seven dwarfs, bearing numerous little babies for them. Kurahashi's rewriting does in fact emphasize sex and violence—it also includes her rewriting of "How Some Children Played at Slaughtering," a gruesome tale removed by the Grimms after the first edition of their collection—but does so paradoxically in order to lay bare the culturally constructed nature of the sexist ideas underlying traditional tales, and it is in this sense that her fairy-tale collection, generally regarded as separate from the Grimm boom, can be compared with such postmodern retellings as Carter's *The Bloody Chamber,* Donald Barthelme's *Snow White* (1967), and Robert Coover's *Pricksongs and Descants* (1969).

The work that marks the beginnings of the Grimm boom is Yūko Matsumoto's rewriting of the Grimms' and Andersen's tales, collected under the title of *Tsumi bukai hime no otogibanashi* (1996, Fairy Tales of Sinful Princesses) and illustrated by the artist Kumiko Higami. Matsumoto's collection, to which Kiryū's work is heavily indebted,[4] can be said to have shaped the Grimm boom in its textual as well as nontextual form; the combination of her female-centered fairy tales and Higami's sensual portraits of young women in princess-like dresses set a vogue for illustrated story collections for adults, especially addressing a female readership. In a hypertextual manner characteristic of the Grimm boom, Matsumoto indicates in the moral at the end of each tale and in the afterword that her stories are based on the older editions of the Grimms' tales and are informed by the recent fairy-tale criticism by Tatar, Zipes, Bottigheimer, and other Western scholars, which also echoes the late twentieth-century trend of blurred boundaries between fairy-tale retellings and fairy-tale criticism delineated by Vanessa Joosen in *Critical and Creative Perspectives on Fairy Tales* (2011).

The feminist perspective of Matsumoto's collection is reflected in the titles of the stories: "When Sleeping Beauty Awakens to Sexuality," "The Witch Trial in Snow White," "Precocious and Pretty Little Red Riding Hood," "Cinderella and Her Big-Footed Sisters," "Bluebeard's Paradise Lost," "The Little Mermaid Goes to the World of Men," and "The Little Match Whore." "The Witch Trial in Snow White," for example, identifies the fate of the queen with that of the victims of medieval witch trials and exposes the injustices perpetrated on women by male-dominated society. "Snow White" indeed seems to be the pivotal story in the Grimm boom, which was largely led by female writers and readers, who, like Sandra M. Gilbert and Susan Gubar in *The Madwoman in the Attic* (1979),[5] regarded the Grimms' "Snow White" as a patriarchal fairy tale par excellence. "Snow White" tells the story of woman's life reflected in the mirror, representing the male-centered standard according to which women are judged exclusively by their physical beauty and are set against each other in competition for men's love. Although, like Kiryū, Matsumoto enhances the cruel and sexual elements in the Grimms' "original" tales in order to entertain adult readers, her emphasis lies more strongly on feminist revisions than the other Grimm boom writers.

The combination of sex, violence, and feminism in rewriting fairy tales reminds us of Carter's strategy in *The Bloody Chamber,* but the emphatically sensationalistic approach of both Matsumoto's and Kiryū's collections is targeted at a much wider audience than Carter's. Although *The Bloody Chamber* was translated into Japanese in 1992, none of the Grimm boom writers, including even Matsumoto, mentions Carter's rewriting. The translation of *The Bloody Chamber* was reissued as a paperback in 1999, largely due to the Grimm boom, but Carter's fairy tales seem to have been appreciated not so much by the popular readership who enjoyed the works associated with the Grimm boom as by literary scholars, feminist or otherwise.

Misao Kiryū is the pseudonym of two women, Sachiko Tsutsumi and Kayoko Ueda. Until Tsutsumi's death in 2003, they coauthored more than forty populist books about cruel and erotic episodes in European history and literature in which women, invariably characterized as femme fatales, play the leading part. Kiryū's fairy-tale collection, which directly gave rise to the Grimm boom, consists of female-centered, sensationalized retellings of "Snow White," "Cinderella," "The Frog King," "Bluebeard," "Sleeping Beauty," and "The Juniper Tree," with *shōjo*-manga-style illustrations in romanticized European settings (Figure 3).

Each tale is followed by a synopsis of psychoanalytic, folkloristic, socio-historical, and literary interpretations by such scholars as Bruno Bettelheim, Maria Tatar, and Carl-Heintz Mallet. "In the light of these scholars' varied interpretations," writes Kiryū in the preface, "we tried to re-create a more vivid and graphic version of Grimms' tales in our own fashion by keeping the cruel and violent expressions found in their first edition and by bringing out the depths of the psyche and the hidden meanings" (Kiryū 3).[6] Almost all the works that contributed to the Grimm boom derived a large part of their ideas from the psychoanalytic, sociohistorical, literary, and/or feminist in-terpretations of fairy tales by Western scholars that had become available in Japanese translation from the late 1970s. It can be said that the Grimm boom popularized these new interpretations of "traditional" fairy tales, of which the Grimms' were regarded as the quintessential examples. As is evident in the illustrations accompanying these books, Kiryū's work is imbued with Occidentalist fantasies, which is also a major characteristic of the Japanese Grimm boom in general, whose obsession with violence and sexuality can be regarded as a projection of disavowed desires onto the Other.

In Kiryū's "Snow White: The Battle against the Real Mother for Love," the queen, when she finds out that her daughter is having an affair with her husband, tries to kill her three times in the guise of a witch. Snow White for her part is portrayed as a beautiful but cruel girl who indulges in the incestuous relationship with her father and who finds pleasure in torturing people, including her own parents. Kiryū explains that this rewriting is based on the Grimms' first edition in which the wicked queen is not the heroine's stepmother, as the later editions have it, but her biological mother. By going

Figure 3. Cover of *Hontō wa osoroshii Gurimu dōwa* by Misao Kiryū. Illustration by Sumika Yumimoto. Tokyo: KK Bestsellers, 1998. Courtesy of KK Bestsellers.

back to the Grimms' older editions, Kiryū tried to offer alternatives to the well-known versions including the Disney films.

Kiryū describes in detail Snow White's sexual exchanges with her father and the seven dwarfs as well as her cruelty, especially toward her mother, who, in the red-hot iron shoes she is forced to wear by her own daughter, "danced and danced amid the nauseating smell of burning human flesh until she exhausted all her energy and fell flat on the floor" (Kiryū 46). Kiryū's rewritings in general focus on the antagonistic relationship between women in the Grimm tales, recasting it in the most transgressive forms imaginable. In the commentary on "Snow White," however, Kiryū suggests another possible interpretation: the queen drives her daughter away from home in order to rescue her from her husband's sexual abuse.[7] Following Matsumoto's rewriting, Kiryū also points out that the punishment using red-hot iron shoes was an actual punishment inflicted on women charged with witchcraft in medieval Europe.

The year 1999, which followed the publication of Kiryū's collection, saw a burst of publications of populist books on the "horrific" aspects of the Grimms' fairy tales. Related titles include *Hontō wa shiritaku nakatta Gurimu dōwa* (Grimms' Fairy Tales We Did Not Really Want to Know), *Otona mo zottosuru shohan Gurimu dōwa* (The Grimms' First Edition That Would Frighten Even Adults), and *Gurimu dōwa 99 no nazo: Dōwatte hontō wa zankoku* (Ninety-Nine Mysteries of the Grimms' Tales: Fairy Tales Really Are Cruel). Moreover, this new approach to the Grimms' tales led to a reevaluation of the fairy tales of other writers such as Andersen and Charles Perrault as well as a rediscovery of Japanese and other cultures' folktales as sensational literature for adults.[8] It is as if adult readers, who had once been familiarized with the sanitized versions of the Grimms' tales in their childhood, needed to know what the "real" stories were in order to better access their own conflicting desires and fears arising from the realm of the unconscious to which the fairy tale seemed to hold the magic key. However, in their attempt to reinterpret the stories of women's lives, female writers and readers often felt the need to reach even beyond the Grimms' original tales to undermine their presupposed patriarchal gender hierarchies.

As the Grimm boom began to die down after the end of the past century, the Grimm tales may seem to have lost much of their attraction as sensational literature, but their popularity among adult readers with more serious tastes does not seem to have suffered. By revealing the presence of the repressed content as well as the nonmonolithic nature of "traditional" fairy tales, the Grimm boom has inspired a new generation of writers and artists, especially women, to start telling their own versions. Unlike the works associated with the Grimm boom that excluded children by emphasizing their immoral content in their titles, many of the post–Grimm boom writers and artists do not place any particular emphasis on either the moral or the immoral aspect of the Grimms' tales. At the same time, they seem to be moving away from the Occidentalist exoticization of the Grimms' tales, which has continued to fascinate the Japanese in varied forms since the late nineteenth century.

In 2001, the first three volumes of *Gurimu dōwa* (Grimms' Tales) *Artist Book Series,* based on "Cinderella," "The Wolf and the Seven Kids," and "Rapunzel," respectively, were published. This ongoing series combines the Grimms' tales with the work of contemporary Japanese artists working in such diverse fields as costume design, graphic art, rock music, and flower arrangement. The publication of "Hansel and Gretel," "The Six Servants," and "Snow White" in 2002 was followed by "The Frog King" and "The Star Coins" in 2005. This innovative series is interesting in terms of its blurring of the boundaries between child and adult audiences and between visual and narrative texts. On the one hand, it uses Yazaki's poetic translation of the Grimms' seventh edition for children, published nearly half a century before the Grimm boom; on the other hand, the artworks by cutting-edge Japanese artists are intended mainly for adults. The visual artist Tabaimo's *Kaeru no ōsama* (The Frog King; Figure 4), for example, consists of a long sheet of paper folded to the size of a book; one side of the sheet has both text and pictures, the other has only pictures. As the story proceeds, a row of connected images unfold from right to left, revealing one image of the grotesquely distorted or dismembered body of the princess or the frog after another; these images, which only partially follow the story line, foreground the intensely tactile—and not necessarily sexual—sensation evoked by this story. The images in this series can be regarded more as artworks collaborating with the Grimms' tales to bring out a new aesthetic dimension than as mere visual aids to illustrate the stories.

Another interesting example of the recent visual recasting of the Grimms' tales can be found in Miwa Yanagi's *Fairy Tale* series of photographs, made between 2004 and 2006, which reinterpret the Grimms' tales as stories not only of antagonism but also of bonding between women belonging to

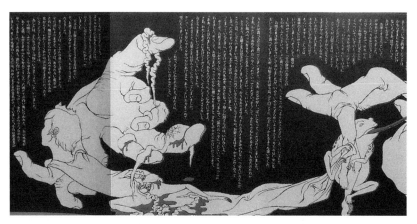

Figure 4. *Kaeru no ōsama* (The Frog King) by Jacob and Wilhelm Grimm and translated by Genkurō Yazaki. Illustration by Tabaimo. Tokyo: Wacoal Art Center, 2005. © Tabaimo and Wacoal Art Centre.

different generations. While the Grimms' tales tend to set women against each other by presenting the older woman as evil and the younger one as good, Yanagi's visual recastings render these two opposite images of women as more complex and ambiguous.

In her "Snow White" (Figure 5), for example, the young girl and the old woman are shown as the mirror image of each other. A figure with her back to the camera appears to be the young Snow White, and the figure confronting the girl looks like her wicked stepmother. A closer look, however, will reveal that the masked figure is the reflection of the girl in the mirror. In Yanagi's version, the two stages of woman's life are compressed into one figure in which the young/beautiful/good side coexists with the old/ugly/evil side, and their common destiny is symbolized by the apple that they are going to share, as one side of the apple must be as poisonous as the other.

Literary adaptations of the Grimms' tales also continued to flourish after the Grimm boom began to wane. In 2001, *Ehon: Shinpen Gurimu dōwa shū* (Picture Book: Newly Edited and Selected Grimms' Tales) by nine contemporary women writers came out. It is a collection of rewritings of the Grimms' tales illustrated with *Bilderbogen* and other nineteenth-century European illustrations and accompanied with short scholarly essays on the

Figure 5. *Snow White* by Miwa Yanagi. Gelatin silver print, 100 x 100 cm, 2004. © Miwa Yanagi. Courtesy of the artist and Seigensha Art Publishing.

Grimms' tales, including Yoshiko Noguchi's feminist analysis of the representations of the two archetypal evildoers in the Grimms' tales, the witch and the stepmother. Although clearly intended for adult readers, this collection does not particularly emphasize the cruel or sexual aspects of the tales; instead, they explore more subtle literary implications. For example, Kaoru Takamura, without altering the actual content of the story, transforms "The Bremen Town Musicians" into a strangely realistic contemporary story by adding a frame narrative in which a first-person narrator visits a friend in Bremen, who tells her or him the story about the famous local band consisting of four animals in a matter-of-fact, everyday tone. Takamura's subtle reframing of the story makes the reader realize how ubiquitous and powerful the storytelling tradition still is in contemporary society.

In 2006, the novelist Yōko Ogawa published a collection of fairy tales titled *Otogibanashi no wasuremono* (Lost and Found Fairy Tales) with illustrations by Kumiko Higami, who had also illustrated Matsumoto's fairy-tale collection about sinful princesses. This project was initiated by Higami, who first drew illustrations inspired by four classic Western stories, "Little Red Riding Hood" (Figure 6), "The Little Mermaid," *Alice's Adventures in Wonderland,* and *Swan Lake.* Ogawa's "Hood Club," based on "Little Red Riding Hood," begins with the narrator–heroine's first encounter with a woman wearing a fashionable hood and accompanied by her handsome wolf-colored dog. The heroine soon finds out that the woman makes her living as a seamstress who specializes in making new dresses out of old—which is suggestive of the craft of rewriting stories—and is the founder and president of the "Hood Club," a group of people obsessed with hoods. At the club's annual "Hood Festival," the president makes a speech while wearing what she claims to be the "original" red riding hood worn by the heroine of the Grimms' story. What distinguishes this "original" red riding hood from others, she explains, is the somber color and sliminess caused by the wolf's blood and gastric juices that testify to the heroine's life-and-death struggle inside the wolf's belly. At the end of the story, the heroine visits the president's flat and finds her wolf-colored dog lying dead with his belly cut open, apparently having been sacrificed for his owner's (re)invention of the bloody hood.

"The Hood Club" can be seen as a parody of the Grimm boom writers' "horrific" reinterpretations of "Little Red Riding Hood," which overemphasized the violent and sexual aspects of the story and whose traces still linger in Higami's illustration based on "Little Red Riding Hood" but titled "Salome," likening the hooded woman to the classic femme fatale by making her raise the severed, still bleeding head of the wolf-dog overhead and wear a wolf fur coat on her bare skin. In Ogawa's subtly surreal story, however, the hood ceases to be a mere metaphor of violence and sexuality and regains its materiality as a piece of clothing; as an object to be studied, made, and worn, the hood becomes the central motif of the story. By faithfully (re) constructing the hood worn by the fairy-tale heroine, the president of the Hood Club reduces the red riding hood, heavily metaphorized by psychological interpretations, to its literal meaning, that is, a piece of headdress that, the Grimms' story tells us, is sewn by the girl's grandmother. What

Figure 6. Cover of *Otogibanashi no wasuremono* by Yōko Ogawa. Illustration by Kumiko Higami. Tokyo: Hōmusha, 2006. Courtesy of the artist and Hōmusha.

is found in Ogawa's retelling is not merely the lost or expurgated parts in the Grimms' tales but their inexhaustible potential for generating different stories and desires.

These works by post–Grimm boom artists and writers, as we have seen, are different from the Grimm boom's sensationalist and Occidentalist reinterpretation of the Grimms' tales, but they certainly would not have attracted a wide audience or may not even have existed if the Grimm boom had not opened up new possibilities of understanding the Grimms' tales as stories that are not as monolithic and innocent as they had appeared previously.

CONCLUSION

The Grimm boom in Japan, which peaked in the last two years of the twentieth century, can be seen as a revolt by adult readers against the long history of various alterations made to the Grimms' tales for educational reasons and also as their attempt to recuperate what they believed had been lost in the process of Japan's modernization that began in the late nineteenth century. Although the mainstream of stories produced in the Grimm boom did not go beyond the sensationalist treatment of the cruel and sexual elements in older editions of the Grimms' tales, it helped bring a much wider audience than folklore researchers to realize that the stories with which they had been familiar as Grimm tales since their childhood were not single, authentic versions faithfully handed down by oral tradition as they had been led to believe. The Grimm boom sparked off a wide-ranging debate over the nature and history of the fairy tale, the definition of children's literature, and the role of translation in general. Writers and artists who are aware of these post–Grimm boom issues are rereading the Grimms' tales to join the ever-variegating re-creation of the fairy-tale tradition captured by the Grimms' collection.

NOTES

1. All translations from Japanese are my own.

2. In 2010, two Chinese publishers, apparently believing that they had found the "real" versions of Grimm tales, published Kiryū's collection in Chinese, which ended up in the children's book section by mistake.

3. The study of folklore was established as an academic discipline in early twentieth-century Japan under the influence of Western folklorists, especially the Brothers Grimm and George Laurence Gomme.

4. In 1999, Mastumoto in fact sued Kiryū and their publisher for plagiarizing over 100 lines from her story collection. They reached a compromise in court in which Kiryū agreed to rewrite the parts in question. For details, see Maruyama and Ikeda.

5. In "The Queen's Looking Glass: Female Creativity, Male Images of Women, and the Metaphor of Literary Paternity," the opening chapter of *The Madwoman in the Attic*, Gilbert and Gubar see the antagonism between the wicked queen and Snow White as a paradigmatic instance of male-generated twin images of monster-woman and angel-woman. They further argue that the mirror, which represents the voice of the king internalized in the queen's mind, sets the two women against each other.

6. Joosen (2010) discusses a similar intertextual return to the older versions among contemporary Dutch retellings.

7. Pat Murphy's "The True Story" follows the plot suggested by this interpretation.

8. Books on cruelty in folktales and fairy tales other than the Grimms' that came out in 1999 include *Kaidan yorimo Kowai! Nihon to Sekai no Zankoku Dōwa* (More Horrific than Ghost Stories: Cruel Fairy Tales in Japan and the World), *Mazagusutte Zankoku: Gurimu Dōwa yori Kowai* (Mother Goose Is Cruel: More Horrific than Grimms' Tales), *Gurimu Dōwa yori Kowai Nihon Otogi-Banashi* (Japanese Fairy Tales That Are More Horrific than Grimms' Tales), and *Minoke mo Yodatsu Sekai "Zankoku" Dōwa* (Bloodcurdling "Cruel" Fairy Tales in the World).

REFERENCES

Bartheleme, Donald. *Snow White*. New York: Atheneum, 1967.

Carter, Angela. *The Bloody Chamber and Other Stories*. 1979. Harmondsworth: Penguin, 1981.

Coover, Robert. *Pricksongs and Descants*. New York: Dutton, 1969.

Gilbert, Sandra M., and Susan Gubar. *The Madwoman in the Attic: The Woman Writer and the Nineteenth-Century Literary Imagination*. New Haven: Yale UP, 1979.

Grimm, Jacob, and Wilhelm Grimm. *Kaeru no ōsama* [The Frog King]. Trans. Genkurō Yazaki. Illus. Tabaimo. Tokyo: Wacoal Art Center, 2005.

———. "Koyukihime" [Snow White]. Trans. Sazanami Iwaya. *Shōnen sekai* [Boys' World]. 2.8 (1896): 25–29.

Ichihara, Hiroko. "Rapuntsueru" [Rapunzel]. *Grurimu dōwa* [Grimms' Tales]. Tokyo: Wacoal Art Centre, 2001. Artist Book Series.

Ikeda, Kayoko. "*Gurimu kenkyūsha kara mita* hontō wa osoroshii . . . *tōyō-mondai*" [The Problem of Plagiarism in *Grimm's Tales Really Are Horrific* Seen from a Grimm Scholar's Perspective]. *The Tsukuru* 29.11 (1999): 76–79.

Joosen, Vanessa. "Back to Ölenberg: An Intertextual Dialogue between Fairy-Tale Retellings and the Socio-Historical Study of the Grimm Tales." *Marvels & Tales* 24.1 (2010): 99–115.

———. *Critical and Creative Perspectives on Fairy Tales: An Intertextual Dialogue between Fairy-Tale Scholarship and Postmodern Retellings.* Detroit: Wayne State UP, 2011.

Kaneda, Kiichi, trans. *Kan'yaku: Gurimu dōwa shū* [A Complete Translation of Grimm's Tales]. Vols. 1–5. Tokyo: Iwanami Bunko, 1979.

Kawahara, Kazue. *Kodomokan no kindai:* Akai tori to *"dōshin" no risō* [The Concept of the Child in the Modern Era: Red Bird and the Ideal of "Children's Minds"]. Tokyo: Chūōkōron-Shinsha, 1998.

Kawato, Michiaki, and Takanori Sakakibara, eds. *Meijiki Gurimu dōwa hon'yaku shūsei* [A Collection of Grimm's Tales Translated in the Meiji Period]. Vols. 1–5. Tokyo: Nada Shuppan Center, 1999.

Kawato, Michiaki, Yoshiko Noguchi, and Takanori Sakakibara, eds. *Nihon ni okeru gurimu dōwa hon'yaku shoshi* [A Bibliography of the Translation of Grimm's Tales in Japan]. Tokyo: Nada Shuppan Center, 2000.

Kiryū, Misao. *Hontō wa osoroshii Gurimu dōwa* [Grimm's Tales Really Are Horrific]. Tokyo: KK Bestsellers, 1998.

Kurahashi, Yumiko. *Otona no tame no zankoku dōwa* [Cruel Fairy Tales for Adults]. Tokyo: Shinchōsha, 1984.

Maruyama, Noboru. "*Hontō wa osoroshii Gurimu dōwa* Tōyō-mondai, hōtei e!?" [The Problem of Plagiarism in *Grimm's Tales Really Are Horrific* Goes to Court?]. *The Tsukuru* 29.11 (1999): 68–75.

Matsumoto, Yūko. *Tsumibukai hime no otogibanashi* [The Fairy Tales of Sinful Princesses]. Tokyo: Kadokawa Shoten, 1996.

Murphy, Pat. "The True Story." *Black Swan, White Raven.* Eds. Ellen Datlow and Terri Windling. New York: Avon, 1997. 278–87.

Nagura, Yōko. *Nihonn no kindaika to Gurimu dōwa: Jidai ni yoru henka o yomi-toku* [Japan's Modernization and Grimm's Tales: Interpreting the Changes over Time]. Tokyo: Sekaishisōsha, 2005.

Nakagawa, Junko. *"Ōkami to shichihiki no koyagi" no nazo* [The Mystery of "The Wolf and the Seven Young Kids"]. Kawato, Noguchi, Sakakibara, 84–103.

Noguchi, Yoshiko. "Eiyakubon kara jūyaku sareta nihon no Gurimu dōwa: Sashio no hōyakubon o chūshin ni" [Grimm's Fairy Tales Translated from the English in Japan: Focusing on the First Japanese Translation]. *Jidō bungaku hon'yaku sakuhin sōran* [A Source Book of Children's Literature in Translation]. Vol. 4. Eds. Michiaki Kawato and Takanori Sakakibara. Tokyo: Nada Shuppan Center, 2005. 465–85.

———. *Gurimu no meruhyen: Sono yume to genjitsu* [Grimms' Märchen: Dream and Reality]. Tokyo: Keisōshobō, 1994.

Ogawa, Yōko. *Otogibanashi no wasuremono* [Lost and Found Fairy Tales]. Tokyo: Hōmusha, 2006.

Ozawa, Toshio, et al., eds. *Gendai ni ikiru Gurimu* [The Grimms Still Living Today]. Tokyo: Iwanami Shoten, 1985.

Suga, Ryōhō. *Seiyō koji: Shinsen sōwa* [Western Folklore: A Collection of Supernatural Tales]. Tokyo: Shūseisha, 1887.

Takamura, Kaoru, et al. *Ehon: Shinpen Gurimu dōwa shū* [Picture Book: Newly Edited and Selected Grimm's Fairy Tales]. Tokyo: Mainichi Shimbun Sha, 2001.

Tatar, Maria. *The Hard Facts of the Grimms' Fairy Tales.* Expanded 2nd ed. Princeton: Princeton UP, 2003.

Yanagi, Miwa. *Fairy Tale: Strange Stories of Women Young and Old.* Kyoto: Seigensha Art Publishing, 2007.

II

Reframings, Paratexts, and Multimedia Translations

9

Translating in the "Tongue of Perrault"

The Reception of the *Kinder- und Hausmärchen* in France

CYRILLE FRANÇOIS

> My own *early* personal response to Grimms' tales was the re-
> sult of a superficial French cultural bias that favored Perrault's
> tales over the Grimms'. I could not read and understand the
> tales fluently in the original, so I had to rely on French and
> English translations. My approach was prejudiced from the
> start: I assumed that Charles Perrault's *Contes* of 1697 obvi-
> ously "came first," bringing to the world the classic texts of
> some of the most famous fairy tales of our Western culture,
> and that the Brothers Grimm just followed in their French
> predecessor's footsteps.
>
> Barchilon 269

To translate the *Kinder- und Hausmärchen* into French is to confront the specter of Charles Perrault and his *Histoires ou contes du temps passé* (Stories or Tales of Past Times), which have haunted the fairy-tale genre in France since they were first published in 1697. From the end of the eighteenth century onward, new editions of Perrault's tales have multiplied, reaching a high point between 1850 and 1870. Celebrated by literary critics and folklorists for their alleged simplicity and naïveté, his *Contes* have become the paragon of a genre against which fairy tales translated into French are—implicitly or explicitly—measured. For example, Philarète Chasles presented Hans Christian Andersen as "the Scandinavian Perrault" in 1869. Mikhail M. Bakhtin argues that a discourse is always in dialogue with other discourses (93). It is suggested here that such dialogism is particularly important in regard to translation, since the translated text has to fit into the genres of the target culture.[1] And, in France, a "fairy-tale language" corresponding to the expectations of the genre has come to be defined largely by Perrault.

This chapter aims to illustrate the effects of his influence on the reception of the *Kinder- und Hausmärchen* in France and show how his heritage has percolated the choice of the tales that are translated, the titles they are given, the words and expressions they contain, and their written style. After a brief overview of French editions of the *Kinder- und Hausmärchen* and the way these translations relate to Perrault more generally, the analysis will turn to the translations of the tales more specifically.

A Brief Overview of French Translations

Since the nineteenth century, English readers have had the benefit of several complete translations of the *Kinder- und Hausmärchen* as well as of various annotated editions, whereas French readers have had to satisfy themselves with a selective number of tales, more or less faithful to their originals. While there are certainly a large number of children's books in French containing Grimm tales, there are only two complete translations, both relatively recent. Armel Guerne's translation for Flammarion (1967)[2] may be the first integral edition in French, but it is lacking in certain significant aspects: it contains neither the Grimms' foreword and comments nor any critical apparatus, and the editorial choices are based on information on the Grimms that was proven incorrect through the work of Heinz Rölleke, among others (for example in regard to the sources of the tales). Titled *Contes pour les enfants et la maison* (Tales for the Children and the Home), the second complete version of the *Kinder- und Hausmärchen* in French was edited and translated by Natacha Rimasson-Fertin (2009).

This edition includes the so-called omitted tales (i.e., those once published in the *Kinder- und Hausmärchen* but omitted by the Grimms in later editions) and the *Kinderlegenden* (religious tales for children) as well as an insightful commentary, sometimes quoting the Grimms' own annotations. Interestingly, it also contains a solid section on the current state of research on the Grimms and provides a more accurate portrayal of the authors than that given previously. Next to these two complete translations, there are also a number of selective collections of interest for this study. It is frequently possible to infer a link to Perrault in the selection of tales for translation. These choices are sometimes, though not always, explained in the forewords to the collections, and they depend on the way the translators view the Brothers Grimm and the fairy-tale genre more generally.

The First Translations

The first French rendition of the *Kinder- und Hausmärchen* was actually translated from English in 1824. *Vieux contes pour l'amusement des grands et des petits enfans* (Old Tales for the Amusement of Old and Young Children) is an almost literal translation of Edgar Taylor's *German Popular Stories* (1823).[3] Indeed, only the notes at the end of the volume are left out, and the ten-page foreword is replaced by a short text. Even George Cruikshank's engravings are copied, but the book provides neither the names of the Grimms nor those of the English and subsequent French translators. It does not endeavor to hide the loan, however, as is evident in the fact that the table of contents gives the English title in brackets to the tale "Boule de neige" (Snow Drop). Since it is a simple copy of an English edition, it could be expected that this translation would be of little interest for the purposes of this chapter. However, the analysis of the translation of "Dornröschen" (Brier Rose)[4] that follows later shows that, in certain respects, the French translator did not follow the English edition but, rather, was inspired by Perrault.

After this first version of selected Grimm tales in French, two more official collections were published and the Grimms actually had copies of these (Denecke 42; Grimm and Grimm, *Ausgabe letzter Hand* I.25). *Contes choisis de Grimm* (1836, Selected Grimm Tales) was translated by F.-C. Gérard and seems drawn from the *Kleine Ausgabe* (Small Edition), from which seventeen of its eighteen texts were taken.[5] The only addition was the famous tale "The Brave Little Tailor." The book does not contain any foreword, and nothing is known concerning the editorial choices, but the subtitle—"for the use of children"—specifies that, like the *Kleine Ausgabe,* it presents a selection that is particularly appropriate for a young audience.

The next translated selection of tales was published in 1846 and 1848 with a title that is among the very few that are close to the German original: *Contes de la famille par les frères Grimm* (Family Tales by the Brothers Grimm). The translators, Nicolas Martin (under whose sole name the second volume is published) and Pitre-Chevalier, present a selection of tales of which three quarters had gone unpublished in France previously, and the book contains a number of lesser known tales.[6] The foreword gives no clear explanation for this editorial choice, but by insisting on the fact that the Grimms collected rather than wrote their own tales, and by presenting the brothers as explorers who scoured the German countryside in search of material, it suggests that the translators aimed for more exotic tales not yet known in France. The foreword to the second volume explains that some tales were "willfully neglected," however, because they were "too removed from our way of thinking" (viii–ix, my translation).[7] This statement clearly demonstrates that in translating the *Kinder- und Hausmärchen,* consideration was given to the French reader and his or her perception of the genre.

The Second Half of the Nineteenth Century

Published by Hachette in 1855 in the popular collection "La Bibliothèque rose," the *Contes choisis des frères Grimm* (Selected Tales by the Brothers Grimm) was an influential edition in nineteenth-century France: several re-editions of this cheap book bear witness to its success. It was translated by the philologist Frédéric Baudry, who based it on the *Kinder- und Hausmärchen* of 1850, and completed with forty vignettes by Bertall, a very famous artist at the time, who also illustrated tales by E. T. A. Hoffman, Perrault, and Andersen.[8] These *Contes choisis des frères Grimm* are thus part of a trend of illustrated books, which were particularly fashionable in the 1850s and 1860s.

After the popular Hachette edition of 1855, the academic editor Didier et Cie introduced a selection of tales in 1869 containing translations of several German authors and destined for an educated audience. Here, the Grimms were presented as "serious scholars" who were "too well known for it to be necessary to provide all their titles, in respect of scholarly Europe" (Frank and Alsleben 5 and 3, my translation).[9] These *Contes allemands du temps passé* (German Tales of Past Times) were translated by Félix Frank—a journalist and professor of literature—and E. Alsleben.[10] The academic foreword presents, after various philosophical considerations on imagination, the tales as children's poetry (Frank and Alsleben iv) and likens them to Perrault's tales (xi). Moreover, the title of this collection is very similar to that of Perrault

(*Histoires ou contes du temps passé*) and particularly to that of its 1842 Curmer edition (*Contes du temps passé*).

The Twentieth Century

The turn of the century was marked by the *Contes des frères Grimm* (Tales of the Brothers Grimm), translated by Ernest Grégoire and Louis Moland and illustrated by Yan' d'argent, who had also published a French translation of Andersen's tales together. The preface claims that it contains a new choice of tales and a new translation (Grégoire and Moland v),[11] but at the same time it confesses that it was impossible not to include some of the more famous tales, such as "The Fisherman and His Wife," "Snow White," "The Gifts of the Little Folk," and "The Three Green Twigs" (x).[12]

The twentieth century offered numerous translations of the *Kinder- und Hausmärchen*. Some are individual tales or popular collections (especially for children), whereas other volumes lean toward a scholarly tradition and manifest more philological rigor than the nineteenth-century editions, for instance by providing the tales in the same order as in the *Kinder- und Hausmärchen*. An edition from 1959 even contains a "first book" and a "second book," with a selection of tales taken from the first and second volumes, respectively, of the *Kinder- und Hausmärchen*. Nevertheless, these translations continue to forward an opposition between Perrault's literary tales and the more popular tales that the Grimms supposedly only collected and assembled (see Robert, *Contes choisis*; Robert and Amsler). Only Rimasson-Fertin's 2009 and Jean Amsler's 2002 translations make use of Rölleke's work, thereby presenting a more truthful image of the Grimms and publishing the omitted tales. Amsler is careful to place the *Kinder- und Hausmärchen* in the context of European fairy-tale history, mentioning Perrault and Marie-Catherine d'Aulnoy and arguing that the Grimms' French predecessors have to be read in order to properly situate the *Kinder- und Hausmärchen* (260).

Direct Reference to Perrault in the Translations

Many of the forewords to the translations cited above mention Perrault to demonstrate that the *Kinder- und Hausmärchen* are part of the same genre as his tales and even the same species. Baudry, for example, begins his preface by claiming that the Grimms did for Germany at the beginning of the nineteenth century what Perrault had done for France at the end of the seventeenth (i). Frank and Alsleben indicate that the Grimms and Perrault drew from the same source (xi), and Grégoire and Moland place the Grimms' tales in a late nineteenth-century French quarrel over children's literature, calling Perrault to the rescue to justify the educative dimension of the *Kinder- und Hausmärchen*: "The good is always rewarded, and the bad always punished; they provide young souls with the 'desire to resemble those who become happy,' as Ch. Perrault said" (Grégoire and Moland ix–x, my translation).[13]

Perrault is thus a reference point that places francophone readers in a familiar context, but he is also used as a contrast to the Grimms' style. Baudry argues that "Perrault, whose only goal was to amuse his grandchildren, allowed himself to gallantly embroider on a background of legends," whereas "the Brothers Grimm, who aimed for a serious work of erudition, treated their tales with more discretion and respect" (i, my translation).[14] Similarly, Grégoire and Moland's foreword even emphasizes the particular characteristics of the *Kinder- und Hausmärchen* to distinguish the Grimms from the "author" Perrault, claiming that "they are more naïve than perhaps any other work of fairy tales"; that it could be felt that "the authors had no pretension as writers"; and that their aim was mainly to "faithfully reproduce the form in which these tales had been transmitted from generation to generation" (Grégoire and Moland vii, my translation).[15]

Thus seen as having drawn from the same well as Perrault, the Grimms are widely considered to have done so with greater integrity and more authenticity. Embedded in a nineteenth-century French stream of folklorism, the forewords to the translations describe the brothers as travelers, picking up on the Grimms' own foreword and often providing a detailed portrait of Dorothea Viehmann as the ideal storyteller. It is therefore not surprising that some editorial choices aim to demonstrate the differences between the tales of the Grimms and those of Perrault or other well-known French tales. For example, Frank and Alsleben's translation of "Aschenputtel" (Cinderella) contains a note that emphasizes the singularity of the Grimms' text, arguing that it "differs in almost every detail from that of Perrault" and that it was chosen to "illustrate these curious differences on the same subject, reflecting the country's essence" (90, my translation).[16] Generally speaking, French translations have a tendency to avoid tales that are very close to those of Perrault, and it is very revealing that except for Guerne's and Rimasson-Fertin's complete collections, none of the most important French editions translate "Rotkäppchen" (Little Red Cap).

THE INFLUENCE OF PERRAULT
ON THE TRANSLATION OF THE GRIMMS' TALES

Having outlined the main features of the French editions of the *Kinder- und Hausmärchen,* we will now consider more specifically how Perrault's influence can be felt in the translations of the tales. To do so, we will first look at the titles of the texts. Where the tales themselves are very close to those of Perrault, as with "Dornröschen," "Rotkäppchen," and "Aschenputtel," do the translators render the title of the *Kinder- und Hausmärchen* as faithfully as possible, or do they pick up Perrault's familiar title? Second, consideration will be given to the tales themselves and to instances in which words or expressions do not seem to have been translated directly from the German but rather conjure up French tales—intentionally or not. Finally, Perrault's influence will be sought at the stylistic level.

THE TRANSLATED TITLES

As regards the tales' titles, it appears that translators find it difficult to keep closely to the original and often choose a title that the reader would recognize. Guerne even goes so far as to add a parenthesis to the title of "Fitcher's Bird" in the table of contents, explaining that the tale is the German version of the well-known French "Bluebeard": "L'Oiseau d'Ourdi (ou Barbe-Bleue dans la poésie populaire allemande)." "Dornröschen" is another good example. It is frequently translated as "Rosebud" or "(Little) Brier (or Briar) Rose" in English editions. Only Ralph Manheim (1977) adds a parenthesis to the title, calling it "Brier Rose (The Sleeping Beauty)," probably directly influenced by Perrault, Disney, or the folktale index by Aarne-Thompson. While French translations from the nineteenth century, as well as Rimasson-Fertin's, also remain close to the original (translating "Dornröschen" as "Bouton de rose," "Rose d'eglantier," or "Rose d'épine"—Rosebud, Brier Rose, or Thorn Rose), Robert calls her version "La Belle au bois dormant" (The Sleeping Beauty in the Woods) and uses this term—which clearly comes from Perrault—in the main text. Guerne opts for an intermediate solution, and though he uses

The Reception of the Kinder- und Hausmärchen *in France* 185

"Fleur-d'épine" (Thorn-Flower) in the main text, he translates the title itself as "La Belle au bois dormant."

The case of "Rotkäppchen" is subtler. Perrault's "Le Petit Chaperon rouge" is most often translated as "Rotkäppchen" in German, except for Perrault 1761, where it was titled "Die kleine Roth-Kappe" (The Little Red Cap). It is thus difficult to distinguish Perrault's tale from the Grimms' in German. In English, however, Perrault's tale is called "Little Red Riding Hood," whereas the Grimms' is translated as "Little Red Cap." Guerne and Rimasson-Fertin both use Perrault's title "Le Petit Chaperon rouge" to translate the *Kinder- und Hausmärchen* (with Guerne adding a parenthesis in the table of contents, indicating that it is a "Bavarian version" of the tale).[17] One may wonder whether it would be judicious to follow English translations and use more dissimilar titles to distinguish the tales of Perrault and the Grimms, for example by calling the Grimms' tale "Petite Cape rouge." However, the main problem with the French translation of "Rotkäppchen" is that the article "Le" is used, as in Perrault's tale, though the title of the *Kinder- und Hausmärchen* and the name of its heroine are given without an article in German ("Blaubart" and "La Barbe bleue" provide a similar example). Putting the article in the translation of the title in French is not something that can be seen as required by French grammar but rather something inherited from Perrault.

In the case of "Aschenputtel," translators have—without exception—chosen to assume the link with Perrault by using his title "Cendrillon." In English too, the most common translation is "Cinderella" (which is also used for Perrault's tale), with Manheim and David Luke remaining closer to the German with "Ashputtle (Cinderella)" and "Ashiepattle," respectively. With some imagination, it would have been possible to also invent a French name by playing with the word for ashes (*cendre*), for example, "Cendroton." It seems, nevertheless, that when confronted with a well-known story line, translators are induced to choose a familiar title: German translations of Perrault prior to the *Kinder- und Hausmärchen* used the name "Aschenbrödel" for "Cendrillon," as in "Aschen-Brodel, oder der kleine gläserne Pantoffel" (1761, Aschen-Brodel, or the Little Glass Slipper) and "Fräulein Aschenbrödel, oder das Glass-Pantöffelchen" (1790, Miss Aschenbrödel, or the Little Glass Slipper); after the *Kinder- und Hausmärchen* were published, the term "Aschenputtel" became more frequently used.

Arguably, in their rendering of the Grimms' tales, French translators have tended to use equivalent titles from French literature, rather than staying close to the German original. Through such a dialogue, readers are confronted with something they can interpret in the framework of a fairy-tale genre they are accustomed to.

Words and Expressions

Translation is not an exact science, and translators frequently—though not always consciously—make choices that result in more or less significant differences from one edition to another. The line in "Aschenputtel" "So wird dir der liebe Gott immer beistehen" (Then the dear Lord shall always assist you) provides a typical example of this, as it has been translated in a variety of ways:

"alors le bon Dieu te viendra toujours en aide" (Robert, 1959 65)
"et le bon Dieu t'assistera toujours" (Rimasson-Fertin 139)
"et tu pourras compter sur l'aide du Bon Dieu" (Guerne 138)

These differences do not change the meaning of the tales as such but simply reflect a flexibility of expression provided by the French language. There are, however, also examples in which translators have made use of their margin of discretion to render their translations closer to the tales of Perrault, and this even when they ignore or downplay his influence in the foreword.

In the translations of "Rotkäppchen" for a younger audience, the usage of the dated term "mère-grand," rather than the more neutral "grand-mère" (grandmother), directly echoes Perrault. Indeed, the dictionary *Grand Robert* even quotes the beginning of Perrault's "Petit Chaperon rouge" to illustrate the meaning and use of the expression "mère-grand." In the same text, the expression "ein Stück Kuchen" (a piece of cake) is translated by Rimasson-Fertin as "un morceau de gâteau," whereas Guerne, as well as a number of translations for children, pick up on Perrault's famous and more specific "galette" (a round, flat cake). In "Bluebeard," Rimasson-Fertin translates "Kammer" (room) as "chambre," but Amsler employs the antiquated word "cabinet," used in "La Barbe bleue" by Perrault, which designates a special room—the old English "cabinet" or "closet." However, the Grimms use the word "Kammer" in several tales in a more neutral way, simply to designate a room. The use of the word "cabinet" refers to the reality of Perrault's reader, not to that of the Grimms. Whether or not these translation choices are consciously made, they are very likely to be the result of the translators' own conceptions of the genre. Knowing that they are rendering a fairy tale, they are induced into using a "fairy-tale language" associated with antiquated words. While this language mirrors the similarly archaic language of the *Kinder- und Hausmärchen,* the words used have their own specific meanings, based in the reality of Perrault and his contemporaries, rather than in nineteenth-century Germany.

The world of "Once upon a time" impregnated by the medieval imagery that fairy tales represent is also populated, in the imagination of the translators and their readers, by archetypal characters, for which the characters in the *Kinder- und Hausmärchen* are not easily substituted. Thus, the Grimms' "weise Frauen" (wise women) are frequently translated into French as "fées" (*Vieux contes*; Martin and Pitre-Chevalier; Guerne), although the *fée* and the *weise Frau* are not the same kind of being (see François, "Fées et weise Frauen"). The translation of *Stiefmutter* (stepmother) as "marâtre" (Frank and Alsleben; Guerne; Rimasson-Fertin) is also the result of an interpretative choice from a certain conception of the fairy-tale genre inherited in this case from d'Aulnoy, not Perrault. Though the German term can indeed have the negative connotation of *marâtre* (Grimm and Grimm, *Wörterbuch* 18.2806), the word "Stiefmutter" in itself is neutral, whereas "marâtre" has been used exclusively in a pejorative sense since the nineteenth century (*Grand Robert*). It is therefore an interpretative (though not faulty, see Robert, 1959 xv) reading that pushes for the use of "marâtre" rather than the more neutral "belle-mère." An even more apparent example of this is when Rimasson-Fertin translates the neutral term "Mutter" (mother) into the depreciatory "marâtre" (89) in "The Three Little Gnomes in the Forest."

This use of a supposed "fairy-tale language" can be problematic, as it sometimes leads to misunderstandings. Consider, for example, the following translations from "Brier Rose." In Grimm it is stated, "Er wußte auch von seinem Großvater" (Grimm and Grimm, *Ausgabe letzter Hand* I.259; The old man also knew from his grandfather). This is translated as "Le vieux dit au prince qu'il a entendu raconter à son grand-père" (Grégoire and Moland; The old man told the prince he had heard it told to or by his grandfather), or "Ce vieillard se souvenait d'avoir entendu dire à son grand-père"

(Martin and Pitre-Chevalier; That old man remembered having heard it said to or by his grandfather). The reflex with which the translators use Perrault's text (in which the old man says that "il y a plus de cinquante ans que j'ay ouï dire à mon pere" [over fifty years ago I heard said to or by my father]) modifies the sense of the *Kinder- und Hausmärchen*: has the character heard someone tell the story to his father, as in Perrault's tale, or is it the grandfather that tells the story directly to his grandson, as appears to be the case in the Grimms' tale?

Another example can be found in "Bluebeard." Rimasson-Fertin translates "auf der untersten Stufe" (467; on the bottom step) as "sur la première marche du perron," thus picking up the term "perron" that can be found in Perrault's "La Barbe bleue." In this latter tale, the killer tries to escape, but he is stopped on the *perron*, that is, on the stairs that can be found *outside* of his castle (Samber uses "steps of the porch" in his translation of Perrault's tale). The Grimm tale, on the other hand, indicates an *indoor* staircase that leads to the upper floor and Amsler would thus be more correct in his translation "sur la marche du bas de l'escalier" (on the step at the bottom of the staircase). The analysis of particular word choices thus shows that when rendering the *Kinder- und Hausmärchen* in French, translators have not simply picked corresponding words from a dictionary. Rather, they have consulted a fairy-tale vocabulary shaped by the classics of the genre, among which Perrault's work is the most influential.

The Style of Translations

Sometimes sentences are transformed on a larger scale. It is not always easy to clearly distinguish modifications that are linked to differences between German and French from those made to integrate a "fairy-tale language." Nonetheless, the incipits provide particularly telling examples of conscious changes related to the genre. The expressions "Il était une fois" and "Es war einmal" (Once upon a time) are frequently linked to Perrault's and the Grimms' tales. Whereas the former begins nine out of his eleven tales with "Il était une fois"[18] (like many other French authors of the time), only 76 of the 201 *Kinder- und Hausmärchen* from 1857 (38 percent) start this way.[19] Nonetheless, adaptations for children of the Grimms' tales have a tendency to begin systematically with the formula "Once upon a time," which has become synonymous with the fairy-tale genre.

The translations under study here are no different. Guerne and Rimasson-Fertin use "Il était une fois" more often than the Grimms do, though their rates (of 42 percent and 47 percent, respectively) remain reasonable in comparison with other translations: Gérard uses the expression in 89 percent of the tales (although only 33 percent of the tales he translates begin with "Es war einmal" in German), and Grégoire and Moland in 75 percent (46 percent in German).[20] Significantly, the number of tales that begin with "Il était une fois" is obviously linked to the choice of tales that are translated: animal and religious tales do not begin with "Es war einmal" in the *Kinder- und Hausmärchen*; therefore, it is logical that the rates for Martin vol. 2 and Amsler, which focus on such tales, are particularly low (31 percent and 24 percent, respectively). Nevertheless, even in the complete editions, the higher percentage is noticeable. According to Harald Weinrich, "Once upon a time" is essential to the fairy-tale genre, as it marks the border between the real world and that of fiction (48–49). Through their use of the formula, French translators have provided francophone readers with texts that correspond with their expectations.

The main differences between Perrault and the Grimms go beyond particular words and are more about how they tell their stories. The logic of the *Kinder- und Hausmärchen* is chronological, and the actions follow one another almost naturally, generating the impression that the events tell themselves (Benveniste 241). In Perrault's tales, as in those of Andersen, the presence of the narrator is much stronger, and there is a feeling that the tales are being commented on and explained, as well as told. This is done particularly through the use of causal utterances, which describe the reasons behind events and the motivations of the characters. In contrast, the parataxis of the *Kinder- und Hausmärchen* forces readers to reconstruct the causal links themselves. This difference is illustrated by the following extracts from "La Belle au bois dormant" and "Dornröschen":

> A peine s'avança-t-il vers le bois, que tous ces grands arbres, ces ronces & ces épines s'écarterent d'elles-mesmes pour le laisser passer: il marche vers le Chasteau qu'il voyoit au bout d'une grande avenuë où il entra, & ce qui le surprit un peu, il vit que personne de ses gens ne l'avoient pû suivre, parce que les arbres s'estoient rapprochez dés qu'il avoit esté passé. (Perrault, *Contes de Perrault* 22)[21]

Nun waren aber gerade die hundert Jahre verflossen, und der Tag war ge-
kommen, wo Dornröschen wieder erwachen sollte. Als der Königssohn
sich der Dornenhecke näherte, waren es lauter große schöne Blumen,
die thaten sich von selbst auseinander und ließen ihn unbeschädigt hin-
durch, und hinter ihm thaten sie sich wieder als eine Hecke zusammen.
(Grimm and Grimm, *Ausgabe letzter Hand* I.259)[22]

In "La Belle au bois dormant," the narrator assists the reader by explaining
why the thorns open up for the prince ("*to* let him pass through") and why the
men cannot follow the prince through them ("*because* the trees closed again").
In "Dornröschen," the narration follows a temporal succession (*Nun, und, als,
und, und*), and the fact that the thorns open up precisely in order to let the prince
through remains implicit. Guerne translates "und ließen ihn unbeschädigt hin-
durch" as "pour lui ouvrir le passage" (287), adding a causal relationship, and
Rimasson-Fertin uses the exact words of Perrault, "pour le laisser passer." In the
translation from Grégoire and Moland, the last *und* is replaced by a *mais*, something that gives readers an element of interpretation instead of leaving them to
infer by themselves what the closing of the thorns means for the prince. Martin
and Pitre-Chevalier make the most changes in this regard, by explicitly developing that which was only implied in the *Kinder- und Hausmärchen*:

Il se trouvait que ce jour même complétait les cent ans pendant lesquels
devait durer *le charme jeté par la méchante fée. Aussi,* dès que le jeune prince
s'avança vers la haie d'épines, celle-ci *se changea* en une innombrable quan-
tité de fleurs ravissantes qui s'entr'ouvrirent d'elles-mêmes *afin de* lui livrer
passage; *puis quand il fut entré,* elles se refermèrent de nouveau en haie
brillante derrière lui. (Martin and Pitre-Chevalier 120, my emphasis)[23]

The addition of conjunctions and the suppression of temporal adverbs elim-
inate the effect of the parataxis that distinguishes the writing of the Grimms.
The voice of the Grimms' tale is therefore replaced by that of a more evident
narrator who provides further explanations.[24]

CONCLUSION

Literature is governed by a dialogical principle and every new oeuvre owes
a good deal to literary exchange and translation.[25] In this regard, the case of

the *Kinder- und Hausmärchen* is particularly interesting: the Grimms were influenced by Perrault and French tales more generally (Velten; François, "Echanges et dialogues intertextuels"), but in return they also had an impact in France, as demonstrated, for example, by Gustave Doré's engravings for the 1862 Hetzel edition of Perrault's tales, which were clearly inspired by the Grimms' world.

The Grimms and Perrault seem inseparable in the history of tales in France, and when the *Kinder- und Hausmärchen* were translated into the French, Perrault was a great influence. The forewords to the translations often evoke his *Contes* to show a tie of familiarity with the *Kinder- und Hausmärchen* but also to insist on their differences. On the one hand, Perrault has come to play an integrating role, linking foreign texts to the French literary heritage and thereby facilitating their reception. Indeed, as the *Kinder- und Hausmärchen* were to be sold as fairy tales, the translators needed them to be recognized as such, and for this they had to fit into the French perception of the genre. On the other hand, Perrault is also used as a contrast to highlight the originality of the Grimms and emphasize cultural differences. Translators have, for example, chosen texts with the least resemblance to those of Perrault or, conversely, opted for very similar ones in order to underline the singularity of the Grimms' tales by comparison. However, even when Perrault is referred to for contrasting purposes, his presence informs the translation: the selection of tales, the choice of titles, and even the style clearly depend on Perrault's influence.

More generally, there is an impression that the translators do not translate the Grimms' tales directly but that they transcribe them in a "fairy-tale language," a subsystem of the French language in which Perrault's *Contes* play an important role. In some extreme cases, such as in certain adaptations for children, the translations mix elements from Perrault and the Grimms to such an extent that the notion of an author at all no longer seems relevant. For example, some versions of "Rotkäppchen" use Perrault's formula "tire la chevillette, et la bobinette cherra" (Pull the bobbin, and the latch will go up; Perrault, *Histories, or Tales of Past Times* 4) or present a lumberjack instead of a hunter and a galette and butter instead of a piece of cake and wine (Jeanneret 26).

Henri Meschonnic has argued that Europe is born in and from translation (32), and Cay Dollerup has underlined the importance of translations for the creation of an international fairy-tale genre (x). Indeed, the Grimms' reception in France demonstrates the great extent to which translation does not consist of a simple act of transcription from one language to another. On the contrary, it is dependent on cultural and discursive facts, such as genres, which means that the *Kinder- und Hausmärchen* have not been translated just into French, into the "tongue of Molière," but also into a "fairy-tale language," the "tongue of Perrault."

NOTES

1. Riitta Oittinen also refers to Bakhtin's dialogism and shows how well this concept applies to the process of translating for children that includes authors, translators, readers, and illustrators (25–32).

2. When titles are not indicated, dates are used to refer to translations of the *Kinder- und Hausmärchen*. The name of the first translator is used when they are referred to in the text.

3. The thirty-one texts pick up thirty-three of the *Kinder- und Hausmärchen* (eighteen of which can be read in the *Kleine Ausgabe*), since one of the tales is a compilation of three Grimm tales. The second volume of *German Popular Stories*, published in 1826, was translated in 1830 by the same editor.

4. The English titles and quotations of the *Kinder- und Hausmärchen* refer to Jack Zipes's translation (Grimm and Grimm, *Complete Fairy Tales*). When quoting the *Kinder- und Hausmärchen* in German, the page number refers to Grimm and Grimm (*Kinder- und Hausmärchen. Ausgabe letzter Hand*).

5. KHM 1, 110, 129, 6, 14, 10, 25, 15, 51, 37, 55, 59, 69, 98, 106, 20, 124, 151.

6. They represent only 20 percent and 22 percent, respectively, of the *Kleine Ausgabe,* and three of the tales translated were not even published in the *Kinder- und Hausmärchen. Volume 1*: KHM 57, 53, 78, 98, 60, 40; KL 8; KHM 142, 9, 177, 122, 50, 129, 35, 54, 49, 52, 191, 151, 200, 28, 184, 192, 180, 189, 44, 14, 16, 175, 176, 62, 97, 85, 118, 186, 152, 145, 109, 160, 155, 6. *Volume 2*: KHM 3; KL 6; KHM 161, 33, 123, 133, 70; and "Le Meilleur Souhait" (The Best Wish). "Le Meilleur Souhait" is also published with the title "Chanson de H. Heine" translated by N. Martin in *L'Artiste* (30 May 1847); it is in fact Johann Hebel's "Drey andere Wünsche" (170). KHM 121, 169, "La mort la plus douce pour les criminels" (The Sweetest Death for Criminals; from Hebel 268–69); *Deutsche Sagen* 362; KHM 92, 48, 130, 107, 86, 83, 72, 87, 182a; KL 5; KHM 154, 150, 29, 174, 8, 63; KL 7; KHM 88, 75, 77, 156, 103, 116, 124, 104a, 115, 73, 1, 101, 134, 17, 99, 135.

7. "Parmi les contes que j'ai négligés à dessein, les uns s'éloignent trop de notre genre d'esprit."

8. Fourteen tales can be found in the *Kleine Ausgabe* (35 percent). The tales are provided in subcategories. Moral tales: KHM 182, 161, 62, 78, 6, 107, 19, 145, 156, 184, 83; short religious legends: KHM 3, 153, KL 5, 6, 8, 9; fantastic and facetious tales: 101, 14, 29, 37, 36, 71, 39, 70, 24, 188, 179, 181, 11, 167, 110, 20, 10, 90, 178, 187, 195, 102, 27.

9. "graves savants"; "trop connus pour qu'il soit nécessaire de rappeler ici tous leurs titres au respect de l'Europe savante."

10. This translation, edited three times, contains around 50 percent of the tales in the *Kleine Ausgabe,* and only three of its seventeen tales were previously unpublished in France: KHM 53, 182a, 39, 97, 106, 14, 52, 179, 24, 17, 11, 44, 116, 21, 12, 49, 13.

11. Originality seems to be a common argument; see also Martin (*Contes de la famille par les frères Grimm* xvi) and Baudry (*Contes choisis des frères Grimm* vi–vii).

12. This translation was reedited several times: KHM 182, 89, 15, 169, 165, 129, 101, 195, 97, 44, 92, 161, 52, 19, 81, 166, 71, 25, 53; KL 6; KHM 11, 83, 110, 4, 27, 3, 91, 116. Half of the tales are contained in the *Kleine Ausgabe.*

13. "le bien y est toujours récompensé et le mal toujours puni; elles font naître dans les jeunes âmes 'le désir de ressembler à ceux qui deviennent heureux', comme disait Ch. Perrault."

14. "Mais Perrault, qui ne se proposait d'autre but que d'amuser ses petits-enfants, s'était permis sur le fond légendaire des broderies galantes, conformes au goût de son temps. Les frères Grimm, qui voulaient faire une oeuvre sérieuse d'érudition, ont traité leurs récits avec plus de discrétion et de respect." An article from *Journal des Débats* that presented the German edition of the *Kinder- und Hausmärchen* in 1832 runs along the same lines.

15. "ils ont la naïveté à un plus haut degré peut-être qu'aucun autre ouvrage de la littérature féérique. On sent que les auteurs n'ont aucune prétention d'écrivains, et que, tout en mettant sur pied, bien entendu, les récits qu'ils entendaient, ils ont tâché de reproduire fidèlement la forme sous laquelle ces récits s'étaient transmis de génération en génération."

16. "Le conte allemand diffère dans presque tous ses détails du conte de Perrault; c'est pour cela que nous l'avons choisi, afin de montrer ces différences curieuses d'un même sujet, suivant le génie du pays."

17. This addition is particularly interesting, as the Grimms state, "aus den Maingegenden" (from the Main area), meaning that the story comes from the Grimms' friend Marie Hassenpflug, who lived in Hanau, in the Main area.

18. One of which is actually a novella rather than a tale.

19. As a reminder, there are 201 tales, not 200 as suggested by the number of the last one, since there are 2 tales numbered 151 in the 1857 edition. The percentage is similar for the *Kleine Ausgabe,* but in the 1810 manuscript around 50 percent of the tales began with "Es war einmal."

20. Martin vol. 1: 44 percent, 1824: 49 percent; Frank: 53 percent; Robert: 51 percent.

21. "Scarce had he advanced towards the wood, when all the great trees, the bushes and brambles gave way of themselves to let him pass through: he walked up to the castle that he saw at the end of a large Avenue which he went into; and what a little surprised him, was, that he saw none of his people could follow him, because the trees closed again, as soon as he had passed through them" (Samber 44).

22. "Now the hundred years had just ended, and the day on which Brier Rose was to wake up again had arrived. When the prince approached the brier hedge, he found nothing but beautiful flowers that opened of their own accord, let him through, and then closed again like a hedge" (Zipes 174).

23. "It was the same day that completed the hundred years that *the spell* cast *by the evil fairy* should last. *Therefore*, as soon as the young prince approached the thorn hedge, it *changed* into a countless mass of ravishing flowers that half-opened by themselves *in order to* let him through; *then when he had entered*, they closed again as a shiny hedge behind him" (my translation).

24. In general, French translations tend to remove or simplify sentences and avoid the repetitions that are characteristic of the language of the Brothers Grimm, thereby bringing the style even closer to that of Perrault.

25. For example, it was the first English translation that gave the Grimms the idea for the *Kleine Ausgabe* (Grimm and Grimm, *Nach der zweiten vermehrten und verbesserten Auflage von 1819*, 554–55).

References

Amsler, Jean, trans. *Nouveaux contes.* By Jacob Grimm and Wilhelm Grimm. Paris: Gallimard, 2002.

Aulnoy, Marie-Catherine Le Jumel de Barneville d'. *Contes des fées; suivis des contes nouveaux ou les fées à la mode.* Paris: H. Champion, 2004.

Bakhtin, Mikhail M. *Speech Genres and Other Late Essays.* Trans. Vern W. McGee. Eds. C. Emerson and M. Holquist. Austin: U of Texas P, 1986.

Barchilon, Jacques. "Personal Reflections on the Scholarly Reception of Grimms' Tales in France." *The Reception of Grimm's Fairy Tales.* Ed. D. Haase. Detroit: Wayne State UP, 1993. 269–82.

Baudry, Frédéric, trans. *Contes choisis des frères Grimm.* By Jacob Grimm and Wilhelm Grimm. Paris: Hachette, 1855.

Benveniste, Emile. *Problèmes de linguistique générale.* Vol. 1. Paris: Gallimard, 1966.

Blamires, David. "The Early Reception of the Grimms' *Kinder- und Hausmärchen* in England." *The Translation of Children's Literature.* Ed. G. Lathey. Clevedon: Multilingual Matters, 2006. 163–74.

Chasles, Philarète. "Le Perrault scandinave et les petits enfants." *Encore sur les contemporains, leurs œuvres et leurs mœurs.* By Chasles. Paris: Amyot, 1869. 195–209.

Denecke, Ludwig, Teitge Irmgard, and Friedhilde Krause, eds. *Die Bibliothek der Brüder Grimm: Annotiertes Verzeichnis des festgestellten Bestandes.* Weimar: Herman Böhlaus Nachfolger, 1989.

Die Blaue Bibliothek aller Nationen. Vol. 1. Gotha: Ettinger, 1790.

Dollerup, Cay. *Tales and Translation. The Grimm Tales from Pan-Germanic Narratives to Shared International Fairytales.* Amsterdam: John Benjamins, 1999.

François, Cyrille. "Echanges et dialogues intertextuels: l'exemple des contes de Perrault et des frères Grimm." *É/change: transitions et transactions dans la littérature française/Ex/change: Transitions et Transactions in French Literature.* Eds. M. Bragança and S. Wilson. Oxford: Peter Lang, 2011. 43–57.

———. "Fées et weise Frauen. Les faiseuses de dons chez Perrault et les Grimm, du merveilleux rationalisé au merveilleux naturalisé." *Des* Fata *aux fées: regards croisés de l'Antiquité à nos jours.* Eds. M. Hennard Dutheil de la Rochère and V. Dasen. Lausanne: U de Lausanne P, 2011. 259–78. Etudes de Lettres 289.3–4.

Frank, Félix, and E. Alsleben, trans. *Contes allemands du temps passé. Extraits des recueils des frères Grimm, et de Simrock, Bechstein, Franz Hoffmann, Musæus, Tieck, Schwab, Winter, etc. avec la légende de Loreley.* By Jacob Grimm, Wilhelm Grimm, et al. Paris: Librairie académique Didier et Cie, 1869.

Gérard, F.-C., trans. *Contes choisis de Grimm, à l'usage des enfants, traduits de l'allemand.* By Jacob Grimm and Wilhelm Grimm. Paris: J. Langlumé et Peltier, 1836.

Grégoire, Ernest, and Louis Moland, trans. *Contes des frères Grimm.* By Jacob Grimm and Wilhelm Grimm. Paris: Garnier frères, n.d.

Grimm, Jacob, and Wilhelm Grimm. *Deutsches Wörterbuch.* 33 vols. Munich: Deutscher Taschenbuch Verlag, 1984.

———. *Die älteste Märchensammlung der Brüder Grimm: Synopse der handschriftlichen Urfassung von 1810 und der Erstdrucke von 1812.* Ed. H. Rölleke. Geneva: Fondation Martin Bodmer, 1975.

———. *Kinder- und Hausmärchen. Ausgabe letzter Hand.* Ed. H. Rölleke. 3 vols. Stuttgart: Philipp Reclam, 2001.

———. *Kinder- und Hausmärchen. Kleine Ausgabe.* Berlin: Franz Dunder, 1858.

———. *Kinder- und Hausmärchen; nach der zweiten vermehrten und verbesserten Auflage von 1819.* Ed. H. Rölleke. Cologne: Eugen Diederichs Verlag, 1986.

———. *Les Veillées allemandes.* Trans. l'Héritier. Paris: impr. de Mme Huzard, 1838.

———. *Traditions allemandes.* Trans. Napoléon Theil. Paris: A. Levavasseur, 1838.

Guerne, Armel, trans. *Contes.* By Jacob Grimm and Wilhelm Grimm. 2 vols. Paris: Flammarion, 1967.

Hebel, Johann P. *Schatzkästlein des rheinischen Hausfreundes.* Tübingen: Cotta, 1811.

Jeanneret, Thérèse. "Une approche linguistique de la simplicité du texte." *Langage et pratiques* 31 (2003): 22–35.

"Littérature allemande." *Journal des Débats* [Paris] (4 Aug. 1832): 1–3.

Luke, David, trans. *Selected Tales.* By Jacob Grimm and Wilhelm Grimm. Harmondsworth: Penguin Classics, 1982.

Manheim, Ralph, trans. *Grimms' Tales for Young and Old.* By Jacob Grimm and Wilhelm Grimm. Garden City: Doubleday, 1977.

Martin, Nicolas, trans. *Contes de la famille par les frères Grimm.* By Jacob Grimm and Wilhelm Grimm. Vol. 2. Paris: J. Renouard, 1848.

Martin, Nicolas, and Pitre-Chevalier, trans. *Contes de la famille par les frères Grimm.* By Jacob Grimm and Wilhelm Grimm. Vol. 1. Paris: J. Renouard, 1846.

Meschonnic, Henri. *Poétique du traduire.* Lagrasse: Verdier, 1999.

Oittinen, Riitta. *Translating for Children.* New York: Garland, 2000.

Perrault, Charles. *Contes.* Paris: Hetzel, 1862.

———. *Contes de fées avec des moralités—Erzählungen der Mutter Loye von den vergangenen Zeiten.* Berlin: Arnold Wever, 1761.

———. *Contes de Perrault.* Geneva: Slatkine Reprints, 1980.

———. *Contes du temps passé.* Paris: L. Curmer, 1842.

Rimasson-Fertin, Natacha, trans. *Contes pour les enfants et la maison.* 2 vols. By Jacob Grimm and Wilhelm Grimm. Paris: José Corti, 2009.

Robert, M., trans. *Contes.* By Jacob Grimm and Wilhelm Grimm. Paris: Le Club français du livre, 1959.

———. *Contes.* By Jacob Grimm and Wilhelm Grimm. Paris: Gallimard, 1976.

———. *Contes choisis.* By Jacob Grimm and Wilhelm Grimm. Paris: Gallimard, 2000.

Robert, Marthe, and J. Amsler, trans. *Contes.* Ed. J.-M. Sapet. By Jacob Grimm and Wilhelm Grimm. Paris: Gallimard, 2006.

Robert, Paul, and Alain Rey. "Grand-mère." Le Grand Robert de la langue française. Version numérique 2.2. Paris: Dictionnaires Le Robert. http://gr.bvdep.com. 10 Oct. 2011.

Robert, Paul, and Alain Rey. "Marâtre." Le Grand Robert de la langue française. Version numérique 2.2. Paris: Dictionnaires Le Robert. http://gr.bvdep.com. 10 Oct. 2011.

Samber, R., trans. *Histories, or Tales of Past Times. With Morals.* By Jacob Grimm and Wilhelm Grimm. London: J. Pote and R. Montagu, 1729.

Taylor, E., trans. *German Popular Stories.* By Jacob Grimm and Wilhelm Grimm. London: C. Baldwyn, 1823.

Velten, Harry. "The Influence of Charles Perrault's *Contes de ma mère l'oie* on German Folklore." *Germanic Review* 1 (1930): 4–18.

Vieux contes pour l'amusement des grands et des petits enfans. Ornés de 12 Gravures comiques. Paris: A. Boulland, 1824.

Weinrich, Harald. *Tempus. Besprochene und erzählte Welt.* Stuttgart: W. Kohlhammer, 1977.

Zipes, Jack, trans. *The Complete Fairy Tales of the Brothers Grimm.* By Jacob Grimm and Wilhelm Grimm. New York: Bantam, 2003.

10

Skeptics and Enthusiasts

Nineteenth-Century Prefaces to the Grimms' Tales
in English Translation

RUTH B. BOTTIGHEIMER

Nineteenth-century English translations of Jacob and Wilhelm Grimm's folktales and fairy tales nearly always began with a preface of some sort, and when a newly translated edition appeared, its preface generally talked at length about fairy tales themselves as well as about the Grimms' own tales. For today's readers these prefaces reveal their authors' conceptualization of fairy tales, their reception of the Grimms' theories, and their formulations of oral transmission and fairy-tale history. These English prefaces also articulate tensions between two schools of thought: a historical one dating from the scientific revolution of the seventeenth and eighteenth centuries that relied on logic and evidence and a Romantic one that increasingly accepted the Grimms' nineteenth-century concept of fairy tales as folk creations.

In their early prefaces to the *Kinder- und Hausmärchen* (Children's and Household Tales) the Grimms had acknowledged that certain tales first appeared in Giovan Francesco Straparola's *Piacevoli notti* (Pleasant Nights, 1551, 1553). Although these tales were not documented in the Middle Ages, the Grimms firmly believed and actively asserted that they had existed in that period, reasoning that their absence from *written* records proved their presence in an unlettered *oral* tradition (Bottigheimer, *History* 36–37). In England educated reasoning since the scientific revolution had required evidence. But the Grimms' conclusions about fairy tales' oral circulation rested on a large lacuna. In the foreword to the first edition of the *Children's and Household Tales* in 1812, Wilhelm had written that it was "certain that tales

[*Märchen*] have constantly regenerated themselves over the course of time, and for just that reason their foundations must be very old. They are proven to be nearly three hundred years old by traces in Fischart and Rollenhagen, as we have remarked in the notes to the tales. It is doubtless, however, that they are far older, even though an absence of references to them makes direct proofs impossible" (xiii–xiv, my translation).

The Grimms' lack of proof for that ancient oral circulation created a stumbling block for early nineteenth-century English preface authors, and their prefaces demonstrate ambivalence about the Grimms' theories. In the second half of the nineteenth century, however, such ambivalence gave way to acceptance, celebration, and even extension of the Grimms' concepts. How should twenty-first-century critics understand an evolving nineteenth-century propensity to accept a history of fairy tales' peasant creation and subsequently to create theories about illiterate storytellers' millennia-long oral transmission of those same fairy tales? Why might earlier nineteenth-century British preface authors have been reluctant to accept those concepts? I will argue that their initial caution resulted from lingering memories of the harsh controversies surrounding the eighteenth-century *Poems of Ossian*.

JAMES MACPHERSON, *POEMS OF OSSIAN*

In the 1760s, thoughts about Britain's ancient past arose with an urgency that befitted an emerging economic power's desire for a cohesive national identity and persuasive historical roots. It was then that James Macpherson (1736–1796) imposed on British credulity by forging a literary document that satisfied contemporary longings for links to Britain's ancient past. Macpherson was a young, ambitious schoolteacher, an unstoppable writer of verse, and an enthusiastic reciter of Gaelic poetry. He claimed to have collected ancient Gaelic manuscripts containing epic poetry recounting adventures of the mythic hero Fingal, and he announced their author to be a third-century Irish bardic singer, whom he identified as Ossian, son of the cattle-rustling hero Finn McCool. Macpherson began publishing the poetry in late 1761 and by 1765 had gathered the poems into a single volume.

A sensation in Europe as a whole as well as in Britain, the Ossianic poems entered J. W. von Goethe's widely read novel *Die Leiden des jungen Werther* (1774, The Sorrows of Young Werther), whose pan-European success gave the poems, soon translated into Italian, Spanish, French, Dutch, Danish,

German, Russian, Polish, and Hungarian, an added impulse among youthful Romantics all over Europe. A few skeptics demurred. They pointed out that neither traditional poetry nor documentary history provided evidence for a son of Finn McCool named Ossian, and they argued that Macpherson had simply created poetry to fill an empty, and thus available, space in the corpus of Gaelic legends. From the first, the poetical works of Ossian excited heated controversy about their genuineness (Gaskill, Magnusson, Moore).

One of the doubters was a bright young Irish Protestant named Thomas Keightley (1789–1872). As a boy he had loved the Ossian poems and as an adult he felt betrayed when he learned that they were "an audacious and successful forgery" (*Popular Fictions* 169). Keightley took comfort in a sense of a superior *English* reliance on reason when he pointed out that the "forgery, which although disproven, is still believed by many Continental scholars" (169). Celtic antiquities, "the wildest and most improbable figments and deductions that have ever come to my knowledge" were such "incredibilities" that "rational men" seem to have flung off all the restraints of common sense and reason, he wrote (175–76). When Keightley needed a job at the age of twenty-five, he moved to London and joined Thomas Crofton Croker (1798–1854) in his production of the *Fairy Legends and Traditions of the South of Ireland*.[1]

In Keightley's view, Croker's *Fairy Legends and Traditions* had been "intended to be nothing more than a work of amusement," from which nothing could be learned about the Irish people (*Popular Fictions* 180). After listing the tales and verses that he had contributed to Croker's *Fairy Legends and Traditions,* Keightley admitted committing a forgery himself by having knitted together remembered bits and pieces and passing them off to Croker as genuine oral tradition from the Ireland of his youth (*Fairy Mythology* 362–67). Keightley's account of his sophomoric trick revealed a not altogether innocent amusement; it was in a sense a conscious repeat of Macpherson's offense at the expense of the "improbable figments and deductions" of otherwise rational men whose unquestioning beliefs he decried. Although much smaller in scale than Macpherson's affront, Keightley's eagerness to fool his English contemporaries was a forgery nonetheless, and it remained in Croker's 1825 book. Jacob Grimm, deeply impressed by Croker's scholarship, translated it into German as *Irische Elfenmärchen* (Irish Fairy Stories). Thus Keightley's forged tale lived on as evidence of folk literary creation not only in the English original but also in an influential German translation.

Keightley, little more than five years younger than the Grimms themselves, differed from them in important respects. Although a Protestant, Keightley was an Irishman in London and thus a cultural *outsider.* He felt excluded and wrote bitterly of the ways in which his Irish education at Trinity College Dublin resulted in Cambridge and Oxford historians' rejection of the history books he wrote. The Grimms, poor young men living in Cassel and employed by a king whom the hated oppressor Napoleon Bonaparte had set on the Hessian margrave's throne, were economic and—for the moment—national *outsiders,* but as Reformed German Protestants in a Hessian duchy whose legitimate monarch and power elite was also Reformed German Protestant, they were cultural *insiders.* Thus the Grimms proceeded from a different mental and emotional foundation. They did not ridicule credulousness about national roots, as Keightley had done; instead they actively searched for and asserted national German identity, which they explained and expressed in the preface to their *Children's and Household Tales.*

EDGAR TAYLOR, *GERMAN POPULAR STORIES*

Edgar Taylor (1793–1839), the first translator of the Grimms' tales into English,[2] was—like Keightley—a cultural outsider, whose Dissenter religion excluded him from studying at Oxford or Cambridge. However, he received a solid education in classics at a Dissenter academy, the Palgrave School, and as an adult he was, unlike Keightley, an intellectual insider. Taylor read several modern languages (Italian, French, Spanish, and German) and, with his broad intellectual interests, contributed regularly to journals such as *Morning Chronicle, New Monthly, Retrospective Review,* and *Westminster Review* (Stephen 407). In 1823 Taylor translated and published some of the Grimm tales as *German Popular Stories,* with a second volume three years later.

A senior partner in a prosperous law firm, Taylor was an unlikely translator for a book of amusement for children, and indeed, his name did not appear in the book either as translator or editor. The title page of Taylor's *Popular German Tales* devoted half its printed space to an image of a jolly reader entrancing rapt hearthside listeners. An epigraph from a 1621 chapbook, the *History of Tom Thumbe the Little,* followed directly: "Now you must imagine me to sit by a good fire, among a companye of good fellowes, over a well spiced wassel bowle of Christmas ale, telling of these merrie tales which hereafter followe." The title page image linked *oral delivery* to a *written book* via *reading to assembled listeners.* Thus Taylor associated an artifact (book) with a process (telling tales), two categories long considered to be socially distinct (books as possessions for the privileged) and mutually exclusive (telling tales among unlettered folk).

With a book source for storytelling, as the illustrator George Cruikshank depicted it on the title page, Taylor's English publisher C. Baldwyn contextualized storytelling within literate practices (Sumpter 131; Schenda 131–32). The illustration communicated an expectation that the Grimm tales that Taylor's translation would tell would also be read, either silently by an individual reader or aloud to assembled listeners, who were probably literate or preliterate children. In the preface that followed, Taylor categorized the Grimms' tales as "popular fictions and traditions" (iii) and spoke of "the wide and early diffusion of these gay creations of the imagination," whose origin he located in "some great and mysterious fountain head" (iv) from which "Calmuck, Russian, Celt, Scandinavian, and German . . . [had] imbibed their earliest lessons of moral instruction" (iv).

This sounds like the Grimms' hypothesis that ancient tales were subsequently disseminated orally throughout the world. Taylor accepted Wilhelm Grimm's account of the tales' collection and wrote that they came "for the most part from the mouths of German peasants" (vi), which fitted comfortably with a mythologized British history, in which "Hengist and Horsa, and Ebba the Saxon" had brought "Jack the Giant Killer, and Thomas Thumb" to England's shores (vi).[3] At first blush it seems that Taylor accepted claims about peasant origins for the Grimms' tales, even though he found them "sometimes overstrained" (viii).

Taylor knew about the "resemblances" of the "strongest and [most] minute" sort between tales in Giambattista Basile's *Pentamerone* and magical tales in "The Nights of Strapparola" (*sic*) that subsequently became "so popular in [t]he French fairy tales" on the one hand and in certain German tales on the other hand (ix). But the claim that plots and stories from the early seventeenth-century Neapolitan Basile were present among native and illiterate German peasants also raised serious doubts in Taylor's mind: "How far," he wanted to know, "[were] the well-known vehicles of the lighter southern fictions . . . current at an early period in Germany?" When Taylor wrote, "vehicles of lighter southern fictions," he seems to have meant books, since he was unlikely to have referred to living individuals with this term of inanimacy, and by "current" he meant circulating in Germany.

In other words, Taylor appears to have subscribed to theories of dissemination via books rather than by voices, despite his comments about Hengist and Horsa. Knowing that some of Basile's tales had appeared in Straparola's collection seventy-five years before the *Pentamerone,* Taylor was troubled by the Grimms' implying that Basile had relied on oral sources in their statement within a discussion of oral transmission that "[Basile's] contents leave almost nothing out and are without artificial additions, the style overflowing in good speeches and proverbs" (1812 xvii–xviii, my translation) when, Taylor indicated, Straparola's published tales had been available both to Basile and directly or indirectly to Basile's informants. When it came to Near Eastern narrative elements within German tales that had supposedly been handed down orally from ages past, Taylor queried the Grimm theories once again. There were gaps in the Grimms' chain of evidence, and Taylor wished that Wilhelm had spent more time explaining the combination of oriental and "Northern" features (viii):

> In these popular stories, they are sanguine enough to believe, is concealed the pure and primitive mythology of the Teutons, which has been considered as lost for ever; and they are convinced that if such researches are continued in the different districts of Germany, the traditions of this nature that are now neglected, will change into treasures of incredible worth, and assist in affording a new basis for the study of the origin of their ancient poetical fictions. On these points their illustrations, though sometimes overstrained, are often highly interesting and satisfactory. Perhaps more attention might have been directed to illustrate the singular admixture of oriental incidents of fairy and romance, with the ruder features of Northern fable; and particularly to inform us how far the well-known vehicles of the lighter southern fictions were current at an earlier period in Germany. It often seems difficult to account for the currency, among the peasantry on the shores of the Baltic and the forests of the Hartz, of fictions that would seem to belong to the Entertainments of the Arabians, yet involved in legends referable to the highest Teutonic origin. (viii–ix)

What, Taylor is asking, could account for a German-speaking peasant on the Baltic shores or in the Harz mountains having access to material from "Entertainments of the Arabians" and putting it into "legends referable to the highest Teutonic origin" (ix)? Taylor required proof and evidence to support conclusions and raised important questions about the similarities between the fairy tales by Straparola, Basile, Perrault, Madame d'Aulnoy, and the Grimms' German peasant informants.

THOMAS KEIGHTLEY AGAIN

Thomas Keightley, who outlived Edgar Taylor by many years, continued to write about tales and popular fictions. Six years after *Fairy Mythology* (1828), he brought out *Tales and Popular Fictions* (1834), in which he tried to account for the presence noted by Taylor of the same or similar tales in cultures distant and different from one another. Keightley reasoned that two forces were at work to produce the same or similar tales among different populations. In his view, people's behavior is everywhere much the same, and they are consequently likely to value similar qualities and to speak in similar metaphors.[4] Keightley also recognized a competing model for the dissemination of tales: on some occasions a single originary tale from the past had spread over time and through space and was responsible for the existence of a contemporary tale, a process that would later be labeled "monogenesis."

Keightley, acknowledging that certain similarities could *not* be accounted for by polygenetic parallel creations, developed a protocol to distinguish between the two processes: "When, in a tale of some length, a number of circumstances are the same, and follow in the same order, as in another, I should feel disposed to assert that this is a case of transmission [i.e., monogenesis]. Brief fictitious circumstances, such as shoes of swiftness and coats of darkness, might . . . be independent, and be referred [i.e., polygenetically] to what I termed the poverty of human imagination, which, having a limited stock of materials to work on, must of necessity frequently produce similar combinations" (*Popular Fictions* 6–7).[5]

Keightley then created an objective standard for understanding and analyzing similarities among fairy tales in different national traditions and for measuring differences between transmitted (monogenetic) narratives and independently invented (polygenetic) narratives.[6] In distinguishing between "transmitted" and "independent" tales, Keightley allowed for both literate and oral creation and for both published and oral dissemination (*Popular Fictions* 12–13). If his views had taken hold, they would have affected the understanding of the complex and distinct histories of individual fairy tales and hence the writings of prefaces to the Grimms' tales in the later nineteenth century. But having compromised his academic integrity with a youthful forgery, Keightley's writings were generally ignored by contemporary scholars, and in later years his pragmatic approach survived only within John Edward Taylor's 1846 preface to *The Fairy Ring*.

JOHN EDWARD TAYLOR AND THE CHANGE IN THINKING ABOUT THE GRIMMS' THEORIES

Little is known of the life of John Edward Taylor (flourished 1840–1855), except that he translated and published additional tales from the Grimm collection as *The Fairy Ring* (1846) and that his name is associated with some children's books and several translations from German and Italian into English. In his preface to *The Fairy Ring,* Taylor pointed out that more than twenty years had "passed since a selection from the 'Kinder- und Hausmärchen' of Jacob and Wilhelm Grimm . . . first appeared in English, translated by my kinsman the late Mr. Edgar Taylor and Mr. Jardine*" (iii–iv). The asterisk pointed readers to a note confirming the book's continuing market success, after which Taylor expressed the hope "that a new collection from the same source may be an acceptable sequel to that work" (iv). "Acceptable sequel" meant that John Edward Taylor's optimistically commercial 1846 project was intended to build on the success of his kinsman's earlier publications.

John Edward Taylor had no interest in the issues of fairy-tale origins and dissemination that had occupied both Edgar Taylor and Thomas Keightley: his preface seemed to follow in their footsteps automatically rather than by conviction or logic. His selection of tales was meant to suit the tastes of young readers, and to do so, he made a great effort "to preserve as strictly as possible that simple style of narrative and language" that gave these tales their "peculiar charm" (*Fairy Ring* iv). He added a few notes from the Grimms' "rich storehouse of legendary lore" and recorded his indebtedness "to the works of my friend Mr. Keightley, who has so ably explored the regions of classical and fairy mythology [and] . . . to Mr. Richard Doyle," the book's illustrator (v).

John Edward Taylor's reference points were the Grimms' tales as translated by Edgar Taylor; Thomas Keightley, whose books sold well among England's middlebrow book buyers in the nineteenth century; and the vastly popular Punch illustrator "Dickie Doyle." In other words Taylor sought market acceptance by invoking successful predecessors and popular personalities but generally avoided dealing with theoretical questions.

Just two years after *The Fairy Ring,* John Edward Taylor published a selection of tales from Basile's *Lo cunto de li cunti* (The Tale of Tales) as *The Pentamerome, or, The Story of Stories: Fun for the Little Ones.* In Germany the *Pentamerone* had been translated from its original Neapolitan into German by Felix Liebrecht and published in 1846, with an imposing preface by Jacob Grimm. There Grimm stated that Basile's tales had been unmistakably taken from oral tradition, like those of Straparola before him (vii), and that the tales (*Märchen*) were beyond a shadow of a doubt the final echoes of ancient myths that had taken root all over Europe (ix). It was a fully developed theoretical position known by German-reading English scholars, but one that had been previously inaccessible to England's general public. (Edgar Taylor's mention of Hengist and Horsa having brought Jack the Giant Killer and Tom Thumb to England's shores [see above] was, after all, a jocular aside, not a generalized assertion about oral origins.)

John Edward Taylor propagated Jacob Grimm's views in the preface (v–xvi) to his 1848 book of Basile tales, and in so doing, he validated the Grimms' theories of origins and transmission. Taylor incorporated earlier translations of Basile's tales from Keightley's *Tales and Popular Fictions* and *Fairy Mythology* and drew on Keightley's ongoing translations. He was also assisted by "a friend from Naples, Mr. Rosetti" (xiii). These borrowings and aids, along with repeated claims that he had translated from Basile's Neapolitan and not from Liebrecht's German translation,[7] strongly suggest that insofar as Taylor translated Basile's tales, it was, in fact, from Liebrecht's German rather than from Basile's Neapolitan, and we may regard as disingenuous the surprise he expressed "that two unrelated translations [Liebrecht and his own] should appear within two years of one another" (xi). Like his preface in *The Fairy Ring,* Taylor's preface to the *Pentamerone* suggests that marketing concerns were paramount. He flattered his readers' sensibilities, and he valorized his omission of the objectionable stories or coarse passages that Liebrecht had maintained. He cast his *Pentamerone* project as more than "a mere collection of children's stories" (xv) and claimed for it "a philosophical character and worth, which acquires for them a much larger and more general acknowledgment, including serious adult interests" (xvi).

John Edward Taylor's preface mined Wilhelm Grimm's extensive notes to the *Children's and Household Tales* for biographical material about Basile

(*Pentamerome* v); drew heavily on Wilhelm's prefatory remarks to the *Children's and Household Tales* to drive home the idea that oral narrative tradition at that period was more complete than in the nineteenth century; and incorporated Jacob Grimm's comments on Basile's tales in the Liebrecht translation (399–404) into his own notes to the individual tales. Finally, he praised Basile for having faithfully transcribed the tales with "scarcely a single addition of any importance" (*Pentamerome* vi), a claim the Grimms had made about their own work. The bulk of Taylor's historical and theoretical remarks derive from Jacob Grimm's preface to the Liebrecht translation,[8] and thus John Edward Taylor's preface effectively delivered an uncritical representation of Jacob and Wilhelm Grimm's thinking about fairy tale origins and transmission to the English fairy-tale public.

John Ruskin's Introduction to *German Popular Stories*

By the 1860s it had been more than forty-five years since Edgar Taylor's skeptically tinged preface to the 1823 translation of *German Popular Stories* first appeared, and its successor publisher John Camden Hotten approached Edgar Taylor's widow to request that a new preface by John Ruskin (1819–1900) replace her late husband's introductory essay. She apparently agreed. Whereas Edgar Taylor's preface had wrestled with the logical implications of the Grimms' theories about the origins of tales and their oral transmission, the eminent art critic and author Ruskin, like John Edward Taylor in his preface to the Basile tales, accepted those theories as a given. Ruskin's preface represents a sea change in acceptance of the Grimms' thought. He built on it, adopted their assumptions, and appeared to find in them a relevance to his views of an ideal childhood.

Like the Grimms, Ruskin believed that a rural economy's lean conditions promoted the telling and retention of tales and praised the Grimm tales for their simple directness, implying that these qualities mimicked the conditions from which they arose, that is, from the uncomplicated lives of ordinary illiterate peasants. Ruskin's language, like the Grimms', leapt from peak to peak: he spoke of "tales" and left readers to fill in the blanks about what kind of tales peasants might have told—coarse anecdotes, ribald jokes, exemplary folktales, or hope-inducing and structurally complex fairy tales. Ruskin noted that every child could observe and learn from the structural morality of the Grimms' tales. There, he wrote, virtue was rewarded and vice punished with little further commentary, so unlike the piously overt morality that Ruskin deplored in contemporary children's books. He idealized children as pure and innocent, their moral development evolving from a benign nature. Ruskin's artistic eye created an ideal past, in which walled medieval towns were surrounded by "bright and unblemished" fields, pastures, and woods, features that in his view promoted the instinctive invention of fairy tales (xii).

Ruskin's understanding of fairy tales represented a break with earlier prefatory discussions of the Grimms' tales but was consistent with John Edward Taylor's 1848 preface to his translation of Basile's *Pentamerone.* Ruskin's words recall the Grimms' phrasing: fairy tales were "remnants of a tradition" and have "naturally arisen out of the mind of a people under special circumstances" (ix). God, immanent in nature and present in the spirits of the simple and the innocent, formed part of fairy tales to the extent that they were related to the people's "sphere of religious faith" (ix). As a "minor tradition, a rude and more or less illiterate tone will always be discernible; for all the best fairy tales have owed their birth, and the greater part of their power, to narrowness of social circumstances" (xii). Ruskin cited neither Jacob nor Wilhelm Grimm but expressed the self-evidence of his views. His thoughts on fairy tales chart a markedly different direction from the one that had begun with Edgar Taylor in 1823.

ANDREW LANG'S INTRODUCTION TO *GRIMM'S HOUSEHOLD TALES*

Andrew Lang (1844–1912) had been a brilliant student of classics at Oxford. Soon after graduation, however, he turned to anthropology, and at twenty-nine published an essay titled "Mythology and Fairy Tales" (1873). In it he refuted Max Müller's fairy tale–related solar theories, such as Red Riding Hood's release from the wolf's belly as a representation of the rising sun's daily emergence from nighttime darkness. From this point onward, Lang linked fairy tales (his generic term for brief tales with or without magic) to the folk and to an oral tradition that he and many fellow literary scholars of his generation had come to believe had existed continuously for centuries, or even for millennia.[9] Like Keightley and others, Lang observed that the same tales occurred in different cultures in Europe, Africa, and Asia, which led him to embrace a concept of polygenesis. More importantly, he espoused the Grimms' theory that fairy tales collected in Germany in the early nineteenth century were surviving examples of ancient Mediterranean myths. Lang factored folk and fairy tales from the far reaches of the British Empire (some of which bore striking resemblances to familiar European folk and fairy tales) into his mix of evidence about tales in general and fairy tales in particular.

Overall, Lang synthesized *late* nineteenth-century observations (of similarities between European and colonial tales) with the Grimms' views (that early nineteenth-century tales were remnants of Greek myths). He also went beyond the Grimms' argument into a more ancient past by reasoning that Greek mythology of the classical period had grown from a simpler—and older—body of stories. Having posited the existence of an earlier body of tales that had preceded Greek mythology as known in the modern world, Lang surmised that tales being collected in India and other British colonial possessions at the end of the nineteenth century were remnants of the same ancient folk narratives from which classical Greek mythology had grown. He elaborated his theory in detail in *Custom and Myth* (1884), which may be viewed as a response to Jacob Grimm's *Teutonic Mythology,* three of whose four volumes had by then appeared in English translation.

For Lang a central issue involved the age of *Märchen.* Were contemporary *Märchen* the youngest and most recent form of ancient myth, as the Grimms, Johann Georg von Hahn, and Max Müller believed? Or were the *Märchen* that were being recorded in the nineteenth century survivals from *precursors* of ancient myth, a hypothesis that would make them older than Greek myths themselves? Lang, an anthropologically oriented student of fairy tales, was firmly of the latter opinion. His conceptualization of fairy tales as surviving instances of stories from preclassical Greece was deeply attractive to late nineteenth-century historical positivists, who relished the possibility of locating links between contemporary storytellers and even more ancient peoples.

Lang's 1884 "Introduction" to *Grimm's Household Tales*[10] brought together the main points of his *Custom and Myth.*[11] Locating *Märchen* origins in humanity's savage state of life and mind ("Introduction" xli, xliii) not only made it impossible to determine how the stories had been transmitted and/ or disseminated but also made it illogical to do so (xli–xlii, xliii). Lang proposed as theory, and then stated as fact, that the Grimms' *Household Tales* (as he termed the collection) "occupy a middle place between the stories of savages and the myths of early civilizations" (xliii), a conclusion that accounted for his observation that the "same" *Märchen* exist all over the world in similar forms, among Aryans and non-Aryans, in the storytelling repertoires of both civilized and savage, and among "people so far apart, so long severed by space, and so widely different in language as Russians and Celtic Highlanders" (xiii).[12] The similarities between Aryan European and non-Aryan African folktales raised questions that Lang said "have not yet been seriously considered by mythologists" (xlvii), and so he undertook that analysis. Lang created a chart of correspondences between civilized Aryan "European" customs and beliefs and "savage" non-Aryan African ones (liv, lvii–lix) as they occurred in the Grimms' tales.

In the case of a European tale in which a "girl marries a frog" and a corresponding "savage" tale in which a "girl [is] wooed by [a] frog," he concluded that both tales were survivals from a past of savagery, with the European tale incorporating social development that had taken place between the time of savage conditions and the present (lx). This mixing of chronological and cultural categories enabled him to express the view that the Grimm tales developed continuously within a peasant milieu, surviving "in peasant tales from the time when the ancestors of the Germans were like Zulus or Maoris or Australians" (lxx).

Lang might, in theory, have theorized fundamentally different developmental paradigms for fairy tales. Using the same evidence (about similarities between tales printed in Europe and subsequently recorded in Europe's African and Asian colonial empires), he might have imagined that fairy tales created in Europe had been sluiced into "non-Aryan" schools via colonial educational systems that delivered their European plots and characters intact. He might have considered colonial marketplaces as locations where purveyors of cheap print sold European stories with nativized plots, characters, and internal references, such as "The Match-Making Jackal" by the Reverend Lal Behari Day (1824–1892). Published in 1883 in Day's *Folktales of Bengal*, it was a restoration fairy tale based on the "Puss in Boots" plot with a jackal instead of a cat as an animal helper. Rather than considering this tale as a colonial adaptation of a Western story, Lang republished this tale in his introduction to *Perrault's Popular Tales* (1888) and cited it as proof that "Puss in Boots" had originated in India, even though the respected scholar Theodor Benfey had found no evidence of a "Puss in Boots" tale type there (lxiv–lxxvi). Such paradigms, however, would have required different assessments of relationships between seventh- and sixth-century BCE Greeks and nineteenth-century Germans, Indians, and Zulus, as well as thorough readings of the range of printed literatures available in the colonies. But Lang lived at the high-water mark of positivist thinking with its powerful image of unbroken chains of transmission, and he proposed paradigms that accorded with that thinking.

Because Lang's conceptual framework integrated the Grimm collection into a schema applicable to the entire world, it universalized the Grimms' tales for English-speaking readers, just as the Grimms had done for German-speaking ones seventy years earlier, when they often blurred distinctions between specifically German and international tale provenance and character in the tales in their collection. Lang translated the Grimms' German title *Hausmärchen* as "household tales," making it into a generic term that he used so broadly in his "Introduction," that it is often unclear whether he is discussing the Grimm collection, collections from other countries patterned on the Grimm collection, the genre of brief tales told in preliterate and aliterate societies (that had no writing at all), or the genre of brief tales told in illiterate subgroups within literate cultures. By further conflating all tales—whether ancient or modern, with or without magic—into a single genre called "fairy tales," Lang effectively fostered an ahistorical timelessness within the study of fairy tales and affirmed the irrelevance of chronologies of creation and transmission in the study of both folktales and fairy tales.

Lang gave the Grimm collection pride of place within all historically significant tale collections by calling it "scientific and exact," which he contrasted with "merely literary collections in which the traditional element is dressed up for the sake of amusement" like "Somadeva, The Thousand and One Nights, Straparola, the Queen of Navarre, Perrault, and others" ("Introduction" xv). Lang thus confirmed the Grimms' assessment of the transcendent significance of their German collection and helped set in place future British folklorists' and literary scholars' views both of tales in general and of the Grimms' own tale-collecting activity.

In the sixty-odd years from 1823 to 1884, scores of imprints of the Grimm collection appeared in England. Additional ones were published in the United States, which were almost entirely based on, that is, pirated from, preexisting English editions. The numbers of English imprints of Grimm tales rose steeply decade by decade throughout the nineteenth century. In the 1850s, when the Grimm tales had become an English publishing phenomenon, the balance tipped from the skepticism of early preface writers (who had looked askance at theories that posited fairy tales as surviving remnants of ancient myth) to the enthusiasm of later translators, publishers, and preface writers (who accepted Jacob and Wilhelm Grimm's theories as the basis for further theorizing).

Of the many imprints of the Grimms' tales in English translation, I have discussed the prefaces of only four, which differ fundamentally from one another in their approach: Edgar Taylor's generally skeptical evidence-requiring preface (despite his notion that the giant-killing Jack had arrived along with Hengist and Horsa), John Edward Taylor's neutral presentation of the Grimm tales, John Ruskin's warmly appreciative enthusiasm, and Andrew Lang's politically and culturally charged anthropological one. Lang united his Romantic acceptance of the undocumented segments of the Grimms' theories with the traditional English requirement for evidence by augmenting and buttressing the Grimms' nationalistically based theory with late nineteenth-century anthropological observations from European colonies.

CONCLUDING THOUGHTS

The four prefaces to the Grimms' tales treated here—from 1823, 1846, 1868, and 1894—provide a measure of views as they shifted from skeptical consideration to enthusiastic acceptance. The requirement of skeptical rationalists for evidence undercut later Romantic impulses to link stories that had been edited, and subsequently collected, in the modern world to ancient and precivilized lives and experience. How had intellectuals beyond the literary community bridged that deep divide? Edgar Taylor, Thomas Keightley, and John Edward Taylor had expressed caution about links between modern and prehistoric stories.

Following John Edgar Taylor's wholehearted acceptance of Jacob Grimm's theory of fairy-tales origins as expressed in his preface to the 1846 German Liebrecht translation of Basile's *Pentamerone* and its delivery to English readers in 1848, John Ruskin and Andrew Lang unquestioningly assumed the truth of the Grimms' views as set down in the prefaces to the *Children's and Household Tales*. Was it solely John Edward Taylor's 1848 introduction of Jacob Grimm's thought in English translation that removed earlier caution? Or did issues beyond the present discussion condition thinking about folktales' and fairy tales' creation, transmission, content retention, and international dissemination? We are left to wonder about the history of acceptance of the

Grimms' theories in other countries. France had no *Ossian* fraud to inspire early caution. Did early French prefaces reflect skepticism as Edgar Taylor's English one did? By what routes did the Grimms' theories gain footholds in other national discussions about the history of folktales and fairy tales? Prefaces to nineteenth-century translations of the Grimms' tales into other European languages may demonstrate different patterns. In England, however, there was a clear progression from early nineteenth-century skepticism to a later unquestioning belief in the peasant creation and oral transmission of tales in the Grimm collection.

Notes

1. As was written in the *New York Times* of 18 Nov. 1872 (http://query.nytimes. com/mem/archive-free/pdf?res=F40712FE3D5F1A7493CAA8178AD95F468784F9).

2. It is possible that a few undated single tales appeared earlier.

3. Those mythic heroes may have brought large numbers of Saxons to England's shores, but tiny Tom and valiant Jack were not among them. Taylor did not know, nor did anyone else at that time seem to know, that Richard Johnson had composed and published Tom Thumb's tale in 1621 and that "Jack the Giant Killer" made its first appearance as we now know it in the early 1700s, a thousand years or so after Hengist, Horsa, and Ebba. Ignorant of England's national tradition of cheap print, Taylor's mistake in associating Hengist, Horsa, and Ebba with Tom and Jack was an honest one that misled future generations.

4. This iteration of polygenesis was given further impetus in 1888 by T. F. Crane (14). Its premises were adopted by Carl Jung and his followers to support assertions about universal images and metaphors, but this approach has been largely abandoned or ignored in scholarly circles (Chesnutt 1162–63).

5. Keightley also acknowledged a "third class of fictions, such as Whittington and his cat,—a legend to be found . . . in more countries than one,—I professed myself to be unable to dispose of to my own satisfaction: they might be transmitted, they might be independent" (*Popular Fictions* 7).

6. See also Joseph Jacobs's similar, but more concise, formulations from 1894 (143), which were also ignored by subsequent scholars.

7. John Edward Taylor, in his preface to *The Pentamerome*, claimed to find it "remarkable" that the *Pentamerone* had not been translated into any language outside Italy and asserted that his translation was "unrelated" to Liebrecht's (xi). He further claimed that he had no assistance in translating it from the Neapolitan and that he had used not the Liebrecht translation but the original Neapolitan (xii), which he had gone through "word by word," adding a translation of Mr. Liebrecht's

acknowledgement of the difficulty of the Neapolitan dialect (xiii; which undercut his arguments by showing that he had made use of the Liebrecht translation). He did acknowledge the help of a friend from Naples, Mr. Rosetti, as well as his indebtedness to Mr. Keightley, who gave him permission to reproduce Basile stories he had already published and who also shared stories he was in the process of translating. He also recounted his efforts to keep to the Neapolitan sense of phrasing, because of the example of the popular German tales, i.e., Grimm (xiv).

8. Wherever Taylor went off on his own to create a theoretical history for fairy tales, he sank into a morass of internal contradictions. On the one hand he believed that the *Pentamerone* stories might be perhaps from Crete and were not indigenous to the south of Italy (*Pentamerome* x) but contradicted that by stating that they their authentically Neapolitan style showed that they had been circulating among the Neapolitan folk (xiv). The particular Neapolitan-ness he claimed for the tales undermined Taylor's demonstration a few pages earlier that Basile's style shared in the English Baroque metaphorical extravagance of Philip Sidney's *Arcadia* (ix). Taylor defended the folk's literary taste as demonstrated in the tales by stating that Basile's literary conceits turned "absurdity into humour" by burlesquing the faults of seventeenth-century writers rather than exemplifying bad taste among its purported folk authors.

9. Articles in the journal *Folk-Lore* in its first ten years richly corroborate this statement.

10. In 1882 the Grimms' tales appeared in a new translation by Lucy Crane, the sister of the celebrated illustrator Walter Crane. One of the book world's most gorgeous books ever produced for children, a perfect exemplar of Walter Crane's theory of the book as art work and Lucy Crane's theory of art as acculturation, it has, however, no preface.

11. Lang devoted the first forty pages of the "Introduction" to his (earlier published) refutation of the theories of "Mr. Max Müller" (*Oxford Essays*, 1856, and *Selected Essays*, 1881, including the concepts of polyonymy and synonymy, xxx–xxxvi). He counterposed their theories to those of "Sir George Cox" (*Mythology of the Aryan Nations*, 1870), "M. Husson," and "Mister Tylor" (*Primitive Culture, Early History of Man*, n.d.), and others.

12. "Aryan" and "non-Aryan," accepted as fundamental categories, were commonplace reference points in the nineteenth century, although today they are regarded as dubious.

REFERENCES

Basile, Giambattista. *Lo cunto de li cunti*. 1634–1636. Ed. Michele Rak. Milan: Garzanti, 1987.

———. *Der Pentamerone oder: Das Märchen aller Märchen von Giambattista Basile. Aus dem Neapolitanischen.* Trans. Felix Liebrecht. Breslau: Josef Max und Komp., 1846.

———. *The Pentamerome, or, The Story of Stories: Fun for the Little Ones.* Trans. and introd. John Edward Taylor. London: David Bogue and J. Cundall, 1848.

Bottigheimer, Ruth B. *Fairy Tales. A New History.* Albany: State U of New York P, 2009.

———. "France's First Fairy Tales: The Rise and Restoration Narratives of 'Les Facetieuses Nuictz du Seigneur François Straparole.'" *Marvels & Tales* 19.1 (2005): 17–31.

Chesnutt, Michael. "Polygenese." *Enzyklopädie des Märchens.* Vol. 10: *Nibelungenlied—Prozeßmotive.* Ed. Kurt Ranke et al. Berlin: de Gruyter, 2002. 1161–64.

Crane, T. F. "The Diffusion of Popular Tales." *Journal of American Folk-Lore* 1 (1888): 8–15.

Croker, Thomas Crofton. *Fairy Legends and Traditions of the South of Ireland.* London: J. Murray, 1825–28.

———. *Irische Elfenmärchen.* Trans. Jacob Grimm. Leipzig: Friedrich Fleischer, 1826.

Day, Lal Behari. "The Match-Making Jackal." In *Folktales of Bengal.* London: Macmillan, 1883.

Dollerup, Cay. *Tales and Translation: The Grimm Tales from Pan-Germanic Narratives to Shared Universal Narratives.* Amsterdam: John Benjamins, 1999.

Gaskill, Howard, ed. *The Reception of Ossian in Europe.* London: Continuum, 2004.

Goethe, Johann Wolfgang von. *Die Leiden des jungen Werther.* Leipzig: Weygand, 1774.

Grimm, Jacob. Preface. *Der Pentamerone oder: Das Märchen aller Märchen von Giambattista Basile. Aus dem Neapolitanischen.* Trans. Felix Liebrecht. Breslau: Josef Max und Komp., 1846. v–xxiv.

———. *Teutonic Mythology.* 1835. Ed., trans., and notes James Steven Stallybrass. 4 vols. Vol. 1, London: W. Swan Sonnenschein & Allen, 1880; vols. 2–4, London: George Bell, 1882–88.

Grimm, Jacob, and Wilhelm Grimm. 1846. *The Fairy Ring: A New Collection of Popular Tales.* 2nd ed. Trans. John Edward Taylor. Illus. Richard Doyle. London: John Murray, Albemarle Street, 1847.

———. *German Popular Stories.* 2 vols. Trans. Edgar Taylor. Illus. George Cruikshank. London: C. Baldwyn, 1823, 1826.

———. *German Popular Stories.* Trans. Edgar Taylor. Introd. John Ruskin. London: John Camden Hotten, 1869.

———. *Grimm's Household Tales.* Trans. Margaret Hunt. Introd. Andrew Lang. London: George Bell, 1884.

―――. *Kinder- und Hausmärchen.* 2 vols. Berlin: Georg Reimer, 1812, 1815.

―――. *Kinder- und Hausmärchen.* 2nd ed. Berlin: Georg Reimer, 1819.

―――. *Kinder- und Hausmärchen. Originalanmerkungen, Herkunftsnachweise, Nachwort.* 3 vols. Ed. Heinz Rölleke. Stuttgart: Reclam, 1980.

Jacobs, Joseph. "The Problem of Diffusion. Rejoinders." *Folk-Lore* 5 (1894): 129–46.

Johnson, Richard. *The History of Tom Thumbe the Little.* London: Thomas Langley, 1621.

Keightley, Thomas. *Fairy Mythology.* London: W. H. Ainsworth, 1828.

―――. *Fairy Mythology.* London: H. G. Bohn, 1850.

―――. *Tales and Popular Fictions. Their Resemblance and Transmission from Country to Country.* London: Whittaker, 1834.

Lang, Andrew. *Custom and Myth.* London: Longmans Green, 1884.

―――. Introduction. *Grimm's Household Tales.* Trans. Margaret Hunt. London: George Bell, 1884.

―――. "Mythology and Fairy Tales." *Fortnightly Review* 13 (1873): 618–31.

―――. *Perrault's Popular Tales.* Oxford: Clarendon, 1888.

Macpherson, James. *The Songs of Selma. From the Original of Ossian, the Son of Fingal.* London: R. Griffith, 1762.

―――. *Temora, an Ancient Epic Poem, in Eight Books, Together with Several Other Poems Composed by Ossian, the Son of Fingal.* London: T. Becket and P. A. De Hondt, 1763.

―――. *The Works of Ossian, the Son of Fingal: Translated from the Gaelic Language.* London: T. Becket and P. S. Dehondt, 1765.

Magnanini, Suzanne. "Postulated Routes from Naples to Paris: The Printer Antonio Bullifon and Giambattista Basile's Fairy Tales in Seventeenth-Century France." *Marvels & Tales* 21.1 (2007): 78–92.

Magnusson, Magnus. *Fakers, Forgers, and Phoneys.* Edinburgh: Mainstream, 2006.

Moore, Dafydd. *Enlightenment and Romance in James Macpherson's the Poems of Ossian: Myth, Genre, and Cultural Change.* Aldershot: Ashgate, 2003.

Rölleke, Heinz. "The 'Utterly Hessian' Fairy Tales by 'Old Marie': The End of a Myth." *Fairy Tales and Society: Illusion, Allusion, and Paradigm.* 1976. Trans. Ruth B. Bottigheimer. Philadelphia: U of Pennsylvania P, 1986. 287–300.

Ruskin, John. Preface. *German Popular Stories.* Trans. Edgar Taylor. London: John Camden Hotten, 1869. v–xiv.

Schenda, Rudolf. "Semiliterate and Semi-Oral Processes." Trans. Ruth B. Bottigheimer. *Marvels & Tales* 21.1 (2007): 127–40.

Second Part of the Pleasant History of Jack and the Giants [and How He Got Leave of the King to Go in Pursuit of Adventures, How He Reliev'd a Knight and His Lady, and How He Distroy'd the Inchanted Castle]. Newcastle: publisher unknown, 1711.

Stephen, Leslie, ed. *Dictionary of National Biography.* London: Oxford UP, 1885–1900.

Straparola, Giovan Francesco. *Le piacevoli notti*. Venice: Comin da Trino, 1551, 1553.

Sumpter, Caroline. "Comment: Reflections on Oral and Literary Relations in the Fairy Tale." *elore* 2 (2010): 127–37.

Taylor, Edgar. Preface. *German Popular Stories*. London: C. Baldwyn, 1823. iii–vii.

Taylor, John Edward. Preface. *The Fairy Ring*. London: John Murray, 1846. iii–iv.

———. Preface. *The Pentamerome, or, The Story of Stories: Fun for the Little Ones*. London: David Bogue and J. Cundall, 1848. v–xiv.

11

German Stories/British Illustrations

Production Technologies, Reception, and Visual Dialogue across Illustrations from "The Golden Bird" in the Grimms' Editions, 1823–1909

SARA HINES

When Arthur Rackham reillustrated the Grimms' collection for his 1909 edition of *Grimm's Fairy Tales,* he included a short prefatory note in which he stated, "Some years ago a selection of *Grimm's Fairy Tales* with one hundred illustrations of mine in black and white was published - in 1900, by Mssrs. Freemantle and Co., and afterward by Mssrs. Archibald Constable & Co., Ltd. At intervals since then I have been at work on the original drawings, partially or entirely re-drawing some of them in colour, adding new ones in colour and in black and white, and generally overhauling them as a set, supplementing and omitting, with a view to the present edition" (Rackham viii). By 1909, Rackham was a highly respected illustrator and had sustained a career solely on book illustration for over twenty years. Rackham's decision to rework his Grimm illustrations deserves consideration because major technological changes had occurred in book printing between 1900 and 1909, not the least of which was the development of the halftone color process, first used commercially in 1901. This process allowed printers to reproduce color illustrations quickly and "provided, for the first time, pictures that have every appearance of verisimilitude" (McKitterick 90).

Rackham first used this process in 1905 with a de luxe illustrated book of Washington Irving's *Rip van Winkle,* followed the next year by J. M. Barrie's *Peter Pan.* Rackham's de luxe editions are clearly designated as gift books, as suggested by their material formats, including size, weight, paper quality, gilt-stamped cloth bindings, elaborate endpapers, and extensive illustrations. Indeed, his 1909 Grimm edition is substantial. As one reviewer writes, "The size and weight of the book will make a miniature Pickford's van or a trolley indispensable in the nursery if small people are to move it from place to place without considerable physical exertion" ("Fairy Stories"). The edition was marketed as Rackham's "masterpiece" ("Rackham's Fairy Tales") and advertisements demonstrated not only the significance of Rackham's name but also that the title, *Grimm's Fairy Tales,* needed no further description. Whalley and Chester explain that gift books in this period tended to reproduce texts with "classic status," and by 1909 the Grimm collection qualified (152). Rackham's illustrations of the Grimms' stories, which in the early twenty-first century have received their own classic status, followed a long and arguably distinguished tradition of coupling illustrations with English translations of the Grimms' stories.

This chapter examines a range of illustrated Grimm editions to contextualize key elements that appear in Rackham's two sets of illustrations. From George Cruikshank's iconic etchings, included in Edgar Taylor's first English translation in 1823, respected and popular artists such as Walter Crane produced illustrated editions of the Grimms' collection. Cruikshank's, Crane's, and Rackham's illustrations are still widely known, but throughout the nineteenth century a number of other British artists also illustrated the Grimms' stories. I will focus on nine English Grimm editions illustrated by British artists such as George Cruikshank, Richard Doyle, Edward Wehnert, Hablot K. Browne, W. J. Wiegand, Walter Crane, and Gordon Browne and explore how Rackham's illustrations are rooted in the visual history of the collection.

In Britain the immediate reception of the various Grimm translations registered an appreciation of the visual components of the various editions. A review of the first Grimm edition in the *Examiner* ignored Edgar Taylor and David Jardine's translation entirely; instead it commented that Cruikshank's "particular talent is strongly exhibited in that grotesque humour and forcible character that he so happily contrives to unite with ease and natural grace" ("Newspaper Chat" 22 Dec.). Reviews of later editions continued to discuss the visual along with the textual: a reviewer of Wehnert's 1853 edition mentioned its "admirable illustrations" and the "general elegance of production" ("Reviews" 248). Regarding Crane's artistic contributions, a reviewer in the *Glasgow Herald* wrote enthusiastically: "His head-pieces and tail-pieces owe nothing but to printers' ink, and yet they are little, if anything short of being perfect" ("Christmas Books" 1882), expressing an opinion repeated throughout reviews on Crane's edition. Alluding to the stylistic similarity between Cruikshank's and Gordon Browne's illustrations, one reviewer described Browne as "particularly successful in illustrating the grotesque and fantastic elements of the story" ("Christmas Books" 1894). Unsurprisingly, a review praised Rackham's "most desirable edition" noting, "The illustrations are full of life and action," which also echoes reviewer descriptions of Cruikshank's etchings ("Rev. of *Grimm's Fairy Tales*" 8).

Publishers' advertisements demonstrated that editions often prioritized different aspects of the book; for some editions the reputation of the translator took precedence, whereas others minimized the translator and accentuated the contributions of the illustrator. In either scenario, however, illustrations were not ignored. Prefaces frequently commend the illustrator's contributions; publishers included the illustrator's names within advertisements; and reviewers discussed illustrations alongside the translated text. The integral role illustrations have in the history of the Grimms' collection in Britain provides a framework for Rackham's gift editions. A comparative analysis of visual approaches to the Grimms' collection demonstrates that Rackham's two editions capitalized on trends that emerged across the previous illustrated editions.

One of the illustrations that Rackham updated in the 1909 edition accompanied the story "The Golden Bird" (KHM 57). This fairy tale, which has neither retained lasting popularity nor received extensive critical attention, is often overlooked in favor of its more famous siblings. The narrative combines a number of familiar fairy-tale motifs. The youngest son of the king discovers that a golden bird has been stealing apples from the palace garden. In a quest to capture the golden bird for the king, the two eldest sons ignore a fox's advice and fail. The young prince, however, treats the fox kindly and in return the fox offers the prince a ride on his tail to find the bird. The prince halfheartedly heeds the fox's advice and fails in his quest. Nevertheless, the fox helps the prince again, allowing the prince a second chance to pass three tests successfully. At the fox's request, the prince—now in possession of the golden bird, a golden horse, and a golden princess—shoots the fox and cuts off his head and feet and thus reveals the fox to be the princess's brother. This story is repeatedly visualized in nineteenth-century English editions. It is one of the ten illustrations that Cruikshank contributed to the 1823 edition; Rackham and Wehnert illustrated it twice; and in the interim, Crane, Wiegand, and Gordon Browne all chose to illustrate "The Golden Bird" for their respective editions.

Due to the consistency with which artists represent this story, illustrations from "The Golden Bird" not only facilitate informative comparative analysis of the variance in artistic style but also exhibit the range of book production techniques that existed in the nineteenth century. Rackham's 1900 and 1909 editions showcase the major development of photomechanical reproduction that occurred in the twentieth century; however, this development follows eighty years of technological advancements in printing techniques. From 1823 onward each decade of the nineteenth century witnessed at least one new translation of the Grimms' stories. Concurrently, changes in printing ensured that each decade also utilized new and different techniques to reproduce illustrations. The perennial retranslation of the Grimms' collection into English, therefore, was always paired with illustrations produced using the latest technologies,[1] inciting reviewers to describe editions as "modern," "ever fresh," and appealing to "the modern child" in 1861, 1882, and 1909, respectively ("Fairy Books," "First," and "Juvenile").

The remainder of this study surveys eleven English translations of the Grimms' collection chronologically. Each survey provides production and reception contexts for the respective editions through brief descriptions of the current printing technologies and critiques of publishers' advertisements. Advertisements indicate ways that publishers used the translator, the illustrator, or both as selling points. Finally, analyses of illustrations from "The Golden Bird" suggest that the artists, including Rackham, use visual references to engage with and to comment on each other's artistic interpretations and, moreover, that this ongoing visual dialogue was instrumental in elevating the Grimms' collection to its "classic status."

George Cruikshank, Richard Doyle, and Edward Wehnert: Etchings, Woodcuts, and Engravings

C. Baldwyn of London published *German Popular Stories* in 1823, which was anonymously translated by Edgar Taylor and David Jardine and included ten illustrations from Cruikshank (1792–1878).[2] The Grimm edition appeared early in Cruikshank's book illustration career, although he had already established his reputation as a caricaturist. Muir describes Cruikshank as "without question one of the greatest of all the fine illustrators" (37), a reputation augmented after he illustrated Charles Dickens's *Oliver Twist* (1837–1839). The *Examiner* review of the first Grimm edition, quoted above, mistakenly states, "The book acquires a completeness from twelve wood-cut embellishments designed by M. George Cruikshank" ("Newspaper Chat" 22 Dec.). That the illustrations were produced by copper etchings, and not woodcuts, was corrected in the *Examiner* the following week ("Newspaper Chat" 29 Dec.). The self-correction highlights the significance that production technique had on Cruikshank's artistic style.

Copper etching, an intaglio technique, is a process in which a copper plate is cut into with a burin or acid (Gascoigne 10). Unlike relief printing, in which ink sits above the surface, in intaglio printing, the ink sits below and fills the etched portion of the plate. Transferring the ink to the paper, therefore, demands considerable pressure (Scally 53). This method, not common in children's book illustrations, created "the almost magical quality of his pictures" (Whalley and Chester 51). According to contemporary reviews, Cruikshank's etchings were "whimsical" and "executed with admirable freedom and spirit" ("Literary Notices"). Indeed, Cruikshank's etchings convey a striking amount of energy. His ability to capture moments in the middle of action—people throwing their hands in the air, running in fear, dancing—is exemplified in his image for "The Golden Bird." This image shows the fox in midstride, with the prince's cape flowing behind him. Using one hand to steady himself on the fox's tail, the prince holds down his own hat with the other hand to keep it from being blown off by the wind. The image conveys action, vitality, and speed. Cruikshank's influence on subsequent illustrators is best demonstrated by their continual return to and reimagination of this scene.

The humor and energy present in Cruikshank's etchings testify to his talent and confidence with his medium. The significance of the production method to Cruikshank's illustrations becomes evident when compared to the publication of *Gammer Grethel or German Fairy Tales and Popular Stories,* published in 1839 by John Green in London. The edition rearranges Taylor's 1823 and 1826 translations although it retains Cruikshank's illustrations along with the vignette derived from his famous 1823 title page. Because this image has been cropped, however, Cruikshank's signature is absent from the *Gammer Grethel* title page. Furthermore, according to the preface, his "old designs" are "now engraved on wood by Byfield" and the difference between the results is striking (Taylor vi).

Cruikshank possessed the technical skills required to etch his images for *German Popular Stories,* allowing him control over his own illustrations. Conversely, the engravings in *Gammer Grethel* were subject to Byfield's interpretation. As Gascoigne explains, "The craftsmen churning out thousands of wood blocks to meet the deadlines on the presses were not themselves the originating artists. . . . Wood engraving became a purely reproductive medium, though one of extraordinary skill" (6b). The wood engraving of "The Golden Bird" (in this edition retitled "The Fox's Brush") appears far less textured and complex than Cruikshank's original etching. Cruikshank's castle, for example, contains extensive details and the shadows along one side cause it to appear three-dimensional and more realistic. In the revised wood engraving, the castle contains minimal detail and appears flat and two-dimensional. Furthermore, the prince's shape has changed and the distance between the fox and the ground has decreased. Because of these two alterations, the fox is no longer spritely and energetic; instead, the prince seems heavy and the fox tired.

The quality gap between Cruikshank's copper etchings and Byfield's wood engravings has little to do with the two media—wood engraving techniques can produce extremely intricate illustrations—but demonstrates instead the diminishing returns of an illustration the further it is separated from the originating artist. The intermediary engraver, despite his skill, alters the artist's work. It is Cruikshank's technical skill with copper engraving along with his artistic skill that render his 1823 illustrations so appealing.

John Edward Taylor's 1846 edition of the Grimms' stories, titled *The Fairy Ring,* contains ten illustrations by Richard Doyle (1824–1883). Doyle is known for illustrating several nineteenth-century fairy-tale books, including John Ruskin's *The King of the Golden River* (1851), "Sleeping Beauty" in J. R. Planché's *An Old Fairy Tale Told Anew in Pictures and Verse* (1856), and William Allingham's poem *In Fairyland* (1870). Gleeson White observes that Doyle "evidently felt the charm of fairyland, and peopled it with droll little folk who are neither too human nor too unreal to be attractive" (19). *The Fairy Ring* contains a "List of Illustrations" that includes the names of the different engravers who,[3] like Byfield, interpreted Doyle's illustrations and mediated between Doyle's art and the final product. Nevertheless, Doyle receives full credit from reviewers, who described his illustrations as "wonderfully clever" and "in R. Doyle's best manner" (Rev. of *The Fairy Ring*; "Miscellaneous Notes" 250). Each of Doyle's ten illustrations serves as a title page for the individual stories.[4] The words of the title are integrated into the illustration and he designed different decorative font styles for each title. Wehnert adopted Doyle's tendency to frame his images with illustrations of pieces of wood and Crane recalls Doyle's illustrations by integrating the story titles into his illustrations.

Addey and Co. released a two-volume edition of *Household Stories Collected by the Brothers Grimm* in 1853. No translator is listed on the title page; there is, however, a note stating that the edition contains "Two Hundred and Forty Illustrations by Edward H. Wehnert." Wehnert (1813–1868) was a watercolor painter. He studied informally at the British Museum and also spent two years studying art in Paris. In addition to the Grimm edition, Wehnert contributed illustrations to *History of the Bold Robin Hood* (1850), Samuel Taylor Coleridge's *Ancient Mariner* (1857), John Bunyan's *Pilgrim's Progress* (1858), Hans Christian Andersen's *Eventyr* (as *Fairy Tales,* 1861), and Daniel Defoe's *Robinson Crusoe* (1862). According to F. M. O'Donoghue, Wehnert's paintings did not sell particularly well and he was more successful as a book illustrator. Addey's edition reproduces images by the wood engraving method. No engraver is mentioned in the book, and it is unknown whether the images are interpretations or if Wehnert possessed the technical skills to engrave his own work.

The anonymous preface maintains, "Any praise of Mr. Wehnert's Illustrations is quite unnecessary. They are so full of character, and so happily in accordance with the spirit of the work, that every one who admires the stories must be delighted with the pictures" (*Household Stories* iv). Nevertheless, by returning to many of the same scenes that Cruikshank illustrated, Wehnert invites comparison. In Wehnert's illustration from "The Golden Bird"[5] the energy and levity apparent in Cruikshank's original etching are absent. In Wehnert's interpretation, the prince is leaning forward, almost doubled over, thus making him appear thick and cumbersome. The fox is descending, rather than ascending as he is in Cruikshank's etching. The image conveys minimal movement and the prince has removed his hat completely, thereby reducing the humor. He appears comfortable, casually observing his nondescript surroundings, rather than intently looking forward as the prince in Cruikshank's etching does. Wehnert draws the prince's face turned away, which disengages the viewer. This image, unlike Rackham's later versions, does not invite the reader to join the prince's adventure. Overall the image lacks the humor and energy that permeates Cruikshank's etching.

If, as Brian Alderson suggests, the translators for this Grimm edition were Wehnert's family members (5), then, like Crane's and Rackham's editions, Wehnert's edition should be regarded as an exhibition platform for the artist, prioritizing the visual over the literary. Such an interpretation is further supported by advertisements and reviews. In 1853, Addey marketed this book alongside other popular storybooks "With Beautiful Illustrations by Eminent Artists" ("Christmas Books for Young People"). The publisher's advertisements include Wehnert's name and mention the number of illustrations he contributed with no reference to the translator(s). Indeed, the number of illustrations in this edition far exceeds those in previous Grimm editions. Wehnert has not retained a lasting reputation and yet his illustrations, despite the ambiguity of their artistic quality, kept this edition in print in various formats until the mid-1880s.[6] In the interim, three further editions of the Grimms' collection appeared and each one utilized newly developed printing technologies, some of which included color.

HABLOT K. BROWNE, W. J. WEIGAND, AND KRONHEIM: THE ADVENT OF COLOR

George Vickers of London published a series titled "Fairy Books for Boys and Girls" in weekly numbers. *Grimms' Goblins,* the first installment, appeared on 19 December 1860 for one penny. Despite the title, not all the stories within are derived from the Grimms' collection, a phenomenon true of other Grimm editions. The illustrator, "Phiz," the pseudonym for Hablot K. Browne (1815–1882), already had a solid reputation based on his illustrations for Charles Dickens and Harrison Ainsworth. His illustrations for *Grimms' Goblins* received mixed reviews. The *Isle of Wight Observer* "strongly recommends our readers not to purchase it" ("Literature," 16 Mar.). Nonetheless, it did merit brief mention in the *Morning Chronicle* specifically because of its use of recent printing technologies: "The peculiar feature of the present work is that every sheet is illustrated by an engraving from a design by Phiz, and *printed* in colours. These pictures ought to be charming to young eyes, since they are immensely superior to anything that has hitherto been prepared in the shape of coloured story-book illustrations" ("Literature," 28 Feb., emphasis in original).

Grimms' Goblins reproduced illustrations using Edmund Evans's color process,[7] also known as chromoxylography (color from wood), which uses blocks of wood etched on the grain side: "The makers of colour wood engravings tended to break up their colours into ever more intricate overlapping patterns of finely engraved hatching" (Gascoigne 23a–c). The illustrations were overprinted with three colors—red, yellow, and blue—plus black. The color illustrations, described by the preface as "a singular and successful novelty" (n.p.), are printed on cheap paper. Due to technological advancements, color images could now be mass-produced and made available at a lower cost. According to Vickers's advertisements in *Reynolds's Magazine,* this edition is "designed to give children of all rank the amusement, instruction, and delight hitherto confined, by high prices, to the favoured few" ("Fairy Books for Boys and Girls"). The prices of Grimm editions had remained consistently in the midlevel price range[8]: *German Popular Stories* (7s), *Gammer Grethel* (3s 6d), *The Fairy Ring* (7s 6d). The gift edition of Wehnert's *Household Stories* was priced as high as 12s. The low price and the colored illustrations were the two primary selling points for *Grimms' Goblins* and are indicative of the state of publishing at the time. Technological changes cause this edition to appear far more modern than its black-and-white predecessors; moreover, the capacity to mass-produce color illustrations made the edition available to a wider readership.[9]

Frederick Warne and Company published Mrs. Paull's *Grimms' Fairy Tales* in 1872 as part of its Fairy Library. This edition includes "Sixteen Original Illustrations By W. J. Wiegand," although no further mention is made of Wiegand (flourished 1869–1882) in the preface. His illustrations are full-page drawings, bordered by a simple line frame, and signed by the illustrator and engraver. The overall emphasis of these illustrations, in a volume noted to be "specially adapted and arranged for young people" on the title page, is on the juvenile or child characters. Furthermore, there is minimal action in these images; indeed, Wiegand tended to draw figures in portrait poses—either seated or standing still. Although Wiegand did illustrate "The Golden Bird," he did not select the same scene as Cruikshank or Wehnert. There is a tremendous amount of detail in Wiegand's image, but the scene itself is entirely passive. Despite claims in the preface that "the tales are full of incident and wonderful adventures" the only action in this illustration is a flying bird (Paull iii). The prince stands still with his back to the viewer; he carries a bow but does not appear to be using it. Although the technology existed, Wiegand's illustrations were not printed in color.

Publisher advertisements clearly prioritize Paull's contributions over Wiegand's by placing her name, along with her other publications, in a much larger font than and several lines above Wiegand's name. Paull "had an extraordinary prolific output as both writer and translator" (Sutton 231). Moreover, she reminds the reader in her preface that this edition is meant as a companion volume to her translation of *Hans Andersen's Fairy Tales* (1867), also part of Warne's Fairy Library. Priced at 5s, this edition offers an interesting counterexample to other editions discussed. Unlike Wehnert's lavishly illustrated gift book and Browne's colorful penny magazine, this edition focuses on translation and adaptation. The relative obscurity of this edition is likely due to its lack of inspiring illustrations as well as the market competition. Wehnert's edition was still being reprinted, and in 1868 John Camden Hotton republished Edgar Taylor's 1823 and 1826 editions, complete with Cruikshank's original illustrations and a preface written by John Ruskin. Hotton's edition, in the same price range as Paull's translation, was still appearing in advertisements through the mid-1870s and was considered a better purchase.

In 1876 Routledge published an edition titled *Household Stories*. The color illustrations, printed by the company Kronheim, were produced using a technique known as lithography, a type of planography. Scally explains that "planographic processes print on the surface. The action of transferring an image to the printing surface therefore relies on chemical differences" (57). Chromolithography (color from stone) uses stones covered in grease; texture is added by either scraping through the grease, or by stopping out parts of the stone before the grease is added. Like chromoxylography, color is separated on different stones and then overlaid in printing (Gascoigne 27–28). "Lithography in England was eventually debased to a level of cheap nastiness that touched possibly the lowest point in book illustration. . . . The firm of Kronheim was the most prolific source of this wretched process," Percy Muir explains (156). Like Wiegand's illustrations, the few images in this edition are passive and do not engage the viewer with the energy or humor present in other Grimm illustrations. Nevertheless, the intensity of the color immediately calls attention to the production techniques. As such, the illustrations exemplify the vast changes in technology that had occurred since Browne and Evans's color edition of *Grimms' Goblins* fifteen years earlier, although the novelty of color supplants artistic quality.

Routledge capitalized on modern color-printing techniques in two subsequent editions. In 1879 the firm issued a ten-volume series titled *Grimm's*

Fairy Library that included Wehnert's 1853 illustrations. Each volume, titled after one tale, included ten to twenty stories. One-color wood-block illustration, derived from the title story, appeared as a frontispiece for each volume. For "The Golden Bird and Other Tales," Wehnert revisited this story and contributed an additional color illustration. Representing a scene later in the narrative than those mentioned earlier, this color image shows the prince and princess riding on a horse, with the fox running alongside. Wehnert introduced a new visual interpretation of the narrative, but one that is revisited by Crane a few years later. In 1883, Routledge combined Wehnert's black-and-white illustrations with Kronheim's chromolithographic illustrations from 1876 in an edition titled *Grimm's Fairy Tales*. The title page of this edition, however, drops references to Kronheim and mentions Wehnert only. By this time versions of Wehnert's Grimm illustrations had been in print for thirty years. This 1883 edition, however, was the last printing, possibly due to the success of Walter Crane's illustrated edition now available.

WALTER CRANE AND GORDON BROWNE: ARTISTIC STYLE AND PHOTOMECHANICAL REPRODUCTION

In 1882, Lucy Crane translated *Household Stories from the Collection of the Bros. Grimm,* for Macmillan, which her brother Walter Crane (1845–1915) amply illustrated. The Crane edition is a gift book notable more for its artistic value than the textual quality.[10] Crane's illustrations are black and white, a departure from the color illustrations that solidified his reputation. The prioritization of Crane's visual contributions over his sister's translations is unmistakable; the book contains a list of illustrations, rather than a table of contents. Each story is coupled with two illustrations: a headpiece and a tailpiece. A small selection of stories also includes an additional full-page illustration. Advertisements further prioritize Walter's contributions, placing his name above the Grimms' and the title, often leaving Lucy's name out entirely.

In this edition, three illustrations accompany "The Golden Bird." For the headpiece, Crane reillustrates the scene of the prince riding the fox, in which he incorporates many of the same devices present in previous images. Once again, the prince holds his hat on to his head and steadies himself by grasping the fox's tail. The fox is parallel to the ground, posing in midstride and conveying agility and speed. The intensity of the prince's expression echoes Cruikshank's etching; it serves to connect the viewer to the prince's experience and magnifies the adventure of this scene. In the full-page illustration, the scale is altered. The fox, in the foreground, now appears much smaller than the prince, thereby heightening the fantastical element of the prince's ride. This illustration contains other visual references to previous editions.

Crane reillustrates the scene that Wehnert added to his color frontispiece. The castle that appears in the background recalls Cruikshank's etching and there is a similarity between the landscapes of both illustrations. Furthermore, this image is elaborately framed and, like Doyle's illustrations, integrates the title of the story into the overall design. Crane's illustrations were immediately commended for their artistic quality; nevertheless, it is notable that he reproduced these particular scenes from "The Golden Bird" so exactly, especially given that Cruikshank's and Wehnert's illustrations were still available in print. Such repetition reiterates that Crane's illustrations incorporate visual motifs from previous artists' interpretations and should be examined within this context.

In 1895, Wells Gardner, Darton & Co. produced a gift book of the Grimms' stories titled *Fairy Tales from Grimm*. Sabine Baring-Gould (1834–1924) wrote a lengthy introduction, and Gordon Browne (1858–1932) contributed illustrations and designed the endpapers. This edition draws on three sellable points: the status of the Grimms' stories, Baring-Gould's scholarly reputation, and Browne's artistic popularity. Variants in advertisements reveal the importance of both Baring-Gould and Browne to the production of this edition. An advertisement in the *Saturday Review* lists the edition as "Grimms Fairy-Tales. With an Introduction by S. Baring-Gould, MA" (*Grimm's Fairy-Tales*), whereas one in the *Athenæum* refers to the book as "Mr Gordon Browne's Fairy Tales" ("Mr Gordon Browne's").

Previously, Browne had illustrated other works of fiction such as *Robinson Crusoe* (1885) and *Gulliver's Travels* (1886)[11] along with stories of Mrs. Ewing and Mrs. Molesworth. During his career he also illustrated fairy tales such as *Beauty and the Beast* (1887), Countess d'Aulnoy's *Fairy Tales* (1888), Andrew Lang's *Prince Prigio* (1889), and Andersen's *Fairy Tales* (1902). His Grimm edition makes use of photomechanical reproduction, which became commercially viable in the 1880s. One example of this process is relief halftone, which uses pure black and white to represent shades of gray through wholly photographic means (Gascoigne 34).[12] Because interpretation of an image was not assigned to another engraver, as Whalley and Chester explain, this new process allowed the illustrator more artistic control over the final illustrations. Furthermore, they write, "the new process line block made it possible for more precision and delicacy" (131). Artists, such as Browne, achieved success by embracing the new medium and adapting artistic skills accordingly.

Browne's artistic style varies throughout the book. His illustrations are often integrated into the text in such a way that the words are formatted around the image, something not possible with earlier technologies. Browne also chose to reillustrate "The Golden Bird." The landscape and castle are quite different from Crane's and Cruikshank's, yet Browne employed similar visual devices. The prince holds his hat and steadies himself on the fox; the fox appears to be ascending; and the wind catches the prince's cape in much the same way as it does in Cruikshank's illustration. Other details—the prince's intense expression and the fox's smile—further capture the humor of Cruikshank's first image. Such comparisons acknowledge Browne's skill but also demonstrate that in seventy years Cruikshank's illustrations had not been lost from public memory.

CONCLUSION: RACKHAM'S GIFT BOOKS OF CLASSIC TEXTS

Arthur Rackham (1867–1939) included illustrations of "The Golden Bird" in both his 1900 and 1909 editions. The two images convey the prince's rather precarious position. Awkwardly clenching his knees, with his feet barely holding the fox's body, the prince cuts a humorous figure. His discomfort, in both the physical and emotional sense, is palpable. However, in the 1909 illustration, the perspective of the scene changes slightly, thus accentuating the size difference between the two figures. Although this prince does not appear as heavy as the one in Wehnert's illustration, the size difference echoes Crane's interpretation: the prince may be bigger, but the fox is strong enough to carry him, thereby reinforcing the fantastic quality of the story. Finally, the fox's expression is a combination of determination and delight, whereas the prince is concerned, if not frightened, both of which suggest the humor implicit within the narrative and captured by illustrators since Cruikshank.

The most obvious distinction between the 1900 and 1909 images is the addition of color. The color process employed combines the halftone process with the color separation technique used in chromoxylography and chromolithography. McCleery provides an overview of the process: "Four-colour process work (or full-colour printing) uses the three subtractive primary colours—cyan, magenta and yellow plus black to add detail—to reproduce a facsimile of the original. A separate negative/positive screen film, plate, cylinder or stencil is required for each of the four colors. As the colours are printed on top of one another, the reproduction emerges in the correct tones. As each separation has been screened at a different angle, the printed dots overlap one another to create the optical illusion of solidity in the image" (171). Color allows Rackham to illustrate a detailed background that does not distract from the central figures in the image.[13] The soft yellows and browns of landscape do not compete with the subtle reds and blues of the fox and prince.

The publishers' anticipated success of this edition is evident in the extensive advertisement campaign, and there is no doubt that Rackham's name is a significant selling point for this edition. A review in the *Bookman* observes, "Of this collection of Grimm's Tales (a subject, which we remember, is an old Friend of Mr Rackham) we cannot speak too highly. . . . Mr Rackham's earlier 'Grimm's' were very good, but this is a finished achievement of which he may well be proud" ("Bookman Christmas"). Although the Grimms' stories have continued to be translated, illustrated, and published in Britain throughout the twentieth and twenty-first centuries, the description of Rackham's edition as "finished" is notable and the technological sophistication of Rackham's 1909 illustrations demands a retrospective analysis of the earlier illustrations. Each previously illustrated edition capitalizes on the up-to-date technologies available, inciting reviewers to refer to editions as "modern." The process available to Rackham, however, allowed his edition the distinction of being "finished": an achievement that cannot be claimed for either the wood engraving of the 1830s, the wood color printing of the 1860s, or the chromolithography of the 1870s.

Brian Alderson privileged the literary over the visual in his exhibition "Grimm Tales in English" for the British Library in 1985. In his exhibition notes, he suggests, "The very emphasis on visual formulae (and the publishing prestige of Large Paper copies alongside the trade edition) presage the arrival of illustrators who dominate rather than serve their authors" (6). John Scally offers an alternative understanding of nineteenth-century publishing trends and notes, "If there was one feature that stood out more than any other it was the advances made in the creation of illustration, both in monochrome and colour, in response to the inexhaustible public appetite for a combination of visual and textual material" (49). The various Grimm editions produced in

England during the nineteenth and early twentieth centuries display many of the advances in illustration and printing that occurred over the period and exemplify the combination of visual and textual that Scally discusses. Collectively, the editions employ relief, intaglio, and planographic techniques and the illustrations printed in color utilize nineteenth-century inventions such as wood-block color, chromolithography, and finally the halftone color process. Given the range of printing techniques used to produce Grimm editions, the visual is integral to the textual reception of this collection in English. Not only did the Grimms' stories first appear in Britain alongside illustrations in 1823, but this coupling is continued throughout subsequent editions. Furthermore, repeated illustrations of individual stories, such as "The Golden Bird," exemplify the visual dialogue that occurs across editions and demonstrate the significant contributions illustrations have made in promoting the Grimms' stories to their classic status.

Notes

1. Margaret Hunt's *Grimm's Household Stories* (1884) is one of the more notable exceptions. Her translation, however, was published with a purpose quite distinct from those of other editions discussed, as it was primarily intended for scholars interested in the study of folklore.

2. A second volume appeared in 1826 published by Robbins & Co. Taylor was the sole translator for this volume, and once again Cruikshank contributed a title page and several illustrations.

3. The list of engravers includes H. Vietelly, G. Dalziel, W. T. Green, E. Dalziel, W. J. Linton, L. Martin, J. Thompson, and T. Williams. Each illustration also contains the individual engraver's signature along with Doyle's initials.

4. "The Golden Bird" does not appear in this edition.

5. This image also appears on the title page of volume one.

6. David Bogue of London reissued this book with a new title page in 1857. Routledge subsequently released another "new edition" using Bogue's title page in 1862. The two editions contain different frontispieces.

7. Evans is best known for his color prints produced in collaboration with Walter Crane, Randolph Caldecott, and Kate Greenaway in the 1870s and 1880s.

8. For further information on book prices in the nineteenth century, see Simon Eliot's *Some Patterns and Trends in British Publishing, 1800–1919*.

9. *Grimms' Goblins* does not contain "The Golden Bird," but Browne does illustrate many of the same scenes that Richard Doyle selected for *The Fairy Ring*.

10. Lucy Crane famously translated "Geislein" to "goslings" rather than "kids" or "goats," a mistake noted by contemporary reviewers (Rev. of *Household Stories* 620).

11. Incidentally, both books were also illustrated by his father, Hablot Browne in 1861 and 1879, respectively.

12. Allistair McCleery provides a useful and detailed technical description in *The History of the Book in Scotland*, vol. 4 (171).

13. For his black-and-white illustration, he uses white space to separate the prince and fox from the background, a stylistic technique used by Browne and Wehnert.

References

Grimm Editions

Crane, Lucy, trans. *Household Stories from the Collection of the Bros. Grimm.* Illus. Walter Crane. London: Macmillan, 1882.

Fairy Tales from Grimm. Introd. Sabine Baring-Gould. Illus. Gordon Browne. London: Wells Gardner, Darton & Co., 1895.

German Popular Stories. Translated from the *Kinder und Haus Marchen* [*sic*], collected by M. M. Grimm, from oral tradition. Illus. George Cruikshank. London: C. Baldwyn, 1823.

German Popular Stories. Translated from the *Kinder und Haus-Märchen.* Vol. 2. Illus. George Cruikshank. London: Robbins & Co., 1826.

The Golden Bird and Other Tales Collected by the Brothers Grimm. Illus. E. H. Wehnert. London: George Routledge and Sons, 1879.

Grimm's Fairy Tales. Illus. E. H. Wehnert. London: George Routledge and Sons, 1883.

Grimms' Goblins. Illus. Hablot K. Browne. London: George Vickers, 1861.

Household Stories Collected by the Brothers Grimm. Newly Translated. Illus. Edward H. Wehnert. London: Addey and Co., 1853.

Household Stories Collected by the Brothers Grimm. Newly Translated. Illus. E. H. Wehnert. London: David Bogue, 1857.

Household Stories Collected by the Brothers Grimm. Newly Translated. Illus. E. H. Wehnert. London: Routledge, Warne, and Routledge, 1862.

Household Stories Collected by the Brothers Grimm. Newly Translated. Illus. Kronheim. London: Routledge, 1876.

Hunt, Margaret, trans. *Grimm's Household Tales.* 2 vols. London: George Bell and Sons, 1884.

Lucas, Mrs. Edgar, trans. *Fairy Tales of the Brothers Grimm.* Illus. Arthur Rackham. London: Freemantle & Co., 1900.

———. *Fairy Tales of the Brothers Grimm.* Illus. Arthur Rackham. London: Constable & Company, 1909.

Paull, H. H. B., trans. *Grimms' Fairy Tales. A New Translation.* Illus. W. J. Wiegand. London: Frederick Warne and Company, 1872.

Rackham, Arthur. Prefactory Note. *Fairy Tales of the Brothers Grimm.* By Jacob and Wilhelm Grimm. Ed. Mrs. Edgar Lucas. London: Constable & Company, 1909. viii.

Taylor, Edgar, trans. *Gammer Grethel, or German Fairy Tales, and Popular Stories.* Illus. George Cruikshank. London: John Green, 1839.

Taylor, John Edward, trans. *The Fairy Ring: A New Collection of Popular Tales.* Illus. Richard Doyle. London: John Murray, 1846.

Secondary Material

Alderson, Brian. "Grimm Tales in English." *British Library Exhibition Notes.* London: British Library, 1985.

Baring-Gould, Sabine. Introduction. *Fairy Tales from Grimm.* London: Wells Gardner, Darton & Co., 1895. vii–xxii.

"Bookman Christmas 1909." Rev. of *Grimm's Fairy Tales. Bookman.* Dec. 1909: 58. *British Periodicals.* http://britishperiodicals.chadwyck.co.uk. 17 Nov. 2011.

"Christmas Books." Rev. of *Fairy Tales from Grimm. Supplement to the Saturday Review.* 1 Dec. 1894: 579. *British Periodicals.* http://britishperiodicals.chadwyck. co.uk. 17 Nov. 2011.

"Christmas Books." Rev. of *Household Stories. Glasgow Herald.* 16 Nov. 1882: 3. *19th Century British Library Newspapers.* http://find.galegroup.com. 17 Nov. 2011.

"Christmas Books for Young People." Advertisement. *Athenaeum.* 31 Dec. 1853: 1580. *British Periodicals.* http://britishperiodicals.chadwyck.co.uk. 27 Mar. 2012.

Eliot, Simon. *Some Patterns and Trends in British Publishing, 1800–1919.* Occasional Papers No. 8. London: Bibliographic Society, 1994.

"Fairy Books for Boys and Girls." Rev. of *Grimms' Goblins. Era.* 3 Mar. 1861: 6. *19th Century British Library Newspapers.* http://find.galegroup.com. 27 Mar. 2012.

"Fairy Stories and Others." Rev. of *Grimm's Fairy Tales. Saturday Review of Politics, Literature, Science and Art.* 12 Dec. 1909: 10. *British Periodicals.* http://britishperiodicals.chadwyck.co.uk. 24 Nov. 2011.

"First of the Gift-Books." Rev. of *Household Stories. Academy.* 14 Oct. 1882: 475. *British Periodicals.* http://britishperiodicals.chadwyck.co.uk. 17 Nov. 2011.

Gascoigne, Bamber. *How to Identify Prints: A Complete Guide to Manual and Mechanical Process from Woodcut to Ink Jet.* London: Thames and Hudson, 1986.

Grimm's Fairy-Tales. Advertisement. *Saturday Review of Politics, Literature, Science, and Art.* 31 Oct. 1896: 488. *British Periodicals.* http://britishperiodicals.chadwyck.co.uk. 17 Nov. 2011.

Grimms' Goblins. Advertisement. *Reynolds's Newspapers*. 16 Dec. 1860: 13. *19th Century British Library Newspapers*. http://find.galegroup.com. 27 Mar. 2012.

Preface. *Grimms' Goblins*. London: George Vickers, 1861. n. pag.

Preface. *Household Stories Collected by the Brothers Grimm*. London: Addey and Co., 1853. iii–iv.

"Juvenile Literature." Rev. of *Grimm's Fairy Tales*. *Athenaeum*. 20 Nov. 1909: 619. *British Periodicals*. http://britishperiodicals.chadwyck.co.uk. 21 Feb. 2012.

"Literary Notices." Rev. of *German Popular Stories*. *Kaleidoscope, or Literary and Scientific Mirror*. 7 Jan. 1823: 209. *British Periodicals*. http://britishperiodicals.chadwyck.co.uk. 17 Nov. 2011.

"Literature." Rev. of *Grimms' Goblins*. *Isle of Wight Observer*. 16 Mar. 1861: 4. *19th Century British Library Newspapers*. http://find.galegroup.com. 17 Nov. 2011.

"Literature." Rev. of *Grimms' Goblins*. *Morning Chronicle*. 28 Feb. 1861: 3. *19th Century British Library Newspapers*. http://find.galegroup.com. 24 Nov. 2011.

Lucas, Mrs. Edgar. *Fairy Tales of the Brothers Grimm*. Prefatory Note by Arthur Rackham. London: Constable & Company Ltd., 1909. viii.

McCleery, Allistair. "Reproducing Images." *The Edinburgh History of the Book in Scotland*. Vol. 4: *Professionalism and Diversity, 1880–2000*. Ed. David Finkelstein and Allistair McCleery. Edinburgh: Edinburgh UP, 2007. 170–72.

McKitterick, David. "Changes in the Look of the Book." Ed. McKitterick. *The Cambridge History of the Book in Britain*. Vol. VI: 1830–1914. Cambridge: Cambridge UP, 2009. 75–116.

"Miscellaneous Notes." Rev. of *The Fairy Ring*. *Westminster Review*. 41.5 (1846): 250–51. *British Periodicals*. http://britishperiodicals.chadwyck.co.uk. 25 Nov. 2011.

Mr Gordon Browne's Fairy Tales. Advertisement. *Athenæum*. 23 Feb. 1895: 236. *British Periodicals*. http://britishperiodicals.chadwyck.co.uk. 17 Nov. 2011.

Muir, Percy. *Victorian Illustrated Books*. London: B. T. Batsford Ltd., 1971.

"Newspaper Chat." Rev. of *German Popular Stories*. *Examiner*. 22 Dec. 1822: 812. *19th Century British Library Newspapers*. http://find.galegroup.com. 17 Nov. 2011.

"Newspaper Chat." Rev. of *German Popular Stories*. *Examiner*. 29 Dec. 1822: 830. *19th Century British Library Newspapers*. http://find.galegroup.com. 17 Nov. 2011.

O'Donoghue, F. M., and Anne Pimlott Baker. "Wehnert, Edward Henry (1813–1868)." *Oxford Dictionary of National Biography*. Oxford, Oxford UP. 2004.

Paull, H. H. B., trans. Preface. *Grimms' Fairy Tales*. London: Frederick Warne and Company, 1872. iii–iv.

"Rackham's Fairy Tales." Advertisement. *English Review Advertiser*. Nov. 1909: 4. *British Periodicals*. http://britishperiodicals.chadwyck.co.uk. 17 Nov. 2011.

Rev. of *The Fairy Ring*. *Critic*. 3.54 (1846): 27. *British Periodicals*. http://britishperiodicals.chadwyck.co.uk. 25 Nov. 2011.

Rev. of *Grimm's Fairy Tales*. *Bookman*. Dec. 1900: 7–8. *British Periodicals*. http://
  britishperiodicals.chadwyck.co.uk. 27 Mar. 2012.

Rev. of *Household Stories*. *Athenæum*. 11 Nov. 1882: 620–21. *British Periodicals*. http://
  britishperiodicals.chadwyck.co.uk. 17 Nov. 2011.

"Reviews." Rev. of *Household Stories*. *Athenaeum* 26 Feb. 1853: 247–48. *British Periodicals*. http://britishperiodicals.chadwyck.co.uk. 27 Mar. 2012.

Scally, John. "Illustration." *The Edinburgh History of the Book in Scotland*. Vol. 3: *Ambition and Industry, 1800–1880*. Ed. Bill Bell. Edinburgh: Edinburgh UP, 2007.
  49–61.

Sutton, Martin. *The Sin Complex: A Critical Study of English Versions of the Grimms'
  Kinder- und Hausmärchen in the Nineteenth Century*. Kassel: Brüder Grimm-
  Gesellschaft, 1996. Schriften der Brüder Grimm-Gesellschaft. Vol. 28.

Taylor, Edgar, trans. Preface. *Gammer Grethel, or German Fairy Tales, and Popular
  Stories*. London: John Green, 1839. i–vi.

Whalley, Joyce Irene, and Tessa Rose Chester. *A History of Children's Book Illustration*.
  London: John Murray with the Victoria & Albert Museum, 1988.

White, Gleeson. "Children's Books and Their Illustrators." *The Studio*. Special winter
  number. 1897–1898.

12

Marvelous Worlds

The Grimms' Fairy Tales in GDR Children's Films

BETTINA KÜMMERLING-MEIBAUER

After the Second World War there was a fierce debate about fairy tales in general and the Grimms' tales in particular in Germany. In 1945 the occupation forces, especially the British, banned the publication of fairy tales, since they believed that the cruelty often shown in folktales was at least partially responsible for the brutalization of German youth during the Nazi era. This verdict also concerned the Grimms' tales, which were regarded as prototypical German fairy tales. Although the ban was lifted in 1946, the discussion proceeded, since some pedagogues continued to connect the dreadful events depicted in some popular Grimm tales with Nazi ideology. The claim that preschool children find it difficult to distinguish between reality and fantasy also emerged in the postwar period, refuting the moral and cognitive use of fairy tales on the grounds that they transmit a false impression of everyday life (Zipes 341).

After the separation of Germany into two states (the Federal Republic of Germany in the west and the German Democratic Republic, or GDR, in the east) in 1949, the appreciation of the Grimms' tales was subordinated to different ideological viewpoints that also affected the film industry in both countries. However, the fairy-tale films in the Federal Republic of Germany mostly relied on the puppet animation technique established by the Brothers Ferdinand, Hermann, and Paul Diehl in the 1930s, thus demonstrating a rather traditional and old-fashioned attitude toward this genre (Schoemann).[1] The GDR fairy-tale films instead showed a surprisingly innovative approach that was supported by the cultural policy of DEFA.

DEFA was short for the Deutsche Film Aktiengesellschaft (German Film Public Company) and was successor to the famous film studio UFA (Berlin). It was founded in November 1945 by the Soviet occupation force in cooperation with German cultural functionaries, film makers, authors, and other artists. The main purpose of this film company was to build up an antifascist cultural climate (Bock 28ff; Byg and Moore). According to the cultural program formulated by Vladimir Lenin in the 1920s, film production was socialized. Newly created films should communicate the ideas of Social Realism, support political elucidation and topical knowledge about technique and the natural sciences, and expose social and economic disadvantage.

After the foundation of the GDR in 1949, the Soviet occupation force assigned DEFA to the new state. The DEFA studio, as *volkseigener Betrieb* (a company owned by the people), was established in 1953 with its head office in Potsdam. While live action films were produced at Studio Babelsberg in Potsdam, animated films were created at the DEFA animation studio in Dresden from 1955 onward. Moreover, the DEFA studios had their own department responsible for the production of children's films. The executive committee requested that the best directors, authors, and actors be engaged to improve the narrative and aesthetic quality of children's films. Therefore, renowned artists and authors, such as Gerhard Holtz-Baumert, Christa Kožik, Ulrich Plenzdorf, Benno Pludra, Fred Rodrian, and Erwin Strittmatter, contributed to the success of GDR children's films at home and even abroad (Jungnickel 85ff).

The first film projects were realized in 1946, but the production of children's films started later, in 1953.[2] Although many early children's films are based on film scripts that describe the everyday life of children in East Germany, the huge success of the Russian fairy-tale film *Kamennyi svetok* (1946, The Stone Flower, directed by Alexander Ptushko) that was shown in East German cinemas in 1947 called the attention of producers to fairy tales as another possible subject for children's films. The first DEFA fairy-tale film was an adaptation of Wilhelm Hauff's *Das kalte Herz* (The Cold Heart), directed by Paul Verhoeven in 1950. However, this film was advertised not as a children's film but as a film for children and adults alike, stressing the crossover appeal of fairy tales.

More than thirty fairy tales by the Brothers Grimm were adapted for the screen by the DEFA studios, starting with *Das tapfere Schneiderlein*[3] (The Cunning Little Tailor) in 1956 and ending with *Die Geschichte von der*

Gänseprinzessin und ihrem treuen Pferd Fallada (The Goose Girl) in 1989. Some of these fairy tales were adapted twice, for short, animated films and/ or live action films, for example *König Drosselbart* (King Thrushbeard), *Die kluge Bauerntochter* (The Peasant's Wise Daughter), and *Sechse kommen durch die Welt* (Six Made Their Way in the World). Among the adapted fairy tales are both popular Grimm fairy tales, such as *Schneewittchen* (Snow White, 1961), *Dornröschen* (Sleeping Beauty, 1972), and *Der Froschkönig* (The Frog King, 1988), and lesser known fairy tales, such as *Das blaue Licht* (The Blue Light, 1976), *Der Meisterdieb* (The Master Thief, 1978), *Jorinde und Joringel* (Jorinda and Joringel, 1986), and *Der Bärenhäuter* (Bearskin, 1986).[4]

The feature films, whose lengths vary between 50 and 100 minutes, more or less rely on the Grimms' tales, although the scriptwriters and directors include passages referring to historical or contemporary events, such as the Prague Spring and the Cold War. Some remediations exhibit an additional frame story, for instance in *Frau Holle* (Mother Holle, 1953) and *Jorinde und Joringel*. These frame stories function as a threshold between the real world and the fantastic world, with an old woman or man who acts as narrator of the subsequent story. The film version that most deviates from the original tale is *Der Froschkönig* (1988), probably due to the shortness of the original version.

Whereas the first third is a retelling of the Grimms' tale, the subsequent two thirds tell a new story. After the princess Henriette has thrown the frog against the wall, he changes into a beautiful prince. However, since Henriette has not kept her promise, the enchantment has not completely disappeared. He has a cold heart and is therefore not able to love and leaves the princess. Henriette, who deeply regrets her broken promise, travels to the end of the world in search of the prince. She finally arrives at the "Zitadelle der Lieblosigkeit" (citadel of lovelessness), the prince's domicile. Disguised as a boy, the princess, who is called "Heinrich," consecutively becomes apprentice to the cellar man, the cook, and the valet. Hence, she is able to fulfill the requests she formerly rejected: to drink from the same cup, to eat from the same dish, and to sleep in the same bed. The prince finally recognizes the princess but keeps this a secret. He orders instead that she drive him to his pretended bride.

During the drive, the following dialogue that also appears in the original Grimms' tale takes place between prince and disguised princess: "Heinrich, der Wagen bricht!" (Henry, the wheel is breaking!)—"Nein, Herr, der Wagen nicht. Es ist ein Band von meinem Herzen, das da liegt in großen

Schmerzen" (No, Sir, the wheel does not break. It is the band round my painful heart that lies on the ground). After that the magic ban is definitely broken (König, Wiedemann, and Wolf, *Märchen* 374). The fairy-tale film emphasizes the importance of love and the request to keep one's promise much more than the original version and also shows that adhering to authority (the princess's father) is not sufficient. In addition, Henriette has to abandon her royal attitude to win the prince's heart.

These aspects, as well as her gender crossing, significantly emphasize underlying issues, such as the criticism of social and political injustice and concern for oppressed people's welfare, that are typical for the majority of the DEFA fairy-tale film versions. Although they refer to traditional popular fairy tales, the inherent ideological premises are changed to adjust them to the ideology of Social Realism, that is, overcoming social classes in order to build up a society that is governed by general human rules rather than by political and social privileges.

CULTURAL HERITAGE

The interest in fairy tales and their remediation was additionally elicited by the discussion of the so-called cultural heritage in the GDR during the 1950s that led to a shifting view on canonical texts, whether written for children or for adults (Dahlke). In this regard, the fairy-tale collections by Hans Christian Andersen, Ludwig Bechstein, Wilhelm Hauff, and the Brothers Grimm were chosen as suitable reading matter for children. Educators and cultural functionaries regarded the Grimms' *Kinder- und Hausmärchen* (Children's and Household Tales) as part of the cultural heritage for different reasons. One reason was the tales' provenance from oral tradition and therefore from the "folk" in a broader sense.

Another aspect was the depiction of people from lower classes in several Grimm tales. Despite this appreciation, the early editions of the Grimms' tales targeted at a child readership underwent a palpable revision so that they conformed to the ideology and value system of the state. Cruel and violent episodes as well as religious passages were eliminated or diminished, whereas moral statements that matched the political and pedagogical policy of Social Realism were added. The first unabridged version of the *Kinder- und Hausmärchen* in the GDR was published in 1955, but the revisions and censorship of these tales continued.[5] This resulted in a dehistorization of the

Grimms' tales in order to convert them into "pristine" folktales that could be utilized for the moral and political education of children and youth.

In contrast to the literary adaptations, the DEFA films based on the Grimms' tales show a tendency to refer to social and historical events that are not mentioned in the original works. This is because the party leadership encouraged the remediation of the fairy tales into children's films on the condition that they be adapted to the ideology of Social Realism. Artworks considered to be bourgeois were declined or had to be remodeled to adhere to Communist and Socialist ideals. For this reason directors and producers demonstrated a preference for those fairy tales that have protagonists belonging to the laboring class or other minor social classes (peasants, soldiers, maidservants, farm laborers, workers, fishermen, craftsmen, even beggars) who are presented as "heroes of labor," thus praising their hard work as a seminal contribution to society's prosperity. In contrast, the nobility (i.e., kings, queens, princesses, princes, knights, earls, and courtesans) and their staff but also people belonging to the bourgeois class (doctors, mayors, judges, and merchants) are often a target of criticism. In many DEFA fairy-tale films the protagonists belong to the working or craftsmen class.

By means of their skills and cognitive abilities—sometimes supported by magic—they are able to cope with difficult problems, releasing subordinated people from unjust kings or noblemen. In *Das tapfere Schneiderlein,* the brave little tailor outsmarts a giant, a boar, and a unicorn; refuses to marry the king's spoiled daughter; chases the king away; and ascends the throne with his fiancée, a maidservant. Although some film critics and educators criticized the film as *vulgärmarxistisch* (vulgar Marxist) and opposed the somewhat crude and narrow-minded characterization of the protagonists, the film was appreciated by the political and cultural administration as a successful prototype of a fairy-tale film that completely obeyed the requirements of Social Realism (Häntzsche 253–54).[6]

While *Das tapfere Schneiderlein* was praised by the official GDR institutions, *Das singende, klingende Bäumchen* (1957, The Singing, Ringing Tree), based on a fragment by the Grimms, experienced a mixed reception. The audience was fascinated by the innovative film tricks, intense colors, artful sets, and lively play of the actors. The film was even broadcast several times on the BBC (British Broadcasting Corporation) in the 1960s and achieved the status of a cult film in the United Kingdom (Liptay 137). Nevertheless, it was criticized by hardliners as a "bourgeois idyll," representing a "false fairy-tale romanticism" (König, Wiedemann, and Wolf, *Zwischen Marx und Muck* 109). Since the director Francesco Stefani lived in the Federal Republic of Germany—he was invited by the DEFA studio as a guest director for this film—the repudiation of *Das singende, klingende Bäumchen* by cultural functionaries presumably reveals a politically motivated background.

ARTISTIC INFLUENCES ON THE CREATION OF DEFA FAIRY-TALE FILMS

The majority of the DEFA fairy-tale films reveals an astonishing variety of intermedial references, ranging from cartoons to the fairy-tale films in East European countries, the animated films of the Disney studios, and contemporary theater. The animated short films, produced for television and cinema, refer either to the prewar tradition of Lotte Reiniger, who created silhouette fairy-tales films (Giera, "Aschenputtel" 228ff) or to the contemporary animated films for children created in other East European countries, especially Czechoslovakia, Poland, and Russia. Just a few of the East German animated films are cartoons; most of them use stop-motion animation with puppets in the tradition of the Czech puppet maker and director Jiří Trnka, who was also widely acclaimed as an illustrator of children's books. Another model was the Czech director Karel Zeman, who cooperated with Czech avant-garde artists and filmmakers. His animated films are distinguished by beautifully accomplished scenery and an experimental character (Holloway 240ff.).

As for the feature films, several sources of influence are discernible: the Russian fairy-tale films, theater, Bertolt Brecht's concept of "alienation," and the Disney tradition. The famous Russian fairy-tale film *Kamennyi svetok* (The Stone Flower, 1946), which was released in Berlin and other GDR cities from 1947 onward, had a strong impact on the development of East European fairy-tale films in general, and the GDR fairy-tale films in particular. *Kammenyi svetok* was the first Russian color film produced with the newly established three-color procedure. Therefore the colors were extremely brilliant, emphasizing especially the malachite green and copper red (as colors belonging to the Mistress of the Mountain) and the warm red as the color of Katia.

An additional innovative aspect is the combination of frame story and inner story. In the frame story, an old miner tells the village children the tale of Danila and the mountain fairy. This strategy was used to stress the emergence of folktales from oral storytelling. Although the film was produced in a studio, with painted scenery and artificial landscapes, living animals, such as squirrels, rabbits, birds, deer, and foxes, and plants were represented. The juxtaposition of artifacts, natural objects, and animals largely contributes to the creation of a harmonic atmosphere, highlighted by close-ups of the animals and flowers and by sophisticated lighting control that underlines the mystical character of the scenery. The film tricks, for instance cross-fading, double exposure, and the use of a revolving stage to show converse movements, create a puzzling mood and convey the impression that it is not always easy to distinguish between fantasy and reality.

A final innovation in *Kamennyi svetok* is the connection of the film genre with political and social issues, in this case with the ideology of the Soviet regime (Prokhorov 136). Therefore, Danila's individual conflict is juxtaposed with the fate of the people in his village. Although Danila is at first most concerned with becoming a perfect artist on his own, he finally recognizes that he has to establish a balance between his ambition for artistic perfection and his responsibility for and empathy toward the village people (Berger and Giera 152). The schematic presentation of bad versus good people, typical for many folktales and fairy tales, is reduced in favor of a critical depiction of class relationships and a historical perspective on the political and economic conditions of different social groups.

These different issues strongly influenced the development of the DEFA fairy-tale films in the 1940s and 1950s. When comparing the early DEFA films, such as *Das tapfere Schneiderlein* (1956), *Das Zaubermännchen* (Rumpelstiltskin, 1960), *Schneewittchen* (1961), and *Frau Holle* (1963), with *Kamennyi svetok,* the impact of the Russian film is obvious, whether it concerns the depiction of nature, the metaphorical use of colors, the frame story with an old storyteller, the stage-like character of the scenery, or the adaptation of the fairy-tale plot to contemporary political and social constraints.

Since many directors, screenwriters, stage technicians, and stage designers had experience with theater, the majority of the early fairy-tale films are influenced by the stage as well. Films such as *Frau Holle, König Drosselbart,* and *Dornröschen* are produced in studios with a reduced stage design. Painted sets and buildings and trees made of cardboard placed against a monochrome background largely contribute to the artificial character of the settings. This stylization is particularly evident in *Frau Holle,* in which the isolated props, for example paper cutout trees, clouds made of cotton, and an oven made of cardboard, are arranged in geometrical patterns on the stage with scarcely painted sets or monochrome backgrounds whose changing colors indicate the character of the protagonists (white for Mother Holle and Golden Mary; black for Pitch Mary).

The director Walter Beck adopted the reference to the stage for his remediations of *König Drosselbart, Der Prinz hinter den sieben Meeren* (The Singing, Springing Lark), and *Der Bärenhäuter.* He even went a step further by situating the actors and props on a platform with a steady and smooth illumination in order to achieve the impression of infinite space (König, Wiedemann, and Wolf, *Zwischen Marx und Muck* 30). Beck's rather abstract style calls the viewer's attention to the artificiality of the films, prompting a quite distant position toward the protagonists and the fairy-tale plot. In an interview, Beck (59) once indicated that it was his main intention to show "Kunst als vorsätzlich Gemachtes" (art as intentionally made). Moreover, Beck's fairy-tale films are distinguished by their ahistorical and timeless character, in a small act of rebellion against the request to build up connections to Social Realist policy.

Another source of inspiration for Walter Beck (and other directors as well) was Bertolt Brecht, who founded the famous Berliner Ensemble at the Theater am Schiffbauerdamm (Berlin) in 1954. As a playwright he had established the concept of the *Verfremdungseffekt* (alienation effect) in the 1930s. Reacting against the Aristotelian principle of catharsis, Brecht categorically disapproved of performances and plays that appealed to the audience's empathy and displayed a quasinaturalistic stage setting. To destroy any illusory effects and to facilitate a critical distance from the play and its actors, Brecht insisted on antinaturalistic stage design and performance, on the one hand, and the insertion of songs and comments directed toward the audience, which function as interruptions of the stage action, on the other (Fischer 1989).

Several early DEFA fairy-tale films, such as *Frau Holle* and *König Drosselbart,* are distinguished by the "alienation effect" that is established in their combination of songs, dialogue, and comments and in the selection of an abstract stage setting. The reference to Brecht resurfaced in the 1980s, when Wera and Claus Küchenmeister, who were Brecht's "master disciples" at the Berliner Ensemble, wrote the film scripts for *Der Meisterdieb, Gevatter Tod* (Godfather Death), and *Jorinde und Joringel.* In contrast to the early DEFA fairy-tale films, the setting was not situated in a studio but in cityscapes and real landscapes. Nevertheless, Wera and Claus Küchenmeister remained true to Brecht's principles insofar as they inserted passages that invite the viewers to maintain a distance from the film action, thus encouraging them to reflect upon the open and implied meanings of the films.

Although the animated and live action fairy-tale films are regarded as a counterpart to Western fairy-tale remediations, some DEFA films are obviously influenced by Western European and US models. A case in point is *Schneewittchen* (1961), directed by Gottfried Kolditz. While the depiction of nature, the color scheme (every figure has its own typical color), and the subliminal allusions to class struggle refer to the Russian fairy-tale tradition, the portrayal of the seven dwarfs is strongly reminiscent of the famous Walt Disney film *Snow White and the Seven Dwarfs* (1937). The comical behavior and the individual characterization of the dwarfs, their humorous songs, and the design of their wood cabin exactly mirror the animated Disney version.

HISTORICAL REFERENCES AND SUBVERSIVE MEANINGS

In order to adapt the Grimm fairy tales to the ideological prospects of Social Realism, references to social and historical events that are more or less related to the liberation of peasants, craftsmen, and laborers are included in the film versions, although they are not mentioned in the original works, for example, the Peasant War in *Gevatter Tod* (1980), the French Revolution in *Sechse kommen durch die Welt,* bondage in *Wer reißt denn gleich vor'm Teufel aus* (The Devil with Three Golden Hairs, 1977), and the Thirty Years' War in *Jorinde und Joringel, Das blaue Licht,* and *Der Bärenhäuter.*

This strategy led to the appropriation of (German) history and culture by antifascist and Communist ideology. *Jorinde und Joringel* openly shows the brutalization and indifference of people due to the long-lasting Thirty Years' War, resulting in pillage, robbery, murder, and rape. The director intended to create an antiwar parable in light of the ongoing rearmament in Europe. To make this reference clearer, he had primarily intended to situate the fairy-tale plot in the 1980s but refrained from this idea during work on the film script. The historical context that emphasizes the underlying melancholic mood of the original tale ideally suited the director's program to highlight the universal meaning of *Jorinde und Joringel* as a parable for eternal love and mutual commitment, even in dark times and under severe circumstances. Moreover, *Jorinde und Joringel* is distinguished by interpictorial references to Renaissance art and culture.

The three marauding mercenaries who threaten Jorinde's family at the beginning and end of the film are clothed in the manner of the figures presented in Albrecht Dürer's famous copper engraving "Knight, Death, and the Devil" (1513), thus emphasizing the troops' menacing aura (Giera, *Wahrheit* 37). When Joringel finally defeats the three mercenaries and saves his family, the foggy moor landscape, where the family sought refuge, is replaced by a green meadow with dancing children and young maidens, thus creating an idyllic Eden-like setting that emphasizes the peaceful atmosphere after the end of the war.

The changeover from the Middle Ages to the early modern age plays a significant role in the remediation of *Gevatter Tod*. This film was produced in Görlitz, a town with a Renaissance cityscape situated at the frontier with Poland. The struggle between death and his godchild, a renowned doctor who is able to cure fatally ill clients, parallels the conflict between religious superstition and humanist elucidation (Kliems 174ff.). It is no wonder then that one model for the characterization of the main protagonist is the German alchemist Paracelsus. Both he and the tale's protagonist are distinguished by an oscillation between hubris and a concern for other people's suffering, and both finally fail due to the overestimation of their own capacities and their incomprehension and mistrust of their surroundings.

The luxurious and bacchanalian life at royal courts with distinct references to the French Sun King, Louis XIV, is a topic in the film versions of *Dornröschen* and *Sechse kommen durch die Welt*, whereas the oppression of the country folk and poor gentry by aristocratic people and great landowners is presented in the remediations of *Der Meisterdieb* and *Gevatter Tod*, among others. Besides these politically accepted references to important historical events, the directors and screenwriters covertly insert allusions to contemporary political and economic incidents into their films.[7] For instance, the behavior of the unstable, and sometimes even iniquitous, king in *Wie heiratet man einen König?* (The Peasant's Wise Daughter) has been interpreted as a caricature of Walter Ulbricht, president of the GDR State Council from 1960 onward.

Another example is *Sechse kommen durch die Welt*, whose bleak mood refers to the leaden atmosphere under Ulbricht's regime. As a critical commentary on the brutal abatement of the uprising in Czechoslovakia in 1968 (the so-called Prague Spring), the director Rainer Simon offered the Czech actor Jiří Menzel, who was banned from his profession in 1969, the role of the brave soldier who rebels against the king and is therefore threatened by death. The film presents a satirical depiction of the narrow-mindedness of the dominant aristocratic class. This is evident in the opening scene when the king—comparable to Stalinist dictators—bestows several decorations on himself but puts off his soldiers with a starvation wage. On closer consideration, the dialogue reveals an ambivalent meaning, encouraging the attentive viewer to read between the lines.

The subversive message of this film is also evident in the behavior of the soldier's six companions, characterized as a "Bund der ungewöhnlichen Leute" (league of unusual people). In order to avoid the attention of their superiors and members of the noble class, they consciously conceal their special gifts. This attitude can be interpreted as a metaphor for those people in East European countries who came into conflict with the regime because of their critical and independent thinking or their claim for artistic freedom (Schenk 84). These experiences resulted in careful behavior and the decision to deny one's own talents rather than risk being arrested or suppressed. In the film version, the soldier has to use all his persuasion to convince his unusual companions to support him in his endeavor to take revenge on the unjust king, his spoiled and touchy daughter, and the counselors. It is interesting to note that the folk remain passive until the end, although the "revolutionary" group around the soldier intends to free the poor people from the king's exploitative taxes and the nobility's unfair enactments. In contrast to the original tale, in which the king shows some comprehension, letting the soldier and his companions go with the treasure, the film version presents an ambivalent ending. The king orders his guards to chase the soldier and his group to get the royal treasure back. The king's army attacks the corral of the soldier, but the fiddler keeps the guards dancing with his magic fiddle. In the final scene, the companions have left the playing fiddler, everyone departing in different directions. It remains open what will happen with the treasure when the fiddler is too exhausted to play anymore.

The tendency to insert ambiguous scenes and speech into the fairy-tale films that prompt the viewer to read between the lines also crops up in other remediations of the Grimms' tales. The film *Das blaue Licht* was very popular with its audience, since it consists of many side blows against the economy of scarcity in the GDR, while the dialogue in *Gevatter Tod* is an indirect reaction to the contemporary discussion of euthanasia. *König Drosselbart* is characterized by sophisticated dialogue with intertextual allusions to William

Shakespeare's comedies (*The Comedy of Errors*, 1589; *The Taming of the Shrew*, 1594; and *Much Ado about Nothing*, 1598). The verbal exchanges between the snappish princess and her suitors and the asides spoken by the actors include famous citations from Shakespeare's plays that contribute to the humorous effects, on the one hand, but also add references to contemporary gender debates in the GDR, on the other.

The general shortcomings of GDR politics and economics in the 1980s are subliminally evoked in the remediation of *Eisenhans* (1988, Iron John). What is most striking about this film is its ecological perspective, clearly charging mankind for the destruction of nature (Zipes 348). Nature conservation was not on the agenda of the GDR regime, whose coalmining and factories resulted in pollution. However, the awareness of the long-lasting effects caused by heavy industry provoked the growing dissatisfaction of the GDR population, especially young people, with the insufficient conservation of nature. This attitude also determines the film version, in which Iron John is depicted as a guardian of nature. He is never displayed as a whole person; just his face is shown as an image in a rock, thereby stressing his ghostly appearance and his metaphorical character.

Mankind's responsibility for the destruction of nature is clearly indicated at the beginning: a voiceover gives an account of the happy, bygone times when everyone lived in harmony with nature, thus building up a contrast to the following scenes, which show the decadence, laziness, and brutality of modern people, exemplified by the rulers of two neighboring countries who make war on each other, regardless of the consequences for nature and the population. The collapse of both rulers and the reconciliation of their countries occasioned by the love marriage of their children have been interpreted as an anticipation of the political changes in 1989: the fall of the wall and the reunion of both German states in 1990 (Zipes 347).

CHANGES IN SETTING, STYLE, AND AUDIENCE

The claim to adhere painstakingly to the cultural policy of the Communist regime of the GDR meant that directors, set designers, and producers had to conform to ideological constraints with changing, even arbitrary standards due to political developments over several decades. Although the film makers faced rather strict ideological guidelines, they attempted to maintain artistic standards. Despite constriction by the party leadership and the government, many directors created innovative fairy-tale films that are distinguished by their aesthetic quality and experimental character. The animated films are characterized by a subtle poetic style, thus establishing an alternative model to Disney films and American cartoons. Some of these films do not have any dialogue at all; the soundscape just consists of music, so that the images speak for themselves, as in *Frau Holle* by Johannes Hempel and *Dornröschen* by Katja Georgi. Moreover, a survey of the feature fairy-tale films created over the course of four decades reveals three general tendencies: the shift in the choice of setting (from studio to outdoor setting), the increasing interest in the psychological aspects of the respective fairy tales, and the crossover appeal.

The first fairy-tale film whose setting was not just in a studio was *Wie heiratet man einen König?* The request to show more realistic settings led to the relocation of the action outdoors. This development goes hand in hand with an increasing interest in the psychological disposition of the fairy-tale protagonists. As a consequence, interpersonal relationships came to the fore. To stress the psychological aspects of the fairy tale, the producers attempted to avoid the stereotyped depiction of the actors, showing them as ordinary people rather than as beautiful princesses and noble princes. For instance, Rainer Simon's *Wie heiratet man einen König?* focuses on the love affair between the main protagonists and more or less resembles a romantic movie. Another example is the protagonist in *Wer reißt denn gleich vor'm Teufel aus* (who goes through a process of development?). In the beginning he is characterized as a coward, unable to take a risk. But during the course of the story, he becomes increasingly self-confident, thus overcoming the obstacles and eventually cheating the devil. His success is not the result of magic but of his own cleverness and courage. The same applies to *Die Geschichte von der Gänsemagd und ihrem treuen Pferd Fallada,* in which the film script shows a deep interest in the diverse individual relationships between the main characters and the supporting actors. The psychologization of the protagonists, the subversive messages, and double meanings of dialogue and scenes as well as the intertextual and interpictorial references indicate that the DEFA fairy-tale films were targeted at children and adults alike. This evidence demonstrates that these films, although categorized as children's films, actually should be regarded as early examples of cross-filming, a notion referring to the tendency of modern children's films to transgress the boundaries between films for children and films for adults (Kümmerling-Meibauer 14).

After the fall of the Berlin wall in 1989, the DEFA studios still produced children's films until 1993. The DEFA Stiftung (DEFA Foundation), as administrator of the DEFA films, was founded in 2009. Its main purposes are to conserve and propagate the DEFA films, to investigate the history of the DEFA studios, and to support public access to the films. For this reason almost all DEFA fairy-tale films are available on DVD (produced by the company Icestorm). Because of their popularity and aesthetic quality they are still broadcast on German TV channels. This popularity seems to be astonishing at first glance, but in comparison to the fairy-tale films broadcast in the Federal Republic of Germany between 1950 and 1990, which are distinguished by poor equipment, unpalatable direction, and randomly selected actors, the DEFA films reveal a certain timelessness despite the commitment to Social Realism. Since the DEFA children's film studio enjoyed high esteem in the former GDR, only the best actors and directors had been chosen to transform the Grimms' tales into film versions. The artists involved in these film projects took advantage of their artistic freedom to create sophisticated fairy-tale films that are distinguished by multidimensional features. To these key features belong intertextual and intermedial references to the German "cultural heritage," on the one hand, and to different literary and cinematic sources, on the other. In addition, although the films are shallowly obliged to the ideology of Social Realism, an in-depth-analysis shows that they can be interpreted on different levels, thus revealing an approach that might be characterized as an early stage of cross-filming.

NOTES

1. Because of their poor quality these fairy-tale films totally fell into oblivion after the 1970s.

2. Two children's films were produced in 1953, the fairy-tale film *Der kleine Muck* (Little Mook, directed by Wolfgang Staudte), based on a tale written by Wilhelm Hauff, and *Die Störenfriede* (The Troublemakers, directed by Wolfgang Schleif).

3. All German titles refer to the DEFA film titles, which are sometimes different from the titles of the Grimm tales.

4. To date there does not exist a thorough investigation of the DEFA fairy-tale films discussing their historical, cultural, and film aesthetic aspects. Reimann and Zipes give short overviews, while Kannapin discusses the aesthetic of the DEFA films in general without an in-depth study of the fairy-tale films.

5. From 1952 to 1989 more than sixty different editions of the Grimms' tales were published in the GDR, some of them illustrated by renowned artists, such as Josef Hegenbarth, Werner Klemke, and Eva-Johanna Rubin.

6. Considering this, it is not quite clear whether the comparison of the cunning tailor with Wilhelm Pieck, first president of the GDR until his death in 1960, made in some reviews and comments is a tongue-in-cheek joke or a serious assertion (Wolf 182).

7. Scholars specialized in GDR literature and culture refer to the so-called slave language, a term coined by Lenin before the October Revolution of 1918. Critical artists and intellectuals used this notion to subtextually criticize political and social aspects in the GDR (Wardetzky 184ff.). However, the term is perhaps a bit misleading, because the population in the former GDR was never in the position of slaves. For this reason it might be more appropriate to rely on the notion "Aesopian language," created by the Russian satirist Mikhail Saltykov-Shchedrin at the end of the nineteenth century. The author hereby refers to his method to convey a seemingly innocent meaning on the surface but to communicate a concealed meaning to informed members of a conspiracy or to those readers who have learned to read between the lines (Mirsky 294).

FILMOGRAPHY

Shorts and Animated Films (A Selection)

Frau Holle KHM 024 (Mother Holle, 1955). Director: Johannes Hempel.

Die Bremer Stadtmusikanten KHM 027 (The Bremen Town Musicians, 1955). Director: Bruno Böttge.

König Drosselbart KHM 052 (King Thrushbeard, 1956). Director: Bruno Böttge.

Jorinde und Joringel KHM 069 (Jorinda and Joringel, 1958). Director: Johannes Hempel.

Sechse kommen durch die Welt KHM 071 (Six Soldiers of Fortune, 1959). Director: Lothar Barke.

Rumpelstilzchen KHM 055 (Rumpelstiltskin, 1960). Director: Bruno Böttge.

Die kluge Bauerntochter KHM 094 (The Peasant's Wise Daughter, 1961). Director: Wolfgang Bergner.

Das tapfere Schneiderlein KHM 114 (The Cunning Little Tailor, 1964). Director: Kurt Weiler.

Der Meisterdieb KHM 192 (The Master Thief, 1966). Director: Jörg d'Bomba.

Dornröschen KHM 050 (Sleeping Beauty, 1968). Director: Katja Georgi.

Von einem, der auszog, das Fürchten zu lernen KHM 004 (The Story of the Youth Who Went Forth to Learn What Fear Was, 1970). Director: Rudolf Schraps.

Die Geschichte vom Fischer und seiner Frau KHM 19 (The Fisherman and His Wife, 1976). Director: Werner Krauße.

Hänsel und Gretel KHM 015 (Hansel and Gretel, 1976). Director: Katja Georgi.

Rotkäppchen KHM 026 (Little Red Cap, 1977). Director: Otto Sacher.

Rapunzel KHM 012 (Rapunzel, 1982). Director: Christl Wiemer.

Aschenputtel KHM 021 (Cinderella, 1984). Director: Horst Tappert.

Die Wahrheit um den Froschkönig KHM 001 (The Truth about the Frog King, 1986). Director: Siegfried Hartmann.

Die Gänsemagd KHM 089 (The Goose Maiden, 1987). Director: Horst Tappert.

Dornröschen war ein schönes Kind KHM 050 (Sleeping Beauty Was a Beautiful Child, 1988). Director: Katja Georgi.

Live Action Films

Das tapfere Schneiderlein KHM 114 (The Cunning Little Tailor, 1956). Director: Helmut Spieß.

Das singende, klingende Bäumchen. After a fragment of the Brothers' Grimm (The Singing, Ringing Tree, 1957). Director: Franceso Stefani.

Das Zaubermännchen KHM 055 (Rumpelstiltskin, 1960). Directors: Christoph Engel and Erwin Anders.

Das hölzerne Kälbchen KHM 61 (The Little Peasant, 1961). Director: Bernhard Thieme.

Schneewittchen KHM 053 (Snow White, 1961). Director: Gottfried Kolditz.

Frau Holle KHM 024 (Mother Holle, 1963). Director: Gottfried Kolditz.

Die goldene Gans KHM 064 (The Golden Goose, 1964). Director: Siegfried Hartmann.

König Drosselbart KHM 052 (King Thrushbeard, 1965). Director: Walter Beck.

Wie heiratet man einen König? KHM 094 (The Peasant's Wise Daughter, 1969). Director: Rainer Simon.

Dornröschen KHM 050 (Sleeping Beauty, 1971). Director: Walter Beck.

Sechse kommen durch die Welt KHM 071 (Six Soldiers of Fortune, 1972). Director: Rainer Simon.

Das blaue Licht KHM 116 (The Blue Light, 1976). Director: Iris Gusner.

Wer reißt denn gleich vor'm Teufel aus? KHM 0029 (The Devil with Three Golden Hairs, 1977). Director: Egon Schlegel.

Der Meisterdieb KHM 192 (The Master Thief, 1978). Director: Wolfgang Hübner.

Schneeweißchen und Rosenrot KHM 161 (Snow White and Rose Red, 1979). Director: Siegfried Hartmann.

Gevatter Tod KHM 044 (Godfather Death, 1980). Director: Wolfgang Hübner.

Der Prinz hinter den sieben Meeren KHM 088 (The Singing, Springing Lark, 1982). Director: Walter Beck.

Der Bärenhäuter KHM 101 (Bearskin, 1986). Director: Walter Beck.

Jorinde und Joringel KHM 069 (Jorinda and Joringel, 1986). Director: Walter Beck.

Der Froschkönig KHM 001 (The Frog King, 1988). Director: Wolfgang Hübner.

Rapunzel oder der Zauber der Tränen KHM 012 (Rapunzel, 1988). Director: Ursula Schmanger.

Der Eisenhans KHM 136 (Iron John, 1988). Director: Karl Heinz Lotz.

Die Geschichte von der Gänseprinzessin und ihrem treuen Pferd Fallada KHM 089 (The Goose Girl, 1989). Director: Konrad Petzold.

REFERENCES

Beck, Walter. "Über Verantwortung gegenüber den Zuschauern des Märchenfilms." *Medien erzählen Märchen.* Ed. Märchenstiftung Walter Kahn. Leipzig: Märchenstiftung Walter Kahn, 2000. 46–60.

Berger, Eberhard, and Joachim Giera. *77 Märchenfilme. Ein Filmführer für jung und alt.* Berlin: Henschel, 1990.

Bock, Hans-Michael. "East Germany: The DEFA Story." *The Oxford History of World Cinema.* Ed. Geoffrey Nowell-Smith. Oxford: Oxford UP, 1996. 627–39.

Byg, Barton, and Betheny Moore, eds. *Moving Images of East Germany: Past and Future of DEFA Film.* Washington, DC: American Institute for Contemporary German Studies, 2002.

Dahlke, Birgit. *Literaturgeschichte DDR: Kanonkämpfe und ihre Geschichte(n).* Stuttgart: Metzler, 2000.

Fischer, Matthias-Johannes. *Brechts Theatertheorie.* Frankfurt am Main: Peter Lang, 1989.

Giera, Joachim. "Mit Aschenputtel durch die Zeiten: Märchen aus dem DEFA-Trickfilmstudio." *Die Trick-Fabrik: DEFA-Animationsfilme 1955–1990.* Ed. Ralf Schenk and Sabine Scholz. Berlin: Bertz, 2003. 225–62.

———. "Wahrheit wie sie in den alten Märchen steckt. Wera und Klaus Küchenmeister im Gespräch über ihre Märchenfilme mit Joachim Giera." Spec. issue of *Aus Theorie und Praxis des Films* 2 (1989).

Häntzsche, Hellmuth, ed. *. . . und ich grüße die Schwalben. Der Kinderfilm in sozialistischen europäischen Ländern.* Berlin: Henschel, 1985.

Holloway, Ronald. "The Short Film in Eastern Europe: Art and Politics of Cartoons and Puppets." *Politics, Art and Commitment in East European Cinema.* Ed. David W. Paul. London: Macmillan, 1983. 225–51.

Jungnickel, Dirk. "Aspekte des DEFA-Kinderfilmschaffens." *Filmland DDR. Ein Reader zu Geschichte, Funktion und Wirkung der DEFA.* Ed. Harry Blunck and Dirk Jungnickel. Cologne: Wissenschaft und Politik, 1990. 83–94.

Kannapin, Detlef. "Gibt es eine spezifische DEFA-Ästhetik?" *Apropos: Film 2000: Das Jahrbuch der DEFA-Stiftung*. Eds. Ralf Schenk and Erika Richter. Berlin: Das Neue Berlin, 2000. 142–64.

Kliems, Alfrun. "Die slowakische Frau Holle und der deutsche Gevatter Tod: Todeskonzeptionen im Märchenfilm und ihre kulturellen Bezüge." *Filme der Kindheit im Film in Nord-, Mittel- und Osteuropa*. Eds. Christine Golz, Karin Hoff, and Anja Tippner. Frankfurt: Peter Lang, 2010. 165–82.

König, Ingelore, Dieter Wiedemann, and Lothar Wolf, eds. *Märchen: Arbeiten mit DEFA-Kinderfilmen*. Munich: KoPäd, 1998.

———. *Zwischen Marx und Muck. DEFA-Filme für Kinder*. Berlin: Henschel, 1996.

Kümmerling-Meibauer, Bettina. "Einleitung." *Filmgenres. Kinder-und Jugendfilm*. Eds. Bettina Kümmerling-Meibauer and Thomas Koebner. Stuttgart: Reclam, 2010. 9–23.

Lipovetsky, Mark. "Pavel Bazhov's *Skazy:* Discovering the Soviet Uncanny." *Russian Children's Literature and Culture*. Eds. Marina Ballina and Larissa Rudova. New York: Routledge, 2008. 263–84.

Liptay, Fabienne. *WunderWelten. Märchen im Film*. Remscheid: Gardez! Verlag, 2004.

Mirsky, Dmitry. *A History of Russian Literature*. Evanston: Northwestern UP, 1999.

Prokhorov, Alexander. "Arresting Development: A Brief History of Soviet Cinema for Children and Adolescents." *Russian Children's Literature and Culture*. Eds. Marina Ballina and Larissa Rudova. New York: Routledge, 2008. 129–52.

Reimann, Anne. "Märchenfilme in der DDR." *Informationen Jugendliteratur und Medien* 42.2 (1990): 50–60.

Schenk, Ralf. "Sechse kommen durch die Welt." *Filmgenres: Märchen-und Fantasyfilm*. Ed. Andreas Friedrich. Stuttgart: Reclam, 2003. 84–88.

Schoemann, Annika. *Der deutsche Animationsfilm: Von den Anfängen bis zur Gegenwart. 1909–2001*. Remscheid: Gardez! Verlag, 2003.

Wardetzky, Kristin. "Sklavensprache: Märchen und Fabeln in repressiven Gesellschaftssystemen." *Kinder—Lesen—Literatur*. Eds. Monika Platz and Gerd Mannhaupt. Baltmannsweiler: Schneider Verlag Hohengehren, 2008. 179–93.

Wolf, Steffen. *Kinderfilm in Europa. Darstellung der Geschichte, Struktur und Funktion des Spielfilmschaffens für Kinder in der Bundesrepublik Deutschland, CSSR, Deutschen Demokratischen Republik und Großbritannien 1945–1965*. Munich: Dokumentation, 1969.

Zipes, Jack. *The Enchanted Screen. The Unknown History of Fairy-Tale Films*. New York: Routledge, 2011.

13

Retelling "Hansel and Gretel" in Comic Book and Manga Narration

The Case of Philip Petit and Mizuno Junko

MARIANNA MISSIOU

INTRODUCTION

The endurance of fairy tales over the centuries is a testament to their "flexibility" (Van Baaren 217) and "plasticity" (Firth 207).[1] The medium for retelling fairy tales has evolved through literary, theatrical, choreographic, televisual, and cinematographic adaptations to the transformation of the comic book format. In recent years, authors and editors of the ninth art have sought inspiration in the archetypal themes and memorable situations of fairy tales in order to attract a wider readership. Representative works include Art Spiegelman's *Maus,* Bill Willingham's *Fables,* Neil Gaiman's *Sandman,* and Grant Morrison's *Invisibles.*

Scholars and artists have pointed out in various ways the connection between folklore, fairy tales, and comic books. In 1975 Ronald Baker discussed folklore motifs in superhero stories (170–74), while Agnes Curry and Josef Velazquez see superhero stories as "the next step in the fairy tale tradition" (48). In 1987, Harlan Ellison described comic books as "the Grimm's fairy tales of popular culture," and Amanda Banks and Elizabeth Wein induce the folklorist to look for "comic strips, movies, and dime-store literature" as "the functional equivalent(s) of the folktales and myths of the past." Recently, Adam Zolkover examined Bill Willingham's *Fables* to prove that comic books are a postmodern literary endeavor that responds in a multivalent way to the fairy-tale genre (40). Wolfgang Mieder has also noted the resonance of fairy tales in the popular consciousness and the vital relationship between fairy tales and comics, stating that, "Innovative creative works have created a productive new dynamic between traditional tales and visual art in the late 20th and early 21st centuries" (167). Gail de Vos, too, has underlined the penetration of folklore into popular culture (220–23) and has compiled a list of comic book creators who have drawn stories, motifs, themes, and issues from folklore, arguing that "the intersection between the world of folklore and the world of comic books has never been stronger" (222).

It is clear that comic books, as the new form of folklore production, frequently adapt fairy-tale material into a combination of words and images. However, when a story is remediated, there is a dynamic interaction between storytelling practices and the media in which they unfold. As Karin Kukkonen states, in comics, the coexistence of modes—what is shown versus what is told—has a "considerable impact on the storytelling possibilities supported by the medium" (35). Thierry Groensteen argues that comics are a medium based on the "simultaneous mobilization of visual and discursive codes" (7). Thus, the transformation process of any written source to a comic book version includes a visualization of the source through the medium's techniques. The text becomes an illustrated version of plot, characters, and setting. Techniques such as the composition of the page, the shape and dimension of the panels, the thickness of the frames, and the angles of view and perspective are all mobilized to create meaning. Of course, the transformation process also includes condensation, simplification, elimination, shortening, reordering, or addition to the primary source. Furthermore, during the transmediation process, which, according to Maria Nikolajeva (229), precisely emphasizes the crossing from one medium to another, the choice of the medium affects both the form and the content, and changes are dictated by the necessity to adapt to the new medium and the new presumed audience.

As far as the notion of fidelity is concerned between a pure text and its transformation into a comic book format, Stephen Tabachnick states that faithfulness can never be accomplished, as any adaptation from one genre or medium into another necessarily represents various interpretations of the works adapted, due to "intentional and unintentional gaps in the original" (5). For instance, faces, expressions, gestures, and settings are depicted by visual means, allowing many variations. Furthermore, any choice of the creator,[2] showing either fidelity to the original or free adaptation, not only supports the visual interpretation but also gives information about his or her cultural and ideological positions. The selections that are made function as signs of the adaptor's ideology, for there can be no text free from ideology.

The present chapter has a double aim: first, to discuss how the transformative and interpretive elements of comics can promote and expand the readership of fairy tales as a form of literature and, second, to explore what new material a comic book version can bring to a given fairy tale in relation to the notion of fidelity to the primary source. To that end, two contemporary but different versions of "Hansel and Gretel" are analyzed and contrasted as presented though the medium of comics. The first version is a French *bande dessinée* written and illustrated by Philip Petit and published in 2002. The second is the French translation of a Japanese manga by Mizuno Junko, published in English in 2000. Among the other adaptations of the "Hansel and Gretel" story that I am aware of, my specific choice was influenced by the differentiation of the intended audience (children vs. adults) together with the antithesis of the inherent cultural background of the *bande dessinée* and manga. These elements appear to influence the transformation project of the original text. In addition, the two creators mirror antithetical approaches in both style and ideology. Petit follows a traditional approach in both the style of his *bande dessinée* and his ideological position, as he presents a conservative model of gender relations. Mizuno Junko's approach, on the other hand, is more innovative in style and offers a more progressive gender ideology.

The textual history of the Grimms' "Hansel and Gretel" is complex. From the oral tale recorded in 1810 to the version of 1857, the story was subject to various stylistic and thematic changes made by Wilhelm Grimm. Obviously, to be a retelling "a text must exist in relationship to some kind of source," referred to as the "pre-text" (Stephens and McCallum 4). For the purpose of this chapter, the final edition from the *Kinder- und Hausmärchen* of 1857 will be considered as the pre-text.[3] The focus will be on the central characters and the plot's main motifs: famine over the land, the abandonment of Hansel and his sister Gretel by their father and his wife in the woods, their imprisonment by a witch who waylays children to eat them, and their reunion with their father after his wife's death. In Petit's version the basic characters and plotlines have been followed more or less, whereas Mizuno's version includes important subversions. In her story, the characters' personality is reversed. Gretel is a dynamic girl, living in a village with her brother and their parents who run the only local grocery store. The village is blessed with an abundance of food when starvation suddenly occurs. The parents, along with the villagers, leave to find food and get lost. Hansel and Gretel embark on an adventure to rescue them. They meet with the witch, a kind of queen, who has everyone under her spell. Then follows the battle with the witch, the breaking of the spell, and the reunion of the family.

Both comic books use the well-known fairy tale as a starting point. However, they mirror different transformation techniques, personal choices, and cultural backgrounds, thereby applying to a different readership, as will be shown below.

Comic Book Versions of the Fairy Tale as Transage Reading

We will first examine how Mizuno and Petit shape their readership according to their "implied reader," which Wolfgang Iser described as the hypothetical figure of the reader to whom a specific work addresses itself. In comic strip versions of fairy tales, however, the intended readership may be expanded to different age groups.

In the process of identifying and analyzing the elements that support the broad readership of Petit's and Mizuno's books, we begin with Gérard Genette's notion of "paratext" (16) consisting of a visual and textual condensation of information carefully created to catch the reader's and buyer's attention. The peritextual features such as the shape and size of the book, the front and back covers, and the title are vehicles of interpretation even before opening the comic. They often convey the editorial vision of the book and suggest the major theme, style, and tone, while also providing information on the central characters of the story, their relationships, and their personalities.

In Philip Petit's version, "Hansel and Gretel" is designed specifically to appeal to a juvenile readership. At least, this is what is implied by the editor's categorization of the book as part of the collection Delcourt jeunesse. The collection's description on Delcourt's website states: "Whether you are young or old, these adaptations of classic stories and their characters, filled with humor, are true feasts for the eyes and mind."[4] This "paratextual" element (Genette 5) shapes the reader's expectations and suggests particular kinds of interpretation. As far as the peritextual elements are concerned, according to Nodelman, the size, binding, and paper of a book also influence our response

Figure 1. The cover page indicates the creator's unconventional intentions toward the original "Hansel and Gretel" story.

to it (*Words* 44). In Petit's version, the hard cover has a more respectable appearance than Mizuno's paperback with its plastic coating, which looks conventionally popular and disposable. In addition, Petit's drawing style and overall use of pastel colors make the cover look like that of a typical children's picture book. On the cover, the author shows a background view of a little boy and a little girl playing happily in the woods, an image that potentially attracts a younger readership.

Some elements of the cover and endpapers refer by association to the well-known fairy tale on which the book is based, for example the huge pieces of candy in the background of the front cover image. On the back cover, the image of a hideous green-colored visage easily calls the witch to the reader's mind and produces a comic, even grotesque effect. The threat represented by the witch is thus nullified before a reader even opens the book, and a comical appearance mitigates the evil of the character in an effort to keep the book appropriate for young readers and simultaneously wink at older readers. Thus, the author makes an effort to reassure not only young readers but also their parents, who will probably buy the book.

The front endpaper consists of a blue page on which sweets, together with bones, function as metonymies of the witch, and the text of the back cover consists of the well-known dialogue between the parents that reveals their intention to abandon the children in the woods. The reader, who already knows the tale, draws from a "repertoire of plots" (Nodelman, *Pleasures* 10) to enter the interior of the book, probably feeling secure that he will find another version of the well-known story with its familiar hero, motifs, and plot. He thus experiences what Nodelman calls the "pleasure of formula," that is, the repetition of a familiar experience of stories he has enjoyed before (*Pleasures* 20).

In contrast, the peritextual elements of Mizuno's version offer an interesting insight not only into the original story but also into the typical form of a comic book, emphatically making clear the creator's unconventional intentions from the very beginning. On the cover (Figure 1), the reader's eye is drawn to a girl with blatant pink hair, wearing a sailor suit inspired by Japanese school uniforms and holding a bamboo samurai sword. She looks much older than Petit's Gretel, possibly insinuating the intention of the author to address the book to an adolescent readership. The sword she holds functions as a metonym of her character. The sword represents the typical weapon of Japanese samurai comics (Schodt 68), whereas in Western culture it is commonly considered a symbol of male power, strength, and courage as well as a symbol of justice (Becker 290; Evangelista xxiii). Thus, the cover of the book that shows Gretel holding a sword instantly characterizes her as a vital, brave, and independent personality and as a character who will play fair. While the plot unfolds, those characteristics will be affirmed by her acts and speech.

Just in front of and below Gretel's figure, a young boy stands with a tin can on his mouth, held by strings around his ears and garnished with details of the Japanese flag. As becomes clear later in the book, the tin can is used as a cover to keep the boy's mouth shut. The samurai and the flag, as typical Japanese elements, manifest a cultural assimilation of the classic fairy tale and its transmission in a new context. With the characteristic psychedelic flair of Mizuno's art, the threat of the witch is represented on the cover by a fuchsia-colored shape, which forms flames and includes sweets, steaks, and sausages. These elements refer to the food motif of the pre-text as well as to the witch's oven. The low angle shot makes Gretel look powerful and implies an ideological position, as it underlines and presages the girl's predominance in the story. It also adapts the pre-text to the manga genre, where the frequent references to competition and knives have a connection to Japanese samurai tales, in which problems are solved through sword fights (Brau 117).

The title *Hansel & Gretel* anchors, in Roland Barthes's sense (39), the polysemy of Mizuno's image, suggesting a new version of the fairy tale. The text of the back cover, on the other hand, affirms the rebelliousness in the story line and initiates the reader into the subversive character of the book, giving clues to the story and reinforcing what the cover image implies. Often in comic books, due to the usual format of a maximum of forty-six pages, the author has to economize. It is therefore common to find some initial information about the characters on the covers or front pages, so that longer descriptions in the main body of the story can be avoided. Thus, on the back cover, the reader is informed that Hansel is an "élève turbulent et bavard" (a restless and chatty pupil). Later, the story reveals that the tin can over the boy's mouth is there to prevent the shattering of everything around him, as his voice is unnaturally loud. Gretel is presented in the text on the back cover as a "jeune fille impulsive prête à jouer de son sabre en bambou pour défendre la veuve et l'orphelin" (an impulsive young girl ready to use her bamboo sword to save the widow and the orphan).

Inside the book, the story immediately introduces the central character and her special powers to the reader. The first pages show a group of naked girls, with highly stylized silhouettes, taking their shower at school, when a bullying incident arises. This is the pretext for Gretel to show up and be presented to the reader. She too appears naked, as a powerful and sensuous girl in a dominant role, meting out punishment. Just as with the image on the cover, a low angle shot enhances her dynamic and powerful presence. The naïve sensuality of the naked, doll-like characters implies an older audience. However, at the end of the book, the manga includes a playful dimension borrowed from children's picture books, namely naked paper dolls with paper clothes and underwear to dress them in. This dimension once again blurs the line between adult and adolescent readers. Furthermore, compared to the "formula pleasure" that results from Petit's version, here the reader is challenged by the new insight that the paratextual elements typical of manga unveil. Thus, the "pleasures of newness" and of "recognizing similarities between various texts" are mobilized here as well (Nodelman, *Pleasures* 20–21).

In any transformation of an original intended for children, the adaptor may move between pedagogical frames. In reading Petit's comics, the basic priority inferred is that of maintaining the simplicity and clarity of plotline and characters as well as fidelity to the source. The action can then be easily identified and comprehended. Thus, in Petit's version, the transformation of his source into the visual format of a comic leads to redundancy, ensuring that it will not offer any degree of ambiguity in a version intended for a younger readership: images more or less echo words, with few exceptions. General adaptation patterns and the most basic techniques of any adaptation of a written text into visual narration are clearly being followed here: narrative text is reproduced within the caption boxes, while dialogue finds its place in the speech balloons. Furthermore, visual narration is developed so that the eye follows a linear path, which supports young readers. Thus the panels, caption boxes, and balloons are easily distinguishable from each other to ensure that the storyline is clear.

However, Nodelman has shown that pictures add different kinds of information to that provided by the words and often communicate what "words could never convey, no matter how many of them one used" (*Words* 205–8). Furthermore, a drawing is literally and figuratively signed by the artist (Marion 101) and is representative of the artist's idiosyncratic style. A reader reacts in his or her own personal way to a particular style and is not a passive agent but possesses a "contextual knowledge" in order to make sense of visual styles (Lefèvre 16). Thus, if Petit stays faithful to the spirit of the original source, he gives his perspective on the story through his artistic style.

Mizuno's version shows a different approach, since the text is freed from the original source. The motifs from "Hansel and Gretel" that it contains are only a pretext to unfold a new story, one in which the conventions of manga are complex. In general, although manga have their own specific techniques, their visual vocabulary shows consistency and their style is easily accessible to new readers (Cohn 188–90). Nevertheless, some of the graphic signs are difficult to decode. Cohn states, for example, that the graphic signs used in manga to represent emotions or motion go beyond iconic and sensual experiences and are represented through onomatopoeia and mimetic vocabulary (Cohn 192). This is the case with Mizuno's manga. Her version demands that readers be familiar with the conventions, but her treatment of them is experimental. For example, the few captions found in her book are presented in an oval shape without a frame line that looks more like a typical balloon than a caption box, thus confusing the reader. Words are often dominated by artwork that challenges the viewer's imagination, as a variety of lines, fonts, frames, and blatant colors create a psychedelic, dreamlike universe.

Colors function on multiple levels and offer multiple interpretations. For example, in Petit's use of realistic colors, dark colors are used to underline the famine at the family home, while vivid and warm colors are used to underline an abundance of food at the witch's house. In addition, colors have a "communicative" function (Kress and Van Leeuwen 346), as they can guide and clarify the understanding of the action and the characters' emotional and psychological situations. In Mizuno's manga version, colors are vivid and saturated and overflow the page. Colors imply a sophisticated understanding of action and character and delineate the psychological subtext. During the battle of Gretel with the witch, for example, the latter is transformed into a red monster, red being the color of threat and danger. The choice of this color also symbolizes the monster's hatred for Gretel and its need for revenge; a misunderstanding between the two characters has led the witch to consider Gretel her enemy. Furthermore, to emphasize the culminating point of the story and to reinforce suspense, the monster and consequently the color red are stretched all over the page, while the background is dark green, a color associated with "the green-eyed monster," jealousy.

To summarize, various techniques are used in both versions to convey a particular interpretation and, at times, to suggest a particular age group as implied readers. However, inexperienced readers concentrate on the story, whereas more sophisticated readers will focus on how the story is shaped by those techniques.

How Comics Rewrite the Fairy Tale's Characters and Motifs

"Hansel and Gretel" has for many centuries been a fixed item in the literary canon—of Western countries at least (Zipes, *Happily Ever After* 39). In addition, it reflects historical instances such as the abandonment of children due to famine. Maria Tatar points out that "Hansel and Gretel" is less about "a child's fears about starvation, exposure, and abandonment" than a mirror of "the hard facts of the pre-modern era" (Tatar 180). However, the motifs and their relevant problems, such as poverty and the trauma of abandonment, also reflect contemporary problems. According to Jack Zipes those problems remain unresolved both in the fairy tale and in the contemporary world, making "Hansel and Gretel" a "never-ending story" (*Why Fairy Tales Stick* 219–20). It is therefore interesting to look closely at the transformational process to see how Petit and Mizuno attempt to rationalize in their own way the disturbing incidents of the pre-text. During the remediation process, the creators expose their own value systems embedded within their ideological positions on gender roles.

Separation and abandonment feature on the first stage of the story: the father and his wife cast the children from their home, and a heroic journey begins for Hansel and Gretel. As Vanessa Joosen writes, in the 1857 edition of "Hansel and Gretel," the father "is by far more sympathetic to the children's fate" whereas the stepmother is portrayed as "heartless, cold, and bossy" (97). This is the case in Petit's child-friendly version. However, as in the Grimms' edition of 1812, the mother is the actual mother and not a stepmother, although Petit's source does mention a stepmother. But this fact does not reduce the general impact of a version intended for a young readership. Petit uses visual codes to attenuate the cruelty of a mother abandoning her children. Her caricatured depiction deflects the disdain she would otherwise evoke. The traits of her face are exaggerated to create a rather ludicrous effect. Her hair is separated into two red-colored, curly, and bushy pigtails, whereas the children and the father are blond and have straight hair. This visual difference in hair color and style also marks two distinctive antithetical groups:

the father and the children versus the mother. Whereas the mother is presented with angular points, the father is depicted as a fattish man, rounded and curved, a shape that, according to Perry Nodelman, we tend to associate with softness and yielding (*Pleasures* 223). Consequently, if Petit has differentiated himself from the pre-text with the caricatural traits he attributes to the mother, he now reproduces faithfully the personality of the father.

As far as the protagonists are concerned, in Petit's version the children's roles, and consequently their gender roles, do not vary from those of the pre-text. Gretel is a rather passive personality at the beginning of the story, crying and lamenting her fate, whereas Hansel is the one who takes control over the situation, provides comfort to his sister, and prepares a plan to find the way back home. Once again, comic book techniques, such as coloring, refine their actions and personalities. For example, the communicative function of color is used in a symbolic way to express Gretel's despair and fear when abandoned in the woods. Color is used both to emphasize the dramatic situation and to encourage readers to laugh at it. Thus, Gretel cries to the point of becoming "red." The uneasy situation of the little girl has a humorous aspect, expressed by the expansion of the red color all over her body and stressed by the onomatopoeia "*oouiiinn*," reflecting a baby's cry, as well as the depiction of her body in a frenetic position. The same technique— the color red and a frenetic position of the body—is used to depict the witch when she is angry. However, Hansel and the father seem to keep their sangfroid during the story. Thus, it appears that both females, Gretel and the witch, reproduce the negative stereotype of women being ruled by emotion and, in this case, losing their tempers.

In Mizuno's version, the motif of separation and abandonment is totally reversed. Internal family relationships are tender. The mother and father not only bring food for their children but also supply the entire village. The parents do not abandon the children, but they are forced to leave to look for food when starvation is imposed by the witch's spell. This situation forms the impetus for the children's quest. At this stage, Gretel is not the passive little girl of the pre-text who will be transformed only in the end into a dynamic character by saving herself and her brother from the witch. She is a powerful character from the very beginning of the story. Fearless and impulsive and using a sword, she leads all initiatives, including the plan to save her parents and fellow villagers, with the help of her brother. But if she represents power, Hansel is common sense. He is the one who keeps cool and helps Gretel with his wise advice. As far as the parents' personalities are concerned, the mother is strong, whereas the father is weak and spineless. This motif appears to be faithful to the personality of the couple in the pre-text. However, the mother is not an egoistic person who only looks after herself. She is a strong-minded mother who cares about her children and husband. It seems therefore that in the manga version, the dynamic representation of both feminine figures, together with the attenuation of the male's power, enhances gender equality and subverts stereotypes.

With regard to the themes of poverty and starvation, the absence of food constitutes the core around which the "Hansel and Gretel" story is built. It is interesting to see how both authors, Petit and Mizuno, deal with this key issue in today's world of mass consumption. In Petit's comics, the poverty and starvation motif is promptly introduced in the first one-page panel. The problem is immediately displayed and the consequences derived from it will activate plot and characters. The meager house of Hansel and Gretel and the depiction of the children without shoes are easily recognizable signs of penury. Also, while caption boxes inform readers of the hard fact of the shortage of daily bread, the image forewarns them of the difficulties to come by showing two crows, considered to be bearers of bad news (Eason 66), in close-up. However, the birds are depicted humorously: one is sitting on a branch and the other comes and dislodges him. The first bird is depicted with a comic look of surprise and astonishment as he is knocked off the branch. One can see here an instance of the author's effort to undermine the harshness of the situation, since the way he depicts the birds undermines the motifs of poverty and starvation.

In Mizuno's manga, food drives the entire story. As Loris Brau points out, Japan seems obsessed with food (102–27) so that not only are there manga about food, but they are specially designated as *gurume* (gourmet) or *ryôri* (cooking, cuisine; Brau 110). Furthermore, food is a recurrent theme in most of Mizuno's comics and even became the theme of an exhibition at the Narwhal Projects art space in Toronto titled "Venus Cake—Junko Mizuno's food obsession." This fascination with food is not only manifested per se but also reflects contemporary issues regarding food.

Contrary to the pre-text in which starvation is set immediately as the problem to be solved, food is abundant in Hansel and Gretel's small village of Hibari. Baked products and croissants are mined from the bread mountain, a giant pig cuts slices of meat off himself, and two green girls grow spinach from their scalps to feed people. All of these products are intended for the only grocery store in the village, run by Hansel and Gretel's parents. The well-known famine motif appears when the sources of food suddenly dry up and the villagers are lured to a land of plenty called *Mangetout* (eat everything). In this place, where food is offered generously, the villagers are launched into gastronomic excesses. In fact, in *Mangetout,* they experience an illusion, since they only eat earth and are themselves to be eaten later by the witch Queen Marilyn. Thus food reflects the positive and negative sides of life: food is considered a source of life but is also linked to disastrous bulimia.

Furthermore, food is closely related to the witch Queen Marilyn, who appears as the alternative personality of Mari, one of Gretel's schoolmates. The names of Queen Marilyn and Mari perfectly mirror this fragmentation. Queen Marilyn is driven by an incident that once more revolves around food: when Mari and Gretel were classmates, Gretel stole her meatballs. In addition, Mari felt that she was too fat, unloved, and ignored. As a result, ignoble feelings, including jealousy and frustration, grew inside her and took the form of the witch. Queen Marilyn represents the Freudian id of Mari, as she is formed by Mari's dark feelings; she symbolizes the personification of evil and the destructive power of the unconscious. This approach echoes the one presented in Bruno Bettelheim's *The Uses of Enchantment,* in which the witch is "a personification of the destructive aspects of orality" (162). Even the resolution of the story has to do with food: Gretel helps Mari to begin a new life by adopting a slimming diet that will reintegrate her into society. Mizuno's version of the fairy tale seems to mirror perfectly the modern world's preoccupations with external appearance and body image.

A crucial moment in "Hansel and Gretel" is the capture of the children by the witch, followed by her defeat. In Petit's version, life in the witch's house is depicted in the conventional comic strip manner. Pictograms of clouds and lightening, for example, suggest the witch's choleric personality. Together with the use of intertextual elements borrowed from other fairy tales, such devices tend to give a comic aspect to the capture stage, an otherwise rather scary episode of the pre-text's plot. For example, the witch repeats the widely known phrase from "Snow White": "Oh, joli miroir, dis-moi que je suis la plus belle" (Oh, dear mirror, tell me I'm the fairest). The mirror responds: "Mouais, j'en ai vu mieux" ([Mmm, I've seen better] 25). Humor is thus produced by the unexpected use of a phrase in a new context.

Another element that amplifies the comic effect is the witch's facial expression. She is depicted with closed eyes and a face full of enjoyment while feeling the bone Hansel is holding, believing erroneously that she touches the boy himself. The irony, created by the distance between what the character thinks and what is really happening, constitutes one more stimulus for humor. Even the structure of the external appearance of the witch is quite comical, with the protraction of the lower jaw being the dominating characteristic of her face. Resembling the approach to the caricatural drawings of the mother, both these negative women appear somewhat farcical, reinforced by their stereotypical appearance as the "villain" in comics.

The capture stage and the defeat of the witch in Mizuno's work take quite a different form. The children's capture is completely transformed as the witch dominates the entire village, including Hansel and Gretel's parents, in *Mangetout* land. Hansel and Gretel's confrontation with the witch is dictated by their need not to escape but to save the village from the witch's spell. The protagonists confront a series of dangers that they finally overcome. Queen Marilyn is annihilated when Gretel manages to break the spell. To do so, Gretel has made an effort to undo the wrong done to Mari, as mentioned above. Thus, the defeat of the witch takes on a clear psychoanalytic frame, that of fighting our irrational feelings and raising a better self.

The children's return and reunion with the father constitute the final stage of the story. In Petit's comic, when the children return home, they find it empty. In the garden, a grave, implying death, worries the two children at first. However, the appearance of their father fills them with great joy. The final panel is a disproportionally enlarged picture of the father holding his children; his large dimension projects a sense of security, while the big smiles of the children imply the happy ending. The journey is complete, order is reestablished, and the three of them can enjoy life's treasures, literally and figuratively. However there is one plot element that remains unsolved at the end of the book. Ironically, the children do not show any sign of grief at the loss of their mother, and even though initially the father made no attempt to save them, they return to him. One would wonder why the children return without any reservations to their father after his act of neglect. The way this is presented in both comics implies that they have not considered this act as such. The exoneration of the father in Petit's version coincides with that of the pre-text; patriarchal values are thus perpetuated. In contrast in Mizuno's work, community and family bonds as well as solidarity are highlighted. All family members and the village's inhabitants are reunited and the story ending reverts to the initial happy situation. This happy ending marks not only the structural but also the psychological closure of the story, as no questions are left unanswered.

Mizuno's version, through inversions, twists, and subversions, goes beyond the boundaries of the pre-text and highlights differentiations in the quality and the intensity of community and family relationships together with the individuality of its members. In addition, Mizuno builds a story that goes beyond straight role reversals. Not only the female characters, Gretel and the mother, but also the male characters, Hansel and the father, are empowered. Female issues such as relationships with parents, body image, and jealousy are discussed, developing a narrative that encodes feminist themes and values. According to Roberta Trites, characteristics associated with feminist writing are the empowerment of the protagonist regardless of gender (8), the value of community, and the importance of interpersonal relationships (80–84) as well as the mother–daughter relationship (90–100). As Mizuno's manga includes such characteristics, it opens a critical dialogue about gender and values and could therefore be considered a feminist fairy tale.

CONCLUSION

In the "Hansel and Gretel" versions analyzed in this chapter, the comic strip medium transforms the Grimms' fairy tale in various and innovative ways. First, comics transform the pre-text with their particular techniques, codes, and devices found both in words and pictures. The specific selection of image techniques such as illustrative styles, colors, angles of view, and gesture codes together with literary devices such as the subversion of plot and characters mirror the value systems of the new works. Creators use both visual and written devices to articulate their responses to the subjects of poverty, famine, and abandonment. The result is that they either create a ludicrous effect to soften the unpleasant impact of such subjects or attempt to rationalize those facts by transposing them into a contemporary context. In the latter case, transposition illuminates different controversial aspects of the same subject, such as starvation, bulimia, and body image or abandonment versus strong family relations.

Second, the core of the pre-text changes in the course of transition from one medium to the other in order to reflect cultural values and new interpretations. The two forms of comic books, Japanese manga and French *bande dessinée,* with their inherent cultural backgrounds, offer the reader of the Grimms' fairy tale an interaction with different cultures—in this case the Japanese and French cultures. Elements associated with the particular narrative modes of *bande dessinée* and manga, as well as references to the culture of both creators, give the fairy tale new dimensions.

Furthermore, the transformation of the "Hansel and Gretel" story into a comic book format results in a constant negotiation between the reader of the pre-text and the reader of the comic book version. The reader is invited to decode the new work through the synergy between words and images, while continually having recourse to the pre-text. It challenges readers to detect the profound messages found in the comic strip versions according to their reading competency and life experience. Thus, comics can change the impact of the Grimms' pre-text on a specific audience and, as such, broaden the age and competency range of the readership. The medium's own codes and techniques facilitate the crossing of boundaries between children and adolescent and adult readers. Comics take the reader to a literary universe where signs hidden between words and images and their synergy offer multiple readings, new interpretations, and surprising discoveries.

NOTES

1. Firth talks about the "plasticity" of myth. The concept refers to the myth's variation. There are as many different version of a particular myth as there are tellers of that myth. Van Baaren refers to the "flexibility" of myth, namely the myth's ability to change and to be adapted to new situations and challenges in order to be conserved in time.

2. A comic book can be created by one or two persons or a creative team. In this chapter, the term "creator" is used to describe the individual who wrote and drew the comic book.

3. Philip Petit was kind enough to send me a copy of the French version he used for his source. Unfortunately, he was not able to give me more bibliographical details. However, the source is the chapter "Jeannot et Margot" in a book called *Les Contes* (95–103). The French text is a faithful translation of the abovementioned English edition.

4. The translation is my own. The original text states: "Qu'on soit petit ou grand, ses adaptations de classiques et ses récits aux personnages pleins d'humour, sont de vrais régals pour les yeux et l'esprit."

References

Baker, Ronald L. "Folklore Motifs in the Comic Books of Superheroes." *Tennessee Folklore Society Bulletin* 41.4 (1975): 170–74.

Banks, Amanda, and Elizabeth Wein. "Folklore and the Comic Book: The Traditional Meets the Popular." *New Directions in Folklore* 2.1 (1998). http://hdl.handle.net/2022/7218. 2 Jan. 2013.

Barthes, Roland. *Image, Music, Text*. London: Fontana, 1977.

Becker, Udo. *The Continuum Encyclopedia of Symbols*. London: Continuum, 2000.

Bettelheim, Bruno. *The Uses of Enchantment, The Meaning and Importance of Fairy Tales*. London: Penguin, 1991.

Brau, Loris. "Oishinbo's Adventures in Eating: Food, Communication, and Culture in Japanese Comics." *Manga: An Anthology of Global and Cultural Perspectives*. Ed. Toni Johnson-Woods. New York: Continuum, 2009. 102–27.

Cohn, Neil. "Japanese Visual Language." *Manga: An Anthology of Global and Cultural Perspectives*. Ed. Toni Johnson-Woods. New York: Continuum, 2009. 187–203.

Curry, Agnes, and Josef Velazquez. "Dorothy and Cinderella: The Case of the Missing Prince and the Despair of the Fairy Tale." *The Universe of Oz: Essays on Baum's Series and Its Progeny*. Ed. Kevin Durand and Mary Leigh. Jefferson: McFarland, 2010. 24–54.

Delcourt. "Jeunesse." www.editions-delcourt.fr/catalogue/collections/jeunesse. 2 Jan. 2010.

De Vos, Gail. "Folklore in Comics." *Encyclopaedia of Comic Books and Graphic Novels*. Vol. 1. Ed. Keith Booker. Santa Barbara: ABC-Clio, 2010.

Eason, Cassandra. *Fabulous Creatures, Mythical Monster; Animal Power Symbols*. Westport: Greenwood, 2008.

Ellison, Harlan. *Masters of Comic Book Art*. 1987. VHS.

Evangelista, Nick. *Encyclopedia of Sword*. Westport: Greenwood, 1995.

Firth, Raymond. "The Plasticity of Myth: Cases from Tikopia." *Sacred Narrative—Readings in the Theory of Myth*. Ed. Alan Dundes. Berkeley: U of California P, 1984. 207–16.

Genette, Gérard. *Seuils*. Paris: Éditions du Seuil, 1987.

Grimm, Jacob, and Wilhelm Grimm. *Household Tales*. Vol. XVII, Part 2. The Harvard Classic. New York: P.F. Collier & Son, 1909–14. www.bartleby.com/17/2. 10 May 2010.

Groensteen, Thierry. *Système de la bande dessinée*. Paris: PUF, 1999.

Iser, Wolfgang. *The Implied Reader: Patterns of Communication in Prose from Bunyan to Beckett*. Baltimore: Johns Hopkins UP, 1978.

Joosen, Vanessa. *Critical and Creative Perspectives on Fairy Tales: An Intertextual Dialogue between Fairy-Tale Scholarship and Postmodern Retellings*. Detroit: Wayne State UP, 2011.

Kress, Gunter, and Theo Van Leeuwen. "Colour as a Semiotic Mode: Notes for a Grammar of Colour." *Visual Communication* 1.3 (2002): 343–68.

Kukkonen, Karin. "Comics as a Test Case for Transmedial Narratology." *Substance* 40.1 (2011): 34–52.

Lefèvre, Pascal. "Some Medium-Specific Qualities of Graphic Sequences." *SubStance* 40.1 (2011): 14–33.

Marion, Philip. *Traces en cases. Travail graphique, figuration narrative et participation du lecteur. Essai sur la bande dessinée.* Louvain-la-Neuve: Academia, 1993.

Mieder, Wolfgang. "Cartoon and Comics." *The Greenwood Encyclopedia of Folktales and Fairy Tales.* Ed. Donald Haase. Westport: Greenwood, 2008. 164–67

Mizuno, Junko. *Hansel & Gretel.* Paris: Imho, 2005.

Nikolajeva, Maria. *The Aesthethic Approach to Children's Literature.* Lanham: Scarecrow, 2005.

Nodelman, Perry. *The Pleasures of Children's Literature.* 2nd ed. White Plains: Longman, 1996.

———. *Words about Pictures: The Narrative Art of Children's Picture Books.* Athens: U of Georgia P, 1988.

Petit, Philip. *Hansel et Gretel.* Paris: Delcourt Jeunesse, 2002.

Schodt, Frederik. *Manga! Manga! The World of Japanese Comics.* Tokyo: Kodansha International, 1986.

Stephens, John, and Robyn McCallum. *Retelling Stories, Framing Culture: Traditional Story and Metannaratives in Children's Literature.* New York: Garland, 1998.

Tabachnick, Stephen. "The Graphic Novel and the Age of Transition: A Survey and Analysis." *English Literature in Transition, 1880–1920* 53.1 (2010): 3–28.

Tatar, Maria. *The Classic Fairy Tales.* New York: Norton, 1999.

Trites, Roberta. *Waking Sleeping Beauty: Feminist Voices in Children's Novels.* Iowa: U of Iowa P, 1997.

Van Baaren, Theodore. "The Flexibility of Myth." *Sacred Narrative—Readings in the Theory of Myth.* Ed. Alan Dundes. Berkeley: U of California P, 1984. 217–24.

Zipes, Jack. *Happily Ever After: Fairy Tales, Children and the Culture Industry.* New York: Routledge, 1977.

———. *Why Fairy Tales Stick, The Evolution and Relevance of a Genre.* New York: Routledge, 2006.

Zolkover, Adam. "Corporealizing Fairy Tales: The Body, the Bawdy, and the Carnivalesque in the Comic Book Fables." *Marvels & Tales* 22.1 (2008): 38–51.

14

Fairy-Tale Scripts and Intercultural Conceptual Blending in Modern Korean Film and Television Drama

SUNG-AE LEE

Western folktales have circulated in an active, two-way dialogue with Korean culture and folktales for almost a century, and some of the tales have become so embedded in Korean culture that they are as readily used as narrative frames in contemporary film and TV drama as are local Korean folktales. However, as U. C. Knoepflmacher has aptly observed, "Any transmitted narrative that is persistently subjected to multiple cultural revisions must necessarily be impure" (15) in the sense that the narrative accrues traces of often disparate cultures. When Western tales function as a structural frame or recurrent motif, they are often blended with local analogues, with unrelated local traditions, or with each other. At the same time, there seems to be little overt acknowledgment of origins, whether by producers or consumers, and any allusions made to sources within the narrative itself are likely to name Disney. One of the titles most extensively drawn upon as a script in film and television drama in the first decade of this century was "Cinderella," but because these texts reference what I will call a "Cinderella-script," rather than a specific pre-text, audiences will not inevitably associate the tale with the Grimms' *Aschenputtel* (or Perrault's *Cendrillon*), even when they do share common motifs, but will have in mind a blended version, or what Donald Haase terms a "network" or "hypertext" (223). Usually, although not always, even when a pre-text is named the reference is to a script, not to a specific source.

The notion of *script,* in the sense I am using here, is derived from Roger Schank and Robert Abelson: "Specific knowledge exists in detail . . . with respect to every standard situation that [a person] has been in many times" (38). As a recognizable narrative form, David Herman defines a script as "a knowledge representation in terms of which an expected sequence of events is stored in the memory" (10). A script may draw core schemas from several related folktales but will not necessarily be narratively equivalent to any particular version. The "innocent persecuted heroine" script includes the following schemas: a female orphan; physical poverty; persecution by an older woman; one or more female peers as rivals; a helper; a shoe that, linked only with her, is lost and found; a future husband of high birth. As John Stephens and Sylvie Geerts argue, the transmission of stories as scripts enables an adaptation to take a drastically new form while remaining constant to the script.

SIMPLE BLENDING AND CONCEPTUAL BLENDING

The blending of folktales occurs at two levels of complexity. On the one hand, there is a simple merging or combination of components of what is perceived as a common story, whereby, for example, the names "Cendrillon" (Charles Perrault) and "Aschenputtel" (the Brothers Grimm) come to be interchangeable and then, in popular knowledge, one generally displaces the other. This primary blending has readily happened in the West as well and is obvious in the generalizing of the name "Cinderella" for the (now) eponymous heroine of the tale. This practice was effectively naturalized by Jack Zipes's decision to use "Cinderella" in his 1987 translation of the Grimm tales and by his note that the 1812 text was "obviously influenced by Charles Perrault's 'Cendrillon'" and had been "mixed with additional versions" (729). Elisabeth Panttaja's perceptive discussion of the Grimms' tale likewise begins "Modern criticism of the Grimms' 'Cinderella'" (85).

In Korean film and drama, the name "Cinderella" has been similarly generalized to identify any adaptation, however loose, of the script. In addition to this simple blending, there is also a more complex process that falls within the sphere of what, following the work of Gilles Fauconnier and Mark Turner, is referred to as "conceptual blending." This idea describes the mind's capacity to blend different and even apparently contradictory concepts to develop a third, blended concept that contains more and different information than the two initial concepts. Whereas Fauconnier and Turner were primarily interested in blends of seemingly incompatible concepts or stories, there is a comparable, but slightly different, process at work when a narrative uses incompatible scripts. "How can it be that quite incompatible stories do not suppress each other's activation in the human mind?" (118), Turner asks, and he concludes that the mind has a capacity to blend them into another story and even envisage the product as a model for action. When European folktales are naturalized in Korea, the process of intercultural blending can produce that "third story" in striking ways.

A quite self-reflexive depiction of conceptual blending occurs in the sixth episode of the TV drama *Secret Garden* (2010), a production that alludes to and blends several European folktales. The main characters are Kim Joo-Won,[1] a very wealthy upper-class male, and Gil Ra-Im, an independent young woman, orphaned and earning a small wage as a stuntwoman in TV advertisements and music videos. Their accidental meeting through a mistaken identity incident sets the scene for a Cinderella-script to unfold, but the series constantly problematizes that fairy-tale script they are enacting— "Cinderella" or some variations of Hans Christian Andersen's "The Little Mermaid." Hence the story's possible outcome cannot be assumed. In quite a complex movement, indeed, the series uses the Cinderella-script to overthrow the Little Mermaid-script and then shatters happy-ever-after by disclosing the Cinderella outcome to be an illusion. In itself, the Cinderella-script in this series owes much to the Grimms' "Aschenputtel," even though the most overt reference ("These are wedding presents from your fairy godmother") is to Perrault's "Cendrillon."[2] In a rather droll, ironic, and metafictive fashion, "Cinderella" is evoked as an obvious absence by the repeated assertion that "The Little Mermaid" is the *second* best-known story in the history of humankind. The first is presumably "Cinderella," in that the series obviously follows a Cinderella-script.

As Panttaja (91–92) argues, the motif of an enchanted or somehow disguised bride or groom commonly occurs in tales that depict an unusual marriage, and the Cinderella-script adapts this motif so that the disguised or enchanted person is able to enter into a marriage that he or she would not normally enter into, usually one that crosses class lines. *Secret Garden* employs both the "Cinderella" and the "Little Mermaid" variants. Joo-Won meets Ra-Im because in her job as a stuntwoman she is dressed and made up to look like a celebrity actress whom Joo-Won is actually looking for (whereas it is often remarked that Ra-Im is not beautiful and dresses badly when she is not working as a stuntwoman). The pivotal, innovative turn in this series occurs when a strange shamanistic figure (an embodiment of the spirit of Ra-Im's dead father) gives the duo two bottles of flower-steeped wine that, when drunk, causes them to switch bodies and hence to experience the possibility of life as the other.[3] Horrified by the switch, and unable to think of a rational explanation for it, they attempt to undo it by envisaging themselves in a folktale script and invoke the motif of the kiss of disenchantment. The precedents they cite are "The Little Mermaid" (presumably the Disney version, since it is there that Ariel must win "the kiss of true love" to complete her metamorphosis), "Beauty and the Beast," and "The Frog Prince"—although only the third tale actually includes the kiss of disenchantment.

The principle of conceptual blending is at work here as the couple's conversation invokes not only an enchantment/disenchantment script from European fairy tales but also a first kiss script prevalent in Korean social practice and TV drama. In the fairy-tale script, the enchantment theme pivots on an encounter with some supranormal force that both challenges the taken-for-granted nature of the human world and deprives the affected character(s) of subjective agency. When disenchantment is achieved, usually by means of a kiss given without foreknowledge of its consequence, the outcome not only signifies the recovery of identity and subjective agency but is also marked as an indirect consequence of love. In contrast, the Korean first kiss (especially in television drama) is invested with great social significance. The first kiss is a significant, often long-delayed event, and because it is tinged with an aura of taboo, in that public displays of affection are (still) disapproved of in Korean society, the kiss is often marked by furtiveness, surprise, or embarrassment. A dating couple reaches the "light peck" stage after a week or several weeks, and once they begin to kiss it is assumed that marriage will follow. Thus when Joo-Won and Ra-Im are about to pucker up and Ra-Im asks, "Should it be a light peck or something heavier?" her question has a mischievous and complex cultural resonance (Figure 1).

The conceptual blending of entirely disparate kissing motifs transforms the frame of understanding in the disenchantment kiss scene in *Secret Garden* and makes the scene both subtle and comic. The blending is comedically emphasized in that there are two kisses rather than the single kiss of the disenchantment script. The first kiss is a light peck that is so fumbled and clumsy (as convention presupposes) that the couple decides to try again.

Figure 1. Apprehension about the first kiss in *The Secret Garden.*

With the second kiss, they forget what they are supposed to be doing as pleasure takes over and they engage in a cinematic "lip-lock." Needless to say, the kiss does not disenchant, but because the scene prompts its audience to engage in a mental process that Turner describes as "fir[ing] up incompatible mental patterns simultaneously" (118), the scene functions self-reflexively. It foregrounds, somewhat metafictively, that the drama has a folktale base, and it enacts an East-West interplay of cultural possibilities, perceptions, and practices that has an immediately comedic effect as its "third story." The failure of the primary purpose of the experiment (disenchantment) leads to an increased sense of diminished agency and hence further problematizes subjectivity. It also implies that the metanarratives of folktale scripts can only cross-cultural borders if they are blended with local tales and local customs and are thence glocalized. A question as simple as, What are appropriate expressions of affection? thus becomes important for narrative or visual representation.

Cultural models evolve from a dialogic interaction between mental schemas and sociocultural practice, as Bradd Shore and Bruce McConachie have argued, so intercultural interactions are particularly illuminating. Laurence J. Kirmayer offers the following pertinent observation: "Culture is not simply a matter of the spatial or temporal distribution of representations . . . but a dynamic system in which stories have power; stories reshape our perception of the world, drive us to action, and imbue every action (and inaction) with meaning. At the same time, stories act self-reflexively to change the frames through which they are interpreted and understood" (133–34). Intercultural conceptual blending in the disenchantment scene in *Secret Garden* highlights how intercultural fairy-tale adaptations may generate tension between a shift in cognition prompted by the internalization of European folktale schemas and a script that expresses local social beliefs and practices.

FURTHER FORMS OF BLENDING: LOCAL ANALOGUES AND HOMOLOGIES

The Cinderella-script as it appears in Korea also illustrates two other notable forms of blending. The first is a blending with a local script, and this in turn takes two forms. First, it can be blended with an analogue, a popular Korean folktale, "Kongjwi and Patjwi," which in turn is a glocal version of the Chinese tale that is often considered the ultimate source of the European "Cinderella story" (and is doubtless the source of analogues throughout Asia). A "glocal" text, as explained by Anna Katrina Gutierrez (160), emerges when a culture appropriates a global text and localizes it by imbuing foreign elements with local flavor: glocalization exists as a dialectic between the pressure of uniformity and an affirmation of the local. "Kongjwi and Patjwi" glocalizes the Yexian story by means of specific elements of setting and by the Korean neo-Confucian principle of *kwon seon jing ak* (promoting virtue and punishing vice) that underpins the tale and brings moral justification to the brutal execution of the (step-)sister (Patjwi) that concludes versions of the Yexian story everywhere.[4] Thus, as Fay Beauchamp argues in her case for locating the origin of the tale in the ninth century and among the Zhuang people who lived in what is now the border territory between China and Vietnam, it might be best "to avoid Western ethnocentrism" and refer to the story as "the Yexian/Cinderella story" (449).

In Eastern versions, after her marriage the heroine is murdered by her stepsister, who then impersonates her. The heroine then reincarnates (sometimes in two or three forms, always being murdered again), she becomes reunited with her husband, and her enemies are punished (see, for example, Tran Quynh Ngoc Bui's study of glocalized Southeast Asian versions, 37,

44–45). There are many versions of "Kongjwi and Patjwi," but all hinge on Kongjwi's performance of impossible tasks by means of supernatural assistance, the lost shoe that leads to Kongjwi's excellent marriage, and her murder by drowning at the hand of her stepsister. For an audience familiar with both the Western and Korean traditions, the episode in *Secret Garden* where Ra-Im "dies" (she is in a coma and declared to be brain dead) and is miraculously revived can be identified as a somewhat distal structural import from "Kongjwi and Patjwi": after her death, Kongjwi lies in her watery grave in a lotus pond until her husband is induced to find her, at which moment she returns to life.

A second form of blending can occur with a local script that is unknown in the West but that can be considered homologous in that elements of structure coincide with the Western tale. A notable example is the fox-woman script, derived from tales about a *Gumiho* (a creature who transforms between fox and human forms) who wishes to become human and live a human existence. Retellings of this story in Korean film and television are more common than retellings of "Cinderella." I have elsewhere argued that some contemporary retellings adapt and modernize the story by resignifying the otherness of the fox to figure society's ethnic others, such as immigrant workers and immigrant wives, and thence to challenge social classification of people according to their otherness (Lee 138). This trend coincides with Panttaja's argument that "the anxiety of ["Aschenputtel"] lies in the possibility that the prince might marry one of these women [the coarse, ungraceful stepsisters], that class distinctions, here represented as inborn character traits, could be blurred or erased" (94). Recent fox-woman stories, particularly *My Girlfriend Is a Gumiho* (2010), evoke empathy for the *Gumiho* by blending her with Cinderella.

THREE-WAY BLENDS WITH ANDERSEN

The last form of folktale blending, evident in both *Secret Garden* and *My Girlfriend Is a Gumiho,* is the use of the tales of Andersen—the other main source of European fairy-tale adaptations in Korea—not only in the blendings of diverse Eastern and Western sources but in blendings with the Cinderella-script: *My Girlfriend Is a Gumiho* has a three-way blend ("Gumiho," "Cinderella," and "The Little Mermaid") and, as noted previously, *Secret Garden* blends "The Little Mermaid" with a Cinderella-script (itself already a Grimm-Perrault-"Kongjwi and Patjwi" blend). Needless to say, the Grimms' tales can be blended with one another in comparable ways. For example, *King of Baking, Kim Tak-Goo* (2010) brings together "Aschenputtel" and "Snow White," in that a structural similarity is perceived in the pattern of oppression and persecution, although a male character now occupies the victim role. Tak-Goo's stepmother arranges for a company employee to take Tak-Goo far away, where he grows up in an orphanage. He attracts helpers because of his generous spirit; the bakery in which he later becomes an apprentice has seven workers (an intertextual reference to Snow White's seven dwarfs); his stepmother attempts to have him killed; and his stepbrother attempts to poison him. Because the plots of so many of these series focus on the workings of corporations, the task set for Kongjwi to demonstrate her worth is accordingly modernized: instead of sorting lentils ("Aschenputtel") or weeding a field ("Kongjwi and Patjwi"), Tak-Goo is given the task of reviving a moribund factory and inventing and successfully marketing a new product, while the heroine of *Brilliant Legacy* (2009) must take over a declining restaurant and make it profitable.

The appropriation of tales from Grimm or Andersen is not simply the impact of Western culture on the East but a matter of tales that have strong resonance with deep traumas that underlie modern Korean culture or with cultural changes associated with fluctuations in the economy and shifts in gendering and gender roles since the early 1990s. Of particular interest is the folktale motif of the innocent persecuted child, which is often employed to reflect Korea's extreme socioeconomic stratification and the trauma it disregards. At one point in *Secret Garden,* when Joo-Won is coaching Ra-Im to perform as him, there is a wry comment on the power wielded by the third generation of conglomerate families. Joo-Won shows her his recent family genealogy laid out in his cell phone. It is clear that no "Cinderella" will marry into this upper-class family and that Joo-Won's mother will ensure that Ra-Im does not. *Secret Garden* is not just the most self-reflexive of contemporary TV series but also the most acute in its social observations. A key motif is Joo-Won's claustrophobia, which derives from a suppressed trauma—a near-death experience when he was trapped in an elevator in a burning building, in which Ra-Im's father died to save him. The motif functions as a comment not only on the obscene wealth of the *chaebol* families but also on the maintenance of an entrenched underclass, which this entails.

A *chaebol* is a conglomerate of companies clustered around a single parent company. They tend to be family controlled, have risen to power by means of aggressive governmental support and finance, and usually hold shares in each other. In TV dramas the family network, shareholders list, and allies in government are often exploited by senior family members, usually wives or mothers, to maintain their own power or rein in unruly members of the family, such as Joo-Won. A sharp social criticism of the power wielded by *chaebols* in Korean society is made by the final irony of *Secret Garden,* sprung on viewers at the close of the final episode: the blissful fantasy life of marriage and children enjoyed by Ra-Im and Joo-Won at the beginning of the episode never happened and could never happen in a society in which Cinderellas must know their place and stay in it.

Primary sources for abject, persecuted innocents are scripts derived from "Aschenputtel"–"Kongjwi," "Hansel and Gretel," and "Snow White," and then these scripts may be nuanced more bleakly by analogy or blending with darker, local tales of abandonment or loss such as "Oseam," a modern, Buddhist fairy tale with the potential to be a structural counterpoint to "Hansel and Gretel." "Oseam" tells of two orphans, a blind girl, Ga-Mi, and her mischievous younger brother, Gil-Son, who roam the countryside and are subject to random acts of kindness or abuse by strangers, until they are finally taken in by a group of Mahayana Buddhist monks.[5]

The Cinderella-script has almost become a media obsession and it has been the subject of several long-running TV series that include, in addition to those already mentioned, *Secret* (2000; 18 episodes); *Glass Slippers* (2002; 40 episodes); *My Love Patzzi* (2002; 10 episodes), a retelling of "Kongjwi and Patjwi" in which Patjwi is the persecuted innocent; *My Name Is Kim Sam-Soon* (2005; 16 episodes); *Cinderella's Stepsister* (2010; 20 episodes); and *Rooftop Prince* (2012; 20 episodes), which blends "Kongjwi"–"Aschenputtel" with "The Goose Girl" (Tale 89 in Zipes) and "Snow White."

Two of these series overtly evoke Western versions, and part of the blending is the obvious allusion to a detail from Perrault, the "glass" slipper, even though that particular motif is not deployed narratively within the series so named. Likewise, the opening credits of each episode of *Cinderella's Stepsister* play over an out-of-focus, rotoscoped scene in which the stepsister, Song Eun-Jo, runs through the streets as a clock ticks down to midnight, but the motif has more to do with achieving something (saving her dead stepfather's business from *chaebol* predators, for example) than with meeting a curfew.

An early series, *Glass Slippers,* follows the script of "Kongjwi and Patjwi" in developing a storyline beyond the heroine's marriage: the heroine's opponent, Sun-Hee, who had earlier masqueraded as the heroine (in what seems to be another blending of motifs from "The Goose Girl" and "Kongjwi and Patjwi"), disrupts the wedding and inadvertently causes the death of the groom, Chul-Woong, instead of her target, the bride. She consequently faces a life in prison.

This unusual outcome is perhaps not so surprising given that both Chul-Woong and Sun-Hee come from lower social strata: in the Grimm pre-texts the heroine's rise in social status had been preceded by a fall into abjection (working as a goose girl), and the Korean series likewise tend to ensure that the "coarse, petty, and ambitious" do not marry into the upper social echelons. *Secret Garden* makes a characteristic jibe at this assumption in a scene (Episode 20) in which Joo-Won explains (and misreads) some fairy tales. Of "Snow White" he says: "A woman was taking care of seven dwarfs. After she was kissed by an upper-class man, she abandoned the dwarfs in a heartbeat." The clearest exception to such assertion of proper order is the joyfully subversive *My Name Is Kim Sam-Soon,* in which Sam-Soon, the chubby, foul-mouthed heroine with a distinctly peasant name, ends up with the wealthy son of a high-born family.

Dark Retellings: Hauntology and the Uncanny

The South Korean film industry has produced a substantial number of films that in some form have folktales at their core. The films draw these tales from both local and foreign sources and put them to quite diverse uses, although a frequent conceptual blending of horror film and folktale has meant that tales have been chosen for their dark content, or they have been reenvisaged with an emphasis on the elements that are the catalyst for the protagonist's problems or suffering, rather than on the clear moral outcome generally expected of folktale convention. The ambiguity in the closure of several such films confirms that the supernatural elements—either inherent in the source folktales or attributed to them by cinematic appropriation—take the films into the domain of hauntology or, more specifically, what Kathleen Brogan has defined as "cultural haunting"—uncanny stories about ghosts that explore "the hidden passageways not only of the individual psyche, but also of a people's historical consciousness" (152). In other words, a tale from the past (whether local or international) functions intertextually to suggest that the past haunts the present, and, like the ghosts that flicker on the edge of perception in the action of horror films, it is neither wholly present nor wholly absent but lies beneath the present as a suppressed trauma. The notion that in various ways the past, and specifically narrative encodings of past traumas, haunts the present is the primary effect of retelling or incorporating folktales in these films.

In the horror films the past takes a spectral form in accordance with uncanny elements developed out of the evoked folktale. More generally, filmic adaptations—*Cinderella* (2006), directed by Bong Man-Dae; *Hansel and Gretel* (2007), directed by Yim Pil-Sung; and Korean American director So-Yong Kim's bleak Hansel and Gretel story, *Treeless Mountain* (2008)—project a poignant image of what it is like to live in Korea as a child or young adult, and because they interrogate the possibility of any satisfactory outcome, they dwell on a capacity for chaos and mayhem in the tales that reflects the social, political, and economic upheavals of the past half century. Through these representations, Korean society is depicted as materialistic and cruel, lacking concern for the underprivileged such as orphaned or homeless children.

The most positive of these three films is Bong's *Hansel and Gretel,* an uncanny story of three orphans inhabiting an ornate Victorian ("gingerbread"-style) house within a trackless forest that, like the house itself, changes shape and size. At the turn of autumn to winter, the protagonist (Lee Eun-Soo), initially portrayed as socially and morally incompetent, is led to the house after he is involved in a car accident. The house, once an orphanage, is dissociated from time and place and inhabited by three magic-working children who employ mysterious supernatural powers to capture travelers in a quest to build an ideal family. Captured adults are positioned as parents and, in a phantasmagoric dining room, are fed on cake and sweets conjured up by the children (Figure 2). As soon as their entirely solipsistic desires are not met, the children kill their prisoners. The roles of children and witch in the traditional story are thus reversed. The children were abandoned by their biological parents, as in the Grimm tale, and placed in an orphanage. There, they were abused physically and sexually and tortured and starved by the grotesque orphanage director, whom they eventually kill by pushing him into a large oven in the fashion of the Grimms' "Hansel and Gretel."

Figure 2. Eun-Soo positioned as a reluctant parent in *Hansel and Gretel.*

The history of these never-aging traumatized children, born during and just after the Korean War (1950–1953), blends the story of Hansel and Gretel with the horrific events and civilian massacres of modern Korean history. The question they put to their latest adult victim—"Are children happy in your world?"—is part of the transformation from self-regardingness to humane responsibility that enables the adult's safe return to the everyday world and his future life as a husband and parent. The need to overcome self-regardingness—an all-encompassing focus on the self that precludes consideration for or empathy with others—is a theme that recurs throughout contemporary Korean films and dramas, in which self-regardingness is identified as a core defect in Korean society.[6] The problem is again evident in the circumstances of the sequentially abandoned children in *Treeless Mountain* (a more oblique adaptation of "Hansel and Gretel"), who can only find a home with caring grandparents who eke out a bare subsistence living on a small farm. In this case, with no available treasure to transform their lives and no father to go home to, it is the children who develop other-regardingness as they support their ailing grandmother. Their future, however, is uncompromisingly bleak.

To retell a story such as "Hansel and Gretel" that is in some form familiar to the audience prompts questions about teleology—a pattern that emerges from a narrative to affirm that both the narrative and the society it reflects are meaningful. In folktales, whether we think about the tales of the Brothers Grimm or traditional Korean tales, it is common for an audience to assume that good behavior will invariably be rewarded and bad behavior invariably punished. Retelling such tales hence functions as a commentary on the moral perspectives of the society in which it is retold, and such a moral perspective becomes uncertain when the stories are set in a social context that seems nihilistic—where traditional values and beliefs no longer hold sway and everyday existence lacks purpose and sense. Such a context is acutely evoked in Bong Man-Dae's *Cinderella,* in which a blending of fairy tale and horror genres produces a sharp critique of the valorization of "beauty," and hence of mere surfaces, in contemporary Korean society.

This *Cinderella* invokes a relationship with the common script but is not a retelling. The structural homology is quite slight, so that a function of the title is to prompt audiences to seek a connection. Structurally, the connection lies in a stepmother and stepdaughter relationship in which the child has been deprived of any possibility of subjective agency, to the extent that her acute loss of identity has been engraved on her body by the surgical removal of her face. Further, underlying this film is a premise that informs some of the most commonly reproduced Grimm tales—that feminine beauty is important and that there are strong associations between beauty, goodness, and reward. On the basis of an extensive discourse analysis of retellings of the Grimms' tales, Lori Baker-Sperry and Liz Grauerholz concluded, "Those [tales] that have been reproduced the most (*Cinderella* and *Snow White*) are precisely the ones that promote a feminine beauty ideal" (722). In contemporary Korean popular culture, transformation of the self to achieve a better life is commonly associated with drastic makeovers, in which the helper is replaced by a cosmetic surgeon (sometimes explicitly called a "fairy godmother") and clinics that specialize in cosmetic surgery include the Cinderella Plastic Surgery and Dental Clinic, whose website shows a "surgeon" and a pretty young woman standing together outside the clinic, heads leaning toward each other and wreathed in smiles.[7] As in most versions of the Cinderella-script, a girl's primary asset is a pretty face (automatically associated with virtue and good character), and this scene asserts a sense of well-being because of it.

Bong Man-Dae blends the Cinderella-script with a common social script in which cosmetic surgery has been normalized. A link between Cinderella and surgery is also implied in the drama *My Name Is Kim Sam-Soon* (2005), in which Sam-Soon imagines herself accused of "impudence" because she has not undergone cosmetic surgery, and the film *200 Pounds Beauty* (2006; literal title, "Being a Beauty Is Agonizing"), so at the time a script about surgery and fractured subjectivity was emerging more widely, although it was circulating in the region earlier, having entered Japanese manga by the early 1990s (see Hanabusa). Commenting on the responses of a participant in the US *Extreme Makeover* TV series, Brenda R. Weber observes that the procedures offer "a classical sense of the subject, one that is internally coherent and fully autonomous; [the made-over subject] feels fractured no longer, a newfound state that strikes her as liberating and empowering." At the same time, Weber argues, the nature of the program is that by trying to reassure viewers "that it can eradicate embodied anxieties" it foregrounds the flaws that prompt anxiety and thus, exacerbating both anxiety and desire, promises relief only through "beauty."

Bong Man-Dae's *Cinderella* critiques such a preoccupation with surfaces by blending the Cinderella-script with psychological horror film conventions and suggests that there is a concomitant loss of subjectivity. Cinderella's abject life among the cinders is here transformed into lifelong imprisonment in a cellar, after a female plastic surgeon abducts a small orphan and removes her face, grafting it onto her own disfigured daughter. Eventually the victim (Cinderella) kills herself and the surgeon goes mad. This course of events does not merely point to a skeptical or satirical attitude toward the contemporary fashion for cosmetic surgery in Korea, and hence to an assertion that the product is a nonself or inauthentic self, but also raises deeper questions about the constitution of culture. If an individual's behavior is embedded in cultural systems that privilege or enable certain activities, has that individual become oblivious to the practical and moral outcomes of those activities? The question is focused through other young women depicted in the film who have been operated on by the same surgeon and one by one experience acute subjective anxiety that leads to self-mutilation and death.

CONCLUSION

Bong Man-Dae's *Cinderella* is an extreme use of the "Aschenputtel" story, but it well exemplifies the concerns of this chapter. For a script to become the basis of variants and adaptations of a more or less remote pre-text, or bundle of pre-texts, audiences need to recognize, understand, and accept the components, conventions, and structures of the script. Conceptual blending, however, also entails the possibility that a script will develop different meanings when carried over to a new cultural context and blended with other scripts. The self-reflexive dialogism of *Secret Garden* supplies a paradigmatic example with which to conclude. Informed by Joo-Won's mother that she intends to strip him of his position and all his assets if he continues in his resolve to marry her, Ra-Im decides to break off the relationship and does so by leaving a note that affirms that fairy-tale scripts are also life scripts: "The Little Mermaid's hand holding the knife was shaking, but next, she threw the knife far into the waves. The Little Mermaid's sight of the prince faded, and she threw her body into the ocean. And then the Little Mermaid turned into bubbles and disappeared." When he reads this dark version of Andersen's tale (it refuses any possibility of redemption or immortality of the soul), Joo-Won crosses out "disappeared" and writes a different ending, a parody of the local version of the Cinderella-script in which the heroine becomes a successful businesswoman who may no longer be in need of a prince: "At the moment before the Little Mermaid turned into bubbles and disappeared, the prince, knowing the truth, said to the princess from the neighboring kingdom, 'Is this for the best? Are you sure?' Then he broke off the engagement and ran toward the Little Mermaid. The Little Mermaid used bubbles as the basic concept for inventing a washing machine, and became a wealthy and powerful company director. Because the prince wasn't willing to make investments he lost all his money, and became the Little Mermaid's Secretary Kim for a very, very long time. He really lived for a very, very long time."

Intercultural conceptual blendings produce new schemas and give rise to new scripts. The Grimms' tales continue to furnish cognitive and social cultural models but are constantly implicated in a dialectic between internalizations of European folktale schemas, on the one hand, and scripts that express local social beliefs and practices, on the other. Conceptual blending thus utilizes local scripts drawn from analogues, such as "Kongjwi and Patjwi"; tales with homologous structures, such as *Gumiho* tales; or bundles of scripts blending multiple European and local tales. A powerful outcome of the process of conceptual blending is to develop a conceptual position, neither entirely global nor entirely local, which can examine how the past haunts the present, either as tradition or suppressed trauma, and hence can demand a rethinking of many aspects of modern society. The Brothers Grimm's tales continue to play a key role in this rethinking as, integrated within Korean culture over a century, they constitute a group of powerful themes and concerns that have haunted contemporary creative production to an astonishing extent over recent years.

Notes

1. Names in Korean follow the general East Asian convention of placing family name before given name, and that has been followed here throughout.

2. *Secret Garden* works a variation on the "Aschenputtel" story by reassigning the roles of the dead mother and stepmother to the female protagonist's dead father and the male protagonist's domineering mother. Interchangeability of roles between mother-in-law and stepmother has been common in Western folk tradition, as Marina Warner remarks, pointing to "the relation between mothers-in-law and daughters-in-law as the acute lesion in the social body" (228). There are no step-sisters, but the male, Kim Joo-Won, has some rivalry with his male cousin, rightful heir to the family's extensive business interests but more concerned with his career as a pop singer. Warner's comment that "a mother-in-law had good reason to fear her son's wife" is most overtly brought out in Korean TV drama in *Baker King, Kim Tak-Goo* (2010) when the Aschenputtel, Shin Yoo-Gyung, moves into the house of her mother-in-law (Seo In-Sook) and, after learning that Seo In-Sook was responsible for the death of her own mother-in-law, uses the information to bring about a reign of terror.

3. Ra-Im's father has a darker purpose, however. He has foreknowledge of Ra-Im's imminent death when a stunt goes wrong and plans for Joo-Won to die in her place. It is later revealed that he himself had lost his life rescuing Joo-Won from a fire.

4. For a full text of "Kongjwi and Patjwi," see Ha Tae-Hung, *Folk Tales of Old Korea* (12–28). As Vanessa Joosen points out, "structurality"—the reproduction of the structure of a pre-text—is a common form of intertextuality (24).

5. At the story's close, however, Gil-Son accompanies a monk to a small temple in the mountains in search of enlightenment, but when an accident befalls the monk Gil-Son is left alone and snowbound. He starves to death but does so with such equanimity that he becomes a Buddha. An excellent anime version of the story was made in 2003.

6. Self-regardingness is a concept deployed in social discourse, ethics, and moral philosophy. See Marc F. Plattner, who argues that the function of civil associations is to remedy "the self-regardingness of individuals" (173); George Kateb's formulation of self-regardingness as a vice—"people are too self-regarding, and self-regardingness too easily passes into selfishness, while selfishness expresses itself in the limitless pursuit of

goods that do not gratify because they have no relation to any desire but the unappeasable desire for prestige and status" (923)—applies with acute accuracy to the society depicted in Korean film and TV media. See also the contrasts between "other-regardingness" and "self-regardingness" explored by Lisa Tessman in *Burdened Virtues* (2005).

7. The website (in Korean) can be viewed at http://plakr.cindyclinic.com/bbs/board.php?bo_table=plakr_star&wr_id=178&page=0.

References

Baker-Sperry, Lori, and Liz Grauerholz. "The Pervasiveness and Persistence of the Feminine Beauty Ideal in Children's Fairy Tales." *Gender and Society* 17.5 (2003): 711–26.

Beauchamp, Fay. "Asian Origins of Cinderella: The Zhuang Storyteller of Guangxi." *Oral Tradition* 25.2 (2010): 447–96.

Brogan, Kathleen. "American Stories of Cultural Haunting: Tales of Heirs and Ethnographers." *College English* 57.2 (1995): 149–65.

Bui, Tran Quynh Ngoc. "Structure and Motif in the 'Innocent Persecuted Heroine' Tale in Vietnam and Other Southeast Asian Countries." *International Research in Children's Literature* 2.1 (2008): 37–48.

Fauconnier, Gilles, and Mark Turner. *The Way We Think: Conceptual Blending and the Mind's Hidden Complexities.* New York: Basic Books, 2002.

Gutierrez, Anna Katrina. "*Mga Kwento ni Lola Basyang:* A Tradition of Reconfiguring the Filipino Child." *International Research in Children's Literature* 2.2 (2009): 159–76.

Ha, Tae-Hung. *Folk Tales of Old Korea.* Seoul: Yonsei UP, 1970.

Haase, Donald. "Hypertextual Gutenberg: The Textual and Hypertextual Life of Folktales and Fairy Tales in English-Language Popular Print Editions." *Fabula* 47.3–4 (2006): 222–30.

Hanabusa, Miyuki. "Reading Dual Meanings of Power on Young Women's Bodies: The Representation of Cosmetic Surgery in Japanese Manga." *International Research in Children's Literature* 1.1 (2008): 82–98.

Herman, David. *Story Logic: Problems and Possibilities of Narrative.* Lincoln: U of Nebraska P, 2002.

Joosen, Vanessa. *Critical and Creative Perspectives on Fairy Tales.* Detroit: Wayne State UP, 2011.

Kateb, George. "Individualism, Communitarianism, and Docility." *Social Research* 56.4 (1989): 921–42.

Kirmayer, Laurence J. "Beyond the 'New Cross-Cultural Psychiatry': Cultural Biology, Discursive Psychology and the Ironies of Globalization." *Transcultural Psychiatry* 43.1 (2006): 126–44.

Knoepflmacher, U. C. "Introduction: Literary Fairy Tales and the Value of Impurity." *Marvels & Tales* 17.1 (2003): 15–36.

Lee, Sung-Ae. "Lures and Horrors of Alterity: Adapting Korean Tales of Fox Spirits." *International Research in Children's Literature* 4.2 (2011): 135–50.

McConachie, Bruce. "Toward a Cognitive Cultural Hegemony." *Introduction to Cognitive Cultural Studies.* Ed. Lisa Zunshine. Baltimore: Johns Hopkins UP, 2010. 134–50.

Panttaja, Elisabeth. "Going Up in the World: Class in 'Cinderella.'" *Western Folklore* 52 (1993): 85–104.

Plattner, Marc F. "The Uses of 'Civil Society.'" *Journal of Democracy* 6.4 (1995): 169–73.

Schank, Roger, and Robert Abelson. *Scripts, Plans, Goals and Understanding: An Inquiry into Human Knowledge Structures.* Hillsdale: Erlbaum, 1977.

Shore, Bradd. *Culture in Mind: Cognition, Culture, and the Problem of Meaning.* New York: Oxford UP, 1996.

Stephens, John, and Sylvie Geerts. "Mishmash, Conceptual Blending and Adaptation in Contemporary Children's Literature Written in Dutch and English." *Neverending Stories.* Eds. Sara Van den Bossche and Sylvie Geerts. Gent: Academia Press, 2012.

Tessman, Lisa. *Burdened Virtues: Virtue Ethics for Liberatory Struggles.* New York: Oxford UP, 2005.

Turner, Mark. "Double-Scope Stories." *Narrative Theory and the Cognitive Sciences.* Ed. David Herman. Stanford: Center for the Study of Language and Information, 2003. 117–42.

Warner, Marina. *From the Beast to the Blonde.* London: Chatto & Windus, 1994.

Weber, Brenda R. "Beauty, Desire, and Anxiety: The Economy of Sameness in ABC's *Extreme Makeover.*" *Genders* 41 (2005). www.genders.org/g41/g41_weber.html. 2 Nov. 2011.

Zipes, Jack, ed. and trans. *The Complete Fairy Tales of the Brothers Grimm.* New York: Bantam, 1987.

Television Dramas and Films

TELEVISION DRAMAS

Brilliant Legacy (28 episodes). Korea: SBS, 2009.

Cinderella's Stepsister (20 episodes). Korea: KBS, 2010.

Glass Slippers (40 episodes). Korea: SBS, 2002.

King of Baking, Kim Tak-Goo (30 episodes). Korea: KBS, 2010.

My Girlfriend Is a Gumiho (16 episodes). Korea: SBS, 2010.

My Love Patzzi (10 episodes). Korea: MBC, 2002.
My Name Is Kim Sam-Soon (16 episodes). Korea: MBC, 2005.
Secret (18 episodes). Korea: MBC, 2000.
Secret Garden (20 episodes). Korea: SBS, 2010.

Films

200 Pounds Beauty, directed by Kim Yong-Hwa. Korea: CN Entertainment Ltd., 2006.
Cinderella, directed by Bong Man-Dae. Korea: Mini Film Productions, 2006.
Hansel and Gretel, directed by Yim Pil-Sung. Korea: CJ Entertainment, 2007.
Treeless Mountain, directed by Kim So-Yong. Korea: Oscilloscope Pictures, 2008.

CONTRIBUTORS

RUTH B. BOTTIGHEIMER teaches courses on European fairy tales and British children's literature at Stony Brook University, New York. Her ongoing research includes the history of early British children's literature, the seventeenth-century Port-Royalist Nicolas Fontaine, and a new history of fairy tales. She has published several books on the history of fairy tales, including *Fairy Tales: A New History. Fairy Godfather: Straparola, Venice, and the Fairy Tale Tradition,* and *Grimms' Bad Girls and Bold Boys: The Moral and Social Vision of the Tales.*

CYRILLE FRANÇOIS is a PhD candidate in comparative literature and linguistics at the University of Lausanne. His thesis focuses on narrative strategies in the fairy tales of Perrault, the Brothers Grimm, and Andersen as well as in their translations and adaptations for children. He is the author of several articles and scientific reviews on fairy tales.

MARIJANA HAMERŠAK is a postdoctoral researcher at the Institute of Ethnology and Folklore Research in Zagreb (Croatia). Her PhD (2008) was titled *Formations of Childhood and Transformations of Fairy Tales.* She teaches at the University of Zagreb and the University of Dubrovnik. With Suzana Marjanić she edited *Folkloristička čitanka* (2010, *Folklore Studies Reader*).

ISABEL HERNÁNDEZ is a professor of German literature at the Universidad Complutense in Madrid. She attained her PhD there in 1994 for her work on the notion of *Heimat* in German-language literature, with a particular focus on the works of the Swiss writer Gerold Späth. She has taught and conducted research at various universities in Europe and the Americas. She is the editor of *Revista de Filologia Alemana* and a coeditor of *Ibero-amerikanisches Jahrbuch für Germanistik*.

SARA HINES received a PhD from the University of Edinburgh (2013) for her dissertation on the twelve-volume collection of fairy tales edited by Andrew Lang and published by Longmans from 1889 through 1910. She completed an MA in children's literature at Roehampton University and an MA in European culture at University College London. Her article "Collecting the Empire: Andrew Lang's Fairy Books (1889–1910)" appeared in *Marvels & Tales.*

VANESSA JOOSEN is a postdoctoral researcher and lecturer in children's literature at the University of Antwerp (Belgium) and the University of Tilburg (Netherlands). She is the author of *Critical and Creative Perspectives on Fairy Tales: An Intertextual Dialogue between Fairy-Tale Scholarship and Postmodern Retellings* (Wayne State UP, 2011) and coauthor of *Wit als sneeuw, zwart als inkt: De sprookjes van Grimm in de Nederlandstalige literatuur* (White as Snow, Black as Ink: Grimm's Fairy Tales in Dutch Literature; Lannoo-Campus, 2012). She is coeditor of *Changing Concepts of Childhood and Children's Literature* (Cambridge Scholars Press, 2006) and assistant editor of *Modernism* (John Benjamins, 2007).

BETTINA KÜMMERLING-MEIBAUER is professor in the German department at the University of Tübingen, Germany. She was guest professor at the University of Kalmar/Växjö (Sweden) and the University of Vienna (Austria) and served as advisory editor for *The Oxford Encyclopedia of Children's Literature* (Oxford UP, 2006). She has written and edited ten books; her last publication was *Emergent Literacy. Children's Books from 0 to 3* (John Benjamins, 2011).

GILLIAN LATHEY is a reader in children's literature and the director of the National Centre for Research in Children's Literature at Roehampton University, UK. She is the author of *The Impossible Legacy: Identity and Purpose in Autobiographical Children's Literature Set in the Third Reich and the Second World War* (Peter Lang, 1999) and *The Role of Translators in Children's Literature: Invisible Storytellers* (Routledge, 2010). She edited *The Translation of Children's Literature: A Reader* (Multilingual Matters, 2006) and is a series coeditor for Peter Lang's *Europäische Kinder- und Jugendliteratur im interkulturellen Kontext* (European Children's Literature in an Intercultural Context).

SUNG-AE LEE is a lecturer in the Department of International Studies at Macquarie University, Australia, where she teaches mainly Asian cinema and culture. Her research interests are in imagological studies of Korean society, especially as reflected in fiction, film, and TV dramas. She has published widely, with articles in such journals as *Asian Ethnology, CLE, Diaspora,* and *JAAS,* and contributed a chapter on history, memory, and trauma to the collection *Remaking Literary History* (Cambridge Scholars Press, 2010).

DECHAO LI is an associate professor in the Department of Chinese and Bilingual Studies at Hong Kong Polytechnic University. His research interests include literary translation, corpus-based translation studies, and translation pedagogy.

NIEVES MARTÍN-ROGERO is a lecturer in Spanish language and literature at the Teacher Training School of Madrid's Autónoma University (Spain). Her PhD thesis is titled *Travelling to the Middle Ages in Today's Spanish Young Adults' Literature.* Her most recent publications include *Don Quixote for Children and Young Adults. 1905–2008. History, Analysis and Documentation* (U Castilla-La Mancha P, 2009) and "The Construction of Identity in Picture Books in Spanish" (*Bookbird,* 2010).

ALEXANDRA MICHAELIS-VULTORIUS is a doctoral candidate at Wayne State University writing her dissertation on the introduction, dissemination, and reception of the Brothers Grimm's fairy tales in Colombia.

MARIANNA MISSIOU teaches children's literature at the University of the Aegean (Rhodes, Greece). Her research interests are focused in the field of visual narrations such as picture books and comics.

MAYAKO MURAI is a professor in the English Department at Kanagawa University, Japan. She received her PhD in comparative literature from University College London in 2001. Her current research investigates the contemporary recasting of traditional fairy tales in literature and art. She recently edited *Reading Gender Politics: Between Representation and Practice*

(Ochanomizushobo, 2010) and *Literary Fairy Tales by Women Writers: Madame d'Aulnoy, Anne Thackeray Ritchie, and Mary de Morgan* (Eureka Press, 2010), and her chapters on the uses of fairy tales in contemporary Japanese art are included in *Postmodern Fictional Repurposings and Theoretical Revisitings of Fairy Tales and Fantasies* (Edwin Mellen Press, 2010) and *Anti-Tales: The Uses of Disenchantment* (Cambridge Scholars Publishing, 2011).

MALINI ROY has taught English literature at Nanyang Technological University (Singapore). Formerly, she worked at the Sussex Centre for Folklore, Fairy Tales and Fantasy (University of Chichester, UK). She now works as a freelance writer and editor in Frankfurt, Germany.

MONIKA WOZNIAK is an associate professor of Polish language and literature at the University of Roma "La Sapienza" and a visiting professor at the Jagiellonian University of Cracow. Her research has addressed several topics in literary translation, children's translation studies, and audiovisual translation. She has been guest editor of special issues of *Przekładaniec. Journal of Literary Translation* (Cracow) on children's literature translation (2006) and on fairy tales in translation (2010).

DAFNA ZUR is a doctoral candidate at the University of British Columbia, where she is completing her dissertation on the construction of the child in children's magazines in Korea from 1908 until 1950. Her work on the depictions of the Korean War in North and South Korean children's literature has been published by *International Research in Children's Literature* (December 2009) and the *Korea Yearbook 2010*.

INDEX

Page numbers in italics refer to illustrations

Abelson, Robert, 276
Addey and Co., 225, 226
Adoum, Jorge Enrique, 146
"Aesopian language," 253n7
Akai tori (Red Bird) (Japanese children's magazine), 159, 161
Alderson, Brian, 226, 232
Alianza (Spanish publisher), 71
alienation effect, DEFA films, 244, 246–47
Almancenes LEY, 90
Almodóvar, A. Rodríguez, 59, 60–61
Alsleben, E., 182, 184, 188
Alvarez, María Edmée, 96n12
Amicis, Edmondo de, 83, 95n4; *Cuore,* 95n3
Amsler, Jean, 183, 189, 190
An, Kyŏngsik, 106
analogue blending, 280–81, 289
Anaya (Spanish publisher), Laurín Collection, 72
Anczyc, Władysław Ludwik: *Trzy Baśnie* (Three Fairy Tales), 45; version of "Sleeping Beauty," 46
Andersen, Hans Christian, 26, 182; Devsare's translation of tales, 135; *Eventyr,* 6; first collection of selected tales adapted into Polish, 55n4; prominence of tales in Colombia before 1955, 84–85; tales became popular before the Grimm tales, 6; tales in Poland in 1850s, 41
Anderson, Benedict, 142

anonymity: affected nearly every Croatian author in nineteenth century, 22–26; Calleja adaptations, 63; common in children's literature translations, 22; in English newspapers during nineteenth century, 23
Araluce (publisher), 66, 69
Arciniegas, Triunfo: *Caperucita Roja y otras historias perversas* (Little Red Riding Hood and other Perverse Stories), 93
Arnold, Matthew, 147–48
Assmann, Aleida, 5
ATU (Aarne, Thompson, and Uther), 33n9, 185
Aulnoy, Marie-Catherine d', 183
Austen, Jane, 22

Bacchilega, Cristina, 68
Baker, Ronald, 257
Baker-Sperry, Lori, 287
Bakhtin, Mikhail M., 180, 193n1
Baliński, Karol, 43
Banks, Amanda, 257
Bannong, Liu, 120
Baring-Gould, Sabine, 230
Barrenetxea, Iván, 77n33
Barthelme, Donald: *Snow White,* 163
Barthes, Roland, 263
Bartuš, Franjo, 29
Basile, Giambattista: *Lo cunto de li cunti* (The Tale of Tales), 203, 204, 207
Baśnie dla dzieci i młodzieży (Fairy Tales for Children and Young Readers), translated by Cecylia Niewiadomska, 46–47

Baśnie i powiastki dla dzieci (Fairy Tales and Stories for Children), translated by Maria Kreczowska, 46

Baudry, Frédéric, 182, 183–84

Bauman, Richard, 111, 112, 113n19, 114n21

"*Bearbeitungen,*" 14

Beauchamp, Fay, 280

Beck, Walter, 246

Beijing daxue riken (Beijing University Daily), 119

Benfey, Theodor, 211

Bertall, 182

Berwiński, Ryszard, 43, 47

Bettelheim, Bruno, 12, 154, 165; *The Uses of Enchantment,* 269

Biblioteca fantástica, Italy, 91

Biblioteca Perla (Pearl Library), Callejos, 63, 76n20

Bielicka, Emilia, 51

Biswas, Rumjhum, 148n4

Blanca Nieve y otros cuentos (Snow White and Other Tales), Mexico, 89

Blasco Ibáñez, Vicente, 74n4

Bogue, David (London publisher), 233n6

Bošković-Stulli, Maja, 26

Bottigheimer, Ruth, 2, 4, 13, 68, 149n10, 164; *Grimms' Bold Girls and Bad Boys,* 145

Brau, Loris, 268

Bravo-Villasante, Carmen, 72–73

Brecht, Bertolt, concept of alienation, 244, 246

Brentano, Clemens, 142

Briggs, Charles L., 111, 112, 113n19, 114n21

Brilliant Legacy (Korean television drama), 282

Brogan, Kathleen, 284

Browne, Anthony, 12

Browne, Gordon, 220, 221, 230–31; reillustration of "The Golden Bird," 231

Browne, Hablot K., 220, 226, 234n11, 234n13

Bršljan (Ivy) (Croatian children's journal), 26–30

Brüder Grimm-Gesellschaft (Brothers Grimm Society), 2

Bruguera (Spanish publisher), 70

Brzechwa, Jan, 50, 51

Bui, Tran Quynh Ngoc, 280

Burne, Charlotte S.: *The Handbook of Folklore,* 120

Byfield, Graham, 224

C. Baldwyn (English publisher), 203, 222

Caballero, Fernán, 4, 59; *Cuentos, oraciones, adivinanzas y refranes populares e infantiles* (Popular Children's Stories, Prayers, Riddles, and Proverbs), 61; *Cuentos y poesías populares andaluces* (Popular Andalusian Tales and Poems), 61

Caldecott, Randolph, 233n7

Calleja, Saturnino, 59, 76n20, 85–86

Calleja (Casa Editorial Calleja) (Spanish publisher), 63, 74n8; *Cuentos escogidos* (Selected Stories), 86–87, 89; inaccuracies about Grimm Brothers' fieldwork in prefaces, 86–87

Caracol Television, Colombia, 94

Carter, Angela: *The Bloody Chamber and Other Stories,* 163, 164

Castiglione, Baldassare: *The Book of the Courtier,* 45

Chasles, Philarète, 180

Chenbao fukan (literary supplement), China, 128

Chester, Tessa Rose, 220, 230–31

China, reception of Grimm tales in: Chinese translations of the *Kinder- und Hausmärchen,* 122–28; influence of Grimm tales on folk literature movement, 119–31; influence of tales on first-generation Chinese fairy-tale writers, 128–30

Chinese Folk Literature Movement, 119–21

Ch'oe Namsŏn: advocacy of modernity, 111; Grimm translations in *Tongmyŏng,* 100–101, 102–3, 104–6; social Darwinism, 110; "Weguk ŭlossŏ kwihwahan chosŏn kodam" (Old Korean Stories Domesticated from Overseas), 106

chromolithography (color from stone), 228, 231, 233

chromoxylography, 227, 228, 231

"Cinderella": Korean adaptations for film and television, 2–3, 276, 280–81, 281–82, 285, 287–88; Polish versions of, 46

Cinderella (Disney film), 88
Cinderella (Korean film), 285, 287–88
Cinderella Plastic Surgery and Dental Clinic, Korea, 287
Cinderella's Stepsister (Korean television drama), 283
Clarín, Leopoldo Alas, 74n4
Cohn, Neil, 265
Collodi, Carlo: "Pinocchio," 7
Coloma, Father, 59, 62
Colombia, **children's literature:** *Biblioteca fantástica* (Fantastic Library), 91; *Biblioteca ilustrada: cuentes populares* (Illustrated Library: Popular Stories), 85; *Chanchito,* 86; early distribution of Disney films, 87–88; French editions of fairly-tale volumes, 83–84; Premio Enka de Literartura Infantil, 90–91; prominence of Hans Christian Andersen, 84–85; works by Charles Perrault, 84
Colombia, **Grimm tales in,** 81–96; *Blanca Nieves y los siete enanitos* (Snow White and the Seven Dwarfs), Editorial Norma, 89; *Blanca-Nieves y los siete enanitos* (Snow White and the Seven Dwarfs), Latinopal, 91–92; Calleja editions, 85–87; confusion about which tales are Grimm tales, 89–90; *Cuentas infantiles* (Children's Stories), Editorial Bedout, 91, 96n12, 96n14; *Cuentes y leyendas de los hermanos Grimm* (Stories and Legends of the Brothers Grimm), 1893, 85; *Hermanos Grimm: Cuentos* (Brothers Grimm: Stories), Edilux, 91, 92; influence of Disney on post-1950 publications edited in Americas, 89; influences of Grimm tales on contemporary authors, 93; mass media programs, 94; misperceptions of French origins of tales, 87; reception before 1955, 82–83, 85–86; reception of after 1950, 88–94
color illustrations, 219–20, 227, 228, 231–33
comic books: adaptation of fairy-tale material, 2, 12, 257–59, 271–72; rewriting of fairy tale's characters and motifs, 266–71; version of fairy tale as transage reading, 260–66. *See also* French *bande dessinée;* Japanese manga
Contes allemands du temps passé (German Tales of Past Times), translated by Félix Frank and E. Alsleben, 182–83
Contes choisis de Grimm, translated by F.-C. Gérard, 181
Contes choisis des frères Grimm (Selected Tales by the Brothers Grimm), translated by Frédéric Baudry, 182
Contes de la famille par les frères Grimm (Family Tales by the Brothers Grimm), translated by Nicolas Martin and Pitre-Chevalier, 181–82
Contes des frères Grimm (Tales of the Brothers Grimm), translated by Ernest Grégoire and Louis Moland, 183
Coover, Robert: *Pricksongs and Descants,* 163
copper etching, 223, 224
Cortez, Maria Teresa: *Os contos de Grimm em Portugal: a recepção dos* Kinder- und Hausmärchen *entre 1837 e 1910* (The Grimm Stories in Portugal: A Reception of the *Kinder- und Hausmärchen* between 1837 and 1910), 81
Crane, Lucy, 215n10, 229, 234n10
Crane, T. F., 214n4
Crane, Walter, 139, 215n10, 220–21, 225, 229, 233n7; illustrations for *Household Stories from the Collection of the Bros. Grimm,* 229; illustrations for "The Golden Bird," 229–30
Crnković, Milan, 19, 20, 24
Croatia: **children's literature:** first non-Slavic Croatian children's tale, 28; *Mali tobolac raznog cvětja* (A Little Knapsack Full of Flowers) (Croatia), 24
Croatia, **early translation of Grimm tales,** 5, 19–30; anonymous publication of Grimm tales, 21–22, 26–30; based on free exchange, borrowings, and circulations, 22–26; difference in presentation of Andersen and Grimm tales, 27–28; Grimm tales presented as Croatian, Serbian, and/or Slavic, 28–29; pobrvaćenje (Croatization), 24, 29; question of nation and folk narration, 26–30; 1895 translation of

Croatia (*continued*)
"The Seven Ravens," 19, 26, 33n2, 33n8; variant of "Robber Bridegroom" published in 1865, 20

Croker, Thomas Crofton: *Fairy Legends and Traditions of the South of Ireland,* 201

Cruikshank, George, 6, 11, 139, 181; copper etchings for "The Golden Bird," 223–24, 229, 230; illustrations for Dickens's *Oliver Twist,* 223; illustrations for *German Popular Stories,* 203, 220, 222–24

Cuentas de Grimm: ilustrados por Arthur Rackham (Grimm Stories: Illustrated by Arthur Rackham), 89

Cuentas de Grimm (Stories by Grimm), Mexico, 91, 96n12, 96n14

Cuentos y leyendas de los hermanos Grimm (Stories and Legends of the Brothers Grimm), oldest Spanish translation, 85, 89, 95n7

Curry, Agnes, 257

Czartoryski, Adam, 55n3

Danica ilirska (Illyrian Hesperus), 27

d'Argent, Yan', 183

Das blaue Licht, DEFA film, 247, 249

Das singende, klingende Bäumchen (The Singing, Ringing Tree), DEFA film, 243–44

Das tapfere Schneiderlein (The Cunning Little Tailor), DEFA film, 240, 243, 245

Das Zaubermännchen (Rumpelstiltskin), DEFA film, 245

Day, Reverend Lal Behari: *Folktales of Bengal,* 211

De Agostini (Italian publisher), 52

DEFA Stiftung (DEFA Foundation). *See* Deutsche Film Aktiengesellschaft (German Film Public Company) (DEFA)

Dehung, Shen: *Tonghua* (Fairy Tales), 122–23

Delcourt "Jeunesse," 260

Der Bärenhäuter (Bearskin), DEFA film, 247

Der Froschkönig (The Frog King), DEFA film, 241–42

Der kleine Muck (Little Mook), DEFA film, 252n2

Der Meisterdieb, DEFA film, 246, 248

Der Prinz hinter den sieben Meeren (The Singing, Springing Lark), DEFA film, 246

Deutsche Film Aktiengesellschaft (German Film Public Company) (DEFA), 239, 240, 252

De Vos, Gail, 258

Devsare, Harikrishna, 3; "Preservers of Immortal Folklore: The Brothers Grimm," 142; translation of *Grimm Bandhuon Ki Kahaniyan* (The Grimm Brothers' Tales), 5, 13, 135–48; translation of Hans Christian Andersen tales, 135

dialogical principle, 180, 191, 193n1, 279, 289

Díaz Borbón, Rafael, 92

Didier et Cie (French academic editor), 182

Die Geschichte von der Gänseprizessin und ihrem treuen Pferd Fallada (The Goose Girl), DEFA film, 240, 251

Diehl Brothers, puppet animation technique, 239

Die Kinder- und Hausmärchen (KHM), 20, 25; first edition not designed to appeal to youth, 6; first English translation of 1823, 6; labeled by Grimms as book for education, 13, 127, 144; omitted tales, 180; similarities and differences in international reception of, 1

Die kluge Bauerntochter (The Peasant's Wise Daughter), DEFA film, 241

Die Störenfriede (The Troublemakers), DEFA film, 252n2

Disney films, 12; *Cinderella,* 88; films distributed in Colombia, 87–88; films released in Poland, 56n20; *Sleeping Beauty,* 88; *Snow White and the Seven Dwarfs,* 87–88; *Steamboat Willie,* 87

Dollerup, Cay, 192–93

domestication, 24; in adaptations of tales in Spain, 63–64, 65

Dorée, Gustave, 192

"Dornröschen" (Brier Rose), in *Vieux contes pour l'amusement des grands et des petits enfans* (Old Tales for the Amusement of Old and Young Children), 181

Dornröschen (Sleeping Beauty), DEFA film, 245, 248, 251

Doyle, Richard, 206; illustrations for John Edward Taylor's *The Fairy Ring,* 224–25, 230, 233n9; illustrations from "The Golden Bird," 220

"Dumna Księżniczka" (A Proud Princess), Polish variation of "King Thrushbeard," 46–47

Dürer, Albrecht: "Knight, Death, and the Devil," 248

E. C. and T. C. Jack (publisher), 66

Edilux Ediciones (Colombian publisher), 91

Editorial Bedout (Colombian publisher), 91

Editorial Norma (Colombian publisher), 91

Editorial Norma (publisher), 89; *Blanca Nieve y los siete enanitos* (Snow White and the Seven Dwarfs), 89; *El festival de Blanca Nieves* (The Festival of Snow White), 89

Editorial Porrúa (Colombian publisher), 96n12, 96n14

Ehon: shinpen gurimu dōwa shū (Picture Book: Newly Edited and Selected Grimms' Tales), Japan, 169–71

Eisenhans (Iron John), DEFA film, 250

Ellison, Harlan, 257

Erickson, Lee, 23

Ericson, Joan, 112n4, 113n5

Eun-Soo, Lee, 285–*86*

Evans, Edmund, 227, 233n7

Everest (publisher), 71

Extreme Makeover (US television series), 288

Fabbri, 96n13

Fairy Tales from Grimm, Wells, Gardner, Darton & Co., 230

Fauconnier, Gilles, 276–77

Federal Republic of Germany, fairy-tale films, 239

Feldman, Paula, 23

feminism, perspective on fairy tales, 76n24

feminist retellings, 11

Fénelon, François: *Les Aventures de Télémaque, fils d'Ulysse* (The Adventures of Telemachus, Son of Ulysses), 40

Fiabe sonore (Audible Fairy Tales), 96n13

film adaptations of Grimm tales, 2, 10, 12; German Democratic Republic (*see* German Democratic Republic, Grimms' fairy tales in film); Korean (*see* Korea, fairy-tale scripts and conceptual blending in film and television drama); Polish *Snow White and the Seven Dwarfs,* 52; South Korean rendering of "Hansel and Gretel," 8–9

Firth, Raymond, 272n1

Fischart, Burkhard Waldis, 200

Flammarion (French publisher), 180

Folk-Lore, 215n9

folklorism, international, and Grimm tales, 3–6

Folk Song Research Society (Geyao yanjiu hui), 119

folktale blending: conceptual blending of horror film and folktale, 284–88; simple and conceptual, 276–80; three-way blends, 281–84; through local analogues and homologies, 280–81

Formosa, Feliú, 71

Foucault, Michel, 21–22, 22, 33n4, 33n5

Fouqué, Friedrich de la Motte: *Undine,* 84–85

four-color process, 231–323

France, translations of Grimm tales, 179–93; direct reference to Perrault in translations, 183–85; first translations, 181–82; French translations, 180–85; influence of Perrault on style of translations, 189–91; influence of Perrault on translation of tales, 185–93; influence of Perrault on words and expressions, 187–89; translated titles, 185–87; translations of second half of nineteenth century, 182–83; twentieth-century translations, 183

Franco, General, 76n20

François, Cyrille, 2, 3–4, 9, 10

Frank, Félix, 182, 184, 188

Frau Holle (Mother Holle), DEFA film, 241, 245–46, 251

Fredro, Aleksander, 42

French *bande dessinée,* 259. See also "Hansel and Gretel," French *bande dessinée* version (Philip Petit)

French literary fairy tales, 40

"The Frog King": censorship of, 10; Japanese version, *Kaeru no ōsama,* translated by Genkur Yazaki, illustrated by Tabaimo, 168, *169*

Fu, Pinjin, 121, 126

full-color printing, 231–323

Funü zazhi (The Women's Magazine), China, 128

Gaiman, Neil: *Sandman,* 257

Gálvez, Pedro, 71–72

Gammer Grethel, or German Fairy Tales, and Popular Stories, translated by Edgar Taylor, 223–24, 227

Garvey, Ellen Gruber, 23

Gascoigne, 223

Gawiński, Antoni, 50

Gebethner and Wolff, importance in innovation of children's literature in Poland, 7, 44, 46

Geerts, Sylvie, 276

Gendai ni ikiru gurimu (The Grimms Still Living Today), 162

gender: and anonymity of fairy-tale authors, 22, 26; conservative notions of tales adapted in Francoist Spain, 68; gender roles in comic book versions of "Hansel and Gretel," 259, 262–63, 266–68, 271; promotion of gender equality in Devsare's *Grimm Bandhuon,* 138, 144–45; references to contemporary gender debates in the GDR DEFA fairy-tale films, 250; reinterpretation of gender roles in tales written during Japanese Grimm boom, 167; traditional opinion regarding the supposed prevalence of passive heroines, 13; Yumiko Kurahashi's attack on gender stereotypes, 163

Georgi, Katja, 251

Gérard, F.-C., 181

German Democratic Republic, Grimms' fairy tales in films, 239–53; adaptation of tales to ideology of Social Realism, 2, 12, 13, 242–43, 250, 252; artistic influences on the creation of films, 244–47; changes in setting, style, and audience, 250–52; Deutsche Film Aktiengesellschaft (German Film Public Company) (DEFA), 239, 240; historical references and subversive meanings, 247–50

German Popular Stories, translated by Edgar Taylor and David Jardine, 181, 202–5, 220, 222, 227, 230

Gevatter Tod (Godfather Death), DEFA film, 246, 247, 248, 249

Geyao (Folk Song), China, 121

"gift book," 11

Gilbert, Sandra M., 164, 174n5

Glass Slippers (Korean television drama), 283, 284

Gliński, Antoni Józef: *Bajarz polski* (The Polish Tale Teller), 43–44, 55n9, 55n10

glocalization, 2–3, 280–81

Goethe, J. W. von: *Die Leiden des jungen Werther* (The Sorrows of Young Werther), 200

"The Golden Bird," British illustrations from in Grimms' editions, 1823–1909, 2, 11, 221–33; Browne's illustration, 222, 231; Crane's illustrations, 222, 229–30, 231; Cruikshank's copper etchings, 223–24, 229, 230; Doyle's illustrations, 230; Rackham's illustrations, 221, 231–32; Wehnert's illustrations, 221, 225–26, 229, 231; Wiegand's illustration, 227

Gomme, George Laurence, 174n3

Górnicki, Łukasz: *Dworzanin polski* (Polish Nobleman), 45

Grauerholz, Liz, 287

Green, John (London publisher), 223

Greenaway, Kate, 233n7

Grégoire, Ernest, 183, 184, 190, 191

Griffin, Robert, 22, 24–25

Grimm, Jacob: belief that translation could not approach quality of original, 8; death of in Croatian newspaper, 26–27; *German Mythology,* 47; honorary member of Croatian Historical Society *(Arkiv),* 4, 27; notion of folktales as broken ancient myths, 27; preface to German translation of Basile's *Pentamerone,* 207, 208; *Teutonic Mythology,* 210; theories about oral transmission of tales, 207; translation of Croker's work into German, 201

Grimm, Wilhelm, 6; account of the tales' collection, 203; changes to "Hansel and Gretel," 259; German versions of *Altdänische Heldenlieder, Balladen und Märchen* (Old Danish Heroic Songs, Ballads and Fairy Tales), 8; notes to the *Children's and Household Tales,* 207–8; theories about oral circulation of fairy tales, 199–200

Grimm Brothers: acknowledgment that some tales first appeared in Straparola, 199–200; broad international interest in folktales, 4; dissension over nature and purpose of translation, 8; encouraged translation of tales, 114n20; goal of establishing common German heritage, 121; key figures in Germanic Society of Frankfurt, 4; modifications of tales for children, 60, 74n3; reference to early edition as *Erziehungsbuch,* 13, 127, 144; regarded tales as educational, 126–27; romantic idealization of, 4; selection criteria for tales, 127; theories about oral circulation of fairy tales, 199–200, 203, 204–5, 209, 210

Grimms' Fairy Library (Routledge), 228–29

Grimms' Goblins, 226–27, 228, 233n9

Grimm's Household Stories, translated by Margaret Hunt, 233n1

Grimm tales: 1812 edition not designed to appeal to youth, 6; innovations as children's literature, 6–8; narrative structures, 130; nineteenth-century prefaces to in English translation, 199–214; paradox between universal and local form, 3; prefaces, 4; reservations of British fairy-tale translators about origins of, 4; as source of inspiration for international folklorism, 3–6, 111; translation of, 8–10; universal quality, 111–12; use of symbolic numbers, 130

Grimm tales, **international reception:** introduced through literary and folkloristic magazines, 6; often functioned as or blended with local folktales, 5; often mistaken for local tales attributed to translators or adaptors, 5;

often published anonymously, 5; reached broad audience as tales in children's books and collections, 7

Grimm tales, **political and ideological issues,** 12–14, 13; accused of promoting Nazist atrocities, 13; gender roles within tales, 13; manipulation of tales in films to show Socialist ideals, 13; promotion of German national identity and culture, 13

Grimm tales, **visual renderings,** 10–12. *See also* comic books; film adaptations of Grimm tales; French *bande dessinée;* Japanese manga

"Grimm Tales in English," British Library exhibition, 232

Grimm (TV drama), 12

Groensteen, Thierry, 258

Gruppo Edittoriale Fabbri (Italian publisher), 91

Gubar, Susan, 164, 174n5

Guerne, Armel, 180, 184, 185–86, 186, 187, 188, 190, 191

Guido Amedeo, Baron Vitale, 120

Gumiho tales (Korea), 281, 289

Gurimu dōwa (Grimm's Tales) *Artist Book Series,* Japan, 168

Gurimu otogi-banashi (Grimm Tales), Japanese translation, 104

Gutierrez, Anna Katrina, 280

Haase, Donald, 7–8, 111, 114n22, 275

Hachette (French publisher): "La Bibliothèque rose," 182

Haksaenggye (Students' World) (Korea), 103

halftone color process, 219, 231–32, 233

Halub, Marek, 94n1

Hameršak, Marijana, 2, 4, 5, 9

"Hansel and Gretel": French *bande dessinée* version (Philip Petit), 2, 259, 260, 262, 264–65, 266–67, 268, 269–71; Japanese manga version (Junko Mizuno), 2, 259–60, *261,* 262–64, 265, 267–69, 270–71; South Korean film, 8–9; Spanish adaptations, 64, 65–69; textual history, 259

Hansel and Gretel (Korean film), 285–87, *286*

Harries, Elizabeth Wanning, 68, 76n24

Hassenpflug family, 143

Hauff, Wilhelm, 252n2; *Das kalte Herz* (The Cold Heart), 240
hauntology, 284
Hegenbarth, Josef, 253n5
Heinrich Campe, Joachim: *Robinson der Jüngere* (Robinson the Younger), 19
Hellenization, 24
Hempel, Johannes, 251
Herbart, Johann Friedrich, 154, 158
Herder, Johann Gottfried, 26, 27–28, 33n6
Herman, David, 276
Hernández, Isabel, 2, 4, 5, 77n33
Hernando (publisher), 69
Higami, Kimiko, 163, 171; illustration based on "Little Red Riding Hood" titled "Salome," 171
Hines, Sara, 2, 11
Hoepli, 56n16
Hoffman, E. T. A., 182
Hoffmann, Franz Friedrich, 20, 26
Holtz-Baumert, Gerhard, 240
homologies, 281, 289
Hotten, John Camden: edition of Edgar Taylor's 1823 and 1826 translations, 208, 228
Household Stories, Routledge, 228–29
Household Stories Collected by the Brothers Grimm, Addey and Co., 1853, 225, 227
Household Stories from the Collection of the Bros. Grimm, Macmillan, 229
Hu, Yuzhi: "Lun minjian wenxue" (On Folk Literature), 123–25
Hugo, Victor, 22
Hung, Chang-tai, 120, 121, 123
Hunt, Margaret, 233n1

India: Hindi resurrections of Grimm tales in modern era, 135–48; retellings of Indian-origin folktales, 138
intaglio, 223, 233
intercultural conceptual blending, 276–80, 289
Iser, Wolfgang, 260
Italy, first compilation of Grimm tales, 56n16
Ivanišević, I., 23
Iwaya, Sazanami, 101–2, 112n4; translation of "Koyukihime" (Snow White), 156–58, *157*

Jachowicz, Stanislaw, 42
Jacobs, Joseph, 214n6
Janczarski, Czesław, 50
Jan Deubler (Polish publisher), 46
Japan, **folklore in:** development of interest in fairy tales and "folk" voice, 100, 109–10, 113n5; *genbun itchi* movement, 113n12; study of folklore as academic discipline, 174n3
Japan, **reception of Grimm tales,** 102; central role of tales in children's literature, 7, 159; changes in cultural details and stylistic and ethical elements in early translations, 156, 158; development of folkloristic approach to tales in 1920s, 159, 161; first actual collection in Japanese, 155; first Grimm tale to appear in Japanese ("The Nail"), 154; "Grimm boom," 153–54, 164, 165–73; reception of Grimm tales since late nineteenth century, 154–62; reinterpretations of the tales in contemporary era, 9, 153–74; tales first imported for pedagogical content, 7, 154–56; translations of older editions of tales in latter half of twentieth century, 161–62; version of "The Wolf and Seven Young Kids," 102, 155; works anticipating the Grimm boom, 162–64
Japanese manga, 12, 263, 264, 265. *See also* "Hansel and Gretel," Japanese manga version (Junko Mizuno)
Jardine, David, 6, 8, 220, 222
Jatakas, India, 138, 148n7
Jeżewska, Kazimiera, 50
Jicheng, Yan, 128
Jiegang, Gu, 119
Johnson, Richard, 214n3
Joosen, Vanessa: *Critical and Creative Perspectives on Fairy Tales,* 164, 266, 290n4
Jorinde und Joringel, DEFA film, 241, 246, 247–48
Jung, Carl, 214n4
Junko Mizuno: manga version of "Hansel and Gretel," 2, 259–60, *261,* 262–64, 265, 267–69, 270–71
Juventud (Spanish publisher), 66, 71

Kaebyŏk (The Dawn of Civilization), Korean literary magazine, 99

Kaeru no ōsama (The Frog King), translated by Genkur Yazaki, illustrated by Tabaimo, 168, *169*

Kamennyi svetok (The Stone Flower), Russian fairy-tale film, 240, 244–45

Kaneda, Kiichi, 159, 161

Kannapin, Detlef, 252n4

Karadi Tales (Indian publisher), 138, 147

Karłowicz, Jan, integral Polish edition of *Kinder- und Hausmärchen,* 47

Kasdepke, Grzegorz, 53

Katch, George, 290n6

Keightley, Thomas, 206; *Fairy Mythology,* 205, 207; *Tales and Popular Fictions,* 201–2, 205–6, 207, 214n5

Kim, Hwasŏn, 106

Kim, So-Yong, 285

Kinderlegenden, 180

King of Baking, Kim Tak-Goo (Korean television drama), 282, 290n2

Kirmayer, Laurence J., 279–80

Kiryū, Misao (pseud.), 163–64, 174n4; *Hontō wa osoroshii gurimu dōwa* (Grimms' Tales Really Are Horrific), 153, 165, *166,* 173n2; "Snow White: The Battle against the Real Mother for Love," 153, 165, 167

Kleine Ausgabe (Small Edition), 6, 11, 30, 60, 181

Klemke, Werner, 253n5

Knoepflmacher, U. C., 275

Kochanowski, Jan, 45

Kochanowski, Piotr, translation of Tasso's *Gerusalemme liberata,* 45

Kožik, Christa, 240

Kolberg, Oskar, 47–48

Kolditz, Gottfried, 247

"Kongjwi and Patjwi" (Korean folktale), 280–81, 283, 284, 289

König, Ingelore, 246

König Drosselbart (King Thrushbeard), DEFA film, 241, 245, 246, 249–50

Korea, **Grimm tales in early colonial period,** 99–112; Ch'oe Namsŏn translations in *Tongmyŏng,* 100–101, 102–3, 104–6; "Collection Contest," 99–101, 109; Pang Chŏnghwan translations in *Ŏrini,* 99, 100, 101, 102, 103, 106–9; tales linked to nationalism, 5, 13, 109–10; translations based on Japanese ideas of national identity, 100, 101–3

Korea, **fairy-tales in film and television drama,** 12, 275–91; blending through local analogues and homologies, 10, 280–84; Cinderella script, 280–81, 283–84, 285–88; conceptual blending of horror film and folktale, 284–88; folktale motif of innocent persecuted child, 282–83; fox-woman script, 281; simple and conceptual blending, 275–80; three-way blends with Andersen, 281–84

Korean Enlightenment, 107

Kotō, Nakajima, 103

Kowerska, Zofia, 39, 47

Krasicki, Igncavy: *Bajki i przpowieści,* 42

Kreczowska, Maria, 46

Kronheim & Co. (German printer), 228, 229

Krüger, Maria, 50

Küchenmeister, Wera and Claus, 246–47

Kukkonen, Karin, 258

Kümmerling-Meibauer, Bettina, 2, 251

Kunio, Yanagita: *Tōno monogatari* (Tales of Tōno), 102

Kurahashi, Yumiko: *Otona no tame no zankoku dōwa* (Cruel Fairy Tales for Adults), 163

Labor (Spanish publisher), 69

Lang, Andrew: *Custom and Myth,* 120, 210; introduction to Grimm's *Household Tales,* 209–13; introduction to *Perrault's Popular Tales,* 211; "Mythology and Fairy Tales," 209

Las mejores cuentos infantiles del mundo (The Best Children's Stories of the World), Colombia, 90

Lathey, Gillian: *The Role of Translation in Children's Literature: Invisible Storytellers,* 22, 71

Latinopal (Colombian publisher), 91

Lee, Sung-Ae, 2, 10

Lenin, Vladimir, 240, 253n7

Leprince de Beaumont, Jeanne-Marie: *Le Magasin des enfants* (The Young Misses' Magazine), 84
Lewestam, Fryderyk Henryk, 55n4
Li, Dechao, 2, 3, 7
Lieberman, Marcia, 13
Liebrecht, Felix, 207
lithography, 228
Lompa, Józef, 43
Los cuentos de los hermanos (The Tales of the Brothers Grimm) (animated television series), Colombia, 94
Luke, David, 186
Lumen (Spanish publisher), 71

Macaulay, Thomas Babington, 136
Macpherson, James, forging of *Poems of Ossian*, 200–202
The Madwoman in the Attic (Gilbert and Gubar), 164, 174n5
Magisterio Español (Spanish publisher), 72
Mahabharata, India, 138
Mali tobolac raznog cvětja (A Little Knapsack Full of Flowers) (Croatia), 24
Mallet, Carl-Heintz, 165
Man-Dae, Bong, 285, 287
Manheim, Ralph, 185, 186
Martin, Nicolas, 182, 190, 191
Martín-Rogero, Nieves, 2, 4, 5, 7
"The Marvelous Jar: An Irish Tale," Croatia, 28
Matsumoto, Yūko, 174n4; *Tsumi bukai hime no otogi-banashi* (Fairy Tales of Sinful Princesses), 163–64, 167
May Fourth scholars, China, 120
McCleery, Allistair, 231–323, 234n12
McConachie, Bruce, 279
Media Rodzina, Poland, 44
Meiji Restoration, Japan, 155
Menzel, Jirí, 248–49
Meschonnic, Henri, 192
Michaelis-Vultorius, Alexandra, 2, 7, 9, 12
Michał Arct (Polish publisher), 44
Mickiewicz, Adam: *Ballady i romance* (Ballads and Romances), 41–42
Mieder, Wolfgang, 257–58
Mikołajewski, Jarosław, 53

Minsu (Customs) (Chinese quarterly), 119
minzokugaku (Japanese native ethnology), 102
Missiou, Marianna, 2
Moland, Louis, 183, 184, 190, 191
Morrison, Grant: *Invisibles*, 257
Muir, Percy, 222–23, 228
Mukharji, Shravani, 136
Müller, Max, 209, 210
Munsch, Robert: *Paper Bag Princess*, 11
Murai, Mayako, 2, 7
Mussini, Fanny Vanzi, 56n16
My Girlfriend Is a Gumiho (Korean television drama), 281
My Love Patzzi (Korean television drama), 283
My Name Is Kim Sam-Soon (Korean television drama), 283–84, 288
myth, 272n1

Naithani, Sadhana, 137
Nasza Księgarnia (Polish publisher), 49, 51
Navarro, Antonio Roche, 71
Nĕcová, Božena, 26
Netherlands, tension between Romantic ideals of Grimm tales and Enlightenment tradition, 6, 7
New Culture Campaign, China, 120
Niewiadomska, Cecylia, 46–47
Nikolajeva, Maria, 258
Nippon Animation, 94
Niranjana, Tejaswini: *Sitting Translation*, 141
Nodelman, Perry, 264, 267
Noguchi, Yoshiko, 155, 170; *Gurimu no meruhyen: sono yume to genjitsu* (Grimms' Märchen: Dream and Reality), 162–63
Noguer (Spanish publisher), 70
Nórdica (Spanish publisher), 77n33

O Ch'ŏksŏk: "How Six Made Their Way in the World" (Changsa ŭi iyagi), 103
O'Donoghue, F. M., 225
Ogawa, Yōko: "Hood Club," 171, 173; *Otogi-banashi no wasuremono* (Lost and Found Fairy Tales), 171, *172*
Oittinen, Riitta, 193n1
Ölenberg manuscript, 161
Oppman, Artur, 47
Orientalism, 147

Ŏrini (Child), Pang Chŏnghwan's Grimm
translations in, 100, 101, 102, 103, 106–9
Ortabasi, Melek, 112n4, 113n12
"Oseam," Buddhist fairy tale, 283
O'Sullivan, Emer, 5, 7, 75n15, 104, 110
otogibanashi (literary fairy tale), 156
otogi (Japanese oral tradition), 155
Ozawa, Toshio, 162

The Panchatantra, India, 135, 138, 148n7
Pang, Chŏnghwan: Collection Contest,
103, 109, 113n8; efforts to create a new
kind of children's literature, 107, 110;
establishment of Children's Day in Korea,
112n1; Grimm translations in *Ŏrini,*
100, 101, 102, 103, 106–9; influence of
German culture and education on work,
107; musical narrative techniques, 108;
promotion of nationalist, anticolonial
sentiment, 108–10; publication of
children's magazine, *Ŏŭrini,* 101, 112n1;
Sarang ŭi sŏnmul (Gift of Love), 99, 103
Panttaja, Elisabeth, 276, 277, 281
paratext, 260, 264
Pardo Bazán, Emilia, 74n4
Paull, Mrs. H. B., 155; *Grimms' Fairy Tales: A
New Translation,* 227–28
Payarols, Francisco, 69
Peninsular War, Spain, 60
Perrault, Charles, 2, 10, 67, 182; *Histoires ou
contes du tempe passé* (Stories or Tales of
Past Times), 179–80, 183
Petit, Philip, comic book version of "Hansel
and Gretel," 2, 259, 260, 262, 264–65,
266–67, 268, 269–71, 272n3
photomechanical reproduction, 230
Pieciul-Karmińska, Eliza, 53
Pieck, Wilhelm, 253n6
Pil-Sung, Yim, 285
"Pinocchio," Carlo Collodi, 7
Pitre-Chevalier, 182, 191
Pizano, Daniel Samper, 87
planography, 228, 233
Plattner, Marc F., 290n6
Plenzdorf, Ulrich, 240
Pludra, Benno, 240
pobălgarjavane, 24

pobrvaćenje (Croatization), 24
Poland: arrival of Romanticism in 1820s,
41–42; Disney films released in before
1989, 56n20; growth in demand for
children's literature in nineteenth century,
41, 44–45; state control of book market
from 1949 to 1989, 49; tradition of fables
in verse derived from Aesop and La
Fontaine, 42
Poland, **reception of Grimm tales,** 39–54;
animated television series *Simsala Grimm,*
52; *biblioteka groszowa,* 50; Disney books
and DVDs in 1990s, 52–53; first Polish
translations and adaptations in 1890s, 41,
42, 46; "Grimms' canon," 54n1; impact
of tales on Polish folklorists, 43, 47–48;
new edition of tales in 1956, 51; reception
of tales before 1918, 40–48; reception of
tales from 1920 to present, 47, 48–53;
removal of tales from children's literature
after WWII, 13, 50–51; retellings and
adaptations appropriated by adaptors, 39,
45–46; *Snow White and the Seven Dwarfs*
film, 52; versions of "Cinderella," 46
polygenetic narratives, 205, 210, 214n4
Porazińska, Janina, 50
posrbe (domestication), 24
Prague Spring, 248
Pražmowska, Teresa, 47
printing, technological changes in, 219, 222
Pushkin, Alexander, 26, 44, 240

Rackham, Arthur, 139; *Cuentas de Grimm:
ilustrados por Arthur Rackham,* 89;
illustrations of "The Golden Bird,"
231–32; reillustration of 1909 edition of
Grimms' Fairy Tales, 219–20, 221; use of
halftone color process, 219–20
Ramanujan, A. K.: *Folktales from India,*
140–41
Ramayana, India, 138
The Reception of Grimms' Fairy Tales
(Haase), 2
Reichsteinowa, Wanda, 46
Reiniger, Lotte, 244
relay translation, 9, 20, 30
relief halftone, 230–31, 233

Revista credencial historia (Magazine Credential History), 87–88

Riascos Villegas, Riascos: "Los tres pelos del diablo" (The Devil's Three Hairs), 94

Rimasson-Fertin, Natacha:, 180, 183, 184–85, 186, 187, 188, 189, 190, 191; *Contes pour les enfants et la maison* (Tales for the Children and the Home), 180–81

"Robber Bridegroom," first Croatian translation via Czech, 9

Robert, Marthe, 185

Rodrian, Fred, 240

Rölleke, Heinz, 4, 131, 149n12, 154, 180, 183; "The 'Utterly Hessian' Fairy Tales by 'Old Marie': The End of a Myth," 162

Rollenhagen, Georg, 200

Román, Celso: *Los amigos del hombre*, 93

Rooftop Prince (Korean television drama), 283

Rościszewski, Mieczysław, 47

Roth, Klaus, 24

Routledge, 229, 233n6

Roy, Malini, 2, 3, 9

Rubin, Eva-Johanna, 253n5

Ruskin, John, introduction to *German Popular Stories*, 208–9, 213, 228

Russian fairy-tale films, 240, 244–45, 247

Ryu, Kwon-Ha, 94n1

Šabić, Marijan, 20

Šafárik, Pavel Jozef, 26

Sahitya Akademi (the Indian National Academy of Letters), 135, 141

Said, Edward, 147

Saltykov-Shchedrin, Mikhail, 253n7

Samozwaniec, Magdalena, 50

Santa Teresa de Jesús reading room, 67

Savigny, Friedrich Carl von, 8

Scally, John, 232, 233

Schacker, Jennifer, 11

Schank, Roger, 276

Schiavi, Giuliana, 110

Schlegel, Friedrich, 149n13

Schleif, Wolfgang, 252n2

Schmid, Christoph von, 20, 26, 83, 95n3; *La Chartreuse* (The Carthusian), 83

Schneewittchen, DEFA film, 245, 247

Scott, Walter: *Waverley*, 22

script, transmission of stories as, 276, 288–89

Seago, Karen, 10

Sechse kommen durch die Welt (Six Made Their Way in the World), DEFA film, 241, 247, 248–49

Secret Garden (Korean television drama), 277–80, *279*, 281, 282–83, 284, 289, 290n2

Secret (Korean television drama), 283

Ségur, Sophie Comtesse de, 83

Seijo, María Antonia, 72, 73

self-regardingness, in Korean film and drama, 286, 290n6

Shakespeare, William, 250

Shelley, Percy Bysshe, 22

Shimizu, Yoshio, 159, 160

Shōgokumin (Young Citizen), 102

Shōnen Sekai (Children's World), 102

Shore, Bradd, 279

Shuangqiu, Tai, 128

Sicilian tales, 55n11

Siemieński, Lucjan, 43

Simon, Rainer, 248, 251

Sino-Japanese War, 119

Sleeping Beauty (Disney film), 88

Slowacki, Juliusz: *Balladyna*, 42, 55n5

Snow White and the Seven Dwarfs (Disney film), 12, 87–88, 247

Spain, children's literature: *Catálogo critico de libros para niños* (Critical Catalog of Children's Books), Santa Teresa de Jesús reading room, 67; censorship under Franco, 67; dissemination in regional languages, 74n1; influence of Catholicism on, 68–69; influence of didacticism on, 59, 60–62; influence of publishing houses on acceptance of, 65

Spain, Grimm tales in, 5, 7, 59–77; Calleja versions, 62–65, 85–87, 89; complete edition of, 69–70; domestication of, 63–64, 65; Olañeta editions, 72–73; in pocketbook collections for children, 70–72; publishing boom of 1980s, 72–73; Ramón Sopena versions, 65–66, 68; twentieth-century evolution in adaptations, 65–73

Spanish Civil War, 67, 89

Spanish Romanticism, 60, 74n2

Spiegelman, Art: *Maus*, 257
Šporer, Juraj (alias Jure Matić): *Almanah ilirski (The Illyrian Almanac)*, 23
Starkel, Juliusz, 47
Staudte, Wolfgang, 252n2
Steamboat Willie (Disney film), 87
Steedman, Amy, translations, 66
Stefani, Francesco, 244
Stendhal, 22
Stephens, John, 276
"The Story of the Youth Who Went Forth to Learn What Fear Was," Spanish version of *(Periquillo sin miedo)*, 62
Straparola, Giovan Francesco: *Le piacevoli notti* (Pleasant Nights), 199, 203, 204, 207
Strittmatter, Erwin, 240
structurality, 290n4
Subramaniam, Manasi, 147, 148n7
Suga, Ryōhō: *Seiyō koji: shinsen sōwa* (Western Folklore: A Collection of Supernatural Tales), 155–56
Suzuki, Miekichi, 159
Szelburg-Zarembina, Ewa, 50

Tabachnick, Stephen, 258
Tabaimo, illustration of *Kaeru no ōsama* (The Frog King), 168, *169*
Takamura, Kaoru: "The Bremen Town Musicians," 170–71
Tanigawa Ken'icihi, 102
Tanizaki, Jun'ichirō, 159
Tara (Indian publisher), 138
Tarnowski, Marceli, 50, 51, 56n19
Tatar, Maria, 154, 164, 165, 266; *The Hard Facts of the Grimms' Fairy Tales*, 156
Taylor, Edgar, 6, 8, 11, 139; *German Popular Stories* (first English translation), 181, 202–5, 208, 213, 220, 222, 227, 230
Taylor, John Edward: *The Fairy Ring* (translation), 206–8, 227; *The Pentamerome, or, The Story of Stories: Fun for the Little Ones* (translation), 207–8, 209, 214n7; theoretical history for fairy tales, 207–8, 213, 215n8
Taylor Headland, Isaac, 120
television: Korean fairy-tale scripts and intercultural conceptual blending,

275–91; Polish animated television series *Simsala Grimm*, 52
three-color procedure, 244
Tianyi, Zhang: *Dalin he Xiaolin*, 129–30, 131
Tongmyŏng (Eastern Light), 101, 103, 104–6; Ch'oe Namsŏn's Grimm translations in, 100–101, 102–3, 104–6
transmitted narratives, 205
Treeless Mountain (Korean film), 285, 286
Trites, Roberta, 271
Trnka, Jirí, 244
Truchanowska, Małgorzata, 51
Trueba, Antonio de, 61–62
Tsutsumi, Sachiko, 165
Tsuzukihashi, Tatsuo, 102
Tulika (Indian publisher), 138
Turner, Mark, 276
200 Pounds Beauty (Korean film), 288

Ubbelohde, Otto, 53
Ueda, Kayoko, 165
UFA (Berlin), 240
Ulbricht, Walter, 248

Valentí, Eduardo, 69
Valera, Juan, 74n4
Van Baaren, Theodore, 272n1
Varerkar, Chitta, 136
Varma, Anil, 149n9
Velazquez, Josef, 257
Vélez de Piedrahita, Rocío, 92
Verhoeven, Paul, 240
Vickers, George (London publisher): "Fairy Books for Boys and Girls," 226; *Grimms' Goblins*, 226, 227
Vico, Giambattista, 33n6
Viedma, José S., 63
Viehmann, Dorothea, 184
Vieux contes pour l'amusement des grands et des petits enfans (Old Tales for the Amusement of Old and Young Children), 181
Viswanathan, Gauri: *Masks of Conquest*, 136
Volkspoesie (folk poetry), 27
Von Hahn, Johann Georg, 210
Vranich, Anton, 19

Wakabayashi, Judy, 109
Warne, Frederick, and Company, Fairy Library, 227, 228
Warner, Marina, 290n2
Weber, Brenda R., 288
Wehnert, Edward, 220, 225, 227, 234n13; illustrations for Addey and Co. *Household Stories Collected by the Brothers Grimm*, 225; illustrations from "The Golden Bird," 225–26, 229
Wein, Elizabeth, 257
Weinrich, Harald, 190
Wells, Gardner, Darton & Co., 230
Wer reißt denn gleich vor'm Teufel aus (The Devil with Three Golden Hairs), DEFA film, 247, 251
Western fairy-tale scholarship, 165
Whalley, Joyce Irene, 220, 230–31
White, Gleeson, 224
Wiedermann, Dieter, 246
Wiegand, W. J., 220; "The Golden Bird" illustration, 227
Wie heiratet man einen König? (The Peasant's Wise Daughter), DEFA film, 251
Willingham, Bill: *Fables*, 257
Wilson, William, 33n6
Wójcicki, Kazimierz Wojciech, 43, 45, 55n7, 55n8
Wolf, Lothar, 246
wood-block color, 233
wood engraving, 224, 225
World Storytelling Institute, Chennai, India, 138
Wortman, Stefania, 51

Wozniak, Monika, 2, 5, 6, 7, 11–12, 13
Wright, Arthur R.: *English Folklore*, 120
written folklore, 5
Wu, Hongyu, 121, 123, 126
Wydawnicza, Ludowa Spółdzielnia (publisher), 51

Xi, Yang, 121
Xiao pengyou (Little Child), 127–28

Yanagi, Miwa: *Fairy Tale*, 169–71; Snow White, *170*
Yanagi, Miwa: *Fairy Tale*, 168–69, *170*
Yanagita Kunio, 102, 112n4
Yang, Xi, 126
Yazaki, Genkurō, 161, 168
Yepes, Luis Eduardo, 90
Yixin, Wei, 123
Yŏm, Hŭigyŏng, 108–9
Yuxiu, Sun: *Hongfmaoer* (Little Red Cap), 122–23; *Tonghua* (Fairy Tales), 122–23

Zechenter, Witold, 50
Zerman, Karel, 244
Zhang, Zisheng, 128
Zhao, Jingshen, 126, 128
Zhou Guisheng: *Xinan xieyi* (Interesting Stories Translated by Xinan), 122
Zipes, Jack, 13, 23, 111, 138, 154, 164, 252n4, 266, 276
Zmorski, Roman, 43
Zolkover, Adam, 257
Zuoren, Zhou, 119, 120, 121, 125–26, 127–28
Zur, Dafna, 2, 5, 10, 13